The O. Henry Prize Stories 2003

The O. Henry Prize Stories 2003

Edited and with an Introduction by
Laura Furman

Jurors

David Guterson, Diane Johnson,
Jennifer Egan

ANCHOR BOOKS

A Division of Random House, Inc.

New York

AN ANCHOR ORIGINAL, SEPTEMBER 2003

Library of Congress Cataloging-in-Publication Data is on file.

ISBN 1-4000-3131-1

Book design by Debbie Glasserman

www.anchorbooks.com

Printed in the United States of America
10 9 8 7 6 5 4 3 2

Publisher's Note

MANY READERS have come to love the short story through the simple characters, easy narrative voice and humor, and compelling plotting in the work of William Sydney Porter (1862–1910), best known as O. Henry. His surprise endings entertain readers, even those back for a second, third, or fourth look, and one can still say "Gift of the Magi" in conversation about a love affair or marriage, and almost any literate person will know what is meant. It's hard to think of many other American writers whose work has been so incorporated into our national shorthand.

O. Henry was a newspaperman, skilled at hiding from his editors at deadline. He wrote to make a living and to make sense of his life. O. Henry spent his childhood in Greensboro, North Carolina, his adolescence and young manhood in Texas, and lived his mature years in New York City. In between Texas and New York, he served out a prison sentence for bank fraud in Columbus, Ohio. Accounts of the origins of his pen name vary; it may have dated from his Austin days, when he was known to call the wandering family cat, "Oh! Henry!" or been inspired by the captain of the guard in the Ohio State Penitentiary, Orrin Henry.

Porter had devoted friends in New York, and it's easy to see why. He was charming and had an attractively gallant attitude and an easy courtesy to others. He drank too much and neglected his health, which caused his friends concern. He was often short of money; in a letter to a friend asking for a loan of fifteen dollars (his banker was out of town, he wrote), Porter added a postscript: "If it isn't convenient, I'll love you just the same." The banker was unavailable most of Porter's life. His sense of humor was always at home.

Reportedly, Porter's last words were from a popular song, "Turn up the light, for I don't want to go home in the dark."

Eight years after O. Henry's death, in April 1918, the Twilight Club (founded in 1883 and later known as the Society of Arts and Letters) held a dinner in his honor at the Hotel McAlpin in New York City. His friends remembered him so enthusiastically that a committee met at the Hotel Biltmore in December 1918 to establish an O. Henry memorial. The committee decided to award prizes in his name for short-story writers, and it formed the Committee of Award to read the short stories published in a year and to pick the winners. In the words of Blanche Colton Williams (1879–1944), the first of the nine series editors, the memorial intended to "strengthen the art of the short story and to stimulate younger authors."

Doubleday, Page & Company was chosen to publish the first volume of *O. Henry Memorial Award Prize Stories 1919*. In 1927, the Society sold to Doubleday, Doran & Company all rights to the annual collection. Doubleday published The O. Henry Prize Stories, as it came to be known, in hardcover, and from 1984–1996 its subsidiary, Anchor Books, published it simultaneously in paperback. Since 1997 The O. Henry Prize Stories has been published as an original Anchor Books paperback.

Over the years, the rules and methods of selection have varied. As of 2003, the series editor chooses twenty short stories, each one an O. Henry Prize Story. All stories originally written in the English language and published in an American or Canadian periodical are eligible for consideration.

Three jurors are appointed annually. The jurors receive the twenty prize stories in manuscript form, with no identification of author or publication. Each juror, acting independently, chooses a short story of special interest and merit, and comments on that story.

The goal of The O. Henry Prize Stories remains to strengthen the art of the short story.

In her short stories, Mavis Gallant captures the painful paradoxes of the human condition with breathtaking accuracy. Her characters are fools and self-deceivers, unless they are even less fortunate and never feel the comfort of lying to themselves. She writes like no one else about the lies of adults to children, who must believe them because they have no alternative. Her characters are often in exile not only from their native countries but from their own hearts, and they yearn for a different life. Even her complacent stay-at-homes in Montreal and Paris ache for an imaginary country in which everyone plays by the same set of rules and no one steps out of line. It can be said that nothing human surprises her, but Mavis Gallant remains capable of amazement at the ways we tie ourselves in knots and then feel caught.

Her brilliant story "The Latehomecomer" is told by a young German soldier returned from France, where he spent his adolescence as a prisoner of war. With a masterful command of time, Gallant shows the narrator's past, present, and future. In 1950 he turns up at the apartment where his mother is living to find that he has a stepfather whose name is engraved on a polished brass plate outside the door. ("I put my hand over the name, leaving a perfect palm print. I said, 'I suppose there are no razor blades and no civilian shirts in Berlin. But some ass is already engraving nameplates.'") Observing his opportunistic stepfather, his worn-out mother whom he remembers as young and pretty, the latehomecomer recalls his shattering affair with a French girl, and conceives a touching new hope as he watches a child on her father's knee: "She was all light and sheen, and she was the first person—I can even say the first *thing*—I had ever seen that was unflawed, without shadow." The narrator embodies the postwar bitterness of his generation, and he hungers for a future when his spoiled life might be redeemed.

For more than five decades, her readers have been lucky enough to enjoy her austerely passionate stories. *The O. Henry Prize Stories 2003* is dedicated to Mavis Gallant, one of our greatest storytellers.

Acknowledgments

Thanks to Rebecca Bengal, Kathryn Harrigan, Haven Iverson, Emily Rapp, and my other graduate students at the University of Texas at Austin for their invaluable labor; Susan Williamson for excellence above and beyond the call of friendship; and JWB, SCFB, and KS for loving support at home. Special thanks to the editors who support and nurture short-story writers.

Contents

Introduction

A READER, given a moment with a writer, will often pose the question: "Do you have a reader in mind when you write?"

The question is as interesting as the many answers it inspires, for the thrust of the reader's question is, "How did you know me?"

Sometimes a story matches an incident in the reader's life; at other times the congruence is to an emotional, spiritual, or intellectual experience. The short story, even more than the novel, creates an instant and lasting relationship between writer and reader, perhaps because we experience the story and its characters as we do life. Our understanding of the lives of others, even those we think we know well and whom we love, comes over time yet in intense glimpses, revealed most often by stress or loss, the twin capitals of the short story's dominion. The peace of daily life, even the dullness of it, is what is decimated in the short story and replaced by the nightmare or sometimes the consolation of understanding another's existence or our own. The realization, often called compassion, that everybody else lives in their own unique and solitary universe, can feel shattering, liberating, even amusing, depending on how the reader comes to it. Through our experience of the short story, we are better than we are in life, more ready to be empathic, more ready to see why another made the choices he did.

The writer, whose imagination and voice have given us this brief and intense experience through language alone, often becomes a source of curiosity for the reader, who wishes for further clarification. *Do you have an ideal reader? Did I get it? Did you write it for me?* The literal answer has to be no, but literal answers aren't everything.

Years ago, when I had the opportunity to publish a story by Hortense Calisher in *American Short Fiction,* I asked her so many questions about the manuscript that she finally declared, "Posit an intelligent reader." The intelligent reader, she meant, can tolerate waiting for full information and can survive the absence of data. The reader of fiction doesn't have the same expectations as a newspaper reader. The intelligent fiction reader, in fact, wants to suspend judgment and disbelief, to take a vacation from daily attention to gain another kind of attention through the story. As a writer, teacher, and editor, I've come to see that, in fiction, mystery is as important as transparency.

I cannot answer all the questions that readers will have about the twenty stories included in *The O. Henry Prize Stories 2003.* Neither can the writers and neither can our three jurors. As intelligent, perceptive, and interesting as the remarks about the stories by our jurors and writers are, there is no such thing as a final understanding of a good short story. Authors can't know everything, and any good work of art lends itself to revisiting and reinterpretation. In *The O. Henry Prize Stories 2003* two of the three jurors were most taken with the same story—and for quite different reasons.

At its best, the experience of reading a short story is an immersion into the complete world of the story. Mavis Gallant, to whom *The O. Henry Prize Stories 2003* is dedicated, asked readers of her selected stories not to read her book straight through. "Stories are not chapters of a novel," she wrote. "Read one. Shut the book. Read something else. Come back later. Stories can wait." Sometimes, though, the hunger to read trumps everything else, and the reader goes straight on to the next story and the next. The stories in this collection are arranged so that the reader can move from the beginning to the end of the book with pleasure.

Finding the twenty stories for *The O. Henry Prize Stories 2003* meant reading many times that number. I'm an incorrigible reader, so even when a story was not of the quality of a prize story, I often finished it to find out how it ended. After a thousand or so stories, my habit was bent if not broken. Any tedium associated with the necessity of sorting through so much material was balanced by the thrill of finding a prize story. Some of the stories I chose the moment I finished them; some needed two or three readings and comparison to other excellent possibilities. A list of fifteen additional recommended stories appears on page 342. In a vast ocean of published prose, they and their writers are worth remembering.

This year we have welcomed all English-language writers who appeared in North American publications, regardless of citizenship. This means we can include Chimamanda Ngozi Adichie, A. S. Byatt, and William Trevor, whose work rightly belongs in the O. Henry collection. The venerable *O. Henry* is enriched by the inclusion of such wonderful writers in our common English language.

The longest story in *The O. Henry Prize Stories 2003* stretches the conventional idea of the short story. Some might argue that it should be called a novella, yet in the time of Henry James's "Turn of the Screw" and Anton Chekhov's "My Life," "Train Dreams" by Denis Johnson wouldn't have been thought especially long. The shortest story in the 2003 collection, "Kissing" by William Kittredge, would now be called a short short. Both stories evoke decades of personal life and human history. Both achieve a world unto themselves. The *O. Henry*'s mission is not to build walls around the short story, but to demonstrate how generous and flexible the form can be.

Although the twenty stories in this collection are very different, some qualities and concerns are shared. There are folkloric, larger-than-life elements in "The Thing in the Forest," "The Shell Collector," "Swept Away," and "Train Dreams." "Meanwhile" uses every means of communication possible, including e-mail, to illustrate the shapes love can take in extremis. "Two Words," "God's Goodness," and "Lush" are also moving portraits of love molded by a crisis of physical deterioration. In "The American Embassy," "Bleed Blue in Indonesia," "Burn Your Maps," "What Went Wrong," and "The Story," we see characters living with the aftereffects of war and repression, though the thrust of those stories is not primarily political. In "Election Eve," national politics serve as a convenient metaphor for the main character's contentious marriage. A number of stories revolve around the effect of a particular moment or action in a character's life, such as the stunning accident in "Irish Girl" and the foolish benevolent act that brings such desperate trouble to the carver's family in "Sacred Statues." Other stories offer the pattern of the main character's life, like that of the dancer in "The High Road," who understands at last how to suffer for love. As ever, Alice Munro in "Fathers" gives us the short story as a meditation on the past, the considered reflection of a character on the formation of her heart and mind. "Fathers" has in common with "The Thing in the Forest" middle-aged characters wondering who it was that they were so long ago. With the death of one man in "Train Dreams," a history of the world is obliterated.

In 1926, there was a horse race for *The O. Henry Prize Stories* between "Bubbles" by Wilbur Daniel Steele and "My Mortal Enemy" by Willa Cather. "Bubbles" is a readable tale of horror, seen through the blankly innocent eyes of a much-deceived child. "Bubbles" is dated in its idea of human character in a way that older (and better) stories, including "My Mortal Enemy," are not. The stories were neck and neck when the committee of judges learned that Cather's tale was to be published in a separate volume and was therefore unavailable for inclusion. It now seems inconceivable that there was much of a contest between "Bubbles" and "My Mortal Enemy."

All of which is to say that times change and so does taste. I don't know any more than the 1926 judges did what will last. We live in times when some predict the demise of the book entirely. We'll value the songs we love now and let the future sing for its own supper.

The O. Henry Prize Stories 2003

A. S. Byatt

The Thing in the Forest

from *The New Yorker*

THERE WERE once two little girls who saw, or believed they saw, a thing in a forest. The two little girls were evacuees, who had been sent away from the city by train, with a large number of other children. They all had their names attached to their coats with safety pins, and they carried little bags or satchels, and the regulation gas mask. They wore knitted scarves and bonnets or caps, and many had knitted gloves attached to long tapes that ran along their sleeves, inside their coats, and over their shoulders and out, so that they could leave their ten woollen fingers dangling, like a spare pair of hands, like a scarecrow. They all had bare legs and scuffed shoes and wrinkled socks. Most had wounds on their knees in varying stages of freshness and scabbiness. They were at the age when children fall often and their knees were unprotected. With their suitcases, some of which were almost too big to carry, and their other impedimenta, a doll, a toy car, a comic, they were like a disorderly dwarf regiment, stomping along the platform.

The two little girls had not met before, and made friends on the train. They shared a square of chocolate, and took alternate bites at an apple. Their names were Penny and Primrose. Penny was thin and dark and taller, possibly older, than Primrose, who was plump and blond and curly. Primrose had bitten nails, and a velvet collar on her dressy green coat. Penny had a bloodless transparent paleness, a touch of blue in her fine lips.

Neither of them knew where they were going, nor how long the journey might take. They did not even know why they were going, since neither of their mothers had quite known how to explain the danger to them. How do you say to your child, I am sending you away, because enemy bombs may fall out of the sky, but I myself am staying here, in what I believe may be daily danger of burning, being buried alive, gas, and ultimately perhaps a gray army rolling in on tanks over the suburbs? So the mothers (who did not resemble each other at all) behaved alike, and explained nothing—it was easier. Their daughters, they knew, were little girls, who would not be able to understand or imagine.

The girls discussed whether it was a sort of holiday or a sort of punishment, or a bit of both. Both had the idea that these were all perhaps not very good children, possibly being sent away for that reason. They were pleased to be able to define each other as "nice." They would stick together, they agreed.

The train crawled sluggishly farther and farther away from the city and their homes. It was not a clean train—the upholstery of their carriage had the dank smell of unwashed trousers, and the gusts of hot steam rolling backward past their windows were full of specks of flimsy ash, and sharp grit, and occasional fiery sparks that pricked face and fingers like hot needles if you opened the window. It was very noisy, too, whenever it picked up a little speed. The windowpanes were both grimy and misted up. The train stopped frequently, and when it stopped they used their gloves to wipe rounds, through which they peered out at flooded fields, furrowed hillsides, and tiny stations whose names were carefully blacked out, whose platforms were empty of life.

The children did not know that the namelessness was meant to baffle or delude an invading army. They felt—they did not think it out, but somewhere inside them the idea sprouted—that the erasure was because of them, because they were not meant to know where they were going or, like Hansel and Gretel, to find the way back. They did not speak to each other of this anxiety, but began the kind of conversation children have about things they really dislike, things that upset, or disgust, or frighten them. Semolina pudding with its grainy texture, mushy peas, fat on roast meat. Having your head held roughly back over the basin to have your hair washed, with cold water running down inside your liberty bodice. Gangs in playgrounds. They felt the pressure of all the other alien children in all the other carriages as a potential gang. They shared another square of chocolate, and licked their fingers, and looked out at a great white goose flapping its wings beside an inky pond.

The sky grew dark gray and in the end the train halted. The children got out, and lined up in a crocodile, and were led to a mud-colored bus. Penny and Primrose managed to get a seat together, although it was over the wheel, and both of them began to feel sick as the bus bumped along snaking country lanes, under whipping branches, with torn strips of thin cloud streaming across a full moon.

They were billeted in a mansion commandeered from its owner. The children were told they were there temporarily, until families were found to take them. Penny and Primrose held hands, and said to each other that it would be wizard if they could go to the same family, because at least they would have each other. They didn't say anything to the rather tired-looking ladies who were ordering them about, because, with the cunning of little children, they knew that requests were most often counterproduc-tive—adults liked saying no. They imagined possible families into which they might be thrust. They did not discuss what they imagined, as these pictures, like the black station signs, were too frightening, and words might make some horror solid, in some magical way. Penny, who was a reading child, imagined Victorian dark pillars of severity, like Jane Eyre's Mr. Brocklehurst, or David Copperfield's Mr. Murdstone. Primrose imag-ined—she didn't know why—a fat woman with a white cap and round red arms who smiled nicely but made the children wear sacking aprons and scrub the steps and the stove. "It's like we were orphans," she said to Penny. "But we're not." Penny said, "If we manage to stick together . . ."

The great house had a double flight of imposing stairs to its front door, and carved griffins and unicorns on its balustrade. There was no lighting, because of the blackout. All the windows were shuttered. The children trudged up the staircase in their crocodile, and were given supper (Irish stew and rice pudding with a dollop of blood-red jam) before going to bed in long makeshift dormitories, where once servants had slept. They had camp beds (military issue) and gray shoddy blankets. Penny and Primrose got beds together but couldn't get a corner. They queued to brush their teeth in a tiny washroom, and both suffered (again without speaking) suf-focating anxiety about what would happen if they wanted to pee in the middle of the night. They also suffered from a fear that in the dark the other children would start laughing and rushing and teasing, and turn themselves into a gang. But that did not happen. Everyone was tired and anxious and orphaned. An uneasy silence, a drift of perturbed sleep, came over them all. The only sounds—from all parts of the great dormitory, it seemed— were suppressed snuffles and sobs, from faces pressed into thin pillows.

When daylight came, things seemed, as they mostly do, brighter and better. The children were given breakfast in a large vaulted room, at trestle tables, porridge made with water, and a dab of the red jam, heavy cups of strong tea. Then they were told they could go out and play until lunchtime. Children in those days—wherever they came from—were not closely watched, were allowed to come and go freely, and those evacuated children were not herded into any kind of holding pen or transit camp. They were told they should be back for lunch at twelve-thirty, by which time those in charge hoped to have sorted out their provisional future lives. It was not known how they would know when it was twelve-thirty, but it was expected that—despite the fact that few of them had wrist-watches—they would know how to keep an eye on the time. It was what they were used to.

Penny and Primrose went out together, in their respectable coats and laced shoes, onto the terrace. The terrace appeared to them to be vast. It was covered with a fine layer of damp gravel, stained here and there bright green, or invaded by mosses. Beyond it was a stone balustrade, with a staircase leading down to a lawn. Across the lawn was a sculpted yew hedge. In the middle of the hedge was a wicket gate, and beyond the gate were trees. A forest, the little girls said to themselves.

"Let's go into the forest," said Penny, as though the sentence were required of her.

Primrose hesitated. Most of the other children were running up and down the terrace. Some boys were kicking a ball on the grass.

"OK," said Primrose. "We needn't go far."

"No. I've never been in a forest."

"Nor me."

"We ought to look at it, while we've got the opportunity," said Penny.

There was a very small child—one of the smallest—whose name, she told everyone, was Alys. With a "y," she told those who could spell, and those who couldn't, which surely included herself. She was barely out of nappies. She was quite extraordinarily pretty, pink and white, with large pale blue eyes, and sparse little golden curls all over her head and neck, through which her pink skin could be seen. Nobody seemed to be in charge of her, no elder brother or sister. She had not quite managed to wash the tearstains from her dimpled cheeks.

She had made several attempts to attach herself to Penny and Primrose. They did not want her. They were excited about meeting and liking each other. She said now, "I'm coming, too, into the forest."

"No, you aren't," said Primrose.

"You're too little, you must stay here," said Penny.

"You'll get lost," said Primrose.

"You won't get lost. I'll come with you," said the little creature, with an engaging smile, made for loving parents and grandparents.

"We don't want you, you see," said Primrose.

"It's for your own good," said Penny.

Alys went on smiling hopefully, the smile becoming more of a mask.

"It will be all right," said Alys.

"Run," said Primrose.

They ran; they ran down the steps and across the lawn, and through the gate, into the forest. They didn't look back. They were long-legged little girls. The trees were silent round them, holding out their branches to the sun.

Primrose touched the warm skin of the nearest saplings, taking off her gloves to feel the cracks and knots. Penny looked into the thick of the forest. There was undergrowth—a mat of brambles and bracken. There were no obvious paths. Dark and light came and went, inviting and mysterious, as the wind pushed clouds across the face of the sun.

"We have to be careful not to get lost," she said. "In stories, people make marks on tree trunks, or unroll a thread, or leave a trail of white pebbles—to find their way back."

"We needn't go out of sight of the gate," said Primrose. "We could just explore a little bit."

They set off, very slowly. They went on tiptoe, making their own narrow passages through the undergrowth, which sometimes came as high as their thin shoulders. They were urban, and unaccustomed to silence. Then they began to hear small sounds. The chatter and repeated lilt and alarm of invisible birds, high up, further in. Rustling in dry leaves. Slitherings, dry coughs, sharp cracks. They went on, pointing out to each other creepers draped with glistening berries, crimson, black, and emerald, little crops of toadstools, some scarlet, some ghostly pale, some a dead-flesh purple, some like tiny parasols—and some like pieces of meat protruding from tree trunks. They met blackberries, but didn't pick them, in case in this place they were dangerous or deceptive. They admired from a safe distance the stiff upright fruiting rods of the lords-and-ladies, packed with fat red berries.

Did they hear it first or smell it? Both sound and scent were at first infinitesimal and dispersed. They gave the strange impression of moving in—in waves—from the whole perimeter of the forest. Both increased very slowly in intensity, and both were mixed, a sound and a smell fabricated of many disparate sounds and smells. A crunching, a crackling, a crushing, a heavy thumping, combining with threshing and thrashing, and added to that a gulping, heaving, boiling, bursting, steaming sound, full of bubbles and farts, piffs and explosions, swallowings and wallowings. The smell was worse, and more aggressive, than the sound. It was a liquid smell of putrefaction, the smell of maggoty things at the bottom of untended dustbins, blocked drains, mixed with the smell of bad eggs, and of rotten carpets and ancient polluted bedding. The ordinary forest smells and sounds were extinguished. The two little girls looked at each other, and took each other's hand. Speechlessly and instinctively, they crouched down behind a fallen tree trunk, and trembled, as the thing came into view.

Its head appeared to form, or first become visible in the distance, between the trees. Its face—which was triangular—appeared like a rubbery or fleshy mask over a shapeless sprouting bulb of a head, like a monstrous turnip. Its color was the color of flayed flesh, pitted with wormholes, and its expression was neither wrath nor greed but pure misery. Its most defined feature was a vast mouth, pulled down and down at the corners, tight with a kind of pain. Its lips were thin, and raised, like welts from whipstrokes. It had blind, opaque white eyes, fringed with fleshy lashes and brows like the feelers of sea anemones. Its face was close to the ground and moved toward the children between its forearms, which were squat, thick, powerful, and akimbo, like a cross between a washerwoman's and a primeval dragon's. The flesh on these forearms was glistening and mottled.

The rest of its very large body appeared to be glued together, like still wet papier-mâché, or the carapace of stones and straws and twigs worn by caddis flies underwater. It had a tubular shape, as a turd has a tubular shape, a provisional amalgam. It was made of rank meat, and decaying vegetation, but it also trailed veils and prostheses of man-made materials, bits of wire netting, foul dishcloths, wire-wool full of pan scrubbings, rusty nuts and bolts. It had feeble stubs and stumps of very slender legs, growing out of it at all angles, wavering and rippling like the suckered feet of a caterpillar or the squirming fringe of a centipede. On and on it came, bending and crushing whatever lay in its path, including bushes, though not substantial trees, which it wound between, awkwardly. The little girls observed, with horrified fascination, that when it met a sharp stone, or a narrow tree trunk, it allowed itself to be sliced through, flowed sluggishly round in two or three smaller worms, convulsed, and reunited. Its progress was apparently very painful, for it moaned and whined among its other burblings and belchings. They thought it could not see, or certainly could not see clearly. It and its stench passed within a few feet of their tree trunk, humping along, leaving behind it a trail of bloody slime and dead foliage.

Its end was flat and blunt, almost transparent, like some earthworms.

When it had gone, Penny and Primrose, kneeling on the moss and dead leaves, put their arms about each other, and hugged each other, shaking with dry sobs. Then they stood up, still silent, and stared together, hand in hand, at the trail of obliteration and destruction, which wound out of the forest and into it again. They went back, hand in hand, without looking behind them, afraid that the wicket gate, the lawn, the stone steps, the balustrade, the terrace, and the great house would be transmogrified, or simply not there. But the boys were still playing football on the lawn, a group of girls were skipping and singing shrilly on the gravel. They let go each other's hand, and went back in.

They did not speak to each other again.

The next day, they were separated and placed with strange families. Their stay in these families—Primrose was in a dairy farm, Penny was in a parsonage—did not in fact last very long, though then the time seemed slow motion and endless. Later, Primrose remembered the sound of milk spurting in the pail, and Penny remembered the empty corsets of the vicar's wife, hanging bony on the line. They remembered dandelion clocks, but you can remember those from anywhere, any time. They remembered the thing they had seen in the forest, on the contrary, in the way you remember those very few dreams—almost all nightmares—that have the quality of life itself. (Though what are dreams if not life itself?) They remembered too solid flesh, too precise a stink, a rattle and a soughing that thrilled the nerves and the cartilage of their growing ears. In the memory, as in such a dream, they felt, I cannot get out, this is a real thing in a real place.

They returned from evacuation, like many evacuees, so early that they then lived through wartime in the city, bombardment, blitz, unearthly light and roaring, changed landscapes, holes in their world where the newly dead had been. Both lost their fathers. Primrose's father was in the Army, and was killed, very late in the war, on a crowded troop carrier sunk in the Far East. Penny's father, a much older man, was in the Auxiliary Fire Service, and died in a sheet of flame in the East India Docks on the Thames, pumping evaporating water from a puny coil of hose. They found it hard, after the war, to remember these different men. The claspers of memory could not grip the drowned and the burned. Primrose saw an inane grin under a khaki cap, because her mother had a snapshot. Penny thought she remembered her father, already gray-headed, brushing ash off his boots and trouser cuffs as he put on his tin hat to go out. She thought she remembered a quaver of fear in his tired face, and the muscles composing themselves into resolution. It was not much, what either of them remembered.

After the war, their fates were still similar and dissimilar. Penny's widowed mother embraced grief, closed her face and her curtains. Primrose's mother married one of the many admirers she had had before the ship went down, gave birth to another five children, and developed varicose veins and a smoker's cough. She dyed her blond hair with peroxide when it faded. Both Primrose and Penny were only children who now, because of the war, lived in amputated or unreal families. Penny was a good student and in due course went to university, where she chose to study developmental psychology. Primrose had little education. She was always being kept off school to look after the others. She, too, dyed her blond curls with peroxide when they turned mousy and faded. She got fat as Penny got thin. Neither of them married. Penny became a child psychologist, working with the abused, the displaced, the disturbed. Primrose did this and that. She was a barmaid. She worked in a shop. She went to help at various church crèches and Salvation Army gatherings, and discovered she had a talent for storytelling. She became Aunty Primrose, with her own repertoire. She was employed to tell tales to kindergartens and entertain at children's parties. She was much in demand at Halloween, and had her own circle of bright-colored plastic chairs in a local shopping mall, where she kept an eye on the children of burdened women, keeping them safe, offering them just a frisson of fear and terror, which made them wriggle with pleasure.

The house in the country aged differently. During this period of time—while the little girls became women—it was handed over to the nation, which turned it into a living museum. Guided tours took place in it, at regulated times. During these tours, the ballroom and intimate drawing rooms were fenced off with crimson twisted ropes on little brass one-eyed pedestals. The bored and the curious peered in at four-poster beds and pink silk fauteuils, at silver-framed photographs of wartime royalty, and crackling crazing Renaissance and Enlightenment portraits. In the room where the evacuees had eaten their rationed meals, the history of the house was displayed, on posters, in glass cases, with helpful notices and opened copies of old diaries and records. There was no mention of the evacuees, whose presence appeared to have been too brief to have left any trace.

The two women met in this room on an autumn day in 1984. They had come with a group, walking in a chattering crocodile behind a guide. They prowled around the room, each alone with herself, in opposite directions, each without acknowledging the other's presence. Their mothers had died that spring, within a week of each other, though this coincidence was unknown to them. It had made both of them think of taking a holiday, and both had chosen that part of the world. Penny was wearing a charcoal trouser suit and a black velvet hat. Primrose wore a floral knit long jacket over a shell-pink cashmere sweater, over a rustling long skirt with an elastic waist, in a mustard-colored tapestry print. Her hips and bosom were bulky. Both of them, at the same moment, leaned over an image in a medieval-looking illustrated book. Primrose thought it was a very old book. Penny assumed it was nineteenth-century mock-medieval. It showed a knight, on foot, in a forest, lifting his sword to slay something. The knight shone on the rounded slope of the page, in the light, which caught the gilding on his helmet and sword belt. It was not possible to see what was being slain. This was because, both in the tangled vegetation of the image and in the way the book was displayed in the case, the enemy, or victim, was in shadows.

Neither of them could read the ancient (or pseudo-ancient) black letter of the text beside the illustration. There was a typed description, under the book. They had to lean forward to read it, and to see what was worming its way into, or out of, the deep spine of the book, and that was how each came to see the other's face, close up, in the glass, which was both transparent and reflective. Their transparent reflected faces lost detail—cracked lipstick, pouches, fine lines of wrinkles—and looked both younger and grayer, less substantial. And that is how they came to recognize each other, as they might not have done, plump face to bony face. They breathed each other's names—Penny, Primrose—and their breath misted the glass, obscuring the knight and his opponent. I could have died, I could have wet my knickers, said Penny and Primrose afterward to each other, and both experienced this still moment as pure, dangerous shock. They read the caption, which was about the Loathly Worm, which, tradition held, had infested the countryside and had been killed more than once by scions of that house—Sir Lionel, Sir Boris, Sir Guillem. The Worm, the typewriter had tapped out, was an English worm, not a European dragon, and, like most such worms, was wingless. In some sightings it was reported as having vestigial legs, hands, or feet. In others it was limbless. It had, in monstrous form, the capacity of common or garden worms to sprout new heads or trunks if it was divided, so that two worms, or more, replaced one. This was why it had been killed so often, yet reappeared. It had been reported traveling with a slithering pack of young ones, but these may have been only revitalized segments.

Being English, they thought of tea. There was a tearoom in the great house, in a converted stable at the back. There they stood silently side by side, clutching floral plastic trays spread with briar roses, and purchased scones, superior raspberry jam in tiny jam jars, little plastic tubs of clotted cream. "You couldn't get cream or real jam in the war," said Primrose as they found a corner table. She said wartime rationing had made her permanently greedy, and thin Penny agreed it had—clotted cream was still a treat.

They watched each other warily, offering bland snippets of autobiography in politely hushed voices. Primrose thought Penny looked gaunt, and Penny thought Primrose looked raddled. They established the skein of coincidences—dead fathers, unmarried status, child-caring professions, recently dead mothers. Circling like beaters, they approached the covert thing in the forest. They discussed the great house, politely. Primrose admired the quality of the carpets. Penny said it was nice to see the old pictures back on the wall. Primrose said, Funny really, that there was all that history, but no sign that they, the children, that was, had ever been there. Funny, said Penny, that they should meet each other next to that book, with that picture. "Creepy," said Primrose in a light, light cobweb voice, not looking at Penny. "We saw that thing. When we went in the forest."

"Yes, we did," said Penny. "We saw it."

"Did you ever wonder," asked Primrose, "if we really saw it?"

"Never for a moment," said Penny. "That is, I don't know what it was, but I've always been quite sure we saw it."

"Does it change—do you remember all of it?"

"It was a horrible thing, and yes, I remember all of it, there isn't a bit of it I can manage to forget. Though I forget all sorts of things," said Penny, in a thin voice, a vanishing voice.

"And have you ever told anyone of it, spoken of it?" asked Primrose more urgently, leaning forward.

"No," said Penny. She had not. She said, "Who would believe it?"

"That's what I thought," said Primrose. "I didn't speak. But it stuck in my mind like a tapeworm in your gut. I think it did me no good."

"It did me no good either," said Penny. "No good at all. I've thought about it," she said to the aging woman opposite, whose face quivered under her dyed goldilocks. "I think, I think there are things that are real—more real than we are—but mostly we don't cross their paths, or they don't cross ours. Maybe at very bad times we get into their world, or notice what they are doing in ours."

Primrose nodded energetically. She looked as though sharing was solace, and Penny, to whom it was not solace, grimaced with pain.

"Sometimes I think that thing finished me off," Penny said to Primrose, a child's voice rising in a woman's gullet, arousing a little girl's scared smile, which wasn't a smile on Primrose's face.

Primrose said, "It did finish her off, that little one, didn't it? She got into its path, didn't she? And when it had gone by—she wasn't anywhere," said Primrose. "That was how it was?"

"Nobody ever asked where she was or looked for her," said Penny.

"I wondered if we'd made her up," said Primrose. "But I didn't, we didn't."

"Her name was Alys."

"With a 'y.'"

There had been a mess, a disgusting mess, they remembered, but no particular sign of anything that might have been, or been part of, or belonged to, a persistent little girl called Alys.

Primrose shrugged voluptuously, let out a gale of a sigh, and rearranged her flesh in her clothes.

"Well, we know we're not mad, anyway," she said. "We've got into a mystery, but we didn't make it up. It wasn't a delusion. So it was good we met, because now we needn't be afraid we're mad, need we—we can get on with things, so to speak?"

They arranged to have dinner together the following evening. They were staying in different bed-and-breakfasts and neither of them thought of exchanging addresses. They agreed on a restaurant in the market square of the local town—Seraphina's Hot Pot—and a time, seven-thirty. They did not even discuss spending the next day together. Primrose went on a local bus tour. Penny took a long solitary walk. The weather was gray, spitting fine rain. Both arrived at their lodgings with headaches, and both made tea with the tea bags and kettle provided in their rooms. They sat on their beds. Penny's had a quilt with blowsy cabbage roses. Primrose's had a black-and-white checked gingham duvet. They turned on their televisions, watched the same game show, listened to the inordinate jolly laughter.

Seven-thirty came and went, and neither woman moved. Both, indistinctly, imagined the other waiting at a table, watching a door open and shut. Neither moved. What could they have said, they asked themselves, but only perfunctorily.

The next day, Penny thought about the wood, put on her walking shoes, and set off obliquely in the opposite direction. Primrose sat over her breakfast, which was English and ample. The wood, the real and imagined wood—both before and after she had entered it with Penny—had always been simultaneously a source of attraction and of discomfort, shading into terror. Without speaking to herself a sentence in her head—"I shall go there"—Primrose decided. And she went straight there, full of warm food, arriving as the morning brightened with the first busload of tourists, and giving them the slip, to take the path they had once taken, across the lawn and through the wicket gate.

The wood was much the same, but denser and more inviting in its new greenness. Primrose's body decided to set off in a rather different direction from the one the little girls had taken. New bracken was uncoiling with snaky force. Yesterday's rain still glittered on limp new hazel leaves and threads of gossamer. Small feathered throats above her whistled and trilled with enchanting territorial aggression and male self-assertion, which were to Primrose simply the chorus. She found a mossy bank, with posies of primroses, which she recognized and took vaguely as a good sign, a personal sign. She was better at flowers than birds, because there had been Flower Fairies in the school bookshelves when she was little, with the flowers painted accurately, accompanied by truly pretty human creatures, all children, clothed in the blues and golds, russets and purples of the flowers and fruits. Here she saw and recognized them, windflower and bryony, self-heal and dead nettle, and had—despite where she was—a lovely lapping sense of invisible, just invisible life swarming in the leaves and along the twigs.

She stopped. She did not like the sound of her own toiling breath. She was not very fit. She saw, then, a whisking in the bracken, a twirl of fur, thin and flaming, quivering on a tree trunk. She saw a squirrel, a red squirrel, watching her from a bough. She had to sit down, as she remembered her mother. She sat on a hummock of grass, rather heavily. She remembered them all, Nutkin and Moldywarp, Brock and Sleepy Dormouse, Natty Newt and Ferdy Frog. Her mother hadn't told stories and hadn't opened gates into imaginary worlds. But she had been good with her fingers. Every Christmas during the war, when toys, and indeed materials, were not to be had, Primrose had woken to find in her stocking a new stuffed creature, made from fur fabric, with button eyes and horny claws. There had been an artistry to them. The stuffed squirrel was the essence of squirrel, the fox was watchful, the newt was slithery. They did not wear anthropomorphic jackets or caps, which made it easier to invest them with imaginary natures. She believed in Father Christmas, and the discovery that her mother had made the toys, the vanishing of magic, had been a breathtaking blow. She could not be grateful for the skill and the imagination, so uncharacteristic of her flirtatious mother. The creatures continued to accumulate. A spider, a Bambi. She told herself stories at night about a girl-woman, an enchantress in a fairy wood, loved and protected by an army of wise and gentle animals. She slept banked in by stuffed creatures, as the house in the blitz was banked in by inadequate sandbags.

Primrose registered the red squirrel as disappointing—stringier and more ratlike than its plump gray city cousins. But she knew it was special, and when it took off from branch to branch, flicking its extended tail like a sail, gripping with its tiny hands, she set out to follow it. It would take her to the center, she thought. It could easily have leaped out of sight, she thought, but it didn't. She pushed through brambles into denser, greener shadows. Juices stained her skirts and skin. She began to tell herself a story about staunch Primrose, not giving up, making her way to "the center." Her childhood stories had all been in the third person. "She was not afraid." "She faced up to the wild beasts. They cowered." She laddered her tights and muddied her shoes and breathed heavier. The squirrel stopped to clean its face. She crushed bluebells and saw the sinister hoods of arum lilies.

She had no idea how far she had come, but she decided that the clearing where she found herself was the center. The squirrel had stopped, and was running up and down a single tree. There was a mossy mound that could have had a thronelike aspect, if you were being imaginative. So she sat on it. "She came to the center and sat on the mossy chair."

Now what?

She had not forgotten what they had seen, the blank miserable face, the powerful claws, the raggle-taggle train of accumulated decay. She had come neither to look for it nor to confront it, but she had come because it was there. She had known all her life that she, Primrose, had really been in a magic forest. She knew that the forest was the source of terror. She had never frightened the littluns she entertained, with tales of lost children in forests. She frightened them with slimy things that came up the plughole, or swarmed out of the U-bend in the lavatory, and were dispatched by bravery and magic. But the woods in her tales bred glamour. They were places where you used words like "spangles" and "sequins" for real dew-drops on real dock leaves. Primrose knew that glamour and the thing they had seen, brilliance and the ashen stink, came from the same place. She made both things safe for the littluns by restricting them to pantomime flats and sweet illustrations. She didn't look at what she knew, better not, but she did know she knew, she recognized confusedly.

Now what?

She sat on the moss, and a voice in her head said, "I want to go home." And she heard herself give a bitter, entirely grownup little laugh, for what was home? What did she know about home?

Where she lived was above a Chinese takeaway. She had a dangerous cupboard-corner she cooked in, a bed, a clothes-rail, an armchair deformed by generations of bottoms. She thought of this place in faded browns and beiges, seen through drifting coils of Chinese cooking steam, scented with stewing pork and a bubbling chicken broth. Home was not real, as all the sturdy twigs and roots in the wood were real. The stuffed animals were piled on the bed and the carpet, their fur rubbed, their pristine stare gone from their scratched eyes. She thought about what one thought was real, sitting there on the moss throne at the center. When Mum had come in, sniveling, to say Dad was dead, Primrose herself had been preoccupied with whether pudding would be tapioca or semolina, whether there would be jam, and, subsequently, how ugly Mum's dripping nose was, how she looked as though she were putting it on. She remembered the semolina and the rather nasty blackberry jam, the taste and the texture, to this day. So was that real, was that home?

She had later invented a picture of a cloudy aquamarine sea under a gold sun, in which a huge fountain of white curling water rose from a foundering ship. It was very beautiful but not real. She could not remember Dad. She could remember the Thing in the Forest, and she could remember Alys. The fact that the mossy tump had lovely colors—crimson and emerald—didn't mean she didn't remember the Thing. She remembered what Penny had said about "things that are more real than we are." She had met one. Here at the center, the spout of water was more real than the semolina, because she was where such things reign. The word she found was "reign." She had understood something, and did not know what she had understood. She wanted badly to go home, and she wanted never to move. The light was lovely in the leaves. The squirrel flirted its tail and suddenly set off again, springing into the branches. The woman lumbered to her feet and licked the bramble scratches on the back of her hands.

Penny walked very steadily, keeping to hedgerows and field-edge paths. She remembered the Thing. She remembered it clearly and daily. But she walked away, noticing and not noticing that her path was deflected by field forms and the lay of the land into a snaking sickle shape. As the day wore on, she settled into her stride and lifted her eyes. When she saw the wood on the horizon, she knew it was the wood, although she was seeing it from an unfamiliar aspect, from where it appeared to be perched on a conical hillock, ridged as though it had been grasped and squeezed by coils of strength. It was almost dusk. She mounted the slope, and went in over a suddenly discovered stile.

Once inside, she moved cautiously. She stood stock-still, and snuffed the air for the remembered rottenness: she listened to the sounds of the trees and the creatures. She smelled rottenness, but it was normal rotten-ness, leaves and stems mulching back into earth. She heard sounds. Not birdsong, for it was too late in the day, but the odd raucous warning croak. She heard her own heartbeat in the thickening brown air.

It was no use looking for familiar tree trunks or tussocks. They had had a lifetime, her lifetime, to alter out of recognition.

She began to think she discerned dark tunnels in the undergrowth, where something might have rolled and slid. Mashed seedlings, broken twigs and fronds, none of it very recent. There were things caught in the thorns, flimsy colorless shreds of damp wool or fur. She peered down the tunnels and noted where the scrapings hung thickest. She forced herself to go into the dark, stooping, occasionally crawling on hands and knees. The silence was heavy. She found threadworms of knitting wool, unraveled dishcloth cotton, clinging newsprint. She found odd sausage-shaped tubes of membrane, containing fragments of hair and bone and other inanimate stuffs. They were like monstrous owl pellets, or the gut-shaped hairballs vomited by cats. Penny went forward, putting aside briars and tough stems with careful fingers. It had been here, but how long ago?

Quite suddenly, she came out to a place she remembered. The clearing was larger, the tree trunks were thicker, but the great log behind which they had hidden still lay there. The place was almost the ghost of a camp. The trees round about were hung with pennants and streamers, like the scorched, hacked, threadbare banners in the chapel of the great house, with their brown stains of earth or blood. It had been here, it had never gone away.

Penny moved slowly and dreamily round, looking for things. She found a mock-tortoiseshell hairslide, and a shoe button with a metal shank. She found a bird skeleton, quite fresh, bashed flat. She found ambivalent shards and several teeth, of varying sizes and shapes. She found—spread around, half hidden by roots, stained green but glinting white—a collection of small bones, finger bones, tiny toes, a rib, and finally what might be a brainpan and brow. She thought of putting them in her knapsack, and then thought she could not. She was not an anatomist. The tiny bones might have been badger or fox.

She sat down, with her back against the fallen trunk. She thought, Now I am watching myself as you do in a safe dream, but then, when I saw it, it was one of those dreams where you are inside and cannot get out. Except that it wasn't a dream.

It was the encounter with the Thing that had led her to deal professionally in dreams. Something that resembled unreality had lumbered into reality, and she had seen it. She had been the reading child, but after the sight of the Thing she had not been able to inhabit the customary and charming unreality of books. She had become good at studying what could not be seen. She took an interest in the dead, who inhabited real history. She was drawn to the invisible forces that moved in molecules and caused them to coagulate or dissipate. She had become a psychotherapist "to be useful." That was not quite accurate. The corner of the blanket that covered the unthinkable had been turned back enough for her to catch sight of it. She was in its world. It was not by accident that she had come to specialize in severely autistic children, children who twittered, or banged, or stared, who sat damp and absent on Penny's official lap and told her no dreams. The world they knew was a real world. Often Penny thought it was the real world, from which even their desperate parents were at least partly shielded. Somebody had to occupy themselves with the hopeless. Penny felt she could.

All the leaves of the forest began slowly to quaver and then to clatter. Far away, there was the sound of something heavy, and sluggish, stirring. Penny sat very still and expectant. She heard the old blind rumble, she sniffed the old stink. It came from no direction; it was all around; as though the Thing encompassed the wood, or as though it traveled in multiple fragments, as it was described in the old text. It was dark now. What was visible had no distinct color, only shades of ink and elephant.

Now, thought Penny, and just as suddenly as it had begun the turmoil ceased. It was as though the Thing had turned away; she could feel the tremble of the wood recede and become still. Quite rapidly, over the treetops, a huge disk of white gold mounted and hung. Penny remembered her father, standing in the cold light of the full moon, and saying wryly that the bombers would not come tonight, they were safe under a cloudless full moon. He had vanished in an oven of red-yellow roaring, Penny had guessed, or been told, or imagined. Her mother had sent her away before allowing the fireman to speak, who had come with the news. She had been a creep-mouse on stairs and in cubbyholes, trying to overhear what was being imparted. Her mother didn't, or couldn't, want her company. She caught odd phrases of talk—"nothing really to identify," "absolutely no doubt." He had been a tired, gentle man with ash in his trouser turnups. There had been a funeral. Penny remembered thinking there was nothing, or next to nothing, in the coffin his fellow-firemen shouldered. It went up so lightly. It was so easy to set down on the crematorium slab.

They had been living behind the blackout anyway, but her mother went on living behind drawn curtains long after the war was over.

The moon had released the wood, it seemed. Penny stood up and brushed leaf mold off her clothes. She had been ready for it, and it had not come. She felt disappointed. But she accepted her release and found her way back to the fields and her village along liquid trails of moonlight.

The two women took the same train back to the city, but did not encounter each other until they got out. The passengers scurried and shuffled toward the exit, mostly heads down. Both women remembered how they had set out in the wartime dark, with their twig legs and gas masks. Both raised their heads as they neared the barrier, not in hope of being met, for they would not be, but automatically, to calculate where to go and what to do. They saw each other's faces in the cavernous gloom, two pale, recognizable rounds, far enough apart for speech, and even greetings, to be awkward. In the dimness, they were reduced to similarity—dark eyeholes, set mouth. For a moment or two, they stood and simply stared. On that first occasion the station vault had been full of curling steam, and the air gritty with ash. Now the blunt-nosed sleek diesel they had left was blue and gold under a layer of grime. They saw each other through the black imagined veil that grief or pain or despair hangs over the visible world. Each saw the other's face and thought of the unforgettable misery of the face they had seen in the forest. Each thought that the other was the witness, who made the thing certainly real, who prevented her from slipping into the comfort of believing she had imagined it or made it up. So they stared at each other, blankly, without acknowledgment, then picked up their baggage, and turned away into the crowd.

Penny found that the black veil had somehow become part of her vision. She thought constantly about faces, her father's, her mother's, Primrose's face, the hopeful little girl, the woman staring up at her from the glass case, staring at her conspiratorially over the clotted cream. The blond infant Alys, an ingratiating sweet smile. The half-human face of the Thing. She tried to remember that face completely, and suffered over the detail of the dreadful droop of its mouth, the exact inanity of its blind squinnying. Present faces were blank disks, shadowed moons. Her patients came and went. She was increasingly unable to distinguish one from another. The face of the Thing hung in her brain, jealously soliciting her attention, distracting her from dailiness. She had gone back to its place, and had not seen it. She needed to see it. Why she needed it was because it was more real than she was. She would go and face it. What else was there, she asked herself, and answered herself, nothing.

So she made her way back, sitting alone in the train as the fields streaked past, drowsing through a century-long night under the cabbage quilt in the B and B. This time, she went in the old way, from the house, through the garden gate; she found the old trail quickly, her sharp eye picked up the trace of its detritus, and soon enough she was back in the clearing, where her cairn of tiny bones by the tree trunk was undisturbed. She gave a little sigh, dropped to her knees, and then sat with her back to the rotting wood and silently called the Thing. Almost immediately, she sensed its perturbation, saw the trouble in the branches, heard the lumbering, smelled its ancient smell. It was a grayish, unremarkable day. She closed her eyes briefly as the noise and movement grew stronger. When it came, she would look it in the face, she would see what it was. She clasped her hands loosely in her lap. Her nerves relaxed. Her blood slowed. She was ready.

Primrose was in the shopping mall, putting out her circle of rainbow-colored plastic chairs. She creaked as she bent over them. It was pouring with rain outside, but the mall was enclosed like a crystal palace in a casing of glass. The floor under the rainbow chairs was gleaming dappled marble.

They were in front of a dimpling fountain, with lights shining up through the greenish water, making golden rings round the polished pebbles and wishing coins that lay there. The little children collected round her: their mothers kissed them goodbye, told them to be good and quiet and listen to the nice lady. They had little transparent plastic cups of shining orange juice, and each had a biscuit in silver foil. They were all colors—black skin, brown skin, pink skin, freckled skin, pink jacket, yellow jacket, purple hood, scarlet hood. Some grinned and some whimpered, some wriggled, some were still. Primrose sat on the edge of the fountain. She had decided what to do. She smiled her best, most comfortable smile, and adjusted her golden locks. Listen to me, she told them, and I'll tell you something amazing, a story that's never been told before.

There were once two little girls who saw, or believed they saw, a thing in a forest. . . .

Anthony Doerr

The Shell Collector

from *Chicago Review*

T HE SHELL collector was scrubbing limpets at his sink when he heard the water taxi come scraping over the reef. He cringed to hear it— its hull grinding the calices of finger corals and the tiny tubes of pipe organ corals, tearing the flower and fern shapes of soft corals, and damaging shells too: punching holes in olives and murexes and spiny whelks, sending *Hydatina physis* and *Turis babylonia* spinning. It was not the first time people had hired a motorboat taxi to seek him out.

He heard their feet splash ashore and the taxi motor off, back to Lamu, and the light sing-song pattern of their knock. Tumaini, his German shepherd, let out a low whine from where she was crouched under his sleeping cot. He dropped a limpet into the sink, wiped his hands and went, reluctantly, to greet them.

They were both named Jim, overweight reporters from a New York tabloid. Their handshakes were slick and hot. He poured them chai. They occupied a surprising amount of space in the kitchen. They said they were there to write about him: they would stay only two nights, pay him well. How did $10,000 American sound? He pulled a shell from his shirt pocket—a cerith—and rolled it in his fingers. They asked about his childhood: Did he really shoot caribou as a boy? Didn't he need good vision for that?

He gave them truthful answers. It all held the air of whim, of unreality. These two big Jims could not actually be at his table, asking him these questions, complaining of the stench of dead shellfish. Finally they asked him about cone shells and the strength of cone venom, about how many visitors had come. They asked nothing about his son.

All night it was hot. Lightning marbled the sky beyond the reef. From his cot he heard siafu feasting on the big men and heard them claw themselves in their sleeping bags. Before dawn he told them to shake out their shoes for scorpions and when they did one tumbled out. It made tiny scraping sounds as it skittered under the refrigerator.

He took his collecting bucket and clipped Tumaini into her harness, and she led them down the path to the reef. The air smelled like lightning. The Jims huffed to keep up. They told him they were impressed he moved so quickly.

"Why?"

"Well," they murmured, "You're blind. This path ain't easy. All these thorns."

Far off, he heard the high, amplified voice of the muezzin in Lamu calling prayer. "It's Ramadan," he told the Jims. "The people don't eat when the sun is above the horizon. They drink only chai until sundown. They will be eating now. Tonight we can go out if you like. They grill meat in the streets."

By noon they had waded a kilometer out, onto the great curved spine of the reef, the lagoon slopping quietly behind them, a low sea breaking in front. The tide was coming up. Unharnessed now, Tumaini stood panting, half out of the water on a mushroom-shaped dais of rock. The shell collector was stooped, his fingers middling, quivering, whisking for shells in a sandy trench. He snatched up a spindle shell, ran a fingernail over its incised spiral. "*Fusinius colus*," he said.

Automatically, as the next wave came, the shell collector raised his collecting bucket so it would not be swamped. As soon as the wave passed he plunged his arms back into sand, his fingers probing an alcove between anemones, pausing to identify a clump of brain coral, running after a snail as it burrowed away.

One of the Jims had a snorkeling mask and was using it to look underwater. "Lookit these blue fish," he gasped. "Lookit that *blue*."

The shell collector was thinking, just then, of the persistence of nematocysts. Even after death the tiny cells will discharge their poison—a single dried tentacle on the shore, severed eight days, stung a village boy last year and swelled his legs. A weeverfish bite bloated a man's entire right side, blacked his eyes, turned him dark purple. A stonefish sting corroded the skin off the sole of the shell collector's own heel, years ago, left the skin smooth and printless. How many urchin spikes, broken but still spurting venom, had he squeezed from Tumaini's paw? What would happen to these Jims if a banded sea snake came slipping up between their fat legs?

"Here is what you came to see," he announced, and pulled the snail—a cone—from its collapsing tunnel. He spun it and balanced its flat end on two fingers. Even now its poisoned proboscis was nosing forward, searching out his fingers. The Jims waded noisily over.

"This is a Geography Cone," he said. "It eats fish."

"*That* eats fish?" one of the Jims asked. "But my pinkie's bigger."

"This animal," said the shell collector, dropping it into his bucket, "has twelve kinds of venom in its teeth. It could paralyze you and drown you right here."

This all started when a malarial Seattle-born Buddhist named Nancy was stung by a cone shell in the shell collector's kitchen. It crawled in from the ocean, slogging a hundred meters under coconut palms, through acacia scrub, bit her and made for the door.

Or maybe it started before Nancy, maybe it grew outward from the shell collector himself, the way a shell grows, spiraling upward from the inside, whorling around its inhabitant, all the while being worn down by the weathers of the sea.

The Jims were right: the shell collector did hunt caribou. Nine years old in Whitehorse, Canada, and his father would send the boy leaning out the bubble canopy of his helicopter in cutting sleet to cull sick caribou with a scoped carbine. But then there was choroideremia and degeneration of the retina; in a year his eyesight was tunneled, spattered with rainbow-colored halos. By twelve, when his father took him four thousand miles south, to Florida, to see a specialist, his vision had dwindled into darkness.

The ophthalmologist knew the boy was blind as soon as he walked through the door, one hand clinging to his father's belt, the other arm held straight, palm out, to stiff-arm obstacles. Rather than examine him—what was left to examine?—the doctor ushered him into his office, pulled off the boy's shoes and walked him out the back door down a sandy lane onto a spit of beach. The boy had never seen the sea and he struggled to absorb it: the blurs that were waves, the smears that were weeds strung over the tideline. The doctor showed him a kelp bulb, let him break it in his hands and scrape its interior with his thumb. There were many such discoveries: a small horseshoe crab mounting a larger one in the wavebreak, a fistful of mussels clinging to the damp underside of rock. And then, as he waded ankle-deep, his toes came upon a small round shell no longer than a segment of his thumb. His fingers dug up the shell, he felt the sleek egg of its body, the toothy gap of its aperture. It was the most elegant thing he'd ever held. "That's a mouse cowry," the doctor said. "A lovely find. It has brown spots, and darker stripes at its base, like tiger-stripes. You can't see it, can you?"

But he could. His fingers caressed the shell, flipped and rotated it. He had never felt anything so smooth—had never imagined something could possess such deep polish. He asked, nearly whispering, "Who *made* this?" The shell was still in his hand, a week later, when his father pried it out, complaining of the stink.

Overnight his world became shells, conchology, the phylum *Mollusca*. In Whitehorse, during the sunless winter, he learned Braille, mail-ordered shell books, turned up logs after thaws to root for wood snails. At sixteen, burning for the reefs he had discovered in books like *The Wonders of Great Barrier*, he left Whitehorse for good and crewed sailboats through the tropics: Sanibel Island, Saint Lucia, the Bataan Islands, Colombo, Bora Bora, Cairns, Mombasa, Mooréa. All this blind. He skin went brown, his hair white. His fingers, his senses, his mind—all of him—obsessed over the geometry of exoskeletons, the sculpture of calcium, the evolutionary rationale for ramps, spines, beads, whorls, folds. He learned to identify a shell by flipping it up in his hand; the shell spun, his fingers assessed its form, classified it: *Ancilla, Ficus, Terebra*. He returned to Florida, earned a bachelor's in biology, a Ph.D. in malacology. He circled the equator; got terribly lost in the streets of Fiji; got robbed in Guam and again in the Seychelles; discovered new species of bivalves, a new family of tusk shells, a new *Nassarius,* a new *Fragum*.

Four books, three Seeing Eye shepherds, and a son named Josh later, he retired early from his professorship and moved to a thatch-roofed kibanda just north of Lamu, Kenya, one hundred kilometers south of the equator in a small marine park in the remotest elbow of the Lamu Archipelago. He was fifty-eight years old. He had realized, finally, that he would only understand so much, that malacology only led him downward, to more questions. He had never comprehended the endless variations of design: Why this lattice ornament? Why these fluted scales, these lumpy nodes? Ignorance was, in the end, and in so many ways, a privilege: to find a shell, to feel it, to understand only on some unspeakable level why it bothered to be so lovely. What joy he found in that, what utter mystery.

Every six hours the tides plowed shelves of beauty onto the beaches of the world, and here he was, able to walk out into it, thrust his hands into it, spin a piece of it between his fingers. To gather up seashells—each one an amazement—to know their names, to drop them into a bucket: this was what filled his life, what overfilled it.

Some mornings, moving through the lagoon, Tumaini splashing comfortably ahead, he felt a nearly irresistible urge to bow down.

But then, two years ago, there was this twist in his life, this spiral which was at once inevitable and unpredictable, like the aperture in a horn shell. (Imagine running a thumb down one, tracing its helix, fingering its flat spiral ribs, encountering its sudden, twisting opening.) He was sixty-three, moving out across the shadeless beach behind his kibanda, poking a beached sea cucumber with his toe, when Tumaini yelped and skittered and dashed away, galloping down-shore, her collar jangling. When the shell collector caught up, he caught up with Nancy, sun-stroked and incoherent, wandering the beach in a khaki travel suit as if she had dropped from the clouds, fallen from a 747. He took her inside and laid her on his cot and poured warm chai down her throat. She shivered awfully; he radioed Dr. Kabiru who boated in from Lamu.

"A fever has her," Dr. Kabiru pronounced, and poured sea water over her chest, swamping her blouse and the shell collector's floor. Eventually her fever fell, the doctor left and she slept and did not wake for two days. To the shell collector's surprise no one came looking for her—no one called; no taxi-boats came speeding into the lagoon ferrying frantic American search parties.

As soon as she recovered enough to talk she talked endlessly, a torrent of divulged privacies. She'd been coherent for a half hour when she explained she'd left a husband and kids. She'd been naked in her pool, floating on her back, when she realized that her life—two children, a three-story Tudor, an Audi wagon—was not what she wanted. She'd left that day. At some point, traveling through Cairo, she ran across a neo-Buddhist who turned her on to words like "inner peace" and "equilibrium." She was on her way to live with him in Tanzania when she contracted malaria. "But look!" she exclaimed, tossing up her hands. "I wound up here!" As if it were all settled.

The shell collector nursed and listened and made her toast. Every three days she faded into shivering delirium. He knelt by her and trickled seawater over her chest, as Dr. Kabiru had prescribed.

Most days she seemed fine, babbling her secrets. He fell for her, in his own unspoken way. In the lagoon she would call to him and he would swim to her, show her the even stroke he could muster with his sixty-three-year-old arms. In the kitchen he tried making her Mickey Mouse pancakes and she assured him, giggling, that they were delicious.

And then one midnight she climbed onto him. Before he was fully awake, they had made love. Afterward he heard her crying. Was sex something to cry about? "You miss your kids," he said.

"No." Her face was in the pillow and her words were muffled. "I don't need them anymore. I just need balance. Equilibrium."

"Maybe you miss your family. It's only natural."

She turned to him. "Natural? You don't seem to miss *your* kid. I've seen those letters he sends. I don't see you sending any back."

"Well, he's thirty . . ." he said. "And I didn't run off."

"Didn't run off? You're three trillion miles from home! Some retirement. No freshwater, no friends. Bugs crawling in the bathtub."

He didn't know what to say: What did she want anyhow? He went out collecting.

Tumaini seemed grateful for it, to be in the sea, under the moon, perhaps just to be away from her master's garrulous guest. He unclipped her harness; she nuzzled his calves as he waded. It was a lovely night, a cooling breeze flowing around their bodies, the warmer tidal current running against it, threading between their legs. Tumaini paddled to a rock-perch, and he began to roam, stopped, his fingers probing the sand. A marlin-spike, a crowned nassa, a branched murex, a lined bullia, small voyagers navigating the current-packed ridges of sand. He admired their sleekness and put them back where he found them. Just before dawn he found two cone shells he couldn't identify, three inches long and audacious, attempting to devour a damselfish they had paralyzed.

When he returned, hours later, the sun was warm on his head and shoulders and he came smiling into the kibanda to find Nancy catatonic on his cot. Her forehead was cold and damp. He rapped his knuckles on her sternum and she did not reflex. Her pulse measured at twenty, then eighteen. He phoned Dr. Kabiru, who motored his launch over the reef and knelt beside her and spoke in her ear. "Bizarre reaction to malaria," the doctor mumbled. "Her heart hardly beats."

The shell collector paced his kibanda, blundered into chairs and tables that had been unmoved for ten years. Finally he knelt on the kitchen floor, not praying so much as buckling. Tumaini, who was agitated and confused, mistook despair for playfulness, and rushed to him, knocking him over. Lying there, on the tile, Tumaini slobbering on his cheek, he felt the cone shell, the snail inching its way, blindly, purposefully, toward the door.

Under a microscope, the shell collector had been told, the teeth of cones look long and sharp, like tiny translucent bayonets. The proboscis slips out the siphonal canal, unrolling, the barbed teeth spring forward. In victims the bite causes a spreading insentience, a rising tide of paralysis. First your palm goes horribly cold, then your forearm, then your shoulder. The chill spreads to your chest. You can't swallow, you can't see. You burn. You freeze to death.

"There is nothing," Dr. Kabiru said, eyeing the snail, "I can do for this. No antivenom, no fix. I can do nothing." He wrapped Nancy in a blanket and sat by her in a canvas chair and ate a mango with his penknife. The shell collector boiled the cone shell in the chai pot and forked the snail out with a steel needle. He held the shell, fingered its warm pavilion, felt its mineral convolutions.

Ten hours of this vigil, a sunset and bats feeding and the bats gone full-bellied into their caves at dawn and then Nancy came to, suddenly, miraculously, bright-eyed.

"*That*," she announced, sitting up in front of the dumbfounded doctor, "was the most incredible thing ever." As if she had just finished viewing some hypnotic, twelve-hour cartoon. She claimed the sea had gone slushy and snow blew down around her and all of it—the sea, the snowflakes, the white frozen sky—pulsed. "*Pulsed!*" she shouted. "Sssshhh!" she yelled at the doctor, at the stunned shell collector. "It's still pulsing! *Whump! Whump!*"

She was, she exclaimed, cured of malaria, cured of delirium; she was *balanced*. "Surely," the shell collector said, "you're not entirely recovered," but even as he said this he wasn't so sure. She smelled different, like melt-water, like slush, glaciers softening in spring. She spent the morning swimming in the lagoon, squealing and splashing. She ate a tin of peanut butter, practiced high leg-kicks on the beach, sang Neil Diamond songs in a high, scratchy voice.

That night there was another surprise: she begged to be bitten with a cone again. She promised she'd fly directly home to be with her kids, she'd phone her husband in the morning and plead forgiveness, but first he had to sting her with one of those incredible shells one more time. She was on her knees. She pawed up his shorts. "Please," she begged. She smelled so different.

He refused. Exhausted, dazed, he sent her away on a water-taxi to Lamu.

The surprises weren't over. The course of his life was diving into its reverse spiral by now, into that dark, whorling aperture. A week after Nancy's recovery, Dr. Kabiru's motor-launch again came sputtering over the reef. And behind him were others; the shell collector heard the hulls of four or five dhows come over the coral, heard the splashes as people hopped out to drag the boats ashore. Soon his kibanda was crowded. They stepped on whelks drying on the front step, trod over a pile of chitons by the bathroom. Tumaini retreated under the shell collector's cot, put her muzzle on her paws.

Dr. Kabiru announced that a mwadhini, the mwadhini of Lamu's oldest and largest mosque, was here to visit the shell collector, and with him were the mwadhini's brothers, and his brothers-in-law. The shell collector shook the men's hands as they greeted him, dhow-builders' hands, fishermen's hands.

The doctor explained that the mwadhini's daughter was terribly ill; she was only eight years old and her already malignant malaria had become something altogether more malignant, something the doctor did not recognize. Her skin had gone mustard-seed yellow, she threw up several times a day, her hair fell out. Worse yet: she had degenerated rapidly. For the past three days she had been delirious, wasted. She tore at her own skin. Her wrists had to be bound to the headboard. These men, the doctor said, wanted the shell collector to give her the same treatment he had given the American woman. He would be paid.

The shell collector felt them crowded into the room, these ocean Muslims in their rustling kanzus and squeaking flip-flops, each stinking of his work—gutted perch, fertilizer, hull-tar—each leaning in to hear his reply.

"This is ridiculous," he said. "She will die. What happened to Nancy was some kind of fluke. It was not a treatment."

"We have tried everything," the doctor said.

"What you ask is impossible," the shell collector repeated. "Worse than impossible. Insane."

There was silence. Finally a voice directly before him spoke, a strident, resonant voice, a voice he heard five times a day as it swung out from loudspeakers over the rooftops of Lamu and summoned people to prayer. "The child's mother," the mwadhini began, "and I, and my brothers, and my brothers' wives, and the whole island of Lamu, we have prayed for this child. We have prayed for many months. It seems sometimes that we have always prayed for her. And then today the doctor tells us of this American who was cured of the same disease by a snail. Such a simple cure. Elegant, would you not say? A snail which accomplishes what laboratory capsules cannot. Allah, we reason, must be involved in something so elegant. So you see. These are signs all around us. We must not ignore them."

The shell collector refused again. "She must be small, if she is only eight. Her body will not withstand the venom of a cone. Nancy could have died—she *should* have died. Your daughter will be killed."

The mwadhini stepped closer, took the shell collector's face in his hands. "Are these," he intoned, "not strange and amazing coincidences? That this American was cured of her afflictions and that my child has similar afflictions? That you are here and I am here, that animals right now crawling in the sand outside your door harbor the cure?"

The shell collector paused. Finally he said, "Imagine a snake, a terribly venomous sea snake. The kind of venom that swells a body to bruising. It stops the heart. It causes screaming pain. You're asking this snake to bite your daughter."

"We're sorry to hear this," said a voice behind the mwadhini. "We're very sorry to hear this." The shell collector's face was still in the mwadhini's hands. After long moments of silence, he was pushed aside. He heard men, uncles probably, out at the washing sink, splashing around.

"You won't find a cone out there," he yelled. Tears rose to the corners of his dead sockets. How strange it felt to have his home overrun by unseen men.

The mwadhini's voice continued: "My daughter is my only child. Without her my family will go empty. It will no longer be a family."

His voice bore an astonishing faith, in the slow and beautiful way it trilled sentences, in the way it enunciated each syllable. The mwadhini was convinced, the shell collector realized, that a snail bite would heal his daughter.

The voice raveled on: "You hear my brothers in your backyard, clattering among your shells. They are desperate men. Their niece is dying. If they must, they will wade out onto the coral, as they have seen you do, and they will heave boulders and tear up corals and stab the sand with shovels until they find what they are looking for. Of course they too, when they find it, may be bitten. They may swell up and die. They will—how did you say it—have screaming pain. They do not know how to capture such animals, how to hold them."

His voice, the way he held the shell collector's face. All this was a kind of persuasion.

"You want this to happen?" the mwadhini continued. His voice hummed, sang, became a murmurous soprano. "You want my brothers to be bitten also?"

"No. I want only to be left alone."

"Yes," the mwadhini said, "left alone. A stay-at-home, a hermit, a mtawa. Whatever you want. But first, you will find one of these cone shells for my daughter, and you will sting her with it. Then you will be left alone."

At low tide, accompanied by an entourage of the mwadhini's brothers, the shell collector waded with Tumaini out onto the reef and began to upturn rocks and probe into the sand beneath, to try to extract a cone. Each time his fingers flurried into loose sand, or into a crab-guarded socket in the coral, a volt of fear would speed down his arm and jangle his fingers. *Conus tessulatus, Conus obscurus, Conus geographus,* who knew what he would find. The waiting proboscis, the poisoned barbs. You spend your life avoiding these things; you end up seeking them out.

He whispered to Tumaini, "We need a small one, the smallest we can," and she seemed to understand, wading with her ribs against his knee, or paddling when it became too deep, but these men leaned in all around him, splashing in their wet kanzus, watching with their dark, redolent attention.

It was exhausting, but he'd handled cones a thousand times before, and knew how to spin the shell and hold it by its apex, how to do this so rapidly the animal had no time to spear his fingertip. By noon he had one, a tiny tessellated cone he hoped couldn't paralyze a housecat, and he dropped it in a mug with some seawater.

They ferried him to Lamu, to the mwadhini's home, a surfside jumba with marble floors. They led him to the back, up a vermicular staircase, past a tinkling fountain, to the girl's room. He found her hand, her wrist still lashed to the bedpost, and held it. It was small and damp and he could feel the thin fan of her bones through her skin. He poured the mug out into her palm and folded her fingers, one-by-one, around the snail. It seemed to pulse there, in the delicate vaulting of her hand, like the small dark heart at the center of a songbird. He was able to imagine, in acute detail, the snail's translucent proboscis as it slipped free, the quills of its teeth probing her skin, the venom spilling into her.

"What," he asked into the silence, "is her name?"

Further amazement: the girl, whose name was Seema, recovered. Completely. For ten hours she was cold, catatonic. The shell collector spent the night standing in a window, listening to Lamu: donkeys clopping up the street, nightbirds squelching from somewhere in the acacia to his right, hammer-strokes on metal, far off, and the surf, washing into the pylons of the docks. He heard the morning prayer sung in the mosques. He began to wonder if he'd been forgotten, if hours ago the girl had passed gently into death and no one had thought to tell him. Perhaps a mob was silently gathering to drag him off and stone him and wouldn't he have deserved every stone?

But then the cooks began whistling and clucking, and the mwadhini, who had squatted by his daughter nightlong, palms up in supplication, hurried past. "Chapatis," he gushed. "She wants chapatis." The mwadhini brought her them himself, cold chapatis slavered with mango jam.

By the following day everyone knew a miracle had occurred in the mwadhini's house. Word spread, like a drifting cloud of coral eggs, spawning, frenzied; it left the island and lived for a while in the daily gossip of coastal Kenyans. The *Daily Nation* ran a back-page story, and KBC ran a minute-long radio spot featuring sound-bites from Dr. Kabiru: "I did not know one hundred percent that it would work, no. But, having extensively researched, I was confident . . ."

Within days the shell collector's kibanda became a kind of pilgrim's destination. At almost any hour, he heard the buzz of motorized dhows, or the oar-knocking of rowboats, as visitors came over the reef into the lagoon. Everyone, it seemed, had a sickness that required remedy. Lepers came, and children with ear infections, and it was not unusual for the shell collector to blunder into someone as he made his way from the kitchen to the bathroom. His conches were carted off, and his neat mound of scrubbed limpets. His entire collection of Flinder's vase shells disappeared.

Tumaini, thirteen years old and long-settled into her routine with her master, did not fare well. Never aggressive, now she became terrified of nearly everything: termites, fire ants, stone crabs. She barked her voice out at the moon's rising. She spent nearly all her hours under the shell collector's cot, wincing at the smells of strangers' sicknesses, and didn't perk up even when she heard her food dish come down upon the kitchen tile.

There were worse problems. People were following the shell collector out into the lagoon, stumbling onto the rocks or the low benches of living coral. A choleric woman brushed up against fire coral and fainted from the pain. Others, thinking she had swooned in rapture, threw themselves on the coral and came away badly welted, weeping. Even at night, when he tried stealing down the path with Tumaini, pilgrims rose from the sand and followed him—unseen feet splashing nearby, unseen hands sifting quietly through his collecting bucket.

It was only a matter of time, the shell collector knew, before something terrible would happen. He had nightmares about finding a corpse bobbing in the wavebreak, bloated with venom. Sometimes it seemed to him that the whole sea had become a tub of poison harboring throngs of villains. Sand eels, stinging corals, sea snakes, crabs, men-of-war, barracuda, mantas, sharks, urchins—who knew what septic tooth would next find skin?

He stopped shelling. He was supposed to send shells back to the university—he had permits to send a boxful every two weeks—but he filled the boxes with old specimens, ceriths or cephalopods he had lying in cupboards or wrapped in newspaper.

And there were always visitors. He made them pots of chai, tried politely to explain that he had no cone shells, that they would be seriously injured or killed, if they were bitten. A BBC reporter came, and a wonderful-smelling woman from the *International Tribune*; he begged them to write about the dangers of cones. But they were more interested in miracles than snails; they asked if he had tried pressing cone shells to his eyes and sounded disappointed to hear he had not.

After some months without miracles the number of visits fell off, and Tumaini slunk out from under the cot, but people continued to taxi in, curious tourists or choleric elders without the shillings for a doctor. Still the shell collector did not shell for fear he would be followed. Then, in the mail that came in by boat twice a month, a letter from Josh arrived.

Josh was the shell collector's son, a camp coordinator in Kalamazoo. Like his mother (who had kept the shell collector's freezer stocked with frozen meals for thirty years, despite being divorced from him for twenty-six), Josh was a goody-goody. At age ten he grew zucchini on his mother's back lawn, then distributed them, squash by squash, to soup kitchens in St. Petersburg. He picked up litter wherever he walked, brought his own bags to the supermarket, and air-mailed a letter to Lamu every month, letters that filled half-a-page of exclamation-laden Braille without employing a single substantial sentence: *Hi, Pop! Things are just fabulous in Michigan! I bet it's sunny in Kenya! Have a wonderful Labor Day! Love you tons!*

This month's letter, however, was different.

"*Dear Pop!*" it read,

> . . . *I've joined the Peace Corps! I'll be working in Uganda for three years! And guess what else? I'm coming to stay with you first! I've read about the miracles you've been working—it's news even here. You got blurbed in* The Humanitarian! *I'm so proud! See you soon!*

Six mornings later Josh splashed in on a taxi-boat. Immediately he wanted to know why more wasn't being done for the sick people clumped in the shade behind the kibanda. "Sweet Jesus!" he exclaimed, slathering suntan lotion over his arms. "These people are *suff*ering! These poor orphans!" He crouched over three Kikuyu boys. "Their faces are covered with tiny flies!"

How strange it was to have his son under his roof, to hear him unzip his huge duffel bags, to come across his Schick razor on the sink. Hearing him chide ("You feed your dog *prawns?*"), chug papaya juice, scrub pans, wipe down counters—Who was this person in his home? Where had he come from?

The shell collector had always suspected that he did not know his son one whit. Josh had been raised by his mother; as a boy he preferred the baseball diamond to the beach, cooking to conchology. And now he was thirty. He seemed so energetic, so good . . . so stupid. He was like a golden retriever, fetching things, sloppy-tongued, panting, falling over himself to please. He used two days of freshwater giving the Kikuyu boys showers. He spent seventy shillings on a sisal basket that should have cost him seven. He insisted on sending visitors off with care packages: plantains or House of Mangi tea biscuits, wrapped in paper and tied off with yarn.

"You're doing fine, Pop," he announced one evening at the table. He had been there two weeks. Every night he invited strangers, diseased people, to the dinner table. Tonight it was a paraplegic girl and her mother. Josh spooned chunks of curried potato onto their plates. "You can afford it." The shell collector said nothing. What could he say? Josh shared his blood; this thirty-year-old do-gooder had somehow grown out of him, out of the spirals of his own DNA.

Because he could only take so much of Josh, and because he could not shell for fear of being followed, he began to slip away with Tumaini to walk the shady groves, the sandy plains, the hot, leafless thickets of the island. It was strange moving away from the shore rather than toward it, climbing thin trails, moving inside the ceaseless cicada hum. His shirt was torn by thorns, his skin chewed by insects, his cane struck unidentifiable objects: Was that a fencepost? A tree? Soon these walks became shorter; he would hear rustles in the thickets, snakes or wild dogs, perhaps—who knew what awful things bustled in the thickets of that island?—and he'd wave his cane in the air and Tumaini would yelp and they would hurry home.

One day he came across a cone shell in his path, toiling through dust half-a-kilometer from the sea. *Conus textile,* a common enough danger on the reef, but to find it so far from water was impossible. How would a cone come all the way up here? And why? He picked the shell from the path and pitched it into the high grass. On subsequent walks he began coming across cones more frequently: his outstretched hand would come across the trunk of an acacia and on it would be a wandering cone; he'd pick up a hermit crab wandering in the mango grove and find a freeloading cone on its back. Sometimes a stone worked itself into his sandal and he jumped, terrified, thinking it would sting him. He mistook a pine cone for *Conus gloriamaris,* a tree snail for *Conus spectrum.* He began to doubt his previous identifications: maybe the cone he had found in the path was not a cone at all, but a miter shell, or a rounded stone. Maybe it was an empty shell dropped by a villager. Maybe there was no strangely blooming population of cone shells; maybe he had imagined it all. It was terrible not to know.

Everything was changing: the reef, his home, poor frightened Tumaini. Outside the entire island had become sinister, viperous, paralyzing. Inside his son was giving away everything—the rice, the toilet paper, the vitamin B capsules. Perhaps it would be safest to just sit, hands folded, in a chair, and move as little as possible.

Josh had been there three weeks before he brought it up.

"Before I left the States I did some reading," he said, "about cone shells." It was dawn. The shell collector was at the table waiting for Josh to make him toast. He said nothing.

"They think the venom may have real medical benefits."

"Who is they?"

"Scientists. They say they're trying to isolate some of the toxins and given them to stroke victims. To combat paralysis."

The shell collector felt like saying that injecting cone venom into someone already half-paralyzed sounded miraculously stupid.

"Wouldn't that be something, Pop? If what you've done winds up helping thousands of people?"

The shell collector fidgeted, tried to smile.

"I never feel so alive," Josh continued, "as when I'm helping people."

"I can smell the toast burning, Josh."

"There are so many people in the world, Pop, who we can *help.* Do you know how lucky we are? How amazing it is just to be healthy? To be able to reach out?"

"The toast, son."

"Screw the toast! Jesus! Look at you! People are dying on your doorstep and you care about toast!"

He slammed the door on his way out. The shell collector sat and smelled the toast as it burned.

Josh started reading shell books. He'd learned Braille as a Little Leaguer, sitting in his uniform in his father's lab, waiting for his mother to drive him to a game. Now he took books and magazines from the kibanda's one shelf and hauled them out under the palms where the three Kikuyu orphan-boys had made their camp. He read aloud to them, stumbling through articles in journals like *Indo-Pacific Mollusca* or *American Conchologist*. "The Blotchy Ancilla," he'd read, "is a slender shell with a deep suture. Its columella is mostly straight." The boys stared at him as he read, hummed senseless, joyful songs.

The shell collector heard Josh, one afternoon, reading to them about cones. "The Admirable Cone is thick and relatively heavy, with a pointed spire."

Gradually, amazingly, after a week of afternoon readings, the boys grew interested. The shell collector would hear them sifting through the banks of shell fragments left by the spring tide. "Bubble shell!" one would shout. "Kafuna found a bubble shell!" They plunged their hands into the rocks and squealed and shouted and dragged shirtfuls of clams up to the kibanda, identifying them with made-up names: "Blue Pretty! Mbaba Chicken Shell!"

One evening the three boys were eating with them at the table, and he listened to them as they shifted and bobbed in their chairs and clacked their silverware against the table edge like drummers. "You boys have been shelling," the shell collector said.

"Kafuna swallowed a butterfly shell!" one of the boys yelled.

The shell collector continued: "Do you know that some of the shells are dangerous, that dangerous things—bad things—live in the water?"

"Bad shells!" one squealed.

"Bad sheelllls!" the others chimed.

Then they were eating, quietly. The shell collector sat, and wondered.

He tried again, the next morning. Josh was hacking coconuts on the front step. "What if those boys get bored with the beach and go out to the reef? What if they get into some fire coral? What if they step on an urchin?"

"Are you saying I'm not keeping an eye on them?" Josh said.

"I'm saying that they might be looking to get bitten. Those boys came here because they thought I could find some magic shell that will cure people. They're here to get stung by a cone shell."

"You don't have the slightest idea," Josh said, "why those boys are here."

"But you do? You think you've read enough about shells to teach them how to look for cones. You *want* them to find one. You hope they'll find a big cone, get stung, and be cured. Cured of whatever aliment they have. I don't even see anything wrong with them."

"Pop," Josh groaned, "those boys are mentally handicapped. I do *not* think some sea-snail is going to cure them."

So, feeling very old, and very blind, the shell collector decided to take the boys shelling. He took them out into the lagoon, where the water was flat and warm, wading almost to their chests, and worked alongside them, and did his best to show them which animals were dangerous. "Bad sheellllls!" the boys would scream, and cheered as the shell collector tossed a testy blue crab out, over the reef, into deeper water. Tumaini barked too, and seemed her old self, out there with the boys, in the ocean she loved so dearly.

Finally it was not one of the boys, or some other visitor who was bitten, but Josh. He came dashing along the beach, calling for his father, his face bloodless.

"Josh? Josh, is that you?" the shell collector hollered. "I was just showing the boys here this Girdled Triton. A graceful shell, isn't it, boys?"

In his fist, his fingers already going stiff, the back of his hand reddening, the skin distended, Josh held the cone that had bitten him, a snail he'd plucked from the wet sand, thinking it was pretty.

The shell collector hauled Josh across the beach and into some shade under the palms. He wrapped him in a blanket and sent the boys for the phone. Josh's pulse was already weak and rapid and his breath was short. Within an hour his breathing stopped, then his heart, and he was dead.

The shell collector knelt in the sand, and Tumaini lay on her paws in the shade watching him with the boys crouched behind her, their hands on their knees, terrified.

.　　.　　.

The doctor boated in twenty minutes too late, wheezing, and behind him were police, in small canoes with huge motors. The police took the shell collector into his kitchen and quizzed him about his divorce, about Josh, and about the boys.

Through the window he heard more boats coming and going. A damp breeze came over the sill. It was going to rain, he wanted to tell these men, these half-aggressive, half-lazy voices in his kitchen. It will rain in five minutes, he wanted to say, but they were asking him to clarify Josh's relationship with the boys. Again (was it the third time? the fifth?) they asked why his wife had divorced him. He could not find the words. He felt as if thick clouds were being shoved between him and the world; his fingers, his senses, the ocean—all this was slipping away. My dog, he wanted to say, my dog doesn't understand this. I need my dog.

"I am blind," he told the police finally, turning up his hands. "I have nothing."

Then the rain came, a monsoon assaulting the thatched roof. Frogs, singing somewhere under the floorboards, hurried their tremolo, screamed into the storm.

When the rain let up he heard the water dripping from the roof and a cricket under the refrigerator started singing. There was a new voice in the kitchen, a familiar voice, the mwadhini's. He said, "You will be left alone now. As I promised."

"My son—" the shell collector began.

"This blindness," the mwadhini said, taking an auger shell from the kitchen table and rolling it over the wood, "it is not unlike a shell, is it? The way a shell protects the animal inside? The way an animal can retreat inside it, tucked safely away? Of course the sick came, of course they came to seek out a cure. Well, you will have your peace now. No one will come to seek miracles now."

"The boys—"

"They will be taken away. They require care. Perhaps an orphanage in Nairobi. Malindi, maybe."

A month later and these Jims were in his kibanda, pouring bourbon into their evening chai. He had answered their questions, told them about

Nancy and Seema and Josh. Nancy, they said, had given them exclusive rights to her story. The shell collector could see how they would write it—midnight sex, a blue lagoon, a dangerous African shell-drug, a blind medicine guru with his wolf-dog. There for all New York to peer at: his shell-cluttered kibanda, his pitiful tragedies.

At dusk he rode with them into Lamu. The taxi let them off on a pier and they climbed a hill to town. He heard birds call from the scrub by the road, and from the mango trees that leaned over the path. The air smelled sweet, like cabbage and pineapple. The Jims labored as they walked.

In Lamu the streets were crowded and the street vendors were out, grilling plantains or curried goat over driftwood coals. Pineapples were being sold on sticks, and children moved about yoked with boxes from which they hawked maadazi or chapatis spread with ginger. The Jims and the shell collector bought kebabs and sat in an alley, their backs against a carved wooden door. Before long a passing teenager offered hashish from a water pipe, and the Jims accepted. The shell collector smelled its smoke, sweet and sticky, and heard the water bubble in the pipe.

"Good?" the teenager asked.

"You bet," the Jims coughed. Their speech was slurred.

The shell collector could hear men praying in the mosques, their chants vibrating down the narrow streets. He felt a bit strange, listening to them, as if his head were no longer connected to his body.

"It is Taraweeh," the teenager said. "Tonight Allah determines the course of the world for next year."

"Have some," one of the Jims said, and passed the pipe in front of the shell collector's face. "More," the other Jim said, and giggled.

The shell collector took the pipe, inhaled.

It was well after midnight. A crab-fisherman in a motorized mtepe was taking them up the archipelago, past banks of mangroves, toward home. The shell collector sat in the bow on a crab trap made from chicken-wire and felt the breeze in his face. The boat slowed. "Tokeni," the fisherman said, and the shell collector did, the Jims with him, splashing down from the boat into chest-deep water.

The crab boat motored away and the Jims began murmuring about the phosphorescence, admiring the glowing trails blooming behind each other's bodies as they moved through the water. The shell collector took off his sandals and waded barefoot, down off the sharp spines of coral rock, into the deeper lagoon, feeling the hard furrows of intertidal sand and the occasional mats of algal turf, fibrous and ropy. The feeling of disconnectedness had continued, been amplified by the hashish, and it was easy for him to pretend that his legs were unconnected to his body. He was, it seemed suddenly, floating, rising above the sea, feeling down through the water with impossibly long arms into the turquoise shallows and coral-lined alleys. This small reef: the crabs in their expeditions, the anemones tossing their heads, the blizzards of tiny fish wheeling past, pausing, bursting off . . . he felt it all unfold simply below him. A cowfish, a triggerfish, the harlequin Picasso fish, a drifting sponge—all these lives were being lived out, everyday, as they always had been. His senses became supernatural: beyond the breaking combers, the dappled lagoon, he heard terns, and the thrum of insects in the acacias, and the heavy shifting of leaves in avocado trees, the sounding of bats, the dry rasping of bark at the collars of coconut palms, spiky burrs dropping from bushes into hot sand, the smooth seashore roar inside an empty trumpet shell, the rotting smell of conch eggs beached in their black pouches and far down the island, near the horizon—he could walk it down—he knew he would find the finless trunk of a dolphin, rolling in the swash, its flesh already being carted off, piece by piece, by stone crabs.

"What," the Jims asked, their voices far-off and blended, "does it feel like to be bitten by a cone shell?"

What strange visions the shell collector had been having, just now. A dead dolphin? Supernatural hearing? Were they even wading toward his kibanda? Were they anywhere near it?

"I could show you," he said, surprising himself. "I could find some small cones, tiny ones. You would hardly know you'd been bitten. You could write about it."

He began to search for cone shells. He waded, turned in a circle, became quickly disoriented. He moved out to the reef, stepping carefully between the rocks; he was a shorebird, a hunting crane, his beak poised to stab down at any moment, to impale a snail, a wayward fish.

The reef wasn't where he thought it was; it was behind him, and soon he felt the foam of the waves, long breakers clapping across his back, churning the shell fragments beneath his feet, and he sensed the algal ridge just ahead of him, the steep shelf, the rearing, twisting swells. A whelk, a murex, an olive; shell debris washed past his feet. Here, this felt like a cone. So easy to find. He spun it, balanced its flat end on his palm. An arrhythmic wave sucker-punched him, broke over his chin. He spit salt-water. Another wave drove his shin into the rocks.

The thought: God writes next year's plan for the world on this night. He tried to picture God bent over parchment, dreaming, puzzling through the possibilities. "Jim," he shouted, and imagined he heard the big men splashing toward him. But they were not. "Jim!" he called. No answer. They must be in the kibanda, hunkered at the table, folding up their sleeves. They must be waiting for him to bring this cone he has found. He will press it into the crooks of their arms, let the venom spring into their blood. Then they'd know. Then they'd have their story.

He half-swam, half-clambered back toward the reef and climbed onto a coral rock, and fell, and went under. His sunglasses came loose from his face, pendulummed down. He felt for them with his heels, finally gave up. He'd find them later.

Surely the kibanda was around here somewhere. He moved into the lagoon, his shirt and hair soaked through. Where were his sandals? They had been in his hand. No matter.

The water became shallower. Nancy had said there was a pulse, slow and loud. She said she could still hear it, even after she woke. The shell collector imagined it as a titanic pulse, the three-thousand-pound heart of an ice-whale. Gallons of blood at a beat. Perhaps that was what he heard now, the drumming that had begun in his ears.

He was moving toward the kibanda now, he was certain. He felt the packed ridges of lagoon-sand under his soles. He heard the waves behind him collapsing onto the reef, the coconut palms ahead rustling, husk-on-husk. He was bringing an animal from the reef to paralyze some writers from New York, perhaps kill them. They had done nothing to him, but here he was, planning their deaths. Was this what he wanted? Was this what God's plan for his sixty-some years of life led up to?

His chest was throbbing. Where was Tumaini? He imagined the Jims clearly, their damp bodies prone in their sleeping bags, exhaling booze and hashish, tiny siafu biting their faces. These were men who were only doing their jobs.

He took the cone shell and flung it, as far as he could, back into the lagoon. He would not poison them. It felt wonderful to make a decision like this. He wished he had more shells to hurl back into the sea, more poisons to rid himself of. His shoulder seemed terribly stiff.

Then, with a clarity that stunned him, a clarity that washed over him like a wave, he knew he'd been bitten. He was lost in every way: in this lagoon, in the shell of his private darkness, in the depths and convolutions of the venom already crippling his nervous system. Gulls were landing nearby, calling to each other, and he had been poisoned by a cone shell.

The stars rolled up over him in their myriad shiverings. His life had made its final spiral, delving down into its darkest whorl, where shell tapered into shadow. What did he remember, as he faded, poisoned finally, into the tide? His wife, his father, Josh? Did his childhood scroll by first, like a film reel, a boy under the Northern lights, clambering into his father's Bell 47 helicopter? What was there, what was the hot, hard kernel of human experience at his center—a dreamy death in water, poison, disappearing, dissolution, the cold sight of his arctic origins of fifty years of blindness, the thunder of a caribou hunt, lashing bullets into the herd from the landing strut of a helicopter? Did he find faith, regret, a great sad balloon of emptiness in his gut, his unseen, barely known son, just one of Josh's beautiful, unanswered letters?

No. There was not time. The venom had spread to his chest. He remembered this: blue. He remembered how that morning one of the Jims had praised the blue body of a reef fish. "That *blue*," he'd said. The shell collector remembered seeing blue in ice fields, in Whitehorse, as a boy. Even now, fifty-five years later, after all his visual memories had waned, even in dreams—the look of the world and his own face long since faded—he remembered how blue looked at the bottom pinch of a crevasse, cobalt and miraculous. He remembered kicking snow over the lip, tiny slivers disappearing into that icy cleft.

Then his body abandoned him. He felt himself dissolve into that most extravagantly vivid of places, into the clouds rising darkly at the horizon, the stars blazing in their lightless tracts, the trees sprouting up from the sand, the ebbing, pulsing waters. What he must have felt, what awful, frigid loneliness.

The girl, Seema, the mwadhini's daughter, found him in the morning. She was the one who had come, every week since her recovery, to stock his shelves with rice and dried beef, to bring him toilet paper and bread and what mail he had and Uhu milk in paper cartons. Rowing there from Lamu with her nine-year-old arms, out of sight of the island, of other boats, only the mangroves to see, sometimes she would unpin her black wraparound and let the sun down on her shoulders, her neck, her hair.

She found him awash, face-up, on a stretch of white sand. He was a kilometer from his home. Tumaini was with him, curled around his chest, her fur sopped, whining softly.

He was barefoot; his left hand was badly swollen, the fingernails black. She dragged his body which smelled so much like the sea, of the thousands of boiled gastropods he had tweezered from shells, into the surf and heaved him into her little boat, amazed that she could lift him. She fitted the oarlocks and rowed him to his kibanda. Tumaini raced alongside, bounding along the shore, pausing to let the boat catch up, yelping, galloping off again.

When they heard the girl and the dog come clattering up to the door, the Jims burst from their sleeping bags, their hair matted, eyes red, and helped in the best ways they knew. They carried the shell collector in and with the girl's help radioed Dr. Kabiru. They wiped the shell collector's face with a washcloth and listened to his heart beating shallowly and slowly. Twice he stopped breathing and twice one of those big writers put his mouth on the shell collector's and blew life into his lungs.

He was numb forever. What clockless hours passed, what weeks and months? He didn't know. He dreamed of glass, of miniature glass-blowers making cone teeth like tiny snow-needles, like the thinnest bones of fish, vanes on a snowflake. He dreamed of the ocean glassed over with a thick sheet and he skated out on it, peering down at the reef, its changing, perilous sculpture, its vast, miniature kingdoms. All of it—the limp tentacles of a coral polyp, the chewed and floating body of a clownfish—was gray and lonesome, torn down. A freezing wind rushed down his collar. The clouds, stringy and ragged, poured past in a terrible hurry. He was the only living thing on the whole surface of the Earth and there was nothing to meet, nothing to see, no ground to stand on.

Sometimes he woke to chai pouring into his mouth. He felt his body freeze it, ice chunks rattle through his guts.

. . .

It was Seema who warmed him, finally. She visited everyday, rowing from her father's jumba to the shell collector's kibanda, under the white sun, over the turquoise waters. She nursed him out of bed, shooed the siafu from his face, fed him toast. She began walking him outside and sitting with him in the sun. He shivered endlessly. She asked him about his life, about shells he had found and about the cone shell that saved her life. Eventually she began to hold his wrists and walk him out into the lagoon and he shivered whenever air touched his wet skin.

The shell collector was wading, feeling for shells with his toes. It had been a year since he'd been bitten.

Tumaini perched on a rock and sniffed at the horizon where a line of gulls threaded along beneath stacks of cumulus. Seema was on the reef with them, as she had been nearly everyday, her shoulders free of her wrap-around. Her hair, usually bound back, hung across her neck and reflected the sun. What comfort it was to be with a person who could not see, who did not care anyway.

Seema watched as a school of fish, tiny and spear-shaped, flashed just below the surface of the water. They stared up at her with ten thousand round eyes, then turned lazily. Their shadows glided over the rutted sand, over a fern-shaped colony of coral. Those are needlefish, she thought, and that is Xenia soft coral. I know their names, how they rely on each other.

The shell collector moved a few meters, stopped and bent. He had come across what he thought was a bullia—a blind snail with a grooved, high-spired shell—and he kept his hand on it, two fingers resting lightly on the apex. After a long moment, waiting, tentative, the snail brought its foot from the aperture and resumed hauling itself over the sand. The shell collector, using his fingers, followed it for a while, then stood. "Beautiful," he murmured. Beneath his feet the snail kept on, feeling its way forward, dragging the house of its shell, fitting its body to the sand, to the private, unlit horizons that whorled all around it.

Robyn Joy Leff

Burn Your Maps

from *The Atlantic Monthly*

S IX DAYS after Halloween my nine-year-old, Wes, is still dressing in the furry, puffed-out uniform of a Mongolian nomad. He goes to school in the bushy fake fez he ordered off the Internet, tromps across the light Portland snow in his bloated felt boots. What seemed impossibly clever at the end of October has by November grown a bit disconcerting. We threw the gap-toothed pumpkin out two days ago, and Wes merely yawned. But just try to touch his hat—say, to wash his hair—and he turns all claws and parental condemnations.

Wes's father, Connor, is more annoyed than troubled by this unexpected detour into Ulan Bator. Connor, who sells next-generation CAT- and PET-scan equipment to major medical centers, survives on his ability to make up other people's minds, to blunt dissent with reason.

At dinner he shouts at our son, one word at a time: "Who are you?"

"I'm a yak herder, sir."

"Who are you really, though?"

Wes considers the question carefully. "For now," he says, "you can call me Baltnai."

Connor refuses to call his son Baltnai. On the seventh day, at breakfast, we all sit in silence and glare: I at Connor, Connor at Wes, Wes at no one in particular. When Wes is in the bathroom, Connor seriously suggests that we stage a midnight raid, rip off the kid's costume while he's asleep, and toss it in the trash compactor. End of Mongolian story.

"A fledgling imagination is at stake here," I say. "We can't just crush it."

"I've got this weird stomach thing again," Connor says, tossing away his pumpernickel bagel. "Every morning."

"Connor, he's only nine. The developing brain is wacky."

"Wes is not going to be wacky."

I touch my hand to his shoulder. "What I'm saying is, he has a lot of good reasons."

Wes comes out of the bathroom dragging a huge ball of toilet paper, at least three-quarters of the roll, wrapped into an amorphous blob and hitched to his wrist with mint-flavored floss.

"What in the world are you doing?" Connor asks.

"Now I have a flock," Wes says. "A little lamb."

"What about Ethel?" I worry all the time about my son's fading allegiance to our elderly dachshund, about his breaking her very fine heart.

"She's a dog. This is a lamb."

"You're not dragging that pile of crap to school," Connor says with a snort.

"It's not a pile of crap," Wes states, entirely cool. "And Dad, even in Mongolia sheep don't go to school."

In our usual routine, Connor drops Wes in front of Hawkins Elementary and me at the equally dour-looking community center. Wes gets a kiss, but I don't.

"Why don't you ask one of your freaky child-psych friends," he says when I'm already halfway out of the car.

"Connor, you're making too big a deal. Do you know my brother swore he was Spider-Man for a month? One day he started up our garage and he actually thought his hands would stick. The fricking moron broke his leg, pissed off my dad, and ended the superhero summer."

"Lovely. Your brother. Alise, let me ask you something." Connor doesn't even turn off NPR. "You ever had any Mongolian students?"

"Probably. We cover the globe here in the Pacific Northwest."

"You think that has anything to do with it?"

"It's going to be my fault now—is that the concept?" I zip my jacket high over my throat.

"It's just a question," Connor says. "A line of inquiry."

"It was a National Geographic special, Con. That's what Wes says. Ask him yourself, Mr. Inquiry."

"That damned Discovery Channel," Connor says. "They act as if all information is equal."

"I think it's TBS," I say.

"He watches too much TV as it is," Connor says.

"Con, it's not like we let him watch *Wild Police Videos*."

"Let's review this later," he says.

"Have a nice day," I say.

I teach English as a Second Language. My students come from Mongolia or Turkey or Laos, yet I rarely know it. They are the tired, the huddled, the oddly uniform masses who yearn for Oprah and Wolfgang Puck and Intel. They all wear Gap-ish clothing, even if it's secondhand or Kmart. They bring lunches that have nothing to do with where they come from—the Polish woman eats supermarket sushi, the Japanese teenager downs a burger, the Somali carries in boxes of Chinese takeout and snakes cold spicy noodles into his mouth with his equally serpentine fingers.

I used to love all this, used to get off on the very odor of the class-room—a volatile magic of knockoff perfumes, ethnic spices, and cheap wet leather. I could smell the hunger to fit in, to regenerate into fatter, tanner, more legend-worthy versions of themselves, and it aroused me intellectually. I wanted to feed that hunger, wanted to snake American customs and social niceties and the correct use of adjectives into their heads like so many cold spicy noodles. But that was before burnout set in, before I saw too many of my students get nowhere or get terminally frustrated or get deported, their well-taught English turned to spite.

This year, for the first time in a long while, I have a favorite. I actually find myself bouncing to class, pleased to sit authoritatively behind my desk waiting for Ismail to walk in, always with that loose neon-blue backpack bumping toward his high ass, always with the slightest, smoothest shift of the eyes, always catching my eyes with the very corner of his.

He is a Pakistani in his forties, short and lean. He was an engineer in his former life—something to do with mines, I believe, though I fantasize that he is a bridge builder. Earlier in the quarter I asked my students to write a short essay titled "My Advice to New Immigrants Coming to the

USA." I got a lot of funny answers—"There are many bad drivers." "Bring earplugs." "You must have some lucky." "Eat ketchup, yum."—but Ismail's actually stopped me in my tracks. He wrote,

Throw out all maps. Rip them from your books. Rip them from your heart. Or they will break it. I guarantee. Toss all globes from the roof until you have plastic pieces. Burn any atlas. You can't understand them anyway. They are offensive, like fairy tales from another tribe. The lines make no sense and no longer make mountains. You have come to the land where no one looks back. Remember, don't look back. Don't look out the window. Don't dare turn your head. You could grow dizzy. You could fall down. Throw out all your maps. Burn them.

I asked him to stay after class the day I returned the papers. I underlined the A on his essay twice.

"Your essay was so poetic and so sad," I said. "Your written English is quite excellent."

"Yes, it is for crying," he said. "I am this year forty-five, but I am learning like an American boy. Every day I see MTV. Now I rap better than talk. You enjoy Snoop Doggy Dogg, teacher?"

I snorted. He wasn't the gloomy or downtrodden sort I'd expected. "I don't know, we're more into 'NSync at my house. Tell me, Ismail, what are you hoping to do here in America? Return to engineering?"

"No, not one chance. I want to have a coffee shop. Coffee makes all the world happy."

"Not me, actually. Burns my stomach."

He frowned. "For you, for you then, teacher, we have something very special. We have sweet milk, or mint tea, or a drink of almonds. No worries. We make you happy. We will. No doubts."

For some reason in that moment I believed him, and we became friends after that, talking after class about the vagaries of Portland's traffic laws, about the cultural accuracy of *The Godfather*, sometimes even about Connor and Wes. Ismail never talked about his own family, and I didn't push in that area. After all, he was a man who advocated throwing away all maps—and what were families if not sharp demarcations in the flesh?

But on this day, when all the others have shuffled from the room with their admittedly cushy assignment to write a New Year's party menu, I sit on the floor next to Ismail's folding chair and say, "I've never asked, but do you have children?"

"What do you mean with 'have'?" He smiles slyly. It is impossible to know if he is teasing, playing the coy student.

"Are you a father?"

"Of course," he answers. "But my children, they are not with me in my home. So I think I do not 'have' them, as you say."

"Oh," I say. "I'm sorry, then."

"That's no problem," he says. "But you. I think you look very bad. Unhappy."

"No sleep. My son is acting a little weird, and my husband is angry."

"Anger is for husbands," Ismail says with a shrug. "That is the way."

"I know, but this is different. We disagree about Wes. About how best to raise him. You understand?"

Ismail, perched above me in his chair, lowers a hand, seemingly toward my hair, and then lets it slide away. "In this country," he says, "I cannot imagine to be a father. Your problems, they are so—" I think he's going to say "ridiculous"—"decadent."

"Well, Wes wants to be a Mongolian."

"What do you mean by this?" Ismail is no less confused than I.

"He wears a little tunic and pretends he's from Inner Asia. I don't know why—something he saw on TV or read on the Internet. It struck him as, I don't know, a kind of home."

"Mongolia? Like, as in, Mongolia?"

"Yeah, Mongolia."

"Shitty Mongolia?" Ismail shouts. "Dirty, ugly, poor Mongolia?"

We both start to laugh, the kind of musical laughter that feeds on itself, until Ismail puts a long finger to his stilled top lip and settles himself deep into the impossibly flimsy-looking chair beneath him.

It always ends this way. No matter how Ismail and I begin our conversations, they always complete themselves just like this. We both shut up and just sit together. We don't look in each other's eyes. We don't touch. We just slump, staring into space, breathing lightly, together. At first I found it quite odd, disturbing, indefinite; but now I'm beginning to wonder if it isn't some previously undiscovered form of love.

.   .   .

Wes leads his toilet-paper sheep to the dinner table on night number seven. Connor makes strange faces at me, curling and crushing his lips.

"I met a neurosurgeon from the Ukraine today," he begins, spinning yet another tale of MD heroics for Wes's future benefit. "He was all of five-foot-one, ugly little guy, but they say he has magical hands. He can make precise movements of a millimeter or less. You know how big that is?"

"Has he been to Mongolia?" Wes asks.

"Didn't ask. He uses something called a gamma knife. To blast right through tumors. Is that cool or what?"

"Mongolia isn't that far from the Ukraine," Wes points out.

"How was it in Mongolia today?" I ask.

Connor clicks his tongue at me.

"It was cold," Wes says, "but then, it always is. It was windy, too. It's almost time for *dzud*."

"What's *dzud*?"

"It means the slow white death," Wes says.

"Jesus," Connor says. "Are you okay with this?" He is pointing his fork at me, a piece of spinach waving limply.

"Wes," I say, ignoring Connor, "what is it you like so much about being Mongolian?"

He squints at me. "Can I sleep on the stairs tonight?"

"Why, Wes?"

"Baltnai," he corrects. "Because that's where the Mongolians live. On the steps."

"That's s-t-e-p-p-e, you know. It means a plateau, like a high, flat piece of land."

"I know what it is, Mom," he says, in the fierce way of smart boys. "But since I'm here, I got to do what I can to be there."

"Name me one reason," Connor says before bed.

I could name him three, not the least of which is that we are on the verge of separation. On the verge, we say, as if it were a bungee-jumping platform, as if we could just step backward at any point and laugh at what we almost did. But I don't want to start that talk tonight, so I say, "Grandpa Firth."

"Absurd," Connor says. He is lying on top of the covers in his briefs, fingertips jammed just under the band, which incongruously screams JOE

BOXER. He doesn't look as if he could sell firewood to an Eskimo. He looks like a little boy himself. He turns to the right and hugs the bottom of his naked ribs. I toss his half of the blanket over him. He shrinks to a lump beneath it.

"Slow white death," I say. "You think that's a coincidence?"

"Alise," he says.

Two months ago Connor's father died in our television room, surrounded by hospital equipment and cases of Ensure. Before that we saw Grandpa Firth maybe once every other year, guilted into occasional holidays. Wes barely knew him. Hell, I barely know him. Connor used to say he didn't want him spreading his lies to Wes. I knew only that Connor was like a nine-year-old himself in the old man's presence.

"You don't see the connection?"

"Between my old man and Mongolia? You're just pushing any button you can find."

"No—I mean, maybe there's something there. About the incredible transience of human contact. Or something. I mean, I don't know what I mean."

"No shit, Sherlock."

He shuffles and moves in closer, his skin sharp with cold, igniting that lingering instinct to warm what's next to you. It's almost as though we could drop this whole pretense of so many years, wiggle into one another, make sweat-happy teenage love. Instead I slide the sole of a foot onto his icy calf.

"I think Grandpa Firth told Wes that he used to be a CIA agent in Singapore."

"I'd say it was the chemo talking, but that was him. In translation, he meant he once had too many drinks in a bar in Singapore."

"I'm just saying that Wes liked his stories. He's got that storytelling thing now. It's like an addiction."

"My dad was real good with addictions."

"It kills you that anyone could like Will Firth, doesn't it?"

Connor wriggles a little. "You're so wrong it's hilarious, Alise. That's the only thing around here I'm happy about. Wes was the only one who ever made my dad—" He clears his throat as if he's going to cry, but of course he doesn't. "But you know," he goes on, "maybe it's you, and the way you give him so much freedom. He lacks a sense of that one thing Will Firth gave me—boundaries."

I snort, but then suddenly I'm the one who's crying. Lightly, but still crying.

Boundaries. Borders. Maps. I retreat fully from Connor's body, drop my foot off his warming leg, tuck into full fetal position. It could be worse, I suppose. I have a friend, a child psychologist as it happens, who keeps separate bedrooms with her artist husband. He has sleep issues, Krista tells me, and he can't fall asleep if someone else is in the room. So once every two weeks or so they come to each other to make love, but she tells me it's like visiting a stranger's bed: they are awkward and silly, and when they're done, they wipe up and return to their separate islands.

Separate islands, my brain sings near sleep. Then, before I drop off, I begin to wonder just how many young nomad boys in the heart of Inner Mongolia—*most? 50 percent?*—are lying in their yurts right now humming to the Backstreet Boys on some Walkman a tourist left behind, fully engaged in the reverse of Wes's fantasy, certain they were meant to be born American.

I'm sure I have plenty of culpability. Unlike Connor, I don't consider myself that free a parent. Wes may watch some TV shows but not others. A 9:00 P.M. bed curfew is enforced. I've spanked him several times, but never with premeditation. My worst sin may be that I have spent so many nights on Wes's bedcovers, my favorite globe spinning under my fingers. Ismail's nightmare, our little game.

"It's all so close together," Wes said, giggling, in September, because that's what happens when all you do is trace your finger from one land to another: the very shape of distance falls away, becomes an impossible geometry.

"That's just an illusion," I said.

It was a huge error. People of my generation feel we have good excuses for our loneliness. But what about Wes? He flicks through dozens of search-engine hits for Mongolia, and learns that the world's millions are within his reach. So how can he know it's still okay to feel that no one on Earth can understand him, that no one can comfort him if he sits in his room, a micro-lump in the middle of Oregon in the middle of America in the middle of the world, losing it?

.   .   .

Connor doesn't speak at breakfast. He just clutches his slight paunch. "Are you going to call the doctor?" I ask.

"About Wes?"

"About your bellyache, Con. You see a million doctors every day."

"They're head guys. I need a GI man."

"Like G.I. Joe," Wes says.

"'GI' means 'gastrointestinal' in medical talk. Like guts."

"Ew, that's gross," Wes says. He rubs his nubby wool hat violently.

"Bet your hair really itches," Connor teases.

"When it does, I meditate. It's like praying, only you do it to Buddha"—Wes says *"Butt-ah"*—"instead of God."

"Where do you get this stuff?" Connor asks.

"I don't know. Encarta and stuff."

"You know, nomads don't really have the Internet or CD-ROMS."

"Duh, Dad. They don't need it, anyway."

"Why not?"

"Everything they need is right there. They don't have to order stuff from UPS." He is unflinching, standing up to his father. Connor must secretly be proud.

"And where is everything you need, Wes?"

Wes shrugs and squints, making his features so small and pointed that I want to put him back to my breast, grow him all over again. "I don't know," he says. "Where?"

So much purpling blood pours into Connor's face that I am certain he is going to scream. But instead he shuffles quickly toward the bathroom, where he remains until we are all going to be late.

Thank God it is Friday. I'm not exactly looking forward to the weekend, with everything building to a head over Mongolia, but Friday is my student-conference day, when I meet with anyone who makes an appointment to see me. Ismail always makes an appointment.

My Friday slots are almost always filled. Most of my students come desperately seeking help—but not with their English. Today a tall, balding Sri Lankan inquires whether I know any performing-arts agents. His son has an Asian-techno hip-hop band, and if the kid can just snag a record contract, they'll be able to afford a bigger apartment. I tell him to try a book at the library, which makes him belly laugh for a good long minute. At least I'm useful for something.

Sometimes I think I am a fraud, because I myself can barely speak a second language. I can squeak by with some Spanish and a tad of Farsi, and I have painstakingly memorized certain Chinese characters, but I lack that magical ability some annoying linguists have to slide simply between two tongues, easing back and forth between one way of speaking and another. I admit that I am attached to the shapes my tongue makes, to the comforting way my throat opens and closes day after day.

I didn't mean to do this kind of teaching. First I wanted to be a ballet dancer, but my hips bloomed round; then I wanted to be in the Peace Corps, but I met Con; then I fantasized about becoming one of those brilliant private school matrons who mold little geniuses into men and women of the world, only that was just silly. Of course, it was the same for Connor, who wanted to be a brain surgeon but kept failing chemistry. Nothing quite turns out in our lives. But that's what gets me: there might still be a very few remote places in the world—deepest Mongolia, maybe—where a person comes to live exactly the life expected, exactly as offered. I didn't. None of my students has. Wes, child of his times already, doesn't even have a shot at it. And yet somehow it thrills me—and maybe Wes as well—to know that such a thing remains imaginable.

By 3:00 P.M. Ismail should have arrived, but he is late. In his absence I draw thin, malformed yaks on my doodle pad and think about Connor's stomach. Mostly I imagine it's a problem of emptiness. He has lost twenty pounds in the past six months, has started taking a kickboxing class on the weekends, has stopped buying ice cream. I wonder if this has affected Wes at all—his father's slipping away, disappearing, reducing himself. I wonder also if Connor is doing it for me. Is that possible? Is it wicked to hope that his ill health is rooted in thwarted passion?

When Ismail arrives, he is breathless, agitated. He walks right across my office to the window, which looks on a parking lot overgrown with peeling, rusted Subarus.

"You think *you* have some trouble," he says.

"Is something wrong?"

"Lahore has called. A son may be arrested."

I think of going to him, but I know that's not what he wants. His skin—what I can see of it—seems to sag, pulled toward the window and away from me.

"Why?"

"It is not known. Maybe some drugs, maybe some politics, maybe, I don't know how to say, crazy, crazy, crazy."

"Will you go there?"

At last he turns around, and I can see his face, which looks no different—as soft and yielding around the lips and jawline as ever, eyes still shifted to the side.

"I cannot, you see."

"Can I do anything? To help?"

He saunters back to my desk, forcing a slow grin.

"Let us discuss the *Austin Powers*," he says. "I do not get this one."

"Ismail," I say, "I can't talk about *Austin Powers* right now."

"Why so?"

"You've upset me. You're upset. It's outrageous."

He sits on top of my desk, the way a boy with a crush would. "Everything is what you say: outrageous," he says.

He's so damn glib it infuriates me. I scrunch up my doodle page, yaks and all, and throw it at him. Hard.

He glares at me, finally revealing a glint of hurt. Then he grabs a slim paperback off a shelf and hurls it at my shoulder.

I return fire with a catapulted rubber band. Ismail takes up chalk from my board and strafes my side of the desk with several pieces. One hits me square in the cheek, smarting immediately. I rise and move toward the bookshelves. A paper clip ricochets off my breast. Blindly I grab at a stapler. He takes my wrist. I take his wrist.

We crumple into each other, almost hugging. But not. Our arms fall to our sides, the stapler falls to the floor, and we tremble. But we say nothing. We do not touch. We do not look in each other's eyes. We do nothing but stand there.

Finally he steps back and says, "Thank you. You are a good teacher."

"Ismail," I say.

"Shush—we cross no line," he says.

We cross no line, he says. Or at least we pretend not to. You choose your home and you burn all your maps, but that doesn't mean you might not find yourself lost and speechless where the lines fall away and the mountains blur and the silence feels better than years and years of conversation.

Ismail and I walk casually to the parking lot, talking of *Austin Powers*. "Okay," he says. "But why is this funny?"

"Analysis kills humor," I tell him.

"Why does joy break so easy? This is one shitty substance."

I see Connor in the Toyota, biting his nails. I imagine him winking at me. "Try *Groundhog Day*," I say. "And please, your son, if there's anything—"

He laughs, just like the Sri Lankan—the most frequent response to offers of assistance these days.

In the car Connor says, "That your Mongolian?"

"Oh, Lord. He's Pakistani, Con. He was wondering why *Austin Powers* is funny."

"Wrong person to ask."

"What does that mean?"

"Alise. Let's not. Hey, I talked to a doctor today."

"About your stomach?"

"About Wes. A neuropsychologist, top gun, Harvard, the whole schmeer. He says we're in trouble. We have to nip it in the bud."

"Nip what? What about your stomach?"

"He says that obsessions can literally reshape the landscape of the brain. Neurons get stuck in little pathways, draw new maps. It can be permanent."

"Does he have kids?"

"What?"

"Does he have a nine-year-old son on whom he experiments?"

"I don't know, Alise. The point is he knows the brain."

"The brain is just a bit."

"The most important bit," Connor says.

I exhale into my fist. "So what does he say we should do?"

"Take the costume."

"Take the costume," I repeat.

"Throw it away, bury it, burn it. Free Wes of the compulsion."

"Oh, Connor, that seems needlessly cruel."

"Are you saying I'm cruel?"

"Not you, Con. The idea of it."

"Just like that, you know more than the experts, huh?"

"I know my son," I say.

"I know my son too," he says.

The Toyota pulls hard to a halt in front of the library, where Wes waits inside, no doubt reading up on Mongolia. I find myself unable to undo my seat belt. Connor doesn't take his off either. We just sit there a moment, strapped in, he tapping on the dashboard, I fiddling in the cavern of my handbag for something I cannot name.

Saturday afternoon, day nine, Wes walks Ethel the dachshund up and down my back. This is a ritual we began about a year ago, when I started getting fierce cramps in my trapezius. Wes told me he'd read that Gypsies used to walk pet bears up and down people's backs for money. He has always been that kind of kid—digging up weird facts and anecdotes wherever he could find them. Nondiscriminatory about information, I guess, all of it worth paying out.

The truth is that a lot of his info is crap. But with Ethel he hit gold. She loves being the masseuse, and I can tell by the way her sweeping tail draws broad smiles up and down my torso. I, in turn, love the feeling of the paws pressing into my sinews, their animal motion so much more random and unflinching than a human rubdown. Just a walk on the back. Pure, motiveless attention.

I am grateful, as usual, after the mini-hound massage, so I brew Wes a pot of tea, since that is what he says Mongolians drink. Tea and lots of vodka, he says pointedly, but I roll my eyes, so we have Celestial Seasonings Cranberry Cove instead.

Connor is at his kickboxing class, which means that Wes and I can talk about his idea of building a *ger* in the backyard.

"It's like a tent, but it's round," he tells me. "I just need sticks and animal skins."

"Your father will have a cow," I say.

"A cow skin would be good," he says. I wish his smile would last longer.

"Wes," I say. "Are you mad at us?"

"At who?"

"At me. Or your father."

"Not really." He wrinkles his perfectly smooth face. "Not exactly."

"Are you still sad about Grandpa Firth?"

"It's okay, you know. I think he'll be reincarnated. Maybe as a Javanese rhino, but he'll be born in a zoo, because they're almost extinct."

"Wes," I say, "you've got to tell me the truth. Do you hate your life?"

"You're freaking, Mom."

"Really. You can tell me. Do you hate your life with us, with me and your dad, here in America?"

He takes a sloppy sip of tea and then smiles sympathetically at me, as if I'm a hundred moves behind him. "Silly worrywart," he says. "You guys always think it's 'cause of you. But sometimes that's not true. Sometimes a person just wants to be a Mongolian, okay?"

"Okay," I say. "If that's what you feel like."

But it's not okay, because when Connor comes home from his kickboxing class, his forehead is taut and shiny, his cheeks are fat and ruddy, and he stands in the foyer huffing.

"Are you all right?" I ask.

"Stop it with the stomach."

"You seem a little off is all."

"I'm good. I had a great workout." He smells salty and smoky, like winter air.

"Good," I say. "Tougher and stronger every day."

"Are you mocking me?"

"Jesus," I say. "Can't I say something nice?" But I am thinking, *Mocking, the bane of our times,* and *Why don't I ever feel the instinct for niceness first anymore?*

"Let's go to the movies," he says. "It's icy as hell out there, so it won't be crowded. We'll get hot cocoa and popcorn, be a real fam."

"Okay," I say. "Let's be a real fam."

He stands there for a second. "Where's Wes?"

"In his room. On the computer, I think."

"Wes," Connor calls.

"I think he's going to be okay," I say suddenly. I don't know why.

"Wes," Connor calls in a louder voice.

"He's really such a smart kid."

He appears in front of us, a smart kid in a tunic, felt boots, and a wool fez, dragging crumpled toilet paper.

"Do you want to go to the movies?" Connor asks. "That thing with Keanu Reeves?"

"Really?"

"It's not R?" I interrupt.

"Really," Connor says.

"That's so radical, Dad. It's all CGI—computer animation, you know."

"Great. Why don't you put on your jeans and a sweater, and we'll go get the tickets."

"What do you mean?" Wes asks.

"Connor, please," I say.

"I mean, just go change into something normal, and we'll go."

"I'm a nomad, Dad. Take it or leave it."

"I'll leave it," Connor says. The edge has taken over his entire voice, lopped off the soft bits. "You can wear the hat, but the rest is history. That's my final deal."

"I'm going upstairs," Wes says, and shrugs. "I'll be on the modem. 'Night, Mommy."

"No computer," Connor says.

"What?"

"No computer until you take that stuff off."

"Mom?" Wes looks at me urgently.

"Con, let's just rent a video and have a nice night," I plead. I feel like an envoy to the Middle East, my centrist position as dangerous as any.

"I want to see a movie," Connor says.

"Well, I want to see a video," I say.

"Well, I want to have a loving wife and a sane son, but you can't always get what you want."

"Take that back." Wes jumps in his father's face now, looking fierce and ancient in his little nomad uniform. If he had a scimitar, somebody would get hurt.

"Listen, Wes—" Connor says.

"No," Wes says. "I won't. Not till you take it back."

"Take what back?"

"You know what. Take it back."

Connor bends slightly at the waist, and his knees seem to make small circles. I can see how badly he wants to take it back, how the very pull is shredding his innards. But he can't. He can't take it back because he has no more room to stash anything.

"Take it back, Dad," Wes says again in a hoarse whisper.

But his father, my husband, is paralyzed where he stands, in the foyer, at the base of the stairs. Wes pushes past us and races out the front door, whipping it shut on the beat of a sharp sniffle.

I want to say something to Connor, something he won't ever forget, but he looks so bereft that I can't imagine doing further damage. So I button my shirt to the neck and head out into air that has the essence of conscious razor blades, cutting you just for having the gall to breathe it in.

What I find first, on the Swensons' lawn, is a fur cap laced with strands of greasy hair. Then I see the tunic on a tree stump across Ashford Avenue, and the sash and the fat yellow boots near the bus stop. They have been violently strewn, ripped away. Bits of thread are everywhere in the snow, like shrapnel. I follow the line of them, contemplating just how cold it really is, just how long it would take a naked nine-year-old boy to develop hypothermia.

It's amazing how fast he can run in the snow, as if he was born to it. My lungs are like meat in a freezer, all elasticity gone. I am forced to crawl at the bus-stop corner, because the sidewalks are far too icy to get traction with my sneakers.

I almost lose him, but near the school I find a footprint rarely seen in the snow—light as a snow angel, with individual little ellipses of toe shapes. They lead me to an anemic bush inside whose silver arms Wes is huddled, snorting snot into his trembling hands. His body is bright red, but it looks strong. As I get closer, I see that what I thought were white blisters on his belly are actually frail bubbles of water. He looks more inviolate than I ever imagined he could be.

I grab at him anyway, search his limbs for wounds, feel his baby-thin skin for aberrations. Then I catch his eyes, the whites expanding like the universe, and I see him searching for something in mine, for some reason or explanation or even just a nanoglimmer of hope that will set this all back to bearable. He begins to laugh.

"It's not funny," I protest. "You could die out here like this."

"I'm naked in the snow," he giggles. "I'm a naked Mongolian. My butt has ice on it."

This part is true. He is in shockingly dirty blue Gap briefs, which are soaked with snow and sagging off him. I start to laugh too.

We both look up and see Connor approaching, lurching and sliding and completely off-kilter. When he reaches us, his chest heaves; his breath steams out of his mouth.

"What in the hell are you two—" he starts, but then he stops.

That's what gets me. He stops.

"Oh, Christ, you both must be freezing," he says. "Come here."

I scoop Wes in my arms, his wet bottom drenching my shirt. Connor has had the presence of mind to take a wool coat on his way out, and now he wraps it around all three of us, making a kind of mobile cave. For the first time I realize that I am freezing, that my fingers, nipples, and nose are buzzing near numb. Inside the coat Wes and I cling to each other and to Connor's almost fiery warmth. We start walking home, three bodies moving through the night under one cloak, picking up pieces of Mongolia the whole way.

It's very quiet out. The night is so cold and so amply hushed that I can hear the constellations hum like halogen lamps. We say nothing to one another. When we get to the house, before we separate and rush for the door, for a single moment I almost speak. I almost say, "We're home."

But I cannot tell a lie. I don't know that we're home, because it's as if we don't belong anyplace on this Earth, in any country, or any house, or anywhere, really, but in this ragged circle of wool.

Bradford Morrow

Lush

from *Ontario Review*

W HEN MARGOT died a dark maw rose before me, a somber shaft into which I tramped wanting never to return. If ever I'd felt empty during the seven fragile drunken years we were married, I entered a consummate hollowness after she left me with my inheritance of bottles. Vodka was the legacy I embraced behind the drawn shades of our house, because vodka was the one thing I believed I truly understood about Margot—my nickname for Margaret, who hadn't a drop of French in her beyond a thousand sips of Château Margaux. In the months that followed her death I became so saturated by my *cure,* as I called it—I liked renaming the world—that there was no more a dawn to my drinking day than a dusk. Pints, fifths, quarts, gallons, I worked my way through them all like cancer does flesh. Our kitchen counter, not to mention the linoleum floor, was crowded with glass vessels, some yet unsiphoned but most sucked down to a lullaby of disregard. When I managed to sleep it was on that same linoleum, the sofa, the bathroom floor. Slumber was a rare guest that offered my sodden anatomy pause in the otherwise uninterrupted siege of boozing I wreaked upon myself. This bleak therapy, meant to tranquilize the memory of my alcoholic wife and maybe annihilate myself in the bargain, was so exhaustive that the few friends who still put up with me believed I was hot on her heels. Passingly successful in life, I'd be a permanent triumph in suicide. The way I chose to mourn her death, I would soon enough perish in a toxic seizure or else go as unceremoniously as she did. Maybe it was just as well she totaled our car beyond repair and that I didn't get around to replacing it that ugly winter. Our savings and her life insurance policy set me up so that I didn't have to drive anywhere. Before they could fire me I quit my job. The neighborhood bar was within walking distance, but I preferred the privacy of my home and, besides, rarely had the right legs for walking. The liquor store people took good care of me. Television was a solace. Groceries weren't of much concern since I had no appetite for food, but when I did get a craving for crackers, or frozen pizza, I knew the nearby convenience delivered to invalids and the elderly. Not forty, I was a crawling convalescent.

We never met before the day my life changed and hers ended. What a ruthless irony, that I was driving the florist van to the hospital to make deliveries of bouquets and huggy bears and Mylar balloons with the greeting Get Well Soon and that all this florist's freight of cheer was heaved onto the road, flowers everywhere shredded and smashed. I remember how we stared at each other, two women in the snow, how we found each other's gaze through the exploded glass of the wreckage and I remember the look of shock on her face, a look I understand without any words passing between us like she was saying I'm sorry I never meant for us to be lying here in the cold can you believe this is happening? and You gonna be okay over there you don't look that great but one of us should get up and find somebody to help us don't you think? while with all my strength I was trying to ask this woman trapped inside her demolished car the same questions. To this day I don't believe it was any more her fault than mine though the autopsy proved she was way under the influence. Just we each caught a patch of black ice at the same wrong moment and now here we were in the silence after the collision staring mute at each other across a chasm, a mortality gully, believing in our hearts that though we were badly fucked up bleeding on the new-fallen snow, we were both going to make it, were going to survive this, that yeah we'd have to go through some days and weeks of recovery but all would be well in this woman's life and in mine. I think she smiled at me, blinking the blood out of her eyes, smiled encouragement at me since she could see I wasn't moving, was no more able than she to jump up and run to the nearest house for help. Looking back, I should have felt a lot colder than I did. It was blizzarding by the time the ambulance finally arrived. I remember looking over at her while the white blanketed us and this woman who in those

few weird moments had become like a friend, maybe even a best friend, closed
her eyes to rest her head on the pavement beside her overturned car, and think-
ing how very beautiful she must have been this morning when she got up and
dressed for her day never once imagining it might end like this. Her coat was
black caracul, her jeans were faded, which gave me the false impression she was
a woman who was casual and even comfortable living her life, and she wore a
pair of knitted mittens.

Like my wife, I never much liked not being high. It seemed to me a cruel
waste of time not to be drinking. We'd got together on that premise in the
first place, met for a drink, though at the time she had been dry for one
brave month. That a lifelong romance would enter the scene, love at first
sight we both confessed later, was an unexpected blessing; perhaps less so
her freefall off the wagon. She left the city the year before, moved a couple
of hours north, telling herself she would take the riverside train down
often to visit galleries, or go to museums, things she seldom got around to
when living right there in the midst of so much culture. New York, she
said, exhausted her. She was too young for the silver that had begun to
streak her chestnut hair, the oily skiffs under her gray eyes, the fidgety
hands, night sweats, the ashen flesh which shrank on its already slim
frame. Nothing and nobody held her, so she took the chance and rusti-
cated up the Hudson, convinced it would offer a healthy alternative to the
habits she worried were consuming her. Fresh air, birds, the changing seasons—these, Margaret hoped, would reawaken a lightness of heart, an
enchantment with life that had come so easily when she was a girl, but got
lost somehow. She would quit smoking. Would take long walks every day.
Follow a dietary regimen. Read one good book each week. Garden in summer and learn to crosscountry in winter. Above all, she'd stop this over-
drinking business. As she told her mother, she needed to drain the swamp.

Margot did in fact memorize the names of birds that came to her
feeder. Junco, goldfinch, black-capped chickadee. She stopped with the
cigarettes, and after a tough, edgy, migrainous two weeks of hacking,
began to breathe more evenly and notice subtle scents in the rural air, the
rich aroma of the soil around her tiny rented house after a rain shower, the
salt smell of butter on her bread and the rye itself. *Middlemarch* and
Madame Bovary she read with confused pleasure. She planted a small
patch of zucchini, Swiss chard, basil. Through a mutual friend, of all

things—we had few friends—she set the date to meet me, just a guy who worked at a small law firm mostly involved with real estate closings, divorces, and wills. Despite the reasonable argument she'd admit she made with herself against such a slip, she bought cigarettes on her way to the tavern where we agreed to rendezvous, a cozy dark wainscoted cocktail lounge in the nice historic local inn. No doubt chastising herself while making a silent promise she'd again quit the next morning, she smiled as I lit her up and we entered on a dialogue that transformed our night, all our nights from that one forward.

She would later tell me that not only did she think I was smart and frank and wryly funny—my deluded Margot—but were she asked to describe the face she would most love to look at for the rest of her life, mine was that face. She loved, she would later say, my brown hair which lapsed over my forehead when I laughed, and how I combed it back with strong but delicate fingers, fingers of a pianist—Eros again at his confectionery, given a less musical man never existed. My hazel eyes, she said, sweetly sad maybe. My furrowed brow and a mouth whose lips were maybe paler than those of any other man she'd met but sharply drawn. She even liked my name, James Chatham, and said it had an honest ring to it. How love colors everything.

When I ordered another tequila neat I wanted to know was she sure she wouldn't have something besides club soda. Well, she said, she hadn't been drinking much these days . . . but seeing me shrug in such an understanding, empathetic way, she thought why not. She'd have what I was having. Tomorrow would be a new day of abstinence. No smoking, no drinking, she'd been so good she had earned tonight.

I remember asking her about herself, what coaxed her away from the city, a place I professed to love though I never got down there much—in fact deeply feared it. The need for fresh air, she told me, a fresh perspective. Her favorite museum? The Met, of course. How was it possible I'd never been to the Met? She'd love to go through the Met with me sometime. The Egyptian gallery. The wing with the dugout canoes, painted masks, and shields from New Guinea. Sure, another, she answered the bartender, and told me about how this fellow Michael Rockefeller, former Governor Nelson's son, assembled the New Guinea collection before he disappeared, murdered and eaten apparently by the very tribe in Irian Jaya he'd been observing. I told her I thought of studying anthropology when I was in college, but maybe it's better I never pursued it. No, she laughed, her face gone nicely numb with that third drink, a nostalgic warmth I could see rising through her like sap in a spring tree. She hadn't felt so radiantly alive since she moved here, she told me as much, taking the hand I offered her on the varnished rail. The bartender stood us a round as it was an otherwise slow evening.

Turns out we went to school together, her husband and I, and though he's a year or two older I remember thinking he was such a nice guy, quiet and very gentle and unassuming which he still is despite what people say about him and his dead wife being sots. Martin drinks and my father used to disappear into the likable haze of his evening preprandial as he called it but I never held that against either of them, everybody has problems and faults and things they like to do that other people don't. Like Kim Novak said about William Holden in that movie Picnic, *We don't love people because they're perfect. Look at how supportive Martin was after the accident, and I know that if Dad were around he'd have been there for me too. Hard to believe it had been only a week before Martin and I were going to move to the city, where he could really have a chance with his career and I could apprentice with a Fifth Avenue florist, become expert in modern techniques of arrangement, move beyond all these crummy nosegay-style economy vases and dumb carnations and daisy poms and Red Rovers. Give me fresh orchids and phallic calla lilies and heirloom bonsai a hundred years old! was what I thought when Martin first broached the subject last summer of moving, taking the leap, giving life our best shot. Even my mother was all for it, though naturally she mentioned we ought to go ahead and get married before leaving the old burgh for emerald city. I told her we'd try living together first and then if it worked—white long-stemmed roses for everyone. The world was looking up.*

My mother knew his family, Margaret's husband's family. His father was prominent here she says, a member of the town council for many years, hard-working, a skilled stonemason and when season came around quite the deer-slayer. They owned the blue Victorian downtown that had been in their family for years, everybody believed it was haunted and that bad luck befell them because the ship captain who built it for his wife and children was lost at sea in a whaler and their spirits still hovered at the upper-story windows looking out toward the river awaiting his return from Cape Horn. I don't know much about ghosts but I do know that the Chathams never had an easy time despite their Presbyterianism and their reputable roots in the community and a work ethic that seemed part of the very fabric of the family. My mother said that while James's dad liked working with his hands he had the wits to make a good lawyer or anything else he'd have set his mind to, even served in the last year of the Second World War as an ambulance driver in Italy. James went to Albany and got his law degree but rather than clearing out of this little backwater of ours to make his killing in a city where the pockets run deeper, he set himself up with a local firm. After his parents passed, his sister married and moved to Philadelphia, and they sold the big house. End of an era.

We awoke the next morning not knowing how we wound up at her place, but in truth we didn't care. Margaret offered me coffee, which I drank, reluctant to ask if she had any Irish Mist or brandy in the house, something that might keep the buzz on. That night she told me that after I'd dressed and gone off to work, she sat with her head in her hands looking up now and then to see what bird might be at the feeder, thanking god she left her unfinished pack of cigarettes at the tavern. Otherwise it would have been impossible not to have just one with her coffee. She almost made it to noon before getting in her car—the same one that would double as her temporary crypt those years later—and driving to the liquor store in town she had formerly passed, averting her gaze, many times since moving up here. Besides talking about anthropology, Flaubert, perennials, sailing the Hudson, which was an enthusiasm of mine, her work as a graphic designer, we engaged in an excited controversy about which were the best liqueurs, the most memorable wines, the craziest mixed drinks we ever tried. This was far and away a more candid almanac by which we might get to know each other, read one another's souls—a revelatory map of our personal geographies and histories, where we'd been and where we might be going.

The time I first tried retsina, Hyméttos, I remembered its name and the amazing bittersweet resinous stink of it, though I blacked out in Mykonos, then found myself robbed and more or less naked on the beach at Megáli Ámos. That once in her grandfather's house in Burlington, Vermont, when she was six or seven, Thanksgiving it was, she finished everybody's wineglasses, furtive in the kitchen after the dishes had been cleared and the family'd retired to the den to watch some game on the set. Yeah, yeah, I had one like that. The wedding trick all kids play, draining the flutes of flat bubbly the guests left behind, not giving a damn about the soggy butts you'd skim away first, if you happened to notice them. Her first Rob Roy. My brief infatuation with margaritas. Hers with Long Island iced tea. Pink squirrels, kamikazes, grasshoppers, Singapore slings, not to forget the sophomoric sophistication of dry vermouth on the rocks with a lemon twist—god in heaven, the hideous gaudy swill children are willing to irrigate themselves with, before we discover the mature world of manhattans or a dry Bombay martini.

Her intention at the liquor store was simply to stock a kitchen cabinet with some things for me to drink, when I came by next. For her part, she had to stay dry now, having had her little holiday from abstinence. None of the bottles she bought, however, remained capped or corked for long, partly because I dropped over that same night, as excited to carry on with our dialogue as she was, and partly because after I called in the afternoon to tell her how much I loved our night together and asked if I could see her, she needed something to calm her nerves. By the time I arrived with a quaint bouquet of fresh tulips in hand, Margaret was well along in her cups. I noticed, even though I'd had a few stiff courage-builders at a road-side on the way over myself. We were too fatigued from the night before to match the extravagant buoyancy of that first encounter, but this evening brought another kind of gift. Yes, we drank and drank, the chardonnay first, then on to cognac, which had always been one of Margaret's Achilles' heels, but even more than simply wanting to drink, we wanted to drink together. Sworn solitary boozers, forever before preferring that no one stand in judgment of our innocent habit, this was new for both of us. What a breakthrough, we both thought to ourselves. Later, after our love affair fully blossomed, in the depths one night of a liquory confession, we'd disclose this fact and only fall more deeply in love in the aftermath. We were seldom found apart the rest of August and into autumn. I took my beer out into Margot's narrow shaded yard, and helped her weed the unyielding garden. She packed Rose's lime juice and Absolut in an ice chest to mix gimlets out on the water, sailing the Hudson in my old cat-boat, a single-masted wooden affair, my pride and joy. To toast her first visit to my apartment over a gatehouse garage where I dry docked the sail-boat, I brought out a sixteen-year-old Laphroaig, which we finished as the harvest moon poured pale grenadine light through the window. I tried to teach her how to pronounce the name, an old Saxon carbuncle of a word.

Lah-*fragge*, I said. Accent's on the second syllable. But there aren't any syllables, or else way too many, she laughed, then tried, *Lap-fro-age?* No, Lah-*fragge*, I said. *Lah-prfo-agge?*

They say your fate is hidden in your name and while that probably isn't true for everyone it happens to be so for me. My last name Mattie never meant much other than it sometimes gave friends fodder to tease me—Mattie was supposed to be a first name, they said, not a last—but I always liked my real first name Ivy because ivy is such a magical plant. Oh the poison ivy jokes were inevitable but ivy is like a green flower and can grow in the shade and poor soil and climb trees and endure climates as different as those of Africa and the Azores, Japan and Russia, and can live as Lord Byron wrote in one of his poems for two thousand years—well, three hundred anyway, discounting poetic license. Birds like ivy for nesting in and butterflies lay their eggs there. The Greeks thought ivy was a preventative for drunkenness and the best cure for a hangover. It's in Pliny, trust me.

So being Ivy it made some sense that I always wanted to be a florist and loved flowers from as far back as kindergarten when we planted a drift of yellow daffodils in the schoolyard. None of us kids believed in our hearts that the bleak little brown bulbs we'd buried in the October ground would survive the winter and burst into bloom next spring. When they did, that was it for me, and to this day a daffodil bulb is more bewitching and baffling than just about anything in this world. Fly to the moon, map the human genome, do what you will, there is no greater miracle than a drab bulb stuck in the dirt and buried under winter snow which blossoms out of the mud year after year. I remember how after I saw those daffodils bloom in the mucky grounds at school, I told my mother I wanted to plant ivy in our yard and so we did back by the toolshed and it grows there even now. I could see it from the window where I sat day in and day out during the first months of my recovery. I know it's just a wall of vines with fluttering green leaves, my namesake, but it gave me moments of comfort just the same, especially after I agreed with Martin that maybe he ought to go ahead to the city and find us an apartment, get things set up so that I could follow as soon as I was ready. He promised to phone every day and visit every weekend.

And he did so throughout the winter, bringing me brochures from various florist shops and other little presents from time to time. He even got a gig downtown playing backup in some club. My lung and the half dozen ribs that *had punctured it were healing more quickly than the doctors predicted, as were my broken leg and wrist. What wasn't going as well as they'd hoped was, to use their lingo, the series of surgical reconstructive procedures on my face. I'd flown into the windshield hard, and hadn't fastened the seatbelt, which was an insane oversight, but there it was and I paid for it with a long gash on my forehead and another on my cheek, as well as a shattered chin. A surgeon in Cooperstown did most of the work and while I usually loved it when Martin was around, during the months they kept regrafting and revising, and my face went from scarred to swollen-and-scarred to misshapen-and-scarred, I was just as happy when he called saying this weekend or that wasn't good for him to get upstate, he had a crucial stint here or was obligated to finish a five-nighter there, that he loved me and missed me and would come next week for sure. God knows I wasn't used to what I saw in the mirror, and even when girlfriends I'd known since the days of those daffodil plantings came over to keep the invalid company I felt ashamed not merely because my face was a devastated distortion, at least in my eyes, but because this didn't need to have happened. Margaret need not have been drunk, sure, but her responsibility was hers to govern and I had no say in the matter and she already paid for her lack of judgment. For me, my head was a kaleidoscope of moving plans and thoughts of marriage and jostling flowers and wondering if I could get off early to see Martin about some damn thing I've forgotten what possibly it could have been that mattered so much I got distracted, blew through a stop sign and hit that sheet of heartless ice. She was plastered; I was in a rush. Now I live with my mother, and Margaret's husband lives by himself. As for Martin and me, I knew where we were headed by the time April showers brought May flowers.*

I proposed on Christmas, the same day Margot discovered she was pregnant. To celebrate both blessings we had turkey sandwiches and Dom Pérignon. When she called her mother to tell her our news, the woman asked her daughter how went it with the freelancing?—though her graphic design commissions were slowed by the move, she had a few faithful clients and lived modestly on savings between jobs—when would she finally get to meet the famous James? and how was the drinking going? My fiancée said work was fine, promised we'd drive to Vermont sometime soon for a long weekend, but failed to answer the last question. Still, Margot knew she would have to cut back because of the baby. I poured her from a second, cheaper bottle of champagne and phoned my sister in Philadelphia. Both my parents were dead, one of stomach cancer, the other of heart disease, so there wasn't really anybody else for me to share the news with. Margot seldom mentioned her dad except to say she didn't like him, and if she didn't neither did I. I'd always remember thinking that day how my willowy future bride and I had grown inseparable, like the espaliered pears that grew together, latticelike, over at the inn where we first met. We set the wedding for Valentine's Day so the baby, due late April, wouldn't be born out of wedlock.

Sobriety wasn't Margot's calling but with my moral support, I who reminded her it was only a matter of a few lousy dry months, she disciplined herself to stay off the hard stuff, drinking wine and the occasional port. I guess I took up the slack by drinking for both of us, but seldom in her presence. Some good souls I'd known over the years, whenever I bothered to venture out into local bars before I met my wife, became happy hour companions—companions insofar as we drank in the same room. From my stool at the far end of the bar I assumed they no more wanted to chat, pontificate, emote, argue, or in any real way engage than I did. Truth was I missed drinking with Margot, but now that she and I had moved in together—my place because of the catboat—I felt it important not to bedevil my poor darling by hammering right under her nose. When she worried she was becoming fat because of the pregnancy, and that I would meet some beauty at the bar, I could only scoff. She knew as well as I did that bars were for one thing only, especially now that I was living with the mother of my child-to-be.

Her miscarriage in January brought these concerns to an end, and together we went on our first extended bender. When I phoned into work with the tragic news they generously gave me the week off, which I spent behind locked doors with Margot in a fluctuating state of alcoholic philosophizing and comatose despair. Her mother pled to come help see us through our grieving but her daughter told her truthfully we were in no condition to see anyone. My sister sent a magnificent blooming amaryllis, which Margot dropped on the floor, breaking the clay pot and scattering soil and bulbs. We never got around to opening the envelope with her sympathy card. Instead of waiting for Valentine's Day, we pulled ourselves together toward the end of that black week and flew to Reno. We'd later have a good laugh when my sister said Reno was where you went for the quick divorce, not a wedding, but the knot was tied and we were again, after our own fashion, happy.

The first time he came over to see me I'd been three weeks out of my fifth reconstructive and was for a change not feeling all that bad about myself. I'd taken to gardening in the back yard, wearing a huge floppy straw hat because the sun was apparently detrimental to the healing scars, and was tilling soil for a bed of peonies when my mother came out and told me James Chatham was on the line asking if he could visit. Always protective, especially now that Martin and I were no more, she came out back and shook her head No while covering the receiver of the cordless with her palm, as if he could hear her gesture somehow. I told her he was more than welcome. Time had come for us to meet face-to-face and talk. After all, who suffered the most from the accident—his wife aside, whose suffering was over forever—than he and I? It was right that we finally meet, or meet again really since during my months of nights I'd had an abundance of time to think about things, everything imaginable, and during the hours spent wandering the often frustratingly vague halls of memory I remembered him, recalled having known him better than I initially thought in those first confusing days after the collision when I was nothing more than an anaesthetized dreamer who kept herself alive by picturing different roses and assigning them their names, Coral Creeper and Applejack and Marie Bugnet with its pure white tousled petals and a fragrance that would make the devil himself swoon.

Whiskey sours and daiquiris, mint juleps and sloe gin fizzes, the flagrant highball days and even the dull ones of dry Bordeaux having receded into the mist, we settled that spring and summer into the spirits that worked best for us. Margot drank gin on the rocks, her preference being Tanqueray; I became a Scotch man, and while I liked fancy single malts— Oban, Glenfiddich, so forth—my poison of choice was Johnnie Walker. Johnnie walked me where I needed to go, I said, a fatuous joke that never failed to make Margot smile. Johnnie be good. We had things under control. Back at her computer Margot was someone to watch in the graphic design world—uneven, yes, but when she was on her game just brilliant. As for myself, I was reliable, got the job done, worked slow and steady as Aesop's turtle. Binges were masqueraded as the flu, a leveling allergy attack, a sudden family emergency that called us away for a few days.

After we sank our catboat in shallow water, a heavy October wind having pushed the wide-beamed oak and cedar craft into a rock wading distance from the shore, I quit drinking Scotch. The debacle was without question my fault and I'd been through a fifth of Johnnie when I lost control of the *Margot*, as I'd rechristened her the year we were married. To Margaret's respectful bewilderment, I seemed to get away not just from the whiskey but all booze for a few weird months after the accident—that I only drank beer she found both inspiring and frightening. We even managed during this period of remission to take the train down to visit the Met and indulge in hot dogs and beer in Central Park. Margot pointed out a little flock of birds chirping crazily and flailing about in the top of a cherry tree, telling me they were drunk, which made me laugh. No, really, she said, she'd read about this in one of her bird behavior books—they loved consuming berries fermented by the sun in the highest branches. Soused sparrows, go figure. Soon after that I came over to Tanqueray, if only because it made shopping for the liquor much easier and saved money, since we bought by the case.

Evenings eventually witnessed a new routine in which rather than always drinking together we spent some quality time alone, me retiring with a bottle downstairs where the catboat was drydocked, to work on repairing its ruined hull; Margot curled up on the sofa with a magazine, smoking in front of the television. We spoke about having another try at parenthood, and although our lovemaking was sporadic, Margot did get pregnant again, and once more miscarried. As depressing as she found her prior failure to carry our child—I already had names in mind, Margaret if it was a girl, Dylan if a boy—she descended into an inconsolable depression of weeping day and night, bingeing until her speech was too garbled to understand, though I knew the gist of what she might be trying to say. Third time was not going to be the charm in the years that winged by, day by blurry day, since our love evolved into a sibling companionship rather than what in the beginning was something else. I remained beautiful in my wife's eyes despite my puffiness and bloating, while Margot grew gaunt and angular, her skin transparent and long hair now shimmeringly more white than brown, which I frankly adored. We leaned on each other more and more, reflecting one another like the facing mirrors in a García Lorca poem Margaret memorized when she first moved up here, and sometimes recited. *Woodcutter, chop down my shadow.*

Rarely did we argue but when we did the fireworks blinded all measure of reason. The precipitating problem was always some little thing, which, fueled by the gin, turned incendiary. Why couldn't she vacuum once in a blue moon? Instead of pretending to work on my ridiculous boat which was never going to sail again, why didn't I fix the lock on the front door so someone wouldn't murder us in our sleep? Why was this chicken burnt? Why did I come home so late—because I was having an affair? How was it she always accused me of having the affair when she was the one home alone all day, drinking herself blind? How dare I raise my voice about her drinking when I was going through two quarts a night? Violence would follow these words, never visited by one of us on the other, but as inevitable as our morning-after apologies. Margaret smashed crockery and threw books. I punched the wall and stumbled over furniture, breaking my toe and cutting my hands on sharp edges as well as dull. Ordinarily soft-spoken, we thundered and wailed and wept. Usually tender, we spat and raged. Chairs were overturned, bottles flew. I slammed the door screaming I never wanted to see her again. She barricaded herself in the bathroom threatening to slit her wrists. It wasn't until I tripped and fell into the old French doors that separated the living room from our bedroom, and opened up my forehead and cheek with the splintering glass, sending me in an ambulance to the hospital for surgery to remove fragments and getting stitches which would leave me scarred, that we finally sat down to talk.

Scars, I thought. His face was nothing like mine but his flesh had known the same kind of pain. And yes, I was right. I suspected we met before, back when we were young optimistic kids going to school thinking that the world was a place in which reversals of fortune happen to the oldsters but never to us, which in a way wasn't wrong since now we were people we'd have thought of as very old back then. Still, isn't it crazy how stupid young people are and how inevitable is the downfall, the comeuppance, how when we're young we know we're smart and when we're older we know we're not, and how there must be an instant when the transition takes place and how seldom any of us knows just when that moment was or why it happened. My curse and my blessing is that I do know, of course. But when my mother let James Chatham in and he and I shook hands and even tentatively gave each other a victims' hug, I remembered that hand and that same hesitant hug because years ago when we weren't such damaged goods we'd made this same gesture, kissed each other just like a girl and boy who don't know what they're doing do. It was the first time I was ever drunk, the ground whirling and sky spinning and my feet freezing cold, fireworks if I remember right so possibly the Fourth of July, I couldn't have been more than thirteen or fourteen but understood it was a rite of passage, which meant you had to suffer for a higher cause or something idiotic in that vein, but he did kiss me, my first kiss, and I never told a soul pretty much including myself since I erased the moment—it was under a tree, an oak or maple—from my mind until now. Crazy. We sat and talked about my injuries for a while and I asked him how he was getting along and though he said he was doing fine, as good as could be expected, I saw that his eyes were swimming, their rims red as wild poppy petals. I was sorry to see him go and when he asked if he could come back to visit from time to time I told him I wished he would, and he gave me his phone number. My mother and my friends didn't like him and thought it was unhealthy for me to spend any time with him given, as they saw it, his alkie spouse maimed me for life, nearly killed me. What they didn't know and even James would never really know was the ineffable nature of the gaze his wife and I exchanged as we lay there not ten feet from each other in the snow that winter day, a contact so pure and even sublime I will never achieve it again, something so unspeakably marvelous it makes me feel only gratitude that I had it, held it, held her in my eyes, just as she held me in hers, dying. That James must have gazed into her eyes with a similar depth of compassion obsessed me for days after he came by to see me, and when my mother was out one afternoon I took the chance of calling him at work and asked if he'd like to get together again maybe away from my house somewhere. He took to the idea as if it had been his own and when I mentioned I was still shy about being seen in public he asked me if I'd ever been out on the river, and said my scars meant nothing to him if his meant nothing to me. To this day I find it hard to believe he can't remember that time we were kids drinking god knows what and kissed under a tree with not a flaw on either of our bodies nor many strikes against us yet. I suppose it's all just liquor under the bridge.

The drinking had taken Margot and me to a precipice and we had no choice but either to back away into sobriety or jump. A warm May breeze gentled through the room with its promise of summer. In the sane morning light, undecorated by alcohol, we glimpsed for a brief moment just how ravaged, how unexpectedly destroyed, how diminished, how cheated by booze we were. This had to stop. Margot proposed a contract, binding as our marriage vows, in which we would solemnly agree not to partake anymore, until such time we both felt we could do so with restraint, like normal human beings. In complete accord, I typed the agreement and both of us signed and dated it then had one last eulogizing drink before we walked through the house pouring every last bottle down the drain. Afterward we made love and in our exuberance planned a Vermont trip to see her mother and the family homestead, which I still had not visited. Other itineraries came to mind, too. Philadelphia, Atlanta, the Met again. Why not Europe? When I was there I was always too smashed to see anything. From Montmartre to the Bridge of Sighs, from Valladolid's *Ferias Mayores* to the windy Acropolis—all was a perfect tabula rasa cycled into oblivion by Armagnac, grappa, amontillado, and Macedonian *Náoussa*. Maybe the moment had come for me to revisit all those places with my bride—after five years of marriage we were still newlywedded so far as we were concerned—have the honeymoon we talked about but never got around to sharing. See what had lurked beyond the hazy veil.

That first week of sobriety was far harder for Margot than me, not because I wasn't supposed to mix alcohol with the antibiotics—that had never been an impediment—but because of the prescriptions for pain management and the sedatives I'd been given, which nicely blunted the edge of my withdrawal. Seeing the tortured, ennervated glaze that complicated her already nervous eyes, I naturally shared both pills with my wife, figuring what was fair for the gander, and so forth, imagining these would help her decompress a little, ease her back from that cliff we'd articulated and decided to defeat. The turnabout was as immediate as it was shocking. What for Margot was a reminder of that month when she tried this before, was to me pure revelation. The universe of fragrances, for godsake. I never knew my catboat had such a brackish, fish-tangy smell. I'd forgotten that the sheets on our bed, after being washed, would have a scent. The wallpaper in Margot's small study stank: mildew. Our clothes reeked of smoke and of something else, despondency perhaps. Food had taste beyond hot or cold. The bloated travesty I'd grown used to seeing in the mirror whenever I made the mistake of looking had mutated into a familiar face, one my parents, were they alive, might have recognized, even acknowledged. I jokingly told Margot one evening, I remember you, to which she replied,

Oh, no, you don't, you were too drunk. We both regarded it as some kind of miracle that, sober, we loved each other the same as when we were plastered.

As I healed and ran out of the masking drugs, my old craving resurfaced, and with it the terror that it had never receded or withdrawn its deadlock on me for a moment. I was naked again. I was suddenly dying out here. It was a matter not of hour by hour, but instant by instant that I quashed the impulse to return to the bottle. I crammed chocolate, spooned sugar from the canister in the kitchen, chased it with Coke. Knowing in my heart I was going to flunk this experiment—maybe tomorrow, maybe the day after tomorrow—I could only look to Margot as a beacon of hope and strength. She might survive where it was my fate to fail. She was doing so well. Clients loved her again. She spoke often on the phone with her mother. She'd taken to reading at night rather than stare at the television or into amber space.

The afternoon I came home an hour early to discover her lying on the sofa, delirious, clutching an empty quart bottle of Stoli to her chest, was as exhilarating for me as it was devastating. I had every right to yell the way I did and justly accused her of breaking our contract. I wouldn't have felt a more passionate rage, such an excited fury, if she'd been caught embracing my best friend—though, of course, I realized she was doing just that. We slept apart that night, Margot in bed, humiliated, and me on the couch, mortified by the inevitable. For weeks we drank in secret until our need to be together flushed us out of hiding. Life returned to normal as we began to appreciate once more that gift we'd cherished in times past. The gift that two recluses might somehow find a path from their individual hermitages to one they could share, like monks brought together to worship a wrathful, turned-on god.

How strange of Martin to phone the night before James was going to take me out on the river, Martin telling me how much he missed me and how things weren't going so great without his good luck charm as he always called me, despite the fact I never brought him or anybody else much luck and didn't appreciate the sentiment nor that he asked at the dead end of the conversation how my face was doing, as if my face was ever going to do anything other than be a living topographic map of this surgeon's success and that one's failure. Stranger yet was James picking me up in a cab since he didn't drive anymore and taking me to the jetty where his sailboat was moored and helping me step aboard, then getting us out into the flowing Hudson, into the pristine winds that wafted and breathed as if right through me, reminding me what it was to be in the world again, forgetting I had a face. I never meant to like him as much as I did that day, to feel such an intimacy toward him, and resisted what I saw in myself, knowing that people sometimes tend to identify irrationally with others who have been through a kindred crisis. Not that James saw or felt or thought the same things I did. In fact I had to wonder how he thought or felt at all given how much he was drinking while we sailed downwind past Kingston Bridge and the lighthouse and pretty mansions set back on their grassy rises beyond where the train ran along the rockstrewn shore. He offered me something to drink, too, and I accepted a plastic glass full of white wine so as not to look the prude but emptied it overboard when he was tending to the sail, tacking with the unearthly agility of a specter on the deck, thin as the proverbial rail he was though my friends said that before the accident he'd been different, fleshy and flaccid which I found impossible to believe looking at the man who now sailed me through the pelting wake of an oil barge with such easy skill you'd never know he'd ever had a single drink in his life. He weighed anchor and we had lunch, some sandwiches I'd brought along, and as the boat rose and fell gently in the dull brown water we talked about this and that and the other until it came around to her, to Margot as he called her, Margaret whom I associated with Marguerite, the ox-eye daisy, the "day's eye," so-called because the flower opens its petals in the morning to reveal its center then closes them against the night. He asked if he could ask whether she said anything to me when we were alone that day lying there, and I told him he could ask anything but I wasn't sure I could answer in any way that would make much sense but that I'd try. And I did try. I told him we said nothing and everything, that odd as it might sound we made a covenant, became sisters who sensed we were in the midst of knowing something few would have or get to know in their lives, and that I'd hold the memory in myself as long as I could remember my name or hers. He sat quietly for a time and I said nothing either, wondering whether I hadn't already said too much, had misspoken, opened a wound without meaning to do more than help to close it, and he began to cry and I wept with him. It was then he did the strangest rightest thing; he chucked his bottle over the side of the catboat and held me in his arms never kissing me but holding me like a strong wind holds a sail.

. . .

Honoring her with a half-hearted final double shot of who knows what I swore off the stuff, swore on my mother's and father's souls, vowed I was done forever with the nightmare, pledged that Margot wouldn't remain a martyr for nothing, that her spirit's better half, so to speak, would learn from her tragedy, move on toward the life she might have wanted for herself and her husband. I spent two months in rehab, flinching and trembling like a newborn during the first weeks before slowly, incrementally getting an upper hand on what they told me was a disease. Some days seemed so full of strength I doubted that I ever had a problem in the first place; then an ogre would rise in place of the sun the next morning and I would find myself in a cauldron of craving, of aching, simply lusting for liquor. Worse yet were the long days of plateauing—speechless hours spent staring out the window across the lawn or listlessly attending my housemates' testimonial "qualifications" at the noon group meetings. My sister and mother-in-law and Ivy supported me, visiting me at the facility, writing letters of encouragement, and when the time came for me to return home all three were there to help me move into the new place, a studio apartment not far from where I grew up in that great blue Victorian house. It would not be wrong to say I was a new man. Yet it'd be terribly wrong to presume that despite everything I didn't still want to drink, because I did and will always want to retreat into that dreamier, more fluid life.

Ivy was back at the florist shop, managing it in fact, and while too much bad blood had passed between me and the old law firm, I was hired into another outfit, and found myself taking on whatever anyone else didn't want to handle. I threw myself into work and, as well, the inevitably blossoming romance with Ivy whom I adored. Who would have thought horticultural shows, botanical gardens, or even the modest pleasure of having fresh-cut flowers given to you every other day with a note from your affectionate girlfriend could be so sustaining? Who'd have guessed that, sober, I had no stomach for sailing, got seasick as a landlubber and had to sell the catboat? Who might have believed it was possible for me to reemerge from that infernal maw into which I'd descended after Margot died, leaving me to bury her, I who wanted nothing more than to climb into the fresh-dug pit in the cemetery and lie there until snow and gravediggers' soil blanketed us both?

Some months after my small triumph, my return to life, Ivy and I went to Paris and we had a fine time of it as unabashed tourists impatient to visit every monument and museum. We took the train to Berlin then down to Florence and Rome, and on our last day, walking the ancient dirt paths of the Forum aside the invaluable clutter of tumbled columns and broken statuary, I asked her to marry me and she agreed. The bittersweetness of these itineraries, once meant to be toured together with Margot, was somewhat allayed by Ivy's own deep connection with her. But rather than casting a pall on our marriage, which Margot would not, we both believed, have wanted, we took her memory to be affirmative. We bought an eyebrow colonial farmhouse outside town, which had a view of the mountains beyond the river, and fixed it up with our own hands. A year after we were married, Ivy gave birth to our twin daughters. A barn cat adopted us, so we called him Paw because of his fatherly mien. I was made a partner in the firm. Three years elapsed without a drop.

Down in New York on a late November evening I attended a dinner with one of our more important clients, a wealthy weekender whose upstate properties we managed. I'd spent a long day in his midtown offices going over books and records with his accountant and another attorney, reconciling the numbers and discussing an acquisition he was considering—an annual consultation followed by the requisite dinner at a nice French restaurant just off Madison Avenue. We'd had a particularly strong year with him, and all of us were in a festive mood. Although I had a hotel reservation in case things ran late, I still had every hope of catching the last train out of Penn and sleeping in my own bed that night. For all my hard-won sobriety, it was always a little tough to sit with others who were there to enjoy themselves, have wine with dinner like people do, but I never anticipated how uneasy I felt—stunned is the word—when our host ordered a bottle of Château Margaux for the table. The disease was near me, as palpable and alive as the waiter himself, who poured the vintage into crystal stemware set before each of us. Even the crisp starched white of his sommelier's linen was dangerous to me, I knew. I forced myself to concentrate on the vast bouquet of flowers which centerpieced our table, and thought of excusing myself and rushing to a telephone so I could hear Ivy's reassuring voice, but didn't. While normally I would have turned my glass upside down on the tablecloth long before the wine pourer reached me, tonight I failed to do so, allowing him to fill mine in my turn, knowing it was not for me to drink. Yes, I would lift it during the toast and clink my glass against the others'. Yes, I knew it was insulting not to partake after the salutation. But yes, all the same I would have no choice other than to set the untasted wine back on the table and leave it there to decant for the rest of the long evening ahead, unless I believed that just for once in my life, given all I'd been through and learned, I could join my friends in this most simple, convivial act.

Marjorie Kemper

God's Goodness

from *The Atlantic Monthly*

Fɪʀsᴛ, ʟᴀsᴛ, and foremost, Ling Tan thought of herself as a Christian. So when Mrs. Sheriday said, "Tell me a little something about yourself," Ling didn't even draw breath before responding, "I am good Christian." And so saying, she sat up even straighter in her chair, like a star pupil providing the correct answer to a teacher.

But the employment counselor didn't smile. She didn't even look up. She went on regarding the papers on her desk and said, "Well, yes, I'm sure that you are. But what I meant was, tell me more about your work experience. I see that you were enrolled in a practical-nursing program at Long Beach Memorial Hospital but you didn't complete the course of study."

Ling ducked her head.

"Why was that?"

Ling said nothing.

"Why, exactly, did you drop out?"

Ling smiled and shrugged.

The other woman waited.

The silence got too big for Ling. Twisting her hands, she said, "Had late classes. Afraid to ride bus home at night."

"I see." Mrs. Sheriday looked back down at the papers. "Next time try taking morning classes, because you need more credits." She pointed her pen at Ling's thin résumé. "Your references are very good; I can see you're good with patients. But our doctors and care managers like to see more academic training. You still have time to register for some classes at Long Beach Community College."

Ling nodded.

"Even if you were just enrolled, I could list them."

"Next semester I enroll," Ling said, and smiled. Americans liked smiling, and Californians smiled all the time, so Ling made it a habit to smile constantly. She smiled when she was alone; she might even have smiled in her sleep.

As Ling got up to leave, Mrs. Sheriday said, "Check with me midweek—I might have something then. I see you've worked with children. I have a pediatric oncologist who is looking for somebody to live in and provide custodial care for a patient who is terminal. You wouldn't have any expenses, and you could save your wages for next school term."

Ling nodded, and in acknowledgment of the seriousness of this new topic, the mortal illness of a child, atttempted to stop smiling. But this was not quite possible.

Back in her furnished room, two hours later, Ling drank three glasses of water. She drank the first one because she was thirsty from sitting on the bus-stop bench in the hot sun for an hour; she drank the second and third to trick her stomach into thinking she had fed it breakfast and lunch. She sat in a chair she had placed at the uncurtained window of her second-story room. It was spring, and in a yard beyond a shabby garage two plum trees—unpruned for a generation—were struggling into bloom. Ling let her eyes rest on the white blossoms and took the time to thank God for the beauty he had created in every moment and in every place. Even now, even here. Wherever she looked she could see evidence of his goodness. And the flowering plums were beautiful—if Ling looked only at their canopies, if her eye didn't follow the scaling trunks down to the array of old paint cans and junk lumber nestled in the weeds beneath.

Ling took a deep breath and thanked God for his unceasing goodness to her—air in abundance, strong lungs to take it in, the flowering plums, even the water in her plastic glass. Ling sat in her chair and watched the plum trees until dusk fell and the blossoms melted into the darkness. Then, having no food and no money to buy it, she went to bed. In her neighborhood children played late; car alarms went on and off, seemingly at random; police cars and ambulances wailed on their way to St. Mary's Hospital, a block away. Even after she'd pulled the shades down, the orange streetlights cast a hellish glow on the ceiling. Ling shut her eyes and prayed. She was deep in a prayer of thanksgiving for her many blessings when she fell asleep.

Ling called Mrs. Sheriday on Wednesday from a pay phone on the corner of her street. "Ling, I'm glad you called. I got a call from the doctor about that boy. I made a tentative appointment for you to go out and meet his mother, Mrs. Tipton. The parents are divorced."

Ling smiled furiously into the phone.

Martha Tipton, the sick boy's mother, opened the door to Ling Tan. While still in the vestibule, Mrs. Tipton said, "Oh, dear, you don't look very strong—you're shorter than Mike."

"Oh, very strong," Ling said. "Not big, not tall, but very strong. Used to working with children."

"Mike's sixteen. He doesn't weigh what he should, of course, but he's tall for his age."

Ling smiled. "Very strong," she repeated.

Mrs. Tipton led the way into the living room. "Well, if you say so. Mrs. Sheriday said you'd be bringing references. May I see them?"

Ling opened her purse and proffered the letters, and Mrs. Tipton sat down on the edge of the sofa to read them. Ling remained standing. The living room was sparsely furnished—a sofa, a piano, a bare coffee table. All of Mrs. Tipton's domestic efforts appeared to have gone into her yard and her plants. From the sidewalk Ling had already noticed, with approval, Mrs. Tipton's well-kept garden. Now Ling's eyes went to a row of African violets on a low window-sill—pink ones, white ones, purple ones—all blooming! Mrs. Tipton was a good steward.

"These are remarkable," Mrs. Tipton said, handing the letters back to Ling. "Let's go back to Mike's room and see if he's awake." When they got there, Mrs. Tipton stuck her head inside. "He's sleeping," she whispered, closing the door quietly.

"Will I sleep close by, so can hear boy if he call?" Ling asked.

Mrs. Tipton nodded and opened the next door—into a small room containing a bureau, a sewing machine, an ironing board, and a single bed. "I've cleared out the bureau for your things," she said.

The room had French doors. Outside, healthy ferns and fuchsias cascaded from hanging baskets, and nasturtiums bordered the brick wall. God's goodness, as well as Mrs. Tipton's fine stewardship, was much in evidence.

Ling transported her belongings—a green leatherette suitcase and a canvas satchel holding her Bible and her Bible-study books—on the bus later that afternoon. When she arrived, at six, Mike was asleep again, and Mrs. Tipton was preparing to leave for an appointment with her tax man.

"Mike's had his dinner," she said. "He usually eats at five-thirty. Just go in and introduce yourself when he wakes up. And when you do, give him the pills in this paper cup. I've told him about you, and he's expecting to meet you. If you should need me, the number is on the refrigerator, beside Doctor Mackenzie's."

After Mrs. Tipton had gone, Ling checked on Mike. She stood in the doorway to his room and studied her new charge for a long time. He was blond, pale, and tall, as his mother had said—or, more accurate in the circumstances, long. His bare arms were covered with a light blond down. Ling—who had been orphaned at eight and had survived typhus and thirty-two days in an open boat—could not accept the inevitability of the sleeping boy's death. Inevitability was a concept that ran contrary to her experience. That afternoon, while discussing Mike's illness with Mrs. Tipton, Ling had said that she would pray for a miracle for Mike. Mrs. Tipton's brow had furrowed, and she'd said that it was a little late in the day for that. Ling had quickly dropped the subject, but she could not drop the hope. To Ling, who regarded her own life as an unfolding miracle, miracles were a commonplace.

Later, when Ling heard Mike's dry little cough floating down the hall, she ran to his doorway and spoke quietly. "Mike, I Ling Tan. I here to help mother take care of you until you get better." She smiled at the boy—who pushed himself higher on his pillows and studied her face. Ling went on, "Mother just go to see tax man. Back very soon."

"I don't know where you got your information, Ling Tan," Mike said severely, "but I'm not getting better. I'm in the process of getting worse."

"Naughty boy!" Ling exclaimed, laughing as she rushed forward into the room to tuck in a loose cover at the foot of his bed. "Now Ling here, you stop getting worse. Start getting better!"

"You could maybe benefit from a little chat with my oncologist," Mike said, taking a pillow from behind his back and pounding it into a new shape.

"I tell him thing or two. You hungry?"

"No."

"Mother make you little snack. Leave in refrigerator."

Ling went to the kitchen and came back with a bowl of sliced peaches. "Here," she said. "Look good. Eat peach. Give you energy to get better."

"Have you ever heard of white cells?"

"No."

"Lucky you."

Ling nodded. "Lucky all my life—but not luck really. *Grace*." She sat down at the foot of Mike's bed. "Grace better than luck. You pray for grace, Mike. Not look nice to pray for luck."

Mike ate a peach slice. "I'll remember that," he said, and he picked up the TV remote from his bedside table. As the TV sprang to life, a sitcom audience screamed with laughter; Mike muted the TV. "I'd like to know what's so damn funny," he said.

Ling said, "Nothing that funny, don't think. I read in magazine, studio bring crazy people to TV shows in buses, to laugh like pack of monkeys."

"Hyenas," Mike corrected. "The expression is 'pack of hyenas.'"

Ling nodded. "Hyenas," she repeated. "Bring them from crazy house."

"That explains a lot," Mike said. He flipped through the channels until he found a rerun of *M*A*S*H*.

"Oh, like this program," Ling said enthusiastically. "Good doctors on this program. Funny."

"Not very realistic, though," Mike said. "I've yet to meet a doctor with even a rudimentary sense of humor."

Ling nodded brightly.

"Aren't you supposed to bring me my meds?"

Ling looked away from the TV, where Klinger was dressed like a woman. "Oh, I forget! I get them right now."

She handed Mike a glass of water and watched while he transferred six pills from the paper cup to his mouth and swallowed them. She said, "So many!"

"Yes, and they accomplish so little."

"But good for you—make you better."

Mike turned the TV back up. Ling returned to the foot of his bed. She sat sideways and turned her head to watch. "Klinger wear same dress as my auntie," she told Mike, and giggled.

Mike snorted. "I hope it looked better on her."

"Didn't," Ling said with a laugh. "Auntie not look good, but Auntie good inside." Ling tapped her breast. "Here."

She gazed around Mike's room. It had a wall of bookshelves, and a desk and chair by the window. A picture of Mike's parents sat on the bureau, taken when they were much younger. They were holding hands. Ling turned away; photos made her nervous. They were always of things that were over with, gone—a moment, a smile, a person, sometimes a whole country. A poster of an old man with scraggly hair was on the back of Mike's door. The man was sticking his tongue out. Why did Mike have a picture of a crazy person on his door? "Who is that?" she asked cautiously, in case it was a relative.

"Einstein."

Ling smiled and nodded.

"He was a physicist," Mike said. "A genius," he added for Ling's benefit, because she still looked blank. "You've heard of E equals MC squared?"

Ling smiled and nodded. "Are you genius too? Have so many books!"

"I'm smart, but possibly not a genius."

"How come he make that face?"

"Why not?"

"I try go to college, learn more, but my English not very good," Ling confided. "I quit before bad grades get on permanent record." She had never told this to anyone before.

"Your English isn't so bad," Mike said. "Considering."

"Maybe you help me—tell me when I using wrong word."

"It would have to be a crash course. My mother must have told you I'm on my way out. We're talking months here, Ling Tan." Mike ran through the channels with the remote. "Two, maybe three." He clicked the set off. "Tops."

"Mother can't know everything. Doctors either. I wait and see."

"An empiricist in our midst," Mike said.

"A what?"

"An empiricist is someone who draws conclusions from the evidence."

"Not empiricist—Christian. Believe in God's goodness. In miracles."

"That's what it would take."

Ling nodded smartly. "Already praying. Start without you. You see. God is good. He bless us every day."

"You could have fooled me," Mike said.

Ling quickly fit herself into the routine of the Tipton household. Fitting in was what she did best; it was her special gift. She could be quiet, as she had been when her family had hidden from the soldiers in the forest. She could make herself small, as she had in the boat. If necessary, she could even push herself forward and talk fast and loud, as she had in the refugee camp. With Mike she was cheerful as a rule. Early on they developed a vaudeville routine of sorts, with Mike playing Baby Curmudgeon to her Cheerful Naïf.

With Mrs. Tipton, Ling was careful to be quiet and pleasant. Mrs. Tipton's nerves were ragged, and she frequently burst into tears in the course of ordinary conversations. Not wanting Mike to see her cry, she spent a lot of time outside, working in her garden. She came into her son's room at frequent intervals, but rarely stayed long. Usually she rushed off, saying she needed to check on something—just seconds before bursting into tears.

When Mr. Tipton came over, Ling endeavored to make herself invisible. Though she suspected that Mr. Tipton was every bit as sad as his ex-wife, he seemed more angry than sad. He seemed to be angry all the time, at everything and everyone except Mike.

When Ling first met him, she recognized him right away from the photo in his son's room. Unlike poor Mrs. Tipton, Mr. Tipton looked the same as in Mike's photo. When Ling opened the door to him, she said, "Oh! Mike's father! He will be so happy to see you."

"Where's Martha?"

"Go to market. Back soon. I'm Ling Tan."

When she heard Mrs. Tipton's car in the driveway, Ling went out to help carry the groceries. "Mr. Tipton here with Mike," she said. Ling put away the groceries while Mrs. Tipton went back to Mike's room.

Shortly thereafter Mr. Tipton came out to the kitchen. He looked very angry. "Mike tells me you're praying for him."

Ling felt herself accused, and ducked her head. "Yes," she admitted.

"Well, naturally you're free to pray day and night, but I'd appreciate your not talking to Mike about it. Or about miracles. We've spent two years choking on hope around here; hope is ancient history. I appreciate your intentions, but the last thing we need is a latecomer peddling miracles."

Mr. Tipton had spoken quickly and softly, and though Ling had certainly gotten the sense of what he'd said, she'd missed some of the words. What, for instance, did "peddling" mean? Looking down at the floor, she said, "Just try to keep up boy's spirits."

Every morning, when she brought in Mike's breakfast and pills, she opened his drapes and delivered her line: "Look, Mikey! God make another beautiful day just for you. He expect you to *look* at it."

His line was "Close the damn drapes. It's too bright."

"Too bright for moles, maybe," Ling always responded. "You not mole. You boy."

One morning when Ling opened the drapes she saw Mike's mother kneeling in the garden. "Look, Mikey. Mother planting new flowers for you to see out window. Wave at her." Mike rolled his eyes, but he waved. His mother was kneeling in the dirt, transferring pansies from flats into a flower bed around the deodar tree in the side yard. Surprised, she smiled and waved back.

"Your mother best gardener I know," Ling observed. "She love her plants. They feel it and grow big for her."

"She loves me, too, but this is as big as I'm getting."

"You plenty big already," Ling said. "Bigger than me."

"What *is* this?" Mike asked when Ling lifted the lid from a bowl on his breakfast tray.

"Oatmeal."

"I don't like oatmeal."

"Oatmeal good for you. You eat, then maybe I bring something you like."

"Whose bright idea is this?"

"My idea. I read in magazine when we at Doctor Mackenzie's office, oatmeal cleanse the blood."

"Jesus, Ling, get a clue."

"Won't hurt you to eat little bowl of oatmeal," Ling said.

Because Mrs. Tipton took pills and slept soundly, one of Ling's jobs was to listen for Mike during the night. If he needed her, he knocked on their shared wall. After helping him to the bathroom, or getting him something to drink or a pill or—on a bad night—a shot, or rubbing his foot when he had a cramp, Ling kept him company until he was able to sleep again. One night, curled up like a cat at the foot of Mike's bed, Ling asked, "You want to watch TV? Maybe *M*A*S*H* on." It usually was.

"Not really. Has my dad bawled you out about this miracle deal?"

"Not know 'bawled out.'"

"Did he yell at you?"

"Not yell," Ling said. "Father worried for you. Not want me upset you."

"I was afraid of that. I want you to know I didn't complain about you. I only mentioned it to him because I thought he'd get a kick out of it. I was a little off the mark there. Shows you how well I know dear old Dad. Anyway, I hope he didn't hurt your feelings."

"Not hurt my feelings. Don't need Father's permission to pray. Don't need permission for miracle either."

"I wouldn't think so."

"Father love you very much. Tell me getting special doctor for you." Mr. Tipton had informed Ling and Mrs. Tipton that he'd arranged for a psychiatrist who worked with terminally ill children and adolescents to visit Mike.

"You mean the shrink?"

Ling smiled and shook her head to indicate that she didn't know the word.

"S-h-r-i-n-k—that's another word for a head doctor. One of the high priests of humanism."

"Ah," Ling said. "Father's priest?"

Mike snorted. "Close enough. He's supposed to make me feel better about dying."

"He can do that?"

"We shall see." Mike closed his eyes.

"You want me read to you?"

"Sure."

"Same book Father read this afternoon?" Father and son were reading Hegel. Ling had no idea what it was about; all she knew was that it had more hard words than the Bible and no story at all.

"Not this time of night. You pick something."

Ling ran to her room and came back with her Bible. "I read to you from *my* book." Laughing, she held it up for Mike to see.

"Oh, Dad would love this!"

"He say not talk about miracle. Didn't say about *Bible*."

"True," Mike said. "I know—read the Book of Job. Let's get a standard of comparison."

"Oh, Job *sad* story."

"My favorite kind."

But about fifteen minutes into Job's travails Mike's pain pill took effect, and he fell asleep. Ling stopped reading. She sat very still until she was certain that the boy was sleeping soundly, and then she moved to the desk chair. Ling tried to go on reading (she'd left off where Job said, "Wearisome nights are appointed to me"), but the light from the little bedside lamp was too distant to read by, so she shut the book and put her head down on the desk. The miracle she'd been praying for since arriving at the Tiptons' was nowhere in sight, and even Ling, always optimistic, always on the lookout for a blessing, understood that they were running low on time. Mike kept getting thinner, despite the nice meals his mother prepared, meals that Ling spent hours coaxing the boy to eat. Fortunately, she'd been telling Mrs. Tipton the truth when she'd said that she was strong, because nowadays she more carried than walked Mike to the bathroom. They had stopped going downtown to the medical building to see his oncologist. Now Dr. Mackenzie came to the house, rushing in and staying only long enough to rationalize his big bill and to cast a pall over everyone's spirits. Mike's cough had grown worse. At last count nine pills were in the paper cup after dinner, and, most ominous, syringes of pain medicine were now kept in the refrigerator for the relief of Mike's severe headaches, which came on without warning. All in all, Ling had a lot to pray for and about; her head cradled in her thin arms, she was still praying when the sun came up.

The new doctor, Dr. Hanson, the shrink, came to the house three afternoons a week. On his first visit, every time Mike had said anything, Dr. Hanson had responded, "How does that make you feel, Mike?"

"Like death warmed over," Mike had said, trying to fluster him. Or "Makes me want to die," or "Scares me to death." Ling and Mike had exchanged conspiratorial glances, and Ling had laughed behind her hand.

But Dr. Hanson proved to be such a nice young man that teasing him wasn't much fun. In fact, after he'd been coming for a couple of weeks, Mike told Ling that he felt sorry for Dr. Hanson.

"Why sorry for him?" she snapped. "You the sick one."

"Yeah, but he's so damn hopeful, you know?"

"Bible say hope a virtue. Have to hope."

"For what?"

Ling shrugged. "Just hope." She had begun to resent this particular injunction.

"You're saying that this mandatory hope has no object?"

Ling thought for a minute and said, "Hope is to prop open door, so good things can come in. Maybe when you not looking."

"I see. Hope as a metaphysical doorstop. Good one, Ling. Well, anyway, at least Doctor Hanson *talks*. Doctor Mackenzie hasn't said two personal words to me in weeks."

"He lose interest in us, I think."

"I know. I shouldn't have played so hard to get. And probably I should have eaten more *oatmeal*. It's abundantly clear that I've no one to blame for all this but myself."

Ling looked at the floor. She'd thrown the box of oatmeal in the garbage a week before. "Maybe should invite some boys, Mikey, come talk to you. You have some nice friends own age?"

"Not really. Do you?"

"Not really," Ling admitted. "We each other's friend now, I think."

"Works for me."

As Mike grew worse, the room filled with sickroom apparatus—first a walker, then a commode, and finally, after a series of consecutive bad nights, a rollaway bed for Ling. While Mike slept, Ling went through the Book of Job, which had become a favorite of Mike's, with a fine-tooth comb, hoping to find some consolation. After God had let the Devil have his way with Job, after Job had brought credit to him, God took him back. The Bible even said that afterward God gave Job new sons and daughters, new cattle and sheep. And, Ling supposed, cattle were cattle, and one cow was as good as another, but children were not cattle. Children had souls. You could not replace one with another. So where was the comfort in all this?

But Mike read Job over and over. He memorized great hunks of it, and insisted on reading his favorite bits aloud to Ling. Sometimes he stopped midsentence and laughed.

"I'm in your debt for suggesting this, Ling."

"No problem," Ling said. "God's word count for something in this world, but I not go to college, and not a genius, so I not always sure what."

"Yes you are," Mike said.

Ling shook her head.

"You believe in God's goodness still, don't you?"

Ling turned her back on Mike and looked out the window.

"You do, don't you, Ling?"

"Have to believe in that when I look at God's big world," Ling said.

"There you go," Mike said. "The world is very, very big. It stands to reason that it's beyond our understanding, yes?"

"Yes," Ling whispered. "But used to understand."

"And now you don't. You see, you've learned something already."

"What I am learning?"

"That there's more to heaven and earth than oatmeal and a positive attitude. More than Ling Tan was born knowing. Humility—not to put too fine a point on it."

Humility was a hard lesson, worse than English grammar, and Ling missed her old, blithe assurance as keenly as she might have missed a beloved pet. But she believed what she had told Mikey about hope—that you could use it to prop open a door so that something good might come in. So she hoped. And waited. And prayed for something good to slip through their open door. Maybe at night, while they slept.

Dr. Hanson was an even bigger smiler than Ling—who these days had to remind herself to smile, and who thought that the young doctor overdid it.

"Doctor Hanson always so cheerful," Ling remarked one day, while she folded laundry on Mike's bed. She didn't mean it as a compliment.

"And why not?" Mike asked. "He's not the one who's dying. Though I don't know why he doesn't get right on it, since he sees it as such a gigantic opportunity for what he calls 'personal growth.'"

Ling giggled. "I think he already grow big *enough*." The doctor was a little on the plump side.

Mike laughed. "When he was here yesterday, I quoted some Job at him—'Thine hands have made me and fashioned me together round about; yet thou dost destroy me.' I wanted his take on that."

"What did he say?"

"He said, 'Beautiful, beautiful!' With this huge, ecstatic smile plastered on that big round face of his."

"How did that make you feel?" Ling said, joking.

"Like I'd been dead three days," Mike shot back.

"Maybe Job beautiful if not about *you*," Ling said, smoothing a pillowcase. She almost wished she hadn't introduced Mikey to the Bible. She'd certainly had it with Job and his comforters—even Job's God, whom she'd just barely contrived to keep separate from her own. These days, when she had the time and the energy to read, she stuck strictly to the Psalms and the Gospels. But Mike liked Job almost as much as he liked Einstein. Certainly more than Mr. Tipton at this point in the proceedings liked Hegel. Mike had told his mother that Job was his favorite book—which caused Mrs. Tipton to run out of the room in tears, and which she wisely did not pass on to her ex-husband. When Ling brought in Mike's breakfast, he always quoted, in a rising falsetto, "Or is there *any* taste in the white of an egg?"

Folding towels, Ling said, "I think Doctor Hanson look better if he grow beard. Then his face not seem so wide."

"I'll tell him."

"No, Mikey! Then he know we notice his face fat." Piling the folded laundry back in the basket, Ling confessed, "Mikey, worried about miracle. Afraid prayers aren't getting through."

"Sure they are," Mike said. "It's the answers that seem to be snagged up."

"Same thing," Ling said.

"Not necessarily."

Ling nodded. "Study guide say God answer prayers, but his answer not always one we want. No, I say it wrong: it say, maybe not answer we *expect*."

"Ah, the element of surprise. One of his favorite devices. As we've learned."

Ling took a deep breath and tried to smile at Mike's little joke. "Not giving up, Mikey. I keep praying. Promise."

"Everyone should have a hobby," Mike said, "to quote the estimable Doctor Hanson." He flipped on the TV.

Dr. Hanson had asked Mike what his hobbies were, and Mike had said that just lately his hobby was dying.

Undeterred, Dr. Hanson had said, "That's more of a full-time job, isn't it? I'm talking recreation. Do you play chess?"

After that Dr. Hanson and Mike played chess. Mike consistently beat him. But instead of saying "Checkmate," Mike would say, "How does that make you feel?"

"Beat," Dr. Hanson would reply. "Walloped."

"You don't think he's letting me win, do you?" Mike asked Ling later that week. He was having one of what he and Ling were calling his "bad days." He'd had a solid week of them. The smell of Dr. Hanson's after-shave still lingered in the room. Even his after-shave, Ling had protested to Mike, was cheerful.

"Doctor Hanson can't beat genius, Mikey."

"I may not be a genius, Ling. It's impossible at this point to tell for sure."

"Close. Maybe not like old Uncle." Ling pointed at the Einstein poster. "But you not old like him either. Smarter than Doctor Hanson for sure! What he thinking? *Smiling* every minute at boy supposed to be dying!"

"You should talk."

"I know. Used to smile like hyena."

"Monkey! No, monkeys *grin*, don't they? Hyenas laugh. *Lings* smile."

"Ling not so much smiling now. Only when something to smile about. You notice?"

"Actually, I've been meaning to talk to you about that. I think it's time to paste a big old smile on your face and leave it there, because we're definitely running out of reasons. Anyway, on you a smile has always looked good."

Ling smiled. It was an effort.

A month later Dr. Hanson stopped smiling. Mike was in a coma. Still Dr. Hanson came at his appointed times and sat beside Mike's bed and held the boy's hand—now studded like a clove orange with IVs. Dr. Mackenzie came every day, and a registered nurse came morning and evening. Mr. and Mrs. Tipton took turns sitting in Mike's room—Mrs. Tipton crying freely now, her hands clasped in her lap; Mr. Tipton staring at an open book, the pages of which he rarely turned. Ling sat out of the way, in Mike's desk chair, which she had pulled over to the window so that she could look out at Mrs. Tipton's garden.

On the night before he'd slipped into the coma, Ling and Mike had tried to watch *M*A*S*H*, but Mike had a terrible headache, and the light from the TV hurt his eyes. Ling had turned it off.

"We see that one already," she said briskly. By then they'd seen them all. "That one sad anyway. Even Hawkeye cry." Mike, eyes shut, nodded. Ling gave him his pain shot and rubbed his temples with a Chinese herbal lotion that her auntie had used for migraines.

"My God, what is this stuff?" Mike protested. "It smells like a bog!"

"All natural," Ling assured him. "Very good for headache. Cleanse the blood. Good for bad nerves."

"I can't *believe* you're still trying to cleanse this treacherous blood of mine! However," Mike conceded, "my nerves could not be worse."

"Auntie swear by it," Ling said. She smoothed his thin hair back, rubbing his forehead.

Mike looked up into her eyes. "You know where we made our mistake, don't you?"

Ling shook her head.

"Praying for grace instead of luck. We tipped our hand. We indicated we were willing to *settle*."

Ling bit her lower lip and didn't answer.

"Come on, Ling. 'How does that make you feel?'"

Ling giggled weakly. "Don't," she said. "Too tired to joke."

It was three in the morning. The only noise in the house was the refrigerator humming in the kitchen. Mike closed his eyes and quoted: "'God thundereth marvelously with his voice; great things doeth he, which we cannot comprehend.'"

"That not God, that the refrigerator."

"Maybe, maybe not. You'll admit that the universe, or God—whatever you like to call it—*does* stuff we don't get. Hegel didn't get it. I'm not even sure Einstein got it."

"He get it. That's why he stick tongue out."

Mike snorted.

Ling took a long breath. She put the cap back on the bottle of Auntie's lotion and said, "Maybe God blessing us this moment, and we not knowing it."

"Thanks for trying, Ling, but that may be the single most depressing thing you've said to me."

"Not depressing, Mikey. I only mean he bless me with you and he bless you with me."

The morning after Mike died, after she'd packed and before she left Mrs. Tipton's house forever, Ling went into Mike's room. She had made up the empty bed the night before. Now she went to the window and pulled back the drapes.

"God make another beautiful day, Mikey," she said. Then, after blowing her nose and replacing the ragged Kleenex in the pocket of her sweater, she added, "But this one not for you."

Ling stood staring out Mike's window. The dew was still on the grass; though Mrs. Tipton lay sedated in her bed, her lawn shone brightly in the morning light. The little faces of her pansies were turned up to the sun. The beauty of the flowers, and the sunshine they sought, were, Ling still believed, firm and undeniable evidence of God's goodness. Even here and even now. But this knowledge no longer lifted her up. She placed the palm of her hand on Mikey's empty bed and briefly bowed her head.

When she turned to go, her gaze met Einstein's. She had noticed a month before that except for the rude face he was making, Mikey's old scientist looked a lot like the illustrations of God the Father in her Bible-study guide. She had shown Mikey, who had thought this a hilarious coincidence. Now, her hand on the doorknob, Ling looked into the old face that had looked down on them for months, silently regarding everything they had done and suffered.

"Good-bye, Mr. Genius," she said softly. Then, before she sailed out the door, and in recognition, or solidarity, or maybe just farewell, Ling stuck out her little pink tongue.

Adam Desnoyers

Bleed Blue in Indonesia

from *Idaho Review*

I DON'T BELIEVE in this kind of thing anymore. Maybe you only get one. But they met like this:

Will drove the rear flag car for the trucking company. He'd been headed for promotion to lead man until a few trips back, when he rear-ended the two-bedroom on the doublewide. While Will was obviously no longer in high esteem with management, some fluke had occurred where he got to keep driving while they investigated. It was one of those little breaks some people get all their lives and others never get. Usually, he never got them.

The last trip Will took was supposed to be to Ohio but he'd gotten stoned and couldn't keep up with the convoy and didn't see a whole lot of reasons to go to Ohio anyway. He pulled onto the side of the highway at some anonymous point where I saw a car fire the other day and I knew that place because we'd gone by it when we were going west once and Will said, That's where I pulled over that time and then he told me the rest and when he finished telling me I looked back to see it again but it was gone.

When he'd stopped, he left the flag car running and walked through the trees to the chain-link fence which I think starts on one coast and runs all the way to the other. He took a couple steps and jumped, hooking his fingers in the rings, and climbed until he was high enough to throw a leg over. The cars sounded like private planes landing behind him and the concrete hummed like a conveyor belt never to stop and before he knew it he was in a backyard all jungle-lush and maintained by landscaping professionals such as myself and the sun was a second-place prizefighter's eye and with all this beauty Will knew his presence was highly unauthorized. In the middle of that yard was a pool. The Mr., though Will did not know him yet, was asleep on a raft which doodled around over the water. The Mr. had the vestigial musculature of a strong man lost in the folds of middle-age, that skin shining and tan as a belt. But what Will noticed most was the sound of someone banging away and away on a monstrous piano, the notes bridging sharply and smoothly over the din of a tractor-trailer horn howling east. Will stood still to listen to the crash of measure after measure of some monumental prelude or ballad or manifesto and then he was compelled to take baby steps through neon-green grass towards the source. The Mrs. saw him coming from the upstairs window. She scampered downstairs but would be too late. Will reached the house and the sliding glass door, which was open, and peered through the screen door, but was blinded by that trick of light where it's so bright outside it seems infinitely dark inside. A girl played but he couldn't quite make her out. She would explain to him later how the music was that Polish fellow known for piano. He knocked. The girl stopped playing. The sudden silence caused the Mr. to wake. By the time the Mrs. rushed into the room the girl had walked barefoot to face Will, at a distance closer than she would another stranger for there was the netted screen between them, making him seem farther away, but also for other reasons, and she leaned on the glass part with her hand parallel to his, her fingers splayed like bug legs, and when she opened the screen door he could see her. She was half as tall as he was and her black eyes burned and swelled like glass heated until malleable.

I am Ajeng, she said.

I'm Will, he said.

The Mr. and Mrs. intervened. The latter called the police; the former brandished the pool broom. Will made his way off the property. Sent there already, Ajeng watched from her upstairs bedroom window, leaving handprints on the glass which stayed there long after she returned to Indonesia. The gang of purebreds that ran free through the cul-de-sac gathered and began to bark, alerting the rest of their ilk, inside and out. Will noted the name on the mailbox. As the growing dog pack followed and circled, he spied the name on the sign where the road met another. On his way out of town, he noted the last sign. It said *Entering* and then the name of the town he was leaving, and with all that, he hitched the rest of the way home.

He called that night. He said he admired her piano playing very much. She thanked him and said she had played all her life. She said she was an exchange student, from Indonesia, where everyone played piano. He speculated no one owned a radio anywhere in Indonesia because there was so much goddamn piano playing. She said that was true. She said in Indonesia everything was deep and tall and purple. He said it must be some place. She apologized for her poor English, but added that it was her fourth language and that she had not quite reached fluency. He said it was not a problem and added that his Indonesian sucked.

Would you like to be my boyfriend? Ajeng asked. The boys who are American do not like who I am. They say my blue jeans are too blue and too new and that I speak with oddness.

But before Will could answer, the Mr. broke in. He'd been listening in the whole time on the other phone.

Will was forbidden to see her.

My secret was that I hated summer. Because the immortal and attractive all roll out in unisex cadres of four, six, and you tend to see them in the middle of the day when they ought to be at some type of employment, and they're all tan and bursting with sex, and you just get the vibe they're either on their way to or just back from some erotic place so exclusive and profane they're all compelled to wear sunglasses so its secrets aren't revealed in their eyes.

Such a group was stopped at the red in front of me in a stealthlike convertible and they still smoked of erroneous fucking. They floored it at green. I felt profoundly unsatisfied in their wake. I got the truck to chug forward. It was a Thursday and I was on my way home trying to remember if we'd cut down more trees today than I'd planted the day before, when the whole crew—planters, mowers, tree guys—hit the Draper mansion to get it ready for some party Mr. Draper was having. He was our best customer and Pitt would wipe his ass for him if asked. But it meant we were behind in the job we were working on today, and usually this was always the case and no big deal. But today's customer was Mrs. Foderkanz, who was a notorious battle-ax and wouldn't even let us drink from her hose. We double-timed it all day. My ears felt sore from the chainsaw buzz and the woodchipper scream. We hadn't been able to get the chipper down this hill near the pines we were cutting for fear of tire-rutting the lawn—then Mrs. Foderkanz would've really let us have it. So we lugged up the hill. After dragging the logs and brush up that hill all day my body made it clear to me I had two choices. The first was to immediately go to bed. The second was to immediately go to the bar, rage all night, push through, and sleepwalk through the next day cursing every decision made the night before.

Ajeng snuck out her window every midnight and they'd hop in Will's car and go places they would later make special. She was maybe seventeen and Will was however old he was before I met him. Ajeng told him of herself and Indonesia and Will told her of himself and Syracuse, though he admitted he hadn't thought he'd ever need to tell anybody such information and therefore hadn't been paying attention. They'd found high and secluded places to go about all this, places where there was enough wind to keep insects away and from which they could see things in most directions when they weren't looking at each other.

She said in Indonesia they thought her a smart girl but here no one wished to know anything about her. Will said they treated him that way here too. They both had brothers and a mother and a father and they were both middle children and they both had black hair, though her skin was like gold, but she said in Indonesia she did not stand out. She asked if what they were doing was considered right or wrong and Will explained that if they kept doing it they would know the answer any day now.

Ajeng said that's how it was in Indonesia and she kissed him and he wished the sun would stay away from this one night so everyone would be tricked into staying in bed all day until things got back to normal after the next night, the Mr. and Mrs. none the wiser, and they could stay there together that much longer.

It was supposed to be that I pulled up in front of Will and Bianca's and honked once and he was supposed to come out and we would drive away. Instead, I honked once and there was nothing and then I honked a bunch of times and there was nothing and then I went to the door with the truck running and nobody came out and I knocked and rang the bell and then I went and turned off the truck and then I went in.

Bianca was doing dishes. She had been crying or pissed and her face was puffy but made up as if she was going out. She was doing dishes in the way people did sometimes, on principle or to make a statement with the water full blast to prohibit talking and so that one's back could be to the audience the whole time. She never looked at me but I knew she saw me.

I looked all over the house for Will. I didn't see him but somehow I knew he was there. You could just feel him around. I went back into the bedroom. The door had been closed; the only door of the house to be so. I saw him under the bed.

He was long and thin and lay on his back and his feet stuck out.

What are you doing under the bed? I asked.

You know when the mattress and the pillow are too hot? he said.

I suppose.

You know when your body makes them too hot and there's only so many times you can flip the pillow for the cool side?

I guess.

Yeah. Well, eventually the pillow is hot all over. There's not that problem underneath.

Hey, suit yourself.

I will.

You going to come out from under?

In a minute.

After that, are you coming to the Bog?

Is that tonight? he asked.

If we did something, we went to the Bog, so I didn't really see the confusion. Yes, I said.

I need to find my wallet, he said.

All right, I said.

Can you please close the door? he asked.

I shut the door. The water running in the kitchen halted. The television ranted from the living room. The dishes were piled high in the drying rack. As I walked by them, they shifted. A glass dislodged and shattered on the floor. The sound went off on the television, then came back on.

I grabbed a broom quick as I could. I swept furiously. The floor glinted with mica. I figured all that need happen now was for me to cut myself. I swept it into the pan and dumped it into the trash. When I couldn't get the last line of glass dust I shot it right under the stove. I thought somebody would've strolled in by now. But no one had.

I went into the living room. The television was pretty much at grandma volume.

Hey, Cliff, Bianca said. She was half-lying, half-kneeling on the couch, her legs folded up under her knees. Her body had the kind of leanness and long-muscle to it that she always seemed upright and erect.

Sorry about the glass, I said.

What glass?

We had to shout. On the television was a guy in a judge suit. A large, loud woman was suing a larger, louder woman and there was a small, dead dog somehow involved.

I swear it just fell, I said. I didn't even hit it or anything.

I didn't hear you come in, she said.

I knew somebody had to be home, I said.

She stared at the television and on the television both women cried, one for the dog, the other for no clear reason. Bianca's eyes had fossilized into a bleach-white vacancy. She did not look back. Tendons on her neck twitched periodically.

Do you find me attractive, Cliff? Would you take me out, were we to go out, to someplace with style? She stretched the last word out until she had to breathe again.

Strings of sweat progressed down between my eyes and ears into the ticklish hollow of my neck. There were two answers and one was wrong and the other one was wrong.

Of course, I said.

Why?

Because that's what I'd do if I was Will.

Do you find yourself to be a good enough catch to take me away from him?

Don't say that, I said.

That's what I thought. You are all it takes for him to let me down.

Did I do something? I asked, but I knew the answer myself: Will had done something. He'd done something bad or something bad in her mind.

It's the same thing all over again, Bianca said. He has no business being around anymore.

Why don't you two just hang out tonight?

You have no business telling me what to do.

It sounds like it would be a good idea if you two just chilled by yourselves.

How well do you know him? she asked me.

Pretty good, I said, and then I realized it was meant to be one of those rhetorical questions. I shut up the rest of the way.

Do you know what he needs to practice? she asked. Do you know what he needs to improve on? Do you know what he's most afraid of?

She stopped.

It kind of seems like a bad time, I said.

I think Will might need some time to himself, Bianca said.

I remembered Will in the bedroom—I stood up. You're right, I said. I'll be right back.

She looked at the TV. You cut yourself, she said, as if it had just occurred to her.

I walked towards the bedroom, looking at my hands. But there was no blood and I didn't feel anything. I looked at my palms and at the tops. There was no cut anywhere. I looked at my hand as it made a loose fist and knocked on the door of the bedroom. But there was no answer. I opened it.

Will was gone. The window was wide open, the screen laying flat in the crabgrass of the yard. I didn't know how to explain this one. I wondered what the good guy did in this scenario. I walked back over and closed the door. I couldn't remember the last time I'd gone out a window. The gymnastics took a little figuring out. I lowered myself the five feet to the ground. The best thing I could do was pull the window down behind me. The screen was warped to the extent that you needed to fiddle with it for like twenty minutes to learn the singular trick to locking it back in place, so I leaned it neatly against the foundation.

When I walked back around the house, Will was in the truck, looking straight ahead. The truck had been started mysteriously. He seemed better already. His arm was out the window. I had no desire to navigate this one on either front.

When I got in he nodded to me.

What's up, I said.

Nothing, he said. His eyes flicked past me.

I was going to say something, but when I turned to see what he'd looked at, there was Bianca sitting on the porch, glaring vaguely in our direction at some point between us and the sky behind us. I'd been so focused on Will in the truck I'd walked right past her. Then she waved as I pulled the truck forward. At the last moment I waved back. I looked at my hands one last time.

Nothing, I said. Really?

I took us down the road. Will could tell something was up because I was going about two miles an hour.

I want to tell you something, I said. I don't want you to get mad. But if there was like only one thing I could ever tell you, this would be it. All right?

No.

You mean I can't say it?

I think it's better if you didn't. The radio's busted, he added, cranking the knob futilely.

The radio's never worked for as long as I've driven this truck. Don't change the subject.

You got Old Blue tonight, he said, looking at the hole in the floor and all around at what contained us.

Fucking Old Blue, I said.

It was the worst truck my boss Pitt had because it was the oldest and it had no gate and there was a hole in the floor near the brake pedal you could see the road through. The gas gauge didn't work, which was always an adventure, it needed about a quart of oil every ten miles, and the pin never lined up with P, R, N, or D. You had to get the feel for Old Blue before you could get going in the right direction. But it was the first truck Pitt bought when he started the company so he was sentimental about it the way some people are about the place they were born. Unfortunately, the rust had taken over and it was just a matter of time. In fact, the only good thing about Old Blue was you could get in an accident with it and there was pretty much no way for Pitt to tell unless it was still on fire.

I thought Pitt was going to sell it, he said.

He's been saying that for a long time. It's one of those things you say you're going to do but never get around to doing.

After Pitt did finally sell it later in the summer he'd see it around town once in a while and I swear he'd get a tear in his eye. It was like he'd sent one of his daughters off to boarding school. The rest of us felt sorry for the guy who bought it, but not Pitt. To him that guy had the steal of a lifetime.

You better not ever quit this job, Will said. Then you'll have no wheels.

Pitt said I should consider it my benefits package.

Pretty comprehensive, Will said.

He'd done it, gotten me off the subject.

Like I was saying, I started again. I can't believe you don't want to hear what I have to say.

I can. You know, I never knew the bar was this far away.

It's really important.

Then I definitely shouldn't hear it.

I have to say it.

Why? Will it make enough difference for you to say it after you've said it?

I pulled into the bar lot and thought it over. We were there.

Then he said, Is there anything you could know that would be more than I know regarding this situation? And then nothing more was said. I guess I felt a little better because I'd tried. But not really. So we went in. We sat in the stools we always sat in when no one else was sitting in them. We ordered what we always ordered.

My hand look okay to you? I asked a woman next to me.

After we were there for a little while we said something like This place is dead or Weird crowd tonight and Let's get the fuck out of here. It wasn't dead or weird or different, it was one of those arbitrary times when it seemed such or we wanted it to be such even though it was no different from any other night and when one of us voiced the fact that it was some-how different the other agreed and added another observation on how it was different and pretty soon the place was positively foreign and inhospitable and we decided we were unwelcome and we left and probably went the next night and had a grand old time amongst the exact same crowd under the same songs drinking the same drinks.

We got back in Old Blue.

Shit, he said.

What?

What do we do now?

We were quiet for a long a time. It took a couple tries, but I started up the truck and then it was still a little while after that before I had an idea.

I'm never the one with the ideas. Usually it was Will, or some third, alto-gether different person, who we got stuck hanging out with, and after whoever said it said it, we all agreed it was a stupid idea and kept doing whatever it was we'd been complaining about for the rest of the night. Then it came to me.

I know somewhere we can go, I said.

He and Ajeng were in a car accident together and had a pregnancy scare and one time a policeman who stopped them asked if she was being held against her will and she said no it was very much of her will to be with him but that currently the policeman had stopped them very much against her will. He asked for her ID to prove she existed but she explained she was an exchange student from somewhere else and had no such thing and he did not think to ask for her green card or travel visa because it was a small town that never saw people from Indonesia.

Later, she told Will he was a kind of perfect and he said that was a nice way of looking at things and she added they were mostly beautiful and that he took away her fractions. He was not progressing in his study of Indone-sian but that was okay because her English improved by a word every day.

She said in Indonesia she would be married by now with many babies and probably twins and he said in America he should have been somebody by now. She said she believed he was somebody who was with her and that that was another kind of perfect. She said that when she was without him it was as if she had been sliced open and nothing could close the wound and the longer it was she did not see him, the larger the wound grew.

A happy routine had grown into being. The Mr. and Mrs. had improved because they realized they were powerless regarding Will and Ajeng's com-ings and goings. He was allowed over as long as he waited in the running car in the driveway. Many good things had happened in the car so he did not consider it rude. When the Mr. and Mrs. tried to withhold Will from Ajeng she would stop eating and waste away in her bed and miss school and meals alike. The Mrs. suggested a feeding tube, but after talking to the insurance company decided it was easiest to allow her time with Will so as to avert future hunger strikes. The Mr. felt they had failed Ajeng and were perhaps the worst exchange parents ever. They were both barren as the moon and hadn't thought this exchange student business would be such a diminishing return and were glad they couldn't have children after all and canceled next year's Madagascan youth. The Mr. declared that once Ajeng was out, they would get a second dog.

One night Will waited in the car when Ajeng came out looking more stricken than he'd ever seen her. He thought things had been going well between them. But she did not speak as he raced around the hills. Whenever she didn't answer him, he went faster, until even he was scared at their velocity.

He slowed and said that if she didn't tell him what it was she was upset about that he might die instantaneously.

She said she was already dead. She said that she was dead and there was no coming back.

He asked why.

She said she had been looking at the calendar. The Mr. and Mrs. had hiked her departure date up to even sooner than it was supposed to be. She was to be leaving. They had little time.

She asked, What then?

I took us to the lake. We bought some beer on the way and opened one for each of us, which served as conversation. I liked the lake because a lot of people didn't know about it, or at least didn't often have the idea of going there at night.

You had to park in this dirt lot a ways away and walk down this little dirt road which led down a hill to the beach. Some other cars were parked there. I made a point of not looking in the dark interiors because once I'd heard this was a good place to bring a woman and one time I had and we'd made love in the car and I hadn't noticed the other car parked a ways off in the bushes and the person or people in that other car flashed their lights at us for a blazing moment before the night refilled the space between us and them, and the woman and I stopped what we were doing momentarily before starting up again, thinking nothing of it. The next day I'd gotten spooked. It could've been anybody in that other car, and then I wondered what the hell was I doing parking with women in the middle of the woods. Will and I passed quite a few cars as we made our way towards the beach; a veritable orgy.

But it wasn't. The drivers and passengers surrounded a bonfire down on the sand and we saw only their black silhouetted backs or their glowing white fronts. They danced in a circle around the fire to music made by the few who were seated with bongos of some sort and a harmonica and a guitar maybe and their feet left a circle of footprints which filled with round, opaque shadows the way water might collect in firmer ground after a rain. In fact, as we took a wide perimeter around them, they all appeared to have markings neither male nor female, only young, kids in the way Will and I had been so recently but were no longer and that difference was miniature and unmistakable.

They can't see us, I said. They've been looking at the fire too long.

Good, Will said, and I wasn't sure if he meant it was good that we'd not disturbed them, or good that we'd not been discovered ourselves.

Will stashed his shoes and shirt. His watch caught the reflection of the firelight for a second. Ajeng had given it to him. It was his prized possession. Bianca wasn't a big fan of it. But it was his own fault for telling her its origins. The watch was about to ruin both our nights. The goddamn thing didn't even work. He never replaced the batteries after it stopped. People were always asking him if he had the time and for awhile he'd explain that it didn't work until finally he tired of that and just said no.

Don't you want to leave your watch here? I asked.

He didn't look at it. It's waterproof, he said.

Waterproof or water-resistant? I asked. There's a difference, you know.

Why don't you just worry about whether or not you can fucking swim, he said.

Whatever, man.

You're sure there's a dock out there? I can't see anything that's not black out there.

Maybe it sank, I said.

We toed the water. It was too cold to be standing in our shorts but because of that, the water felt warmer than the air, and to go in was actually a relief once we got up to our necks. We each towed a six-pack from the empty ring left from the one we'd each had before. After dog-swimming awhile we saw the blacker silhouette of the dock against the black water.

There's the dock, I said. You have no faith.

It floated at an angle and was both smaller and farther away than I remembered. When we reached it we both put a hand on it to rest.

How was that fun? Will asked no one in particular, our chins dipping into the water from fatigue.

He set his five-pack on the dock and climbed up. I did the same. The dock shifted like it meant to stand on one corner as we climbed up. Water sloshed against its sides.

We shivered and wrapped our arms around our legs. We watched the shapes go around the fire. If you looked at the water just right the reflection of the fire shot towards you across the surface. The sound carried all the way to us and past, their voices audible from drink and the physics of the lake. Once they took a break from the song-and-dance we could hear them talking about us but pretended not to make it out. We looked out and away. The running lights of boats glowed and moved deliberately like lights in a neighborhood going on and off and we stared at them because it was something to do.

I like it here, Will said.

He told her he'd done some thinking and then some more.

He said he couldn't go right away.

He needed more money than he had to go with her. And once he got there, without speaking the language, what could he do? He would need to save up in order to join her; while he saved, he would study the language. Then he would join her, fluent and wealthy.

He knew her to be disappointed. He was disappointed in himself. He would always remember that moment. He would remember it until he died young and she would never know because she had long since gone away.

Will said that he might as well be with Bianca.

I said how he met her in a bar and the difference between her and all the other women at that bar was that something happened to happen between them and he gave and she gave and he took and she took and that the difference now was that she kept taking but had stopped giving and he, well, I had no idea what he was doing these days.

Will didn't respond. Then he sort of grunted and cleared his throat at the same time.

We're out of beer, Will said.

That's not the end of the conversation, I said.

It is until there's more beer. I have to be headed a certain direction; otherwise there's nothing to put words in my mouth.

We were on our backs and above us was the moon. It was one of those moons where you could make out the craters or mountains—all a shade darker. I wondered if anyone I would meet down the road happened to be looking at the moon at the very same time and then I wondered if that was childish. Will reached over and submerged his can in the water. The air gurgled up out of it until it was full and then he let go and it fell down to the bottom where it rested with our other cans and we figured some snorkeling kid would come along someday and redeem them all.

It was still, the way water always was at night, calm too, and every once in a while a fish jumped through the surface a little to engulf a floating beetle. What most people don't mention at times and places like this is the bats. They flew above us, smaller than you'd think, changing directions so much it seemed like they couldn't possibly fly straight. But we didn't mind them. The dock was getting a little uncomfortable, though. My feet had been in the water but Will brought up eels. We were cold. My stomach had a mind for a cheeseburger. Will—he didn't eat much. The kids still raged. They'd go dormant and we'd be afraid they could hear us so we'd whisper and when they started up again we'd raise our voices back to normal. They'd forgotten we were even there.

I can get more beer, I said, realizing that since this was my idea, beer was sort of my responsibility. It's in the truck.

Is it warm?

Warm is better than none.

Let's just go.

No, I said. I'll get it. I need a cigarette anyway.

He sighed.

I got ready to jump in the water but stopped. I looked at him. I couldn't make out his eyes, or maybe they were closed.

Ever since you met Bianca you haven't been the same, I said.

Isn't that what they always say? he said. That's when it's the real deal, right?

I hadn't expected him to answer. They mean in a good way, I said.

How do you know it's not a good way?

Because you never have fun anymore.

I don't see what one thing has to do with another.

When I first met you, you had girlfriends all over the place. You had one at every bar and good thing for you they always went to the same, different bar every night. You even had one in freaking Indonesia.

She was not my girlfriend.

You said you were cheating on her.

I knew I was never going to see her again and she knew I was never going to see her again so it wasn't cheating.

Well, anyway, you were a lot happier then.

Will rolled onto his side, his back to me. I realized maybe I wasn't making the strongest argument. Will was weird back then, too. He did strange things. His mind went off places and he could be positively unapproachable. But this under-the-bed kind of thing? That was new.

I don't know that I was happier, he said. I can't remember when I was really happy. You have to be a little ignorant in order to be really happy.

You said with Ajeng you were, I said and cringed at having said her name. It occurred to me I couldn't remember the last time she'd been brought up and certainly not by Will. I was kind of frightened at what I'd done. But he kept talking.

Yeah, he said. Pretty happy. I didn't know it at the time. It was like This is pretty good.

Will stopped like he would say no more but seemed to think better of it.

You look back on it, he said, and you realize it was way good and what the hell have you been doing ever since? They have a saying or something for it.

Will shook out of it. His head came around my way. I was glad I couldn't make out his face.

What does this have to do with anything? he asked.

I'm just talking.

I don't think so, he said.

I felt willful and knowing. Why didn't you get your ass out there to her? I asked.

You ask me things like I haven't thought of them.

Sorry.

You get back with that beer yet?

I'm going.

I could use a beer.

I dove in. The dock buckled behind me. I opened my eyes underwater even though I couldn't see a thing. I always opened my eyes even though it made them bloodshot. I swam towards the sound of the kids. Swimming was hard and I kept reaching down with a foot hoping for sand and when it finally came I was grateful and my eyes came just over the water and I walked the rest of the way out like a creature. I avoided the kids. There were fewer now; gone home, or passed out, or gone off with somebody. But the ones left were very much into making noise and having a good time. They started up the same song they'd played about five times but that I didn't know. They were the kids with the second wind like me and Will had, the first to arrive and the last to go.

I found our clothes and got a cigarette burning and walked all the way to the truck. The bugs in the woods played the same note all at once and over and over like a metronome. I wondered if I ought to be bringing any of this up with Will. Did I really have the right? I didn't think I did. But friends were supposed to bring up stuff like this. Or at least provide the beer to drink one's way out of it.

Old Blue was empty. I looked all around the cab and felt under the seats. I checked the bed. There was nothing. I could of sworn I'd brought more. I was always prepared. I never left home without it. Then I remembered the kids.

I went down to the bonfire.

You guys take my beer? I said.

Nobody stopped dancing. The women were half-naked but I didn't care. The guys were too but almost all had long hair so it was hard to tell anyway in the firelight. The closest kid not dancing was half-buried in the sand, drinking one of my beers. He made the mistake of making eye contact. I went right up to him.

You took my beer, I said.

I did no such thing.

You're drinking it right in front of me.

I am not. He took a swig and tossed the can.

I should kick your ass.

Don't you try anything. I got more friends than you have teeth.

Give me something to drink, I said.

That's not my problem, he said.

You took my beer.

Maybe your gay lover drank it, he said.

I hope you choke on it, I said.

The rest of them danced around the fire. The kid was way in the sand. I'd never known how to deal with people younger than me. It was the best

I could do at the moment. I unzipped and pissed and made a dark stain in the sand over him where I figured his legs were.

What the hell are you doing? he said.

This hurts me more than it hurts you, I said.

You will pay for that, he said. I own you, man.

I walked back to the water. I didn't know what we'd do when I got back out to Will.

Behind me, the kid in the sand narrated the story to whoever in the group would listen. The water grabbed at my ankles. I took a few steps and dove in. The water was too shallow and I skidded a little, sand getting in my shorts, but soon I was swimming along. Halfway, there was some question about making it back to the dock, I mean, I felt rock-heavy. I thought bodies just floated but that seemed to take work. I thought about all those people who had self-discovery moments while underwater. I thought about how, right before you drown, it was supposed to be like the best orgasm on earth, better than the Asians did it even. I decided I wished I were a better person. Who was on top of shit. Who didn't have friends like Will because their lives had been straightened out for them already. Who had kids who would never steal beer, because it was inconceivable.

Then I made it to the dock. Will was asleep. I didn't think I'd been gone that long.

Let's get out of here, I said.

Their routine was never as happy again as it had been. Her question and his answer had necessitated a kind of pretending for the rest of her stay. They tried to make the best of it. But sometimes they'd not talk and they knew just what the other was thinking.

It was during one of those moments that he asked if anything bad ever happened in Indonesia.

She said in Indonesia, when they come, they come with machetes. They hack you to pieces and they put the pieces in piles and set fire to them and bury them under the earth. When there are no matchetes, they hang you from trees or tie rocks to your legs to sink you underwater or take you up in planes to throw you out from them. If you are lucky and they like you, they let you choose. Sometimes they will let you have your throat cut before you're thrown from the plane if you fear heights. But because there is no air that high in the sky, your blood does not come out red, it comes out blue and that was said to be beautiful and an honorable way to go. But this was all rumor. For no one was ever heard from or mentioned again because they didn't keep track of all the things they did to all these people.

He said, How do you keep that from happening?

She said, You hope they are not coming for you.

He waited to tell me until we'd just about pulled up to his and Bianca's place that he'd lost the watch.

I was more upset than he was.

In the water? I said.

Yeah, like when I was swimming or something. I don't know.

How the hell could you lose it? Watches don't just fall off.

This one did. It must have broke.

Shit, I said. I kept looking at his wrist.

It's all right, he said. Didn't work anyway.

Let's go back.

No, he said as we turned onto his street. I'm home.

Really, I said. We can.

Now I can slit my wrist without anything in the way. He laughed.

There's nothing funny about that or any other part of this.

It's better this way. It made that one arm heavier and I got extra tired at work.

We can go back and find the fucking thing, I said. We'll retrace our steps. That always works.

I watched him walk up to the apartment. The lights were on.

She gave him the watch at the airport. She said that though it was a spiritless, inanimate object, she wished him to pretend it was imbued with some type of energy related to her and so that when he looked upon it he might be reminded of her. He thanked her and promised to do so. They scrunched inside one of those booths that spit out automatic pictures but they cried and kissed while alone inside it and forgot to pull out the pictures. They held each other up all the way into the terminal. When she left his side to go to the ladies' room he missed her already. He wondered if he was doing right by all this. He wished he had a credit card to buy the seat on the plane next to her and just go. They could throw out everything in his apartment and tow his car away and he wouldn't care. His family might miss him a bit but they would understand. His friends would get over it too. He'd just been fired from his job so that wasn't part of the pros and cons either. In fact, there was not a goddamn thing worth staying for. He would get the money. He would not let this slip away. He would do whatever it took.

She came out of the ladies' room and went to the gate. Before he knew it, she was on the plane. He watched it from the window. But it did not take off for a long time. In fact, it sat there, and after a half hour or so, it rolled away. As he made his way to the car, many planes flew in many directions and he hoped one was hers. He wondered if they flew east to Indonesia, or west to Indonesia, over what oceans, and where they might stop around the world along the way.

He got in his car and looked at his watch. He pretended it was a part of her and he wore that part on his body. He went to get gas and when he was all filled up a man walked up and said it cost twenty dollars. He gave the man the twenty dollars. The man walked away. The attendant also said that would be twenty dollars. Will explained that he'd just paid. The attendant asked how was that his problem and waited for the twenty dollars.

When I first met him, Ajeng was still in the picture a little. She would call at the most bizarre hours because she was pretty much on the other side of the world, so when it was night here, it was day there. Her calls scared me at first. When the phone rings that late, the only reason anybody's calling you is because they have some bad news so bad it can't wait until morning. I'd think someone died or something. But it was her. And he would stop everything and put a hand over his other ear and go off as far from me as the cord would stretch. The only time I ever caught any of this was when we'd end up at his place after closing to put down a few more and watch the shows that came on after the late shows. They never talked long. It cost an arm-and-a-leg to call that far. Sometimes he told me he'd called her. Then she stopped calling, or he stopped calling. Then he met Bianca, and he didn't bring her up again.

I didn't see him cover the watch with his hand and slide the watch down his wrist. I didn't see him make a fist around it. I didn't know that he barely looked at it. I didn't know what went through his mind. I didn't know he brought his arm back like the last time he threw a baseball, when he was a kid, and his shoulder winced from the motion, and it didn't go very far and the splash was insignificantly minor, less of a splash than you'd think. I didn't know any of this. It would've saved me a trip. Although maybe I would've gone anyway.

When I got home after dropping off Will, I couldn't sleep. I drank vodka in orange juice because it seemed like it would be morning soon. While it's true drinking makes you tired it's different for me. I'm not tired until I've had what I've wanted to drink. And if it's one of those nights when my mind will not shut off then I'm going to be a hell of a lot thirstier than tired. I felt like I would never be tired again. I felt like I was too awake to feel anything I drank. I felt like I could fix this one a little.

I drove out to the lake. Dawn came in creeping increments. I would go to where we'd left our clothes and walk the way we'd walked out to the water and I'd wade through the water looking for it and then I'd float out towards the dock as the sun came up and caught its silver and if none of that worked I could post a sign and give my number and say reward even though it wouldn't be that much and the same kid that redeemed our beer cans would find the watch.

I shared the highway and then the side roads with few other vehicles. The commuters hadn't come out yet. I needed to get to work soon too. I hoped nobody would recognize that I wore the same clothes. I wished I knew the woman all this effort was about. I wished I could've met her, to know who he was talking about. I knew he'd had pictures of her once. I didn't know anything about Indonesia except that it was underwater mostly and had a bunch of volcanoes. I wanted to see that blue blood, but it sounded like trying to get the refrigerator door open before the light came on.

Mostly, I wished he'd gone there. I wished I'd never known him because he'd gone there before I'd come here. If that wasn't the case, I wished I'd had the money to give him so he could go out there. I figure all the people who have enough money to settle their debts and say fuck it to everything and have enough to buy a ticket to Indonesia probably never even met an Indonesian and are satisfied putting their time in here. The rest of us just wait.

I pulled in the lot. Indonesia was a million miles in both directions.

But I didn't think Bianca ruined it for him. I figured seeing her every day just reminded him he was never going to make it to there. The least I could do was find the watch. Somebody needed to. And you wouldn't catch him thinking any of this stuff. I'm the sentimental one.

I cut the engine on Old Blue. All but a single van were gone from the lot. I walked down. The bonfire was dead and the sand around it black-scarred, and up from it gray vines of smoke were being pulled, hand-over-hand, into the sky. Empty wine jugs lay around on their sides like broken buoys. Someone had forgotten her red towel. Past the bonfire, the kid lay on his back. He was the one who was in the ground. His legs were all dirt-caked.

The sand near his face was darkened from puke. He was blue-gray and it was like the color had gone out of even his brown hair and I remembered the story told to me by a woman whose beau nearly drank himself to death with grain and when she found him he was blue as a fucking alien and the paramedics got to him just in time. Then she said they broke up. Understandable. I figure after something like that you got to either get married or split up.

I didn't see the kid's stomach move. I knelt down and looked at him for a long time like you're supposed to. I wasn't one of those people who knew what to do in situations like this. I'd also never been the first to discover anything—you know, those people always finding wallets, lost dogs, or priceless antiques out of trash heaps. But this was heavy-duty. I was going to have something to talk about for a long time. I felt a little embarrassed that I got to stare at him like this; I wouldn't want to be on the other side of it. Then it occurred to me the authorities would ask me what I'd been doing there, as if I had a part in it or it was my fault or some shit. Then I'd have to tell the whole story about the watch and Will and how it was important to him and all that but at the same time it could be my alibi, I suppose, once they got ahold of Will.

His face was a little stubbly. They say hair grows for about a week after. Finally, I decided it had to be done. I reached down and touched his arm. It was cool, not cold. It felt like anybody's arm. But he squinted and sat up.

Why are you bothering me? he asked.

Edith Pearlman

The Story

from *Alaska Quarterly Review*

"PREDICTABLE," SAID Judith da Costa.

"Oh . . . hopeful," said her husband, Justin, in his determinedly tolerant way.

"Neither," said Harry Savitsky, not looking for trouble exactly; looking for engagement perhaps; really looking for the door, but the evening had just begun.

Harry's wife Lucienne—uncharacteristically—said nothing. She was listening to the tune: a mournful bit from Smetana.

What these four diners were evaluating was a violinist, partly his performance, partly his presence. The new restaurant—Harry and Lucienne had suggested it—called itself The Hussar, and presented piroshki and goulash in a gypsy atmosphere. The chef was rumored to be twenty-six years old. The Hussar was taking a big chance on the chef, on the fiddler, on the location, and apparently on the help; one busboy had already dropped a pitcher of water.

"It's tense here, in the dining room," Judith remarked.

"In the kitchen—don't ask," said Harry.

In some accommodating neighborhood in Paris, a restaurant like The Hussar might catch on. In Paris . . . But this was not Paris. It was Godolphin, a town that was really a western wedge of Boston; Godolphin, home to Harry and Lucienne Savitsky, retired high school teachers; Godolphin, not so much out of fashion as beyond its reach.

One might say the same of Harry. His preferred haberdashery was the Army/Navy surplus store downtown. Lucienne, however, was genuinely Parisian (she had spent the first four years of her life there, never mind that the city was Occupied, never mind that she was hardly ever taken out of the apartment) and she had a Frenchwoman's flair for color and line. As a schoolgirl in Buenos Aires, as a young working woman in nineteen-fifties Boston, she had been known for dressing well on very little money; and she and her brother had managed to support their widowed mother, too. But Lucienne was well over sixty now, and perhaps this turquoise dress she'd bought for a friend's grandson's bar mitzvah was too bright for the present company. Perhaps it was also too tight for what Lucienne called her few extra pounds and Harry called her blessed corpulence. He was a fatty himself.

In the da Costas' disciplined presence Harry was always a little embarrassed about their appetites, his and Lucienne's. Certainly they had nothing else to be ashamed of: not a thing! They were well-educated, as high school teachers had had to be in their day (she'd taught French, he chemistry). Lucienne spoke three languages, four if you counted Yiddish. Harry conversed only in Brooklyn English, but he understood Lucienne in all of her tongues. They subscribed to *The New Yorker* and *Science* and *American Heritage*.

These da Costas, though—they were very tall, they were very thin. Judith with her pewter hair and dark clothing could have passed for a British governess. Justin was equally daunting: a high brow, and a lean nose, and thin lips always forming meaningful expressions. But there were moments when Justin glanced at Judith while speaking, and a spasm of anxiety crossed his face, getting entangled with the meaningful expressions. Then Justin and Harry briefly became allies: two younger brothers who'd been caught smoking. One morning at breakfast Harry had described this occasional feeling of kinship to his wife. Lucienne looked at him for a while, then got up and went around the table and kissed him.

Paprika breadsticks! The waiter's young hand shook as he lowered the basket. Judith took none; Justin took one but didn't bite; Lucienne took one and began to munch; Harry took one and then parked another behind his ear.

"Ha," said Judith mirthlessly.

"Ha ha," said Justin.

Lucienne looked at Harry, and sighed, and smiled—her wide motherly smile, reminding him of the purpose of this annual evening out. He removed the breadstick, brushing possible crumbs from his shoulder. "What do you hear from our kids?" he said to Justin.

"Our kids love it out there in Santa Fe. I don't share their taste for the high and dry," Justin said with an elegant shrug.

"You're a Yankee from way back," said Harry.

The da Costas, as Harry well knew, were an old Portuguese-Dutch family who had begun assimilating the minute they arrived in the New World—in 1800, something like that—and had intermarried whenever an Episcopalian would have them. Fifty years ago Justin studied medicine for the purpose of learning psychiatry. His practice still flourished. He saw patients in a free-standing office, previously a stable, behind their home, previously a farmhouse, the whole compound fifteen miles north of Boston. Judith had designed all the conversions. The windows of Justin's consulting room faced a soothing stand of birches.

The Savitskys had visited the da Costas once, three years ago, the night before Miriam Savitsky's wedding to Jotham da Costa. At that party they discovered that there were backyards in Greater Boston through which rabbits ran, into which deer tripped; that people in the mental health professions did not drink hard liquor (Justin managed to unearth a bottle of Scotch from a recess under the sink); and that the severe Judith was the daughter of a New Jersey pharmacist. The pharmacist was there on the lawn, in a deck chair: aged and garrulous. Harry and his new son-in-law's grandfather talked for a while about synthetic serotonin. The old man had died last winter.

Cocktails! The Hussar did provide Scotch, perhaps knowing no better. The fiddler's repertoire descended into the folk—some Russian melodies. Harry guessed that Lucienne knew their Yiddish lyrics. The da Costas ignored the tunes. They were devotees of Early Music. To give them their due—and Harry always tried to give them their due—they perhaps did not intend to convey the impression that dining out once a year with the Savitskys was bearable, but only marginally. Have pity, he told himself. Their cosseted co-existence with gentle wildlife must make them uncom-

fortable with extremes of color, noise, and opinions. And for their under-
weight Jotham who still suffered from acne at the age of thirty-seven
they'd probably wanted somebody other than a wide-hipped, dense-haired
lawyer with a loud laugh.

"The kids' apartment out there . . . it's adorable," said Lucienne.

"With all that clutter, how can anybody tell?" said Harry.

"Mostly Jotham's paints and canvases, that clutter," Justin bravely
admitted.

"Miriam drops her briefcase in one room, her pocketbook in another,
throws her keys on the toilet tank," said Lucienne. "I raised her wrong," in
mock repentance.

"They like their jobs. They both seem happy," said Judith, turning
large khaki eyes to Harry—a softened gaze. Justin said, "They do," and
Lucienne said, "Do," and for a moment, the maître d' if he was looking,
the fiddler if he was looking, anybody idly looking, might have taken
them for two couples happy with their connection-by-marriage. Sometimes what looked so became so. If Jotham was a bit high-strung for the
Savitskys, if Miriam was too argumentative for the da Costas, well, you
couldn't have everything. Could you? "Many people have nothing," Harry
said aloud, startling Judith, alerting Justin's practiced empathy—"Yes?"
the doctor encouraged—and not at all troubling Lucienne, who was on
her fifth breadstick.

The appetizers came—four different dishes full of things that could kill
you. Each person tasted everything, the Savitskys eager, the da Costas
restrained. They talked about the Red Sox, at least the Savitskys did. The
team had begun the season well, and would break their hearts as always,
wait and see. The da Costas murmured something.

The main course came, and a bottle of wine. Judith poured: everyone
got half a glass. They talked about the gubernatorial race. The da Costas
were staunch Democrats, though it sometimes pained them. "No one
cares enough about the environment," said Judith. Harry nodded—he
didn't care about the environment at all.

The fiddler fiddled. They talked about Stalin—there was a new biography. None of them had read it, and so conversation rested easily on the vil-
lainy they already knew.

Harry finished the rest of the wine.

They talked about movies that both couples had seen, though of course not together.

There were some silences.

Lucienne would tell the story tonight, Harry thought.

She would tell the story soon. The da Costas had never heard the story. She had been waiting, as she always did, for the quiet moment, the calm place, the inviting question, and the turning point in a growing intimacy.

Harry had heard the story scores of times. He had heard it in Yiddish and in French and occasionally in Spanish. Mostly, though, she told it in her lightly accented English.

He had heard the story in many places. In the sanctuary of the synagogue her voice fluted from the bima. She was sitting on a Survivor Panel, that time. She wasn't technically a Survivor, had never set foot in a Camp, but still. He'd heard it in living rooms, on narrow backyard decks, in porches attached to beachfront bungalows, in restaurants like The Hussar. Once—the only instance, to his knowledge, she'd awarded the story to a stranger—he'd heard it in the compartment of an Irish train; their companion was a priest, who listened with deep attention. Once she'd told it at the movies. They and another couple arrived early by mistake and had to occupy half an hour while Trivia questions lingered on the screen. That night she had narrated from his left, leaning towards their friends—a pair of Lesbian teachers—on his right. While she spoke she stared at them with the usual intensity. Harry, kept in place by his wife aslant his lap, stared at her: her pretty profile, her apricot hair, the flesh lapping from her chin.

Whatever language she employed, the nouns were unadorned, the syntax plain, the vocabulary undemanding: not a word that couldn't be understood by children, though she never told the story to children unless you counted Miriam.

He could tell the thing himself, in any of her tongues.

I was four. The Nazis had taken over. We were desperate to escape. My father went out every morning—to stand in line at one place or another, to try to pay the right person.

That morning—he took my brother with him. My brother was twelve. They went to one office and were on their way to a second. Soldiers in helmets grabbed my father. My brother saw the truck then, and the people on it, crying. The soldiers pushed my father toward the truck. "And your son too." One of them took my brother by the sleeve of his coat.

My father stopped, then. The soldier kept yanking him. "Son?" my father said. "That kid isn't my son. I don't even know him." The German still held on to my brother. My father turned away from them both, and started walking again toward the truck. My brother saw one shoulder lift in a shrug. He heard his voice. "Some Goy," my father said.

So they let my brother go. He came running home, and he showed us the ripped place on his sleeve where they had held him. We managed to get out that night. We went to Holland, and got on a boat for Argentina.

The dessert came. Four different sweets: again they shared.
Lucienne said, "We will go to Santa Fe for the Holidays."
Judith said, "We will go for Thanksgiving."
"And the kids will come east for . . . in December," said Justin.
The young couple spent half their vacation with one set of parents, half with the other. "More room in their place," Miriam told Harry and Lucienne. "More food here."
The bill came. They paid with credit cards. The nervous waiter hurried to bring their outerwear—two overcoats, and Judith's down jacket, and Lucienne's fur stole inherited from her mother.
"Judith," said Lucienne. "I forgot to mention your father's death."
"You sent a kind note," said Judith in a final manner.
"My own father died when I was a little girl," said Lucienne. "But when my mother died—I was fifty, already—then I felt truly forlorn, an orphan."
"Dad's life satisfied him," said Judith.
The fiddler had paused. A quiet moment. Justin leaned towards Lucienne.
"You were a little girl?" he said softly. "What did your father die of?"
The patrons were devotedly eating. A calm place. A growing intimacy.
"Where?" he asked.
She lifted one shoulder, and lifted her lip too. "Overseas," she said. She stood up and wrapped herself in her ratty stole; and Harry had to run a little, she was so fast getting to the door.

T. Coraghessan Boyle

Swept Away

from *The New Yorker*

P EOPLE CAN talk, they can gossip and cavil and run down this one or
the other, and certainly we all have our faults, our black funks and
suicides and wives running off with the first man who'll have them and a
winter's night that stretches on through the days and weeks like a foretaste
of the grave, but in the end the only real story here is the wind. The puff
and blow of it. The ceaselessness. The squelched keening of air in movement, running with its currents like a new sea clamped atop the old, win-
nowing, harrowing, pinching everything down to nothing. It rakes the
islands day and night, without respect to season, though if you polled the
denizens of Yell, Funzie, and Papa Stour, to a man, woman, lamb, and
pony they would account winter the worst for the bite of it and the sheer
frenzy of its coming. One January within living memory, the wind blew at
gale force for twenty-nine days without remit, and on New Year's Eve back
in '92 the gusts were estimated at two hundred and one m.p.h. at the
Muckle Flugga lighthouse here on the northernmost tip of the Isle of
Unst. But that was only an estimate: the weather service's wind gauge was
torn from its moorings and launched into eternity that day, along with a
host of other things, stony and animate alike.

Junie Ooley should have known better. She was an American woman—
"the American ornithological woman" is the way people around town
came to refer to her, or sometimes just "the bird woman"—and she hadn't

just barely alighted from the ferry when she was blindsided by Robbie Baikie's old one-eyed tom, which had been trying to inveigle itself across the roof tiles of the kirk after an imaginary pigeon. Or perhaps the pigeon wasn't imaginary, but by the time the cat blinked his eyes whatever he had seen was gone with the wind. At any rate, Junie Ooley, who was at this juncture a stranger to us all, came banking up the high street in a store-bought tartan skirt and a pair of black tights, with a rucksack flailing at the small of her back and both hands clamped firmly to her knit hat, and she never saw the cat coming, for all her visual acuity and the fine-ground photographic lenses she trucked with her everywhere. The cat—his name was Tiger and he must have carried a good ten or twelve pounds of pigeon-fed flesh on his bones—caught a gust and flew off the kirk tiles like a heat-seeking missile locked in on Junie Ooley's hunched and flapping form.

The impact was dramatic, as you would have had reason to testify had you been meditating over a pint of bitter at the rattling window of Magnuson's Pub as we were that day, and the bird woman, before she'd had a chance even to discover the whereabouts of her lodgings or offer up a "Good day" or "How do you do?" to a single soul, was laid out flat on the flagstones, her lips quivering unconsciously over the lyrics to a tune by the Artist Formerly Known as Prince. At least, that was what Robbie claimed afterward, and he's always been dead keen on the Artist, ever since he came by the CD of *Purple Rain* in the used-disc bin of a record shop in Aberdeen and got it for less than half of what it would have cost new. We had to take his word for it. He was the first one out the door and come to her aid.

There she was, flung down on the stones like a wilted flower amid the crumpled stalks of her limbs, the rucksack stuffed full of spare black tights and bird-watching paraphernalia, her kit and dental floss and all the rest, and Tiger just pulling himself up into a ball to blink his eyes and lick at his spanned paws in a distracted way, when Duncan Stout, ninety-two years on this planet and in possession of the first Morris automobile ever manufactured, came down the street in that very vehicle at twice his normal speed of five and a half miles per hour, and if he discerned Junie Ooley lying there was anybody's guess. Robbie Baikie flailed his arms to head off Duncan's car, but Duncan was the last man in these islands to be expecting anything unexpected out there in the middle of the high street designed and reserved exclusively for the traffic of automobiles and lorries and the occasional dithering bicycle. He kept coming. His jaw was set, his cap pulled down to the orbits of his milk-white eyes. Robbie Baikie was not known for thinking on his feet—like many of us, he was a deliberative type—and before he thought to scoop Junie Ooley up in his arms the car was on them. Or just about.

People were shouting from the open door of the pub. Magnus Magnuson himself was in the street now, windmilling his arms and flinging out his feet in alarm, the bar rag still clutched in one hand like a flag of surrender. The car came on. Robbie stood there. Hopeless was the way it looked. But then we hadn't taken the wind into account, and how could any of us have forgotten its caprices, even for a minute? At that crucial instant, a gust came up the canyon of the high street and bowled Robbie Baikie over atop the bird woman even as it lifted the front end of Duncan's car and flung it into the nearby street lamp.

The wind skreeled off down the street, carrying bits of paper, cans, bottles, old bones, rags, and other refuse along with it. The bird woman's eyes blinked open. Robbie Baikie, all fifteen stone of him, lay pressed atop her in a defensive posture, anticipating the impact of the car, and he hadn't even thought to prop himself on his elbows to take some of the crush off her. Junie Ooley smelled the beer on him and the dulcet smoke of his pipe tobacco and the sweetness of the peat fire at Magnuson's and maybe even something of the sheep he kept, and she couldn't begin to imagine who this man was or what he was doing on top of her in the middle of the public street. "Get off me," she said in a voice so flat and calm Robbie wasn't sure he'd heard it at all, and because she was an American woman and didn't commonly make use of the term "clod," she added, "you big doof."

Robbie was shy with women—we all were, except for the women themselves, and they were shy with the men, at least for the first five years after the wedding—and he was still fumbling with the notion of what had happened to him and to her and to Duncan Stout's automobile and couldn't have said one word even if he'd wanted to.

"Get off," she repeated, and she'd begun to add physical emphasis to the imperative, writhing beneath him and bracing her upturned palms against the great unmoving slabs of his shoulders.

Robbie went to one knee, then pushed himself up even as the bird woman rolled out from under him. In the next moment, she was on her feet, angrily shifting the straps of her rucksack where they bit into the flesh, cursing him softly but emphatically and with a kind of fluid improvisatory genius that made his face light up in wonder. Twenty paces away, Duncan was trying to extricate himself from his car, but the wind wouldn't let him. Howith Clarke, the greengrocer, was out in the street now, surveying the damage with a sour face, and Magnus was right there in the middle of things, his voice gone hoarse with excitement. He was inquiring after Junie Ooley's condition—"Are you all right, lass?"—when a gust lifted all four of them off their feet and sent them tumbling like ninepins. That was enough for Robbie. He picked himself up, took hold of the bird woman's arm, and frog-marched her into the pub.

In they came, and the wind with them, packets of crisps and beer coasters sailing across the polished surface of the bar, and all of us instinctively grabbing for our hats. Robbie's head was bowed and his hair blown straight up off his crown as if it had been done up by some mad cosmetologist, and Junie Ooley heaving and thrashing against him till he released her to spin away from him and down the length of the bar. No one could see how pretty she was at first, her face all deformed with surprise and rage and the petulant crease stamped between her eyes. She didn't so much as look in our direction, but just threw herself back at Robbie and gave him a shove as if they were children at war on the playground.

"What the hell do you think you're doing?" she demanded, her voice piping high with her agitation. And then, glancing round at the rest of us: "Did you see what this, this big *idiot* did to me out there?"

No one said a word. The smoke of the peat fire hung round us like a thin curtain. Tim Maconochie's Airedale lifted his head from the floor and laid it back down again. The bird woman clenched her teeth, set her shoulders. "Well, isn't anybody going to do anything?"

Magnus was the one to break the silence. He'd slipped back in behind the bar, unmindful of the chaff and bits of this and that that the wind had deposited in his hair. "The man saved your life, that's about all."

Robbie ducked his head out of modesty. His ears went crimson.

"Saved—?" A species of comprehension settled into her eyes. "I was . . . something hit me, something the wind blew. . . ."

Tim Maconochie, though he wasn't any less tightfisted than the rest of us, cleared his throat and offered to buy the girl a drop of whiskey to clear her head, and her face opened up then like the sun coming through the clouds so that we all had a good look at the beauty of her, and it was a beauty that made us glad to be alive in that moment to witness it. Whiskeys went round. A blast of wind rattled the panes till we thought they would burst. Someone led Duncan in and sat him down in the corner with his pipe and a pint of ale. And then there was another round, and another, and all the while Junie Ooley was perched on a stool at the bar talking Robbie Baikie's big glowing ears right off him.

That was the beginning of a romance that stood the whole island on its head. Nobody had seen anything like it, at least since the two maundering teens from Cullivoe had drowned themselves in a suicide pact in the Ness of Houlland, and it was the more surprising because no one had ever suspected such depths of passion in a poor slug like Robbie Baikie. Robbie wasn't past thirty, but it was lassitude and the brick wall of introspection that made him sit at the bar till he carried the weight of a man twice his age, and none of us could remember seeing him in the company of a woman, not since his mother died, anyway. He was the sort to let his sheep feed on the blighted tops of the heather and the wrack that blew up out of the sea, and he kept his heart closed up like a lockbox. And now, all of a sudden, right before our eyes, he was a man transformed. That first night, he led Junie Ooley up the street to her lodgings like a gallant out of the picture films, the two of them holding hands and leaning into the wind while cats and flowerpots and small children flew past them, and it seemed that he was never away from her for five minutes consecutive after that.

He drove her all the wind-blasted way out to the bird sanctuary at Herma Ness and helped her set up her equipment in an abandoned crofter's cottage of such ancient provenance that not even Duncan Stout could say who the landlord might once have been. The cottage had a thatched roof, and though it was rotted through in half a dozen places and perfervid with the little lives of crawling things and rodents, she didn't seem particular. It was in the right place, on a broad barren moor that fell off into the sea among the cliffs where the birds made their nests, and that was all that mattered.

There was no fuss about Junie Ooley. She was her own woman, and no doubt about it. She'd come to see and study the flocks that gathered there in the spring—the kittiwakes, puffins, terns, and northern fulmars nesting the high ledges and spreading wide their wings to cruise out over the sea—

and she had her array of cameras and telephoto lenses to take photographs for the pricey high-grade magazines. If she had to rough it, she was prepared. There were the cynical among us who thought she was just making use of Robbie Baikie for the convenience of his Toyota minivan and the all-purpose, wraparound warmth of him, and there was no end to the gossip of the biddies and the potboilers and the kind who wouldn't know a good thing if it fell down out of Heaven and conked them on the head, but there were also those who saw it for what it was: love, pure and simple.

If Robbie had never much bothered about the moorits and Cheviots his poor dead and buried father had bred up over the years, now he positively neglected them. If he lost six blackface ewes stranded by the tide or a Leicester tup caught on a bit of wire in his own yard, he never knew it. He was too busy elsewhere. The two of them—he and the bird woman—would be gone for a week at a time, scrabbling over the rock faces that dropped down to the sea, she with her cameras, he with the rucksack and lenses and the black bottles of stout and smoke-tongue sandwiches, and when we did see them in town they were either having tea at the hotel or holding hands in the back nook of the pub. They scandalized Mrs. Dunwoodie, who let the rooms over the butcher's shop to Junie Ooley on a monthly basis, because she'd seen Robbie coming down the stairs with the girl on more than one occasion and once in the night had heard what could only have been the chirps and muffled cries of coital transport drifting down from above. And a Haroldswick man—we won't name him here, for decency's sake—even claims that he saw the two of them cavorting in the altogether outside the cottage at Herma Ness.

One night when the wind was up, they lingered in Magnuson's past the dinner hour, murmuring to one another in a soft indistinguishable fusion of voices, and Robbie drinking steadily, pints and whiskeys both. We watched him rise for another round, then weave his way back to the table, a pint clutched in each of his big red hands. "You know what we say this time of year when the kittiwakes first return to us?" he asked her, his voice booming out suddenly and his face aflame with the drink and the very joy of her presence.

Conversations died. People looked up. He handed her the beer and she gave him a sweet, inquisitive smile and we all wished the smile were for us and maybe we begrudged him it just the smallest bit. He spread his arms and recited a little poem for her, a poem we all knew as well as we knew our own names, the heart stirrings of an anonymous bird-lover lost now to the architecture of time:

> Peerie mootie! Peerie mootie!
>
> O, du love, du joy, du Beauty!
>
> Whaar is du came frae? Whaar is du been?
>
> Wi di swittlin feet and di glitterin een?

It was startling to hear these sentiments from Robbie Baikie, a man's man who was hard even where he was soft, a man not given to maundering, and we all knew then just how far overboard he'd gone. Love was one thing—a rose blooming atop a prickly stem risen up out of the poor soil of these windswept islands, and it was a necessary thing, to be nourished surely—but this was something else altogether. This was a kind of fealty, a slavery, a doom—he'd given her *our* poem, and in public, no less—and we all shuddered to look on it.

"Robbie," Magnus cried out in a desperation that spoke for us all, "Robbie, let me stand you a drop of whiskey, lad," but if Robbie heard him he gave no sign of it. He took the bird woman's hand, a little bunch of chapped and wind-blistered knuckles, and brought it to his lips. "That's the way I feel about you," he said, and we all heard it.

It would be useless to deny that we were just waiting for the other shoe to drop. There was something inhuman in a passion as intense as that—it was a rabbity love, a tup's love, and it was bound to come crashing down to earth, just as the Artist lamented so memorably in "When Doves Cry." There were some of us who wondered if Robbie even listened to his own CDs anymore. Or heeded them.

And then, on a gloomy gray dour day with the wind sitting in the north and the temperatures threatening to take us all the way back to the doorstep of winter again, Robbie came thundering through the front door of the pub in a hurricane of flailing leaves, thistles, matchbooks, and fish-and-chips papers and went straight to the bar for a double whiskey. It was the first time since the ornithological woman had appeared among us that anyone had seen him alone, and if that wasn't sign enough there were those who could divine by the way he held himself and the particular roseate hue of his ears that the end had come. He drank steadily for an hour or two, deflecting any and all comments—even the most innocuous observations about the weather—with a grunt or even a snarl. We gave him his space and sat at the window to watch the world tumble by.

Late in the day, the light of the weltering sun slanted through the glass, picking out the shadow of the mullions, and for a moment it laid the glowing Cross of our Saviour in the precise spot where Robbie's shoulder blades conjoined. He heaved a sigh then—a roaring, single-malt, tobacco-inflected groan it was, actually—and finally those massive shoulders began to quake and heave. The barmaid (Rose Ellen MacGooch, Donal Mac-Gooch's youngest) laid a hand on his forearm and asked him what the matter was, though we all knew. People made their voices heard so he wouldn't think we were holding our breath; Magnus made a show of lighting his pipe at the far end of the bar; Tim Maconochie's dog let out an audible fart. A calm settled over the pub, and Robbie Baikie exhaled and delivered up the news in a voice that was like a scouring pad.

He'd asked her to marry him. Up there, in the crofter's hut, the wind keening and the kittiwakes sailing through the air like great overblown flakes of snow. They'd been out all morning, scaling the cliffs with numb hands, fighting the wind, and now they were sharing a sandwich and a bottle of stout over a turf fire. Robbie had kissed her, a long, lingering lover's kiss, and then, overcome by the emotion of the moment, he'd popped the question. Junie Ooley had drawn herself up, the eyes shining in her heaven-sent face, and told him that she was flattered by the proposal, flattered and moved, deeply moved, but that she just wasn't ready to commit to something like that, like marriage, that is, what with him being a Shetland sheepman and she an American woman with a college degree, and a rover at that. Would he come with her to Patagonia to photograph the chimango and the nandu? Or to the Okefenokee Swamp in search of the elusive ivorybill? To Singapore? São Paulo? Even Edinburgh? He said he would. She called him a liar. And then they were shouting and she was out in the wind, her knit cap torn from her head in a blink and her hair beating mad at her green eyes, and he tried to pull her to him, to snatch her arm and hold her, but she was already at the brink of the cliff, already edging her way down amid the fecal reek and the raucous avian cries.

"Junie!" he shouted. "Junie, take my hand, you'll lose your balance in this wind, you know you will! Take my hand!"

And what did she say then? "I don't need any man to cling to." That was it. All she said and all she wrote. And he stood in the blast, watching her work her way from one handhold to another out over the yawning sea as the birds careened around her and her hair strangled her face, and then he strode back to the minivan, fired up the engine, and drove back into town.

That night, the wind soughed and keened and rattled like a set of pipes through the canyon of the high street on till midnight or so, and then it came at us with a new sound, a sound people hadn't heard in these parts since '92. It was blowing a gale. Shingles fled before the gusts, shrubs gave up their grip on the earth, the sheep in the fields were snatched up and flung across the countryside like so many puffs of lint. Garages collapsed, bicycles raced down the street with no more than a ghost at the pedals. Robbie was unconscious in the sitting room of his cottage at the time, sad victim of drink and sorrow. He'd come home from the pub before the wind rose up in its fury, boiled himself a plate of liver muggies, then conked out in front of the telly before he could so much as lift a fork to them.

It was something striking the side of the house that brought him to his senses. He woke to darkness, the electric gone with the first furious gusts, and at first he didn't know where he was. Then the house shuddered again and the startled bellow of the Ayrshire cow he kept for her milk and butter roused him up out of the easy chair and he went to the door and stuck his head out into that wild night. Immediately the door was torn from his grasp, straining back on its hinges with a shriek even as the pale form of the cow shot past and rose up like a cloud over the shingles of the roof. He had one thought then, and one thought only: *Junie. Junie needs me.*

It was his luck that he carried five hundred pounds of coal in the back of his minivan as ballast, as so many of us do, because without it he'd never have kept the thing to the road. As it was, he had to dodge the hurtling sheep, rabbits that flew out of the shadows like nightjars, posts torn from their moorings, the odd roof or wall, even a boat or two lashed up out of the heaving seas. He could barely see the road for the blowing trash, the wind slammed at him like a fist, and he had to fight the wheel to keep the car from flipping end over end. If he was half looped when he climbed into the car, now he was as sober as a foud, all the alcohol in his veins burned away with the terrible anxiety that drove him. He put his foot to the floor. He could only pray that he wouldn't be too late.

Then he was there, fighting his way out of the car, and he had to hold to the door to keep from being blown away himself. The moor was as black as the hide of an Angus bull. The wind shrieked in every passage, scouring the heather till it lay flat and cried out its agony. He could hear the sea battering the cliffs below. It was then that the door of the minivan gave way, and in the next instant he was coasting out over the scrub like a tobogganer hurtling down Burrafirth Hill, and there'll be men to tell you that it was a tree that saved him from going over, but what tree could grow on an island as stingy as this? It was a thornbush is what it was, a toughened black unforgiving snarl of woody pith combed down to the ground with fifty years of buffeting, but it was enough. The shining white door of the minivan ran out to sea as if it would run forever, an awkward big plate of steel that might as well have been a Frisbee sailing out over the waves, but Robbie Baikie was saved, though the thorns dug into his hands and the wind took the hair off his head and flailed the beard from his cheeks. He squinted against the airborne dirt and the darkness, and there it was, two hundred yards away and off behind him to the left: the crofter's cottage, and with her in it. "Junie!" he cried, but the wind beat at the sound of his voice and carried it away till it was no voice at all. "Junie!"

As for her, the bird woman, the American girl with the legs that took the breath out of you and the face and figure that were as near perfection as any man here had ever dreamed of on the best night of his life, she never knew that Robbie had come for her. What she did know was that the wind was very bad. Very bad. She must have struggled against it and realized how futile it was to do anything more than succumb to it, huddle and cling and wait it out. Where were the birds? she wondered. How would they weather this—on their wings? Out at sea? She was cold, shivering, the fire long since consumed by the gusts that tore at the chimney. And then the chimney went, with a sound of claws raking at a windowpane. There was a crack, and the roof beams gave way, and then it was the night staring down at her from above. She clung to the andirons, but the andirons blew away, and then she clung to the stones of the hearth, but the stones were swept away as if they were nothing more than motes of dust, and what was she supposed to cling to then?

We never found her. Nobody did. There are some who'll say she was swept all the way to the coast of Norway and came ashore speaking Norse like a native, or that a ship's captain, battened down in a storm sea, found her curled round the pocked safety glass of the bridge like a living figurehead, but no one really believes it. Robbie Baikie survived the night and he survived the mourning of her, too. He sits even now over his pint and his drop of whiskey in the back nook at Magnuson's, and if anybody should ask him about the only love of his life, the bird woman from America, he'll tell you he's heard her voice in the cries of the kittiwakes that swarm the skies in spring, and seen her face there, too, hanging over the black crashing sea on the stiff white wings of a bird. Poor Robbie.

Ann Harleman

Meanwhile

from *Southwest Review*

A T THE hospital I take D—he was demoted yesterday from forearm crutches to a walker, and so hates himself slightly more—to the solarium. We process down the second-floor corridor, with its smells of pine and urine, at a bridal pace. From time to time D casts an envious glance at my feet, though at this speed—the speed of the rest of his life, and that's if he is lucky—they might as well be bound.

The room at the end of the corridor lives up to its name, full of golden afternoon light. Amazing for December, the last notes of a long, molten autumn, the warmest on record in Rhode Island and (but they keep no records for this) the most beautiful. Poor D has spent it all in this place.

The blind woman is here again. You'd think one terrible affliction would preclude others; but no: she's in this place—a rehab hospital—to recover from bypass surgery. Her husband—sprightly, cheery, always here—is feeding her lunch. I don't have to do that, yet. They sit by the long windows, sunlight striping the woman's face, seeming to fill her obediently open mouth. How beautiful she is, with her cropped silver hair, her saint's cheekbones, her pale eyes whose blankness gives the effect not of vacancy but of looking inward.

She smiles in our direction—our conjugal shuffle has alerted her—though not so brightly as her husband. Mel—is that his name? I don't know hers, or rather, I've forgotten it; or maybe I don't want to know it. I think of her as Lucy, after the saint whose eyes were gouged out by the Romans. Or did she do it herself? Or was that Agatha?

D and I play cards here every afternoon—simple kids' games, Rat-A-Tat-Cat or Go Fish. That way, we don't have to talk unless we have something to say. He runs a hand over his graying, patriarchal beard, the way he used to when he was working out some complicated sociobiological concept. He is so sad/angry when he loses. One more loss. Should I let you win, darling? But we haven't quite come to that. The room is full of sound: the cassandra mutterings of pigeons on the long window ledge; nurses' hazy voices over the intercom; Christmas carols on a far-off piano. In one corner of the room is a fountain, new since yesterday. Water splashes joyously over red plastic dolphins into a red plastic basin.

What color is it? Lucy asks Mel between mouthfuls.

What color is what? Here, take a sip. Small sip! It's hot.

The fountain.

Blue.

I remember blue.

Her tone is only slightly wistful.

National Family Caregivers Association (NFCA)
1-800/896-3650
www.nfcacares.org

Well Spouse Foundation (WSF)
1-800/838-0879
www.wellspouse.org

Caregivers
847/823-0639
www.caregiving.com

Date: November 28, 1999
From: graywolf@hotmail.com
To: lioness@earthlink.net
Subject: communicado
are you the first person on e mail ive ever wanted to
hear from   you   love

I spring D for the afternoon so that I can take him to see his neurologist. Doctor Jacques: wide, pale, gleamy-eyed, with a tilting, lyrical accent *que j'adore*. It makes the most unpalatable truths sound hopeful. His son has multiple sclerosis (MS) too. When his son's wife divorced him, he was immediately courted by, and very soon remarried to, a nurse at the rehab hospital.

Zis girl—Doctor Jacques says, taking off his flesh-colored glasses for a smile that makes me feel twenty years younger than I am—she ees so close to *le bon Dieu* zat she was still at sirty-sree a virgin.

Prognosis. A word that always makes me think of "snout."

Chronic progressive multiple sclerosis (CPMS). Chronic = always. Progressive = worse and worse. Multiple = many (all up and down the spinal cord—the sine qua non, the marrow of the spine). Sclerosis = hardening (as in, hearts).

Urine urine URINE.

Once, in the summer—it was hot, maybe August?—I got into the car an hour or so after D brought it home. He was still driving then, still going to his office at the University, where he spent mornings shuffling slides he used to teach from and rereading his own book, the one that won the Lamarck Prize, *Animal Dispersion in Relation to Species Behavior*. I drove to the gym. Felt increasingly damp; thought it was the heat. On the StairMaster, my bodysuit and tights felt wet in the seat. Thought it was sweat. Then the odor began to rise.

Why didn't you tell me? I screamed at D when I got home. Just fucking tell me? I could've put down plastic over the seat.

He was sad all evening because I'd lost my temper, sitting in his recliner with his eyes closed, his large head caressing the high cushioned back. Stress, he mentioned, makes MS symptoms worse.

Date: December 1, 1999
From: graywolf@hotmail.com
To: lioness@earthlink.net
Subject: yesterday
dear gorgeous lover
but first a message for the creeps & voyeurs that im told

have access to this e mail since it is unerasable and about
as private as sky writing
if this is the only artifact that survives me into the
millennium then yes, this beautiful woman and ihave
fucked each other and yes, we enjoyed it enjoy
being far too weak a word for the ecstatic abandoned
glorious inventions which delighted us and will ihope
continue to delight us in spite of the inevitability that
you creeps & voyeurs and probably my dean will read
our messages but only to marvel at the endless capacity
of our bodies to surprise and transport each other
now
back to the message which is i cherish you
your precious flowerlike pussy which istudied so devotedly
and all the rest of you

We missed you! Mel cries.

He is walking Lucy down the second-floor corridor, not (say) holding her elbow or linking arms with her, but towing her by the end of a red-and-green plaid scarf tied around her waist. Does he think I don't know meanness when I see it?

I raise my eyebrows unencouragingly.

At the party! Remember? I gave you a flyer? His tone is carefully unre-proachful.

I thought it was next week, I lie.

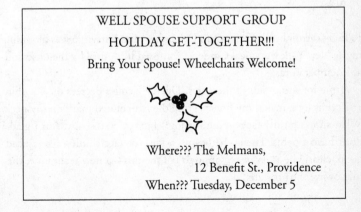

WELL SPOUSE SUPPORT GROUP
HOLIDAY GET-TOGETHER!!!
Bring Your Spouse! Wheelchairs Welcome!

Where??? The Melmans,
12 Benefit St., Providence
When??? Tuesday, December 5

At the bottom, preceded by a pointing finger, is an inspirational quote (all Well Spouse flyers have inspirational quotes). "'I get up. I walk. I fall down. MEANWHILE . . . I keep dancing.'—Rabbi Hillel." Oh, yeah? I think, and write, underneath it, something my lover said yesterday: "'Too long a sacrifice makes a stone of the heart.'—William Butler Yeats." I fold the bright-green paper and write Mel's name on it and leave it for Annie, the charge nurse, to give him in the morning. You won't get me, not that way.

What I am: teacher of English as a Second Language (ESL); wife (W); mother (M); grandmother (GRM); lover (L). What I am not: Well Spouse (WS). But the undertow grows stronger every day.

> Date: December 4, 1999
> From: graywolf@hotmail.com
> To: lioness@earthlink.net
> Subject: delight
> Gorgeous desire 4 yesss ssss dec 8 in nyc is
> what im working on with difficulty as to hotel (ideas)
> maybe joe will help magic flute okay with you?   wear
> something that shows your beautiful arms and under it
> nothing too difficult so that if iwant you urgently it wont
> take too long   you are the bold girl ive always dreamed
> of gorgeous lover soon to be against my body head to head
> foot to foot even if we were to need it for any reason ass
> to ass

Rain by the nightful. Eerie warm December rain. Forsythia was blooming in the New York Botanical Gardens, confused into April by the unseasonable temperatures.

Time for more radical measures, Doctor Jacques decrees on our third visit. (His look makes my fingers go to the iris-colored mark on my neck. What shows on my face—guilt, or joy?) First, a cystoscopy. Am I glad I don't have a penis! Then—he beams, wide pale face shining like a headlamp, clearly he is *vraiment* 'appy to tell me this—a new technique: they microwave the prostate.

.   .   .

My grandson, who is just four, can pee standing up now. He makes us all watch. Often he is called to this task, joyously, in the middle of Sunday dinner.

When I get to the hospital on yet another blue-and-gold afternoon—late, because I gave in to the temptation to bike through Swan Point Cemetery on the path along the Blackstone River—the occupational therapist (OT) is teaching D how to fall. He lifts his head to look at me. Where were you? his eyes ask. You'd think falling lessons would be the province of the physical therapist (PT); but maybe the doctors see falling as an occupation for D now. "Occupation: Gimp," I saw him write last month on the application for Long-Term Disability (LTD). How sad his large body looks, on all fours, head swinging from side to side with the shame of it. I should not, not, not be thinking of the wide bed in New York, the gilt-framed mirror, two lithe bodies bending.

D's roommate, on a bedpan, watches with interest. The OT (Chris? Phil?) looks about twelve, shiny with optimism, asking to be quashed. Learning fast, he says, he's my star pupil—aren't you, Teach? Once D masters these simple techniques, Chris/Phil tells me, he'll be able to fall without breaking a hip. Don't they tell you people what a patient's prognosis is? Once D is in a wheelchair, his neurologist says—and that may be soon—he'll never leave it. Meanwhile, he'll be able (with my help) to pull himself upright. Meanwhile, I won't have to call the Fire Department every time he hits the ground.

I watch for a while, poor D first on his nose, then on his knees. The OT rolls up the sleeves of his blue work-shirt to reveal muscular young forearms. A nurse I haven't seen before pokes her head around the doorway and cries to D's roommate, No poop in the pooper? D shoots me a glance that says, Leave! and I do.

Passing me in the corridor, Annie, the Charge Nurse, smiles approval. So faithful, she says, here every day. By the river, when I stopped my bike to rest, beaky black rocks glittered; I found a discarded snakeskin hanging from an oak tree. Amazed, enchanted, I brought it to show to D, forgetting that he's no longer interested in any manifestations of Nature save his own. Now the pale ochre skin, light and shivery and cool, crackles between my palms when I crush it. It drifts to the floor of the hospital corridor like ash.

The sound of a body falling is unmistakable, like no other. Soft yet

heavy: a dark sound. The whole house quivers in response, like a cam-
panile to its bell. Whenever I dream of D falling, this sound wakes me.
The feel of it in my body, like my own heart beating.

Date: December 9, 1999
From: graywolf@hotmail.com
To: lioness@earthlink.net
Subject: e[ternally your] male
darling lover i was so impatient for you so turned inside
out wanting you im not sure ididnt take away some of your
beautiful flesh in my predatory mouth   ihave slow sweet
designs on your breasts your cunt your toes and consolation
ihope for your difficult situation these days   my birthday
a warm & fine day but some sense of amputation with the
minus of you   tomorrow ill try to console you take the best
care of your beautiful (startlingly beautiful it was like seeing
you for the first time yesterday) body & equally beautiful
soul

Lucy knows all sorts of things:

- the give of linoleum versus carpet beneath paper hospital slippers
- the burble of fish in their violet-lighted tank beside the nurses'
  station
- the changing air: cinnamon rolls for lunch; Lysol; urine (ah!
  urine); the yellow smell of shit

So even though she must hold Mel's hand—which sometimes drags at
hers impatiently, sometimes (more cruelly) lets it drop—she has her own
experience of this place. I know, because I've just walked blindfolded
along the second-floor corridor, sat blindfolded in the solarium. The
nurses, who in fact don't like me much, are impressed: they think I'm
preparing for D's next symptom. What great gulping empathy they attrib-
ute to Well Spouses. Where do they get such a view of human nature?

   Mel would never do this; he stays resolutely outside Lucy's experience,
her pain, as (he told me yesterday) an effective caregiver must. Is that why
I did it—to prove I'm not Mel? Or as a penance for the joy I felt last night?

Or to remind myself where I really live? I don't know. Every day I don't know more (which is not the same thing as knowing, every day, less).

D was an optimistic child, always tasting his gums, waiting for something to happen. Outdoors he'd make a nest in the roots of a maple, then stare upward for whole skies. Under a shawl of dead leaves he'd trace the bones of birds until the cold drove him inside. Bedtimes, the steed of night rubbed against his windows, mentioning tomorrow.

> Date: December 12, 1999
> From: graywolf@hotmail.com
> To: lioness@earthlink.net
> Subject: just to reiterate
> lover not only is the stain evident on the chair the
> blinds are still down and if you are half-crazy like me you
> can discover our scent still on the seat, iwant us to be in
> YOUR office like that too, soon, butterfly thigh   coming
> into you from below was like a welling over really unexpected
> & quiet of love and sex and longing and relief   you did
> we did nothing special to make it happen it just could not be
> held any longer what belongs to you belongs to you

Zere are two kind of woman. Zee kind which divorce zee 'andicapped, and zee kind which marree zem.

Last week his neurologist told me to bring D a book of crossword puzzles graded "Easy," "Medium," "Hard," and have him do one a day. This afternoon D shows the first one to me with a sidelong look.

The brain is part of the spinal cord—we forget that. Conveniently (D used to tell his graduate students) for our insistence on our uniqueness among animals. CUNT. What does D know or guess about my other life? He gazes steadfastly at the opposite wall, where a bulletin board sports a border of bluebirds around the list of today's activities: Bingo, Chapel, Memory Book.

We're sitting at one of the long tables in the solarium while Mel and Lucy work a puzzle at the other and the golden afternoon, outside the window, wanes. In a far corner is the German woman, Lotte; her wheelchair glitters in late sunlight. Every now and then she moans, I vant to go home. The four of us ignore her, having learned from experience that concern invites cursing, spitting, even (if you get close enough) a punch.

Be good! Mel chirps at Lucy, in parting. His grin: solicitous, pitying, evil. She smiles. Not if I get a better offer.

!NEW!   W.S. SUPPORT GROUPS   !NEW!

Warwick, RI (Kent Hospital):
    Catherine, 401/538-2983

Waltham, MA:
    Joe Deschenes, 617/551-7036

Mansfield, MA:
    Bea Thornton, 508/697-1716

"Remember—everything has God's fingerprints on it."

—RICHARD CARLSON

A quick glance around the empty solarium. Then I add, in red ink, at the bottom:

> *"In some primitive cultures women are encouraged to practice*
> *fellatio, for the protein—especially when nursing."*

—Margaret Mead

Date: December 15, 1999
From: graywolf@hotmail.com
To: lioness@earthlink.com
Subject: together
i meant it last night & iwill always mean it
we should we must be TOGETHER   iwish you wanted
to hear this but even if you don't the creeps & voyeurs
probably do and anyway ihave to say it

Pickerel Slough, Wisconsin. A hot, bright day. Ahead of us, that bend in
the river, like Monet's paintings of the Seine. Our rowboat rocked
between wooded banks, the only movement besides the black glitter of
gnats, the red wing of a bird deep in the oak trees. We could hear the far-
off barking of an axe, and the shadowed water pulsed with quick bright
fish. D propped his rod on the gunwale and began to hum "Blue Room,"
putting in the trumpet riffs. Silky strands from the willows brushed our
faces. On either bank: wild roses, dogwood, white birches, honeysuckle. A
sky with thin clouds—peach, mauve, maize—like the inside of a baby's
ear. Looks like rain, D murmured.

There is, in any love, a stretch (like the river just before it turns)
when perfect happiness is possible. We seized it, D and I. Why is that
now no protection? Though the scent of roses stalks me; the sound of
rain on our tent beneath the branches of an oak tree, singing like our two
bodies.

At the Stop & Shop I ram my cart into the cart of a woman smoking, fla-
grantly blowing lazy blue signals into the air above the avocados, making
people cough. I back up and ram her again. The manager (round, young-
old face, chestnut hair) is summoned. Press charges! Go ahead.

But I am merely asked to leave the store and not to return.

Together? How can we ever be that, when I am already together,
with D?

When we were young, D planned his death: a sailboat turned in the direction of Bermuda with no food on board; sunrise; a tape of Thelonius
Monk.

Date: December 17, 1999
From: graywolf@hotmail.com
To: lioness@earthlink.net
Subject: whats wrong
hi heres your e male again   can i say im nervous that
maybe isaid or did something wrong since i have not heard
from you for 3 days now

Sunlight pours through the glass, splashes over the table, the jigsaw puzzle pieces, Lucy's hands. How welcome it would be in a world of snow and ice, a normal mid-December! As it is, outside the long windows buds already deck the branches of the sycamores: tender, red, swollen. Sexual. But of course Lucy, surprisingly strong-looking hands moving among the puzzle pieces, is unaware of this.

I should not, not, not be thinking of this joke:

> Q: How did Helen Keller burn her hand?
> A: Reading a waffle iron

Lotte dozes in her wheelchair at the far end of the room, mercifully silent. D and I are playing Scrabble. Keeps the brain alive, the MS newsletter said; but I doubt they had anything like this in mind:

$$
\begin{array}{c}
\text{D} \\
\text{EAR} \\
\text{I} \\
\text{MAX} \\
\text{TENOR} \\
\text{N}
\end{array}
$$

I put an H on one end of EAR, a T on the other. And my own heart? Is elsewhere, is a tarry lump of resentment and longing.

D plays slowly (I've long since thrown away the little hourglass that times each turn), so I have plenty of time to watch Mel help Lucy with her puzzle, a picture—a country landscape—composed of different textures, specially designed for what Mel calls the Visually Impaired. He sits sideways next to her, legs in dark-red rubbery-looking slacks debonairly crossed.

As usual he looks, not merely cheerful, but happy. How does it feel—to know that your affliction is the source of so much joy? Lucy's fingers interrogate each piece. Her expression reminds me of D, three decades ago, gutting fish at our camp on Pickerel Slough, a hand thrust inside the cold, slick body, rifling its unseen darkness. Quietly, Mel picks up the piece that would fit the spot she's working on, slips it into his pants pocket.

My indrawn breath makes him look at me. Not shame. It's a look of—yes—complicity. The corners of my mouth turn down in revulsion, but he doesn't look away. His shiny little eyes deny my denial.

Lucy yawns. Mel carols, *SOME*body's *SLEEP*y!

D sits back in a gust of glee. He's covered a Triple Word Score with ZEPER.

My third-grade teacher made us study snow. We ran in fours out into the cold, each group carrying a large cloth, a kid at each corner, the way firemen hold a net for people to jump from a burning building. Wisconsin winter air, dry and sparkling, ringing in my lungs, thumping my breastbone. The playground slick with fast-increasing white, and in the margins a wall of white-sugared stones. No birds except the hardy, songless chickadees. Toes burning with cold inside heavy boots; mittened fingers clumsy as sausages. Snow fell slowly onto the dark-green baize, each flake a heartbeat.

> Date: December 19, 1999
> From: graywolf@hotmail.com
> To: lioness@earthlink.net
> Subject: abject
> hey darling gorgeous lover I have a lot of things iwant
> to say to you but the main thing is i love you I LOVE YOU and
> all the thinking ive been doing about how discouraging and
> difficult it seems (i am still depressed from our fight which
> contributes) seems to circle back toward images i cant deny
> like your teeth biting my tongue your thighs sliding wet on
> mine you are wrong to end us WRONG & YOU KNOW IT

Warm, syrupy rain coats the city. Tail-lights gleam in the early evening dark like maraschino cherries.

The wheelchair feels a like a huge heavy stroller. After ten minutes my shoulders ache. I push D past the nurses' station, past the zigzagging fish in their fluorescent tank. It's tricky, those vulnerable knees protruding so far ahead. He won't leave this wheelchair, ever. So many losses, and the one thing I'm sure of now is that I can't add another. I thread our way down the corridor between the parked wheelchairs of less lucky patients, the unvisited, holding my breath against the occasional acrid whiff of pee. They're out here every evening, even the ones who look comatose: the nurses feel an after-dinner change of scene is good for them. The livelier ones have the look I've begun to see on D's face, a look that burns through you, that says you're lying even when you're not. I keep my eyes on the top of D's head with its incipient gleam of baldness, his graying hair raked by nightmares. I can feel the seductive pull of my (relative) youth. Dimmed eyes are drawn upward; white heads swivel. I know, I know, you were like me once, all of you, I know this but I do not believe it. We pass the woman who quacks all day; we pass Lotte, tied into her chair tonight and struggling and shouting (I vant to go home! I vant to go home!); we pass the very thin man who holds out trembling arms and calls me by his daughter's name. Hilary? Hilary!

You can take our sweet Teach home day after tomorrow! Annie, the Charge Nurse (D's favorite), told me this afternoon, beaming, proprietary. He's lucky to have such a faithful wife, aren't you, Teach? Vanguard Medical will deliver a wheelchair just like this one. Why all that practice falling, then? More of D's precious energy wasted. Mel, who'd been standing near the nurses' station, showed me a brochure for a sort of forklift to get D from his bed into his chair. Awesome machine! Annie agreed. Then she taught me how to give D his injection, a new medication called Something Interferon. Sticking needles into oranges; pricking my own finger. Will I sleep for a hundred years? D's eyes met mine above the poised hypodermic, momentarily alive with the knowledge that we can no longer help each other through our very different sorrows.

There's a loud crash behind us. A nurse emerges from the room we're passing and begins to run. I start to look around, then remember. Turn the wheelchair, twit, or D can't see. How heavy it is, how clumsy I am, with this weight that is my life, now. And there at the end of the shining corridor is Lotte, sprawled face down on the floor. Indignation and fury have bounced her right out of her wheelchair. Excitement sweeps the corridor.

Patients twist in their chairs and crane to see; nurses are on the run. Meanwhile, Lotte keeps on howling. I vant to go home! she cries to the linoleum.

Date: December 23, 1999
From: graywolf@hotmail.com
To: lioness@earthlink.net
Subject:
it is painful not to be in touch with you   in this not
invasive medium may i still say iwant you sad or happy,
angry or tender, your rich sensuous mind your conflicted
soul your beautiful gifted golden body

Smell of woodsmoke from our campfire. Pickerel bones and orange rinds on a paper plate. Sex slowly drying on our skin, essential and crusty, like salt.

The rain turned from a simple downpour to a storm. Rain drove sideways against the heavy canvas of the tent. When I pulled aside the flap, pale-gold moths, hundreds of them, throbbed against the dark mesh screen.

Douglas Light

Three Days. A Month. More.

from *Alaska Quarterly Review*

"WHEN YOU turn twelve," Maria says, studying her younger sister Lena's breasts, "I'll give you my bra." Three days, a month. Their mother's left. They've been alone some time, Lena and Maria.

The room, hot from the late-spring sun cutting through the bare windows, smells of burnt onions and bad milk. "You itchy?" Lena asks her sister. She itches, has been itchy ever since Raho spent the night between her and Maria on their dingy, gray-sheeted bed, Raho and Maria squirming about every few hours.

"Why do they always think it's funny to put pants on a monkey?" Maria asks, more to the TV commercial than to Lena. The TV is always on, the sounds of voices, a distant family, issuing from the front room all hours of the day. Maria's father's not Lena's. They've never met either. "They think a monkey with pants," Maria says, "is funny."

Often Lena dreams they are comfortable, that their mother's returned and they are living in a clean apartment with peach-colored carpet, an apartment someplace south of 143rd Street, someplace other than west Harlem.

The TV shows grazing caribou, ice floes, then a woman in a red suit firmly saying, "Drilling in Alaska is our only viable option. The oil there is what we need."

"Shit, Alaska," Maria says. "How come you never meet no one from Alaska?" she asks. "Puerto Rico, yeah, always, everywhere. Manhattan is Puerto Rico on vacation. But Alaska? You never meet people from Alaska."

"You itchy?" Lena asks again, and Maria looks at her surprised, startled, like Lena told her their mother returned.

"Let's," Maria says, standing, "get some ice cream."

Lena remembers her mother leaving, remembers the sound waking her at night. It was a sound of franticness, hurry and fright, of something moving through the walls, a sound similar to the sound of the crazy lady next door trying to cook the way she always cooks, by banging everything around. Then the TV was turned off.

A door shut and someone softly coughed in the hallway. "These sheets," Lena whispered to her sister, feeling the bedding they shared. It was eleven o'clock or midnight or three A.M. "They're suppose to be white."

"She's not coming back," Maria said, lying next to her.

"Where'd she go?" Lena asked.

"Just gone."

Three days, a month passed. "Don't pay no rent," Raho tells them, eyeing Maria as she moves around the kitchen. At age fifteen, he's a man. "The money you got, keep," he says.

The sink's filled with dishes from meals Lena can't remember eating. "You got six months," he says, studying Maria as she leans on the table, "before something happens. A good six months," he slowly says.

The bodega at the corner sells chocolate, vanilla, and coconut ice cream. Maria takes two beers from the standing cooler. "You ain't old enough," the bodega man says, eyeing Maria then Lena as they place the items on the counter.

"But my Mama is," Maria tells him, then asks for a pack of Newport cigarettes and pays in quarters and dimes.

"Tell your Mama," the bodega man says, "I ain't seen her in a while." He winks at Lena, offers her a broken orange popsicle, the wrapper torn. "For free," he says. Maria's cautioned Lena about him, the bodega man, said he was not to be trusted. "He acts like he knows something," she said, "something he'll hold against us."

"Tell her," the bodega man says to Maria, half smiling, "I want to talk with her."

"Tell her," Maria says, grabbing the items, "yourself."

Eating ice cream from the small square box, Lena asks, "What's chocolate look like?" Artificial flavors, sugar, color no. 5, the ice cream box reads. They sit in front of the TV, the news accounting downward economies, a forest fire and a kitten rescued from a storm drain.

"Like this," Maria says, and sticks her ice-cream-covered tongue out.

"I mean, on the tree, or wherever it grows."

Maria pours some beer. "What I don't get," she says, "is why some Puerto Ricans need to wave a Puerto Rican flag all the time."

"Mama's Puerto Rican," Lena says. "We're Puerto Rican." Often she dreams they are comfortable.

"Not that kind of Puerto Rican," she says. "Not the kind that waves a flag." On TV, a white woman says to the black man sitting next to her, "If you're honest with yourself, you'll see that we're all oppressed."

"Tell me something," Maria says. "What's the Alaskan flag look like?"

"I've never seen one," Lena tells her.

"You know why you've never seen one?" Maria asks, pointing her spoon. "Because Alaskans don't go crazy waving them around."

Raho comes by with friends and Chinese food, some beer. "Don't pay the rent," he tells them again.

"Don't you ever wash your sheets?" one of the boys asks Lena, looking at their bed, the dank sheets twisted and rumpled. Lena thinks of her mother, thinks of this boy in her room and the bra she'll get when she turns twelve. "Don't look like they've ever been white," the boy says, lightly kicking the mattress.

Leaving the room, Lena calmly slides her hand under her shirt, into her pants, and scratches. "Shit," the boy says, seeing her. "You too?"

There is no money but somehow Maria has money. Lena takes an old razor of her mother's and shaves her pubic area, the few random strands, but still she itches. Standing in front of the streaked bathroom mirror, she calls to Maria, "When do I get a bra?"

"Let's clean the place," Maria says from the kitchen, staring at the sink filled with dishes. They throw everything out, the dishes, the sheets, old underwear.

"I still need to talk with your Mama," the bodega man says the next time they go for ice cream and beer. Outside, the fire hydrant is open, arcing a spray over the hot summer street, the sweating children, the passing cars. "Ain't seen her in a long while," he says, not smiling. "Tell her I got something she needs."

"You got sheets?" Maria asks him.

"Sheets?" he asks, confused. "What do you mean? Like, for a bed?"

"Listen," Maria says to Lena. "Mama's gone. What do you want?"

They sleep on the bare mattress, scratching through the night. In the front room, the TV blares: "I wish the world would stop." Three days, a month, more. Often Lena dreams they are comfortable.

The landlord comes by. "I'm not all that bad," he says to them. The door barely open, Maria eyes him through the crack. "When is your mother home?" he asks.

"Late," Maria tells him. "She's always working. Two jobs, double shift."

"Then she can afford to pay the rent."

"I'm thirteen years old," she tells him, "my sister's eleven." He seems to understand. They aren't the ones to talk to. They aren't the ones to pay rent.

"Don't pay him shit," Raho says. He is over more and more often, always calm and studying Maria. He buys them a set of sheets, new and dark blue. "They get dirty but it's hard to tell," he says.

"Mama's gone," Maria says to Lena. "What do you want?"

"I want to be a doctor," she tells her, "or a seamstress or someone who whispers on the phone like Mama use to."

"But what do you want," she says, "now that Mama's gone."

The TV speaks of aspirin, Odor-Eaters, pizza and panty hose. "I want one of those purple gowns and square hats like we see people wearing at City College every spring," Lena tells her. She chews at her nails, biting at the tips of her fingers. "I want to be older," she says. "I want a bra."

It is Sunday or Thursday or Monday. Raho moves in. Still, Lena itches. "Listen," he often says, and they stop to listen.

Maria moves Lena into their mother's old room so she and Raho can have the newly sheeted bed to themselves. Mama's room, with its empty air, stripped bed, and scarred bureau, feels like no one has ever lived there. The window and window ledge are marred with pigeon shit. Lena checks the drawers and finds a pair of socks, a T-shirt, a brown blouse, and red shorts, all smelling of a closed space. She can't remember her mother ever wearing these things, can't even picture what she'd look like in them. Can't picture her.

"How much money would you need?" Maria asks her.

The TV comments: "Seventy percent of our oil comes from the Middle East. We've got oil here, our own natural reserves. Not tapping them now is like going out to eat with a refrigerator full of food just waiting to rot."

The landlord starts coming by, knocking on the door every few days, asking for the rent. "I hate to do this," he says. The TV transmits false, empty voices, sounds of a world far away. The noise is the music of the apartment, the music of their lives. "I hate to do this, but we need to talk," the landlord says through the locked door. "I need the rent." Motionless inside, Maria, Raho, and Lena say nothing, remain quiet, like they are elsewhere.

"What do I need money for?" Lena asks Maria. "I have you."

"I'm saying, if you needed money," she asks, "if you were on your own, how much would you need?"

She is not on her own, she tells her. "I don't need money," she says. "I need Mama. I need you."

Three days. A month. Rarely do they leave the apartment. Raho moves about the place, opening closets then slamming them closed. "Why is this always on," Raho asks of the TV, turning it off. "Tell me, why is it always on?"

"Leave it on," Maria calmly tells him. "Mama always had it on. It's home, it's sound," she says. "It's what makes me comfortable when I'm not." He looks to Lena for understanding, and finding none, turns the TV back on.

The issuing voices move from room to room, filling the hollow spaces.

The afternoons pass in a hot stupor, the weak, late-summer breeze failing to cool. "How much would you need?" Maria asks Lena, drinking beer. Barley, hops, yeast, the label reads. "How much?" she asks, her voice tight, strange. She sounds nervous, like the bodega man who has something he'll hold against them.

"Twenty or a hundred or five thousand dollars," Lena tells her. "What does ice cream cost?"

"The cost of ice cream," Maria says, thinking it through. "That's right, ice cream."

Raho buys them new clothing, Rocawear, Sean John, items like everyone else is wearing. "They're real," he says, showing them the labels.

"School started last week," Maria tells Lena.

"When did it end?" she asks, and they both laugh.

Hot baths and alcohol rubs soothe the itching.

"When's your birthday, Lena?" Raho finally asks, standing in the doorway and studying her closely for some time.

She doesn't mind him watching her the way he watches Maria. "What is today?" she asks, lifting her hand to feel her face. Sometimes she forgets the feel of her face. "What day is today?" she asks, lying calmly in the tub, the water warm and her pubic area shaved clean. "What month are we in?"

"OK," Raho says, stepping away, his hands held up as a sign of surrender. "OK."

Three days, a month, more. They throw the mail out, the envelopes bright yellow, the words "final notice" printed in red on the front. Evening comes earlier, the sun setting sooner. It is afternoon, one o'clock or two or five P.M. Sitting on the soiled tile floor, Maria takes her shirt off. "That shit with that Chinese guy lighting himself on fire," she says. "The government say all kinds of stuff and people believe."

"What?" Raho asks. "What the fuck are you talking about?"

There is a knock on the front door, then the rattle of the doorknob. Lena moves softly from the kitchen, stands before the door, one foot socked and her pants unbuttoned. Again, the doorknob rattles. A charge of anxiousness, of fright, cuts over her as she quietly leans to the doorframe, places her cheek to the cool, grimy wood and listens for a sound that is familiar, the sound of breathing or cough that is her mother's.

From the outside hallway, a voice, distant and angry: "Rent by Friday. Tell your mother rent by Friday."

Lena thinks of Raho watching her bathe, thinks of his mouth and what it might taste like on hers.

"Listen," he tells her one afternoon. The day is cool; the leaves are turning the colors they turn when they die for the year. The TV is on, the volume loud. Maria is elsewhere, out buying ice cream or beer, or in the bedroom asleep. They sit next to each other on the couch, Raho and Lena. "Listen," Raho says, his eyes touching her.

Slowly, she lifts her skirt.

The air around them moves then stops moving and his hand is on her thigh, damp and forceful.

Often Lena dreams she is comfortable.

It hurt at first. But then, after some time, it no longer hurt.

"What do you want," Maria asks, moving about the room, "now that Mama's gone?" Her voice is a wall, solid and real. There is something different now. Somehow Maria knows of Raho, knows of Lena. That morning there was shouting, a door slammed, Maria crying. "Raho's not coming back," Maria told her, her eyes red and swollen.

"Where'd he go?" Lena asked.

"Just gone."

No longer are they sisters, Maria and Lena, no longer two girls from the same mother. Now they are two girls of different fathers.

"What do you want?" she asks again.

"I want to be a diplomat," Lena quietly tells her, picking at her toes, "or a model or someone who says 'Hi' to people when they walk into a store." She feels no different, feels no older. Still, she itches. "I want to be older," she says.

"But what do you want?" Maria asks, irritated.

The TV interviewer says, "One can't speak without fear of being castigated for common thoughts, truths that are true even if America doesn't believe them. How was Malcolm X killed? Tell me, who killed him?"

"Ice cream," Lena says.

"Ice cream," Maria answers, then hands her a twenty-dollar bill off a pile of bills. "That's right, ice cream."

The bodega man eyes Lena wearily as she sets the ice cream, a beer, and the twenty-dollar bill Maria gave her on the counter. Baby wipes, bandages, Kool-Aid, and Goya beans. Dust covers the items on the shelf. A Puerto Rican flag hangs over the cash register. Three days. A month. More. "Is your Mama avoiding me?" the bodega man asks, embarrassed. "If she's avoiding me," he says, bagging the items, "tell her to forget about it." He hands her the change. "Tell her it's forgotten."

"You got Alaskan flags?" Lena asks.

"Alaskan flags?" he asks, confused. "What do you mean? Like, for the state?"

Returning home, an awkward stillness clouds the apartment. The TV is off, silence filling the space. Worried, she calls out her sister's name. "Maria," she calls, moving from room to room. The frail autumn sun casts a failing light through the dingy window. West Harlem is on the island of Manhattan. The bed is stripped of the dark blue sheets.

"Maria?" she says. "Maria?" she calls, frightened that she's alone.

There is a loud pounding on the front door, hollow and resounding. Silently, she moves along the hall, her breath still.

The knock sounds again; then the doorknob rattles.

"Maria?" she whispers, slowly leaning her cheek against the cool, grimy doorframe. Today, she turns twelve. Still, she itches. "Maria?" she whispers, listening for a sound of something familiar. "Mama?" she says, listening for a sound that will make her comfortable when she's not.

Joan Silber

The High Road

from *Ploughshares*

MY WHOLE life, it always made me crazy when people weren't sensible. Dancers, for instance, have the worst eating habits. I can't begin to say how many anorexic little girls I used to have to hold up onstage, afraid they were going to faint on me any minute.

I myself was lean and tight and healthy in those days. I went out with different women, and I married one of them. I don't know why she married me, I was never kind to her, but women did not expect much then. She was probably a better dancer than I was, too. I left her, after a lot of nasty fights and spite on both sides, and I went and had my life with men. It was a dirty, furtive, sexy life then—this was before Stonewall—but it had its elations. Infatuation, when it happened, could be visionary, a lust from another zone. From the true zone, the molten center of the earth. I was in my twenties, listening to a lot of jazz, and I thought in phrases like that.

Andre, my lover, was in fact a musician, a trumpeter with a tender, earnest sound, sweet like Chet Baker, although he would have liked to have been as intense as Miles. Well, who wouldn't? I had been with men before him, but only one-night pickups, those flickering hallucinations that were anything but personal. When I met Andre, we were not in a bar but at a mixed party, and we had to signal each other cautiously and make a lot of conversation first. Andre was no cinch to talk to, either. Other white people thought he was gruff or scornful, but actually he was really quite shy.

When we went home together, after the party, we got along fine. For a shy person, he was confident and happy in bed (I was the rough and bumbling one). I could still recount, if I had to, the sequence of things we did that night. I have done them many times since—there isn't that much variety in the world—but the drama was particular and stunning just then. In the morning I made him a very nice breakfast (my wife had been a terrible cook), and he ate two helpings of my spinach omelet, as if he could not believe his good luck. He had a dry sense of humor, and he was quite witty about my makeshift housekeeping and my attempts at décor, the white fake-fur rug and the one wall painted black. We put on music, and we hung around, smoking cigarettes and reading the paper all afternoon. Just passing the time.

I was working in a show on Broadway, skip-skipping across the stage in cowboy chaps and swinging my silver lariat, and he came to see me perform. I suppose the other dancers knew who he was to me. Backstage everybody shook his hand and asked him if it wasn't the dumbest musical he'd ever seen. The girls told me later how nice he was. And sometimes I was in his world, when we went to hear music in the Village or once up to a club in Harlem. Anyone who saw us probably thought I was just some white theater guy wanting to be hip. Had we been a man and a woman, we would have had a much harder time walking together on the street.

Andre stayed with me more nights than not, even if he didn't live with me. But he had to go home to practice. A trumpet is not an instrument that can be played casually in someone's apartment. His own place, up in Morningside Heights, was in the basement (a great cheap find), and he had rigged up a booth lined with acoustic ceiling tile and squares of carpeting for his hours of practice. His chicken coop, I called it, his burrow. I never stayed over with him, and I only visited him there once, but I liked to imagine him hunched over his horn, blowing his heart out in that jerry-built closet.

He wasn't getting gigs yet, but sometimes he sat in with musicians he'd met. To this day, I couldn't say whether he was a great player or not. When he was playing with anyone, I worried like a parent—I looked around to see what people thought. He was okay, I think, but so modest and unflashy that he could be taken for a competent dullard. But he had a rare kind of attention, and sometimes, the way he worked his way in and the way he twisted around what they'd been playing made the other players smile. He was just learning.

In the daytime, he worked as a salesman in a men's clothing store in Midtown. Once I walked in the door and pretended to be a grouchy rich man who needed an ugly suit to wear to divorce court. Something hideous, please, something you wouldn't wear to a dogfight. This cracked Andre up. He laughed through his teeth, hissing softly. That's how bored he was there. He introduced me to the manager as his crazy friend Duncan, this lunatic he knew.

He was quite a careful dresser, from working in that place. A little too careful, I thought, with his richly simple tie and his little handkerchief folded in his pocket. I used to tell people he ironed his underwear, which he stoutly denied. For Christmas he bought me a silk shirt that probably looked silly on me but felt great. We had dinner that day with two of Andre's friends, Reg and Maxmilian. I made a goose, a bird none of us had ever had before. We kept goosing each other all night, a joke that wouldn't die. Reg got particularly carried away, I thought. Andre teased me about the ornateness of my meal—the glazed parsnips, the broccoli polonaise— wasn't there a hog jowl in anything? He wanted the others to be impressed with me, and they sort of were. Andre asked me to put on the record of *Aida* he liked, the one with Roberta Tebaldi.

"Renata Tebaldi," I said.

"Rigatoni Manicotti," he said. "What do I care what her name is?"

But I took to calling him Roberta after that. Just now and then, to needle him. Pass the peas, Roberta. Like that.

We were at the Village Vanguard with a couple he knew when I said, "Roberta, you want another drink?" He turned his beautiful, soft eyes on me in a long stare and said, "Cool it."

I did cool it then, but not for long. He was sleepy in the club, since he had been working at the store all day, and at one point he slumped back in his chair and dozed. Anyone who noticed probably thought he was on drugs. I sang into his ear in a loud, breathy falsetto, "Wake up, Roberta."

The week after this, he refused to take me with him when he went out with his friends. He announced it at breakfast on Saturday. "You don't know respect," he said. "Stay home and study your manners."

He wouldn't say any more. He never got loudly upset as my wife had. I couldn't even get a good fight going.

"Go," I said. "Get away from me, then."

But that night, when the show let out, I took off my satin chaps and rubbed away the greasepaint, and I went walking up and down Bleecker Street, checking out all the clubs that Andre might be in. I just wanted him to be sweet to me again. I wanted to make up. I walked through dark, crowded cellars, peering at tables of strangers who were trying to listen to some moody trio. I must have looked like a stalking animal.

What if he never came back to me? He wasn't in four places I tried, and at the fifth, I sat at the bar and drank a Scotch, but I couldn't stay still. I walked all the way to the river, close to tears. I had never seen myself like this, wretched and pathetic. I could hardly breathe, from misery. I just wanted Andre to be sweet to me again. I couldn't stand it this way.

On the pier I picked up a guy, an acne-scarred blond in a baseball jacket. I didn't have to say more than hi, and I brought him home in a cab to my place in the West Forties. He was just a teenager—the luxury of a cab ride impressed him. I could see he was less excited when we got to my neighborhood with its hulking tenements. My block looked gloomy and unsafe, which it was.

And there on my stoop was Andre, waiting. I was still in the cab paying the driver when I saw him. The boy had already gotten out.

Andre's face was worn and tired—perhaps he had been sitting there a long time—and the sight of us seemed to make him wearier still. He sighed, and he shook his head. I put my arm around the boy, and I walked him past Andre to my front door, where I fished for my key without turning around.

I could hear Andre's footsteps as he walked away—east down the street, toward the subway. I did not turn my head at all. What control I had, all of a sudden. I who had been at the mercy of such desperate longing, such raging torment.

When I got the boy inside, I made him some pancakes—he looked hungry—and then we fooled around a little, but I wasn't good for much. He fell asleep, and I got him up at dawn and gave him some money. He didn't argue about the amount, and he understood that he had to leave.

And what did I do as soon as he was gone? I called Andre on the phone. How sleepy and startled his voice sounded. I loved his voice. When I said hello, he hung up.

And then I really was in hell, in the weeks after that. I woke up every morning freshly astonished that Andre was still gone and that my suffering was still there, the deadweight in my chest. When I phoned Andre again, I got him to talk, and he was rational enough, but he wasn't, he said, "very interested anymore." His language was tepid and somewhat formal. "Not about to embark on another disaster" was a phrase he used in a later conversation. That time I told him he sounded like a foreign exchange student.

So we stopped talking. Even I could see it was no use. But he was never out of my thoughts, he was always with me. I would be on the subway and realize I had shut my eyes in dreamy remembrance of a particular scene of us together, Andre on his knees to me in the shower. How languorous and smug my expression must have looked to riders on the A train. How disappointed I felt when I saw where I was.

I might have gone to find him at work, but I knew how he would be with me. If he was frosty over the phone, he would be a parody of polite disgust in the store, trying to flick me away with noble disdain. I hated the thought of actually seeing him like that, and I didn't want to hear what I might say back.

I didn't really have many friends to talk to. I was late getting to the show a few times, from not really caring and from sleeping too much, and I was fined and given a warning. I was very angry at Andre when this happened. He didn't care what he had done to me. I went down to City Hall, to the Buildings Department, and I looked up the deed to Andre's building to see who the owner was. I phoned the realty company to complain that someone was playing a trumpet very loudly at all hours of day and night. I phoned again and gave them another name, as a different angry neighbor. I phoned again.

On the last of these phone calls a secretary told me that the tenant had been advised he could remain in the apartment only if he ceased to be a noise nuisance, and he had chosen to leave, without paying his last month's rent. I was quite satisfied when I heard this—how often does anything we do in this life attain its goal? And then I remembered that I didn't know now where to find Andre. I didn't have his home phone number anymore.

I wanted to howl at the irony of this, like an anguished avenger in an opera. How had I not known better? Well, I hadn't. There was no new listing for him in any of the boroughs. And he was not at his job, either. Another salesman in the store thought maybe Andre had gone back to

Chicago, where his family was. I didn't see him anymore, not on the street, not in clubs, not in bars. Not then, not later. Perhaps he became famous under another name. Who knows how his playing got to sound? Not me.

All these years later, I don't know if he is still alive. A lot of people aren't, as it has happened. But it may well be that he settled down—he was like that—and a long and sedate monogamy would have kept him safe, if he found somebody early, and he probably did. I wasn't with any one person, after him. I didn't even look for such a thing. I went to bars and took home the occasional hot stranger, and I kept to myself a good part of the time.

For a decade or so I got work pretty steadily on Broadway. Those weren't bad years for musicals, although there was a lot of junk, too. I was hired to slink around as a thirties gangster, to be jaunty with a rake in my hand as a country yokel, and to do a leaping waltz as a Russian general, clicking the heels of my gleaming boots. Only a few male dancers got to be real stars, like Geoffrey Holder or Tommy Tune, and I suppose for a while I thought I could be one of them. I had a strong, clean style, and I was a great leaper. Nothing else anywhere did for me what that sensation of flying did. But my career never made its crucial turn, and then I got older than anyone wanted for the chorus line.

Which was not even that old. I was surrounded, however, by lithe and perfect young boys. Quite vapid, most of them, but decently trained. I was not even attracted to these children, as a rule. Probably I looked like some evil old elf to them, a skinny, brooding character with upswept eyebrows.

For a while I tried teaching in a dance studio, but I didn't get along with the director. She gave me the beginners' classes, and the students really didn't want any grounding in technique, they only wanted someone assuring them they could be professionals overnight. "Ladies," I would say to them, "get those glutes tucked in before you practice your autographs."

I didn't last that long at the school. In the end I gave up the whole idea of teaching, and I got a job in an agency booking dancers for clubs. Go-go girls, in spangled underwear and little white boots. I was the man the girls talked to after they read the classified and came into the office, nervous and flushed or tough and scowling. I sent them to clubs in the outer boroughs, airless caves in the Bronx with speakers blaring disco and red lights on the catwalk. My temper was so bad that people did what I told them, which was the agency's idea of sterling job performance. I was a snarling jerk in these years. Contempt filled my every cell; I was fat as a tick on contempt.

These were not good years, and my drinking got out of hand. One night in a bar, a man threw a chair at me and split open my head. When I missed two weeks' work, the agency hired someone else while I was gone, and there wasn't much I could do about it. It was not a clean or soft business. With my head still shaved and bandaged, I went back to the bar, itching for more trouble, but instead I ran into a dancer I used to know in my Broadway days. We were too old to want to pick each other up, but when I complained of being broke, he told me about a job at the union, answering phones and filing, if I didn't think that was beneath me.

I did, but I took the job, anyway. I used to say the work was bearable because of all those pert young boys who came into the building, but in fact I was in the back offices, hovering over ledgers and, in later years, facing a computer screen. It was a painless job, a reasonable thing to do until I found something else, and then it became what I did.

I didn't go to bars after a while. We knew at the union how many people were dying, even before the epidemic unfurled its worst. Cruising had not been full of glory for me, anyway, so I stayed home and counted myself one of the lucky ones. Staying home suited me. I read more books, and I had a few regular outings. I had brunch once a month with a few theater people I still knew. Through the union I got tickets to plays and sometimes operas. And I helped out backstage at some of the AIDS benefits we sponsored.

In the early years a lot of big names pitched in at these benefits, but later, too, there were people who were impressive in rehearsals. I stayed extra hours one night to listen to a tenor with a clear, mellow voice—he was singing a cycle of songs written by a composer who had just died of AIDS. The accompanist was an idiot, and they had to keep repeating the first song over and over. The singer was a puny, delicate boy, with pale eyebrows and colorless hair in a crewcut. He closed his eyes as he sang—not good form onstage, but affecting nonetheless.

During the break I told him to keep his eyes open, and he said, "Yes, yes. You're right."

"Your Italian sounds good, though," I said.

"I lived in Rome for a year," he said. "It was my idea for Jonathan to set these poems."

The composer had been his lover—I knew this, someone had told me—and the tenor sang with a mournful longing that was quite beautiful. *Amor m'ha fatto tal ch'io vivo in foco*, he sang. Love has made me live in ceaseless fire. I myself had Xeroxed the text for the programs.

His name was Carl, and he was young, still in his twenties. Recent grief had crumpled his face and left a faint look of outrage around his eyes. I began to bring him glasses of water during his break and to keep advising him. *Look at the audience. Watch your diction.* He was quite professional about the whole thing, and he only nodded, even when I praised him.

He let me take him out for a drink after the next rehearsal. We were in an overpriced bar in the theater district, full of tourists. He ordered a Campari and soda. "Isn't that a summer drink?" I said. It was the middle of February.

"It makes me happy to drink it," he said. "It makes me think of Italy."

As I might have guessed, he had gone there to study voice, and he had met his lover Jonathan there. "The light in Rome is quite amazing," he said. "Toasty and golden. Too bad it's so hard to describe light."

He was a boy romantic. Every day he and Jonathan had taken a walk through a park with a beautiful name, the Dora Pamphilj or the Villa Sciarra or the Borghese Gardens, and they had poked around in churches to gaze at Caravaggios or had sat eating gelato in front of some ravishing Bernini fountain. I knew only vaguely what all this was. He glistened and pulsed like a glowworm, remembering it. I did not think any place could be that perfect, and said so.

"It's not," Carl said. "It can be a nightmare city. Noisy, full of ridiculous rules and only one way of doing things, and those jolly natives can be quite heartless. But because Jonathan is dead, I get to keep it as my little paradise."

"*Il paradiso,*" I said, dumbly, in my opera Italian.

He asked me if I had ever toured when I was a dancer. "Only to Ohio and Kentucky," I said. "Nothing exotic. I just remember how tiring that road travel was."

"What keeps me going," he said, "is poetry. I make sure to have a book with me at all times."

I pictured him reading a beat-up paperback of Whitman while everyone else slept on the tour bus. But his favorite poet, he said, was Gaspara Stampa, the Italian whose sonnets I had heard him sing. "She's sort of a 1500s version of the blues," he said. "Love has done her wrong, but she's hanging in there. She thinks all women should envy her because she loves so hard."

I was an undereducated slob, compared to him, but one thing about being a dancer is you know how to pick things up. "I like that line you sing," I said, "about how I'll only grieve if I should lose the burdens that I bear."

"Yes," he said. "Exactly."

I went to more rehearsals. I didn't scold or correct, and I said *"Bravo"* or *"Stupendo"* when he was done. I patted him on the arm, and once I hugged him. We talked about Verdi, which I at least did not sound like a fool about, and about the history of New York office buildings, and about what he had to do to keep his voice in health. I did not ask, really, about his health.

"I am all fire, and you all ice," he sang. I told him they were torch songs. "Gender reversals of the traditional Petrarchan sonnet," Carl said. "A woman bragging about her unquenched longing. Very modern." What a swooner he was, how in love with pure feeling. And he was a huge hit at rehearsals. He had a theory about this, too. "No good words are said anymore," he said, "on behalf of torturing yourself for love. Everybody's told to *get over it*. But a little bleeding is good."

I had noticed that hopeless passion was still in high style in certain corners of the gay world, but I kept this observation to myself. "The pianist needs to practice," I said. "You know that, right?"

I wanted to cook for him, this flimsy little Carl, and I got him to come for dinner on a Sunday night. "Whoa," he said, when he saw my tenement apartment, which had been carved out of the wilderness almost thirty years before. "You've got everything packed in, like a ship." For supper I fed him beautiful food that was good for his vocal cords, no dairy or meat, only bright and cooling flavors. Blue Point oysters, cold sorrel soup, prawns with pea shoots and fresh ginger, purslane and mint salad. Everything vibrant and clarifying. Golden raspberries and bittersweet chocolate for dessert. I had knocked myself out, as he could not fail to notice.

The food made him happy. He said that when he first came to New York, he had been so poor he had eaten nothing but tofu and Minute Rice. Even now I had to show him how to eat a raw oyster. I felt like his uncle. That was not who I wanted to be.

"This is as good as food in Italy," he said. "In my Surviving Partners Group there's a guy who's a chef. I'm sure his food isn't better than this."

"Surely not," I said.

His Surviving Partners Group met every week. It was a great group, he said. But for him personally what was most helpful was meditation.

"Eating is good, too," I said.

"Yes," he said. "I forgot how good it was."

A beautiful suspense hovered around the table when he left for a minute to go off to the bathroom. When he came back into the room, I stood up, and I put my arms around him. He was so wispy and slight, much shorter than I was. He ducked his head, like someone sneaking under a gate, and he slipped right out of my arms.

He did not mean to mock me, he had only been embarrassed. Neither of us moved. I felt old. A vain old queen, a self-deluded old fruit.

I asked if he wanted coffee, and we sat down and drank it. He praised my espresso so lavishly that I couldn't tell if he only felt sorry for me or if he was trying to be friends nonetheless, if such a thing were possible with a grotesque old lech like myself.

At the next rehearsal Carl waved when he saw me. He came over and told me about how much better he sang ever since he'd eaten my dinner. "When I do my vocal exercises now," he said, "my voice is so good I move myself to tears." I thought he did like me. And perhaps I had not allowed him the time that someone like him needed. Perhaps the situation was not entirely hopeless.

When I went home after rehearsal, I lay in bed musing about what might happen between us after all. If I were patient. He had not been with anyone since his lover died, and I had not been with anyone in years. I had underestimated the depth of the enterprise, the large and moving drama involved. He would probably have to make the first move. He would surprise me, and we would laugh at my surprise.

In the middle of the night I got up and looked at the condoms in my night table drawer to see if the dates printed on the packets showed they were past safe use. I threw out the one that was expired. I sat on the edge of the bed in my underwear, hunched over, with my head buried in my hands. I had never asked Carl what his HIV status was. I was ready to go to bed with him without any protection at all, if that was what he wanted. All those years of being so careful I wouldn't risk going out of my own living room, and now I would have bargained away anything to have Carl. I was beyond all reason.

At work the next day the phone rang, and it was Carl inviting me over for brunch on Saturday. He was ashamed to cook for me, he said, but he could buy bagels as well as the next person.

He lived in a remote and dull section of Queens, on a street full of what had once been private houses. He had a nice little back apartment, with a view of the yard. "Welcome to my monkish cell," he said.

It was not cell-like—it was quite cozy and bright—but I was spooked by the shrines in it. On a small table, spread with a white linen cloth, was a collection of photos of his dead lover, who was a pleasant-looking young man, dark-haired and stocky. Jonathan waved from a deck chair on a beach, he stood in front of a Roman ruin and a bright blue sky, he laughed against Carl's shoulder at someone's birthday party. In another corner was an altar to the Buddha, with a stone statue of a thin, pigeon-chested Buddha facing into the room, and a fatter, calmer Buddha embroidered into a square of fringed brocade hanging on the wall. A single deep-blue iris, pure and wilting, stood in a vase. I did not like any of it.

But Carl had clearly wanted me to see it. He gave me a tour of all the photos, naming every guest at the birthday party. He gestured to the Buddhas and said, "Those are my buddies there." He told me that he did Vipassana meditation, adapted from what they did in Burma and Thailand, but that was a Tibetan *tangka* on the wall. "Very nice," I said. "It's the medicine Buddha," he said. "That's his healing unguent in the bowl in his hand." I chewed my bagel and nodded.

I gossiped about the rehearsals, just to get us somewhere else. "Did you see," I said, "how Brice is ogling that first violinist in the quartet? I expect him to drool all over the man's bow any minute. It's not subtle." Brice was the show's organizer.

"I missed it," he said. "I'm bad at noticing who's after who."

"Brice is so obvious."

"What can I tell you?" he said. "I'm away from all that. It's not in my world."

What world was he in?

"People don't think enough about celibacy," he said. "It hasn't been thought about very well in our era. It has a long history as a respected behavior. It has its beauty."

I knew then that he'd brought me here to say this, with the fittings of his cell as backdrop. "The Buddha never had sex?" I said. "I thought he had a family."

"That was before he was the Buddha."

"Don't get too carried away. You know you'll want someone sometime."

"I don't think so."

"It's *unnatural* at your age."

"I'm not unhappy."

Oh, honey, I thought, I didn't tempt you for a second, did I?

"A sexless life will ruin your voice," I said. "I'm not kidding. You'll sound like some wan little old lady. You already have to worry about that."

"Oh," he said. "We'll see."

"You already have some problems in the lower register."

"Oh," he said.

"You'll sound like a squawking hen in a few years."

"No more," he said. "That's enough."

I was depressed after this visit, but lack of hope didn't cure me, either. I didn't stop wanting Carl, and what I wanted kept playing itself out in my mind over and over. At home I would sometimes be slumped in an armchair, reading a book or watching TV, and not even know that I was lost in reverie, until I heard myself say out loud, "Oh, honey." It was terrible to hear my own voice like that, whimpering with phantom love. I was afraid I was going to cry out like this at my desk at work, with other people in earshot, but I never did.

We were civil with each other at the last rehearsal. Actually, Carl was more than civil. He made a decent effort to converse, while the string quartet was busy going through its number. "I read," he said to me, "that Rome is all different now because they've banned cars from parts of it."

"You know what I read?" I said. "I read that there was a man who was very high up in a Buddhist organization who went around sleeping with people and giving them AIDS. Lots of young men. He knew he had it, and he didn't tell anyone he slept with. He thought he could control his karma."

"Oh," Carl said. "That happened years ago. When did you read it?"

"A while ago."

"Why are you telling me now?"

"Those are the guys you want to emulate," I said. "Those are your shining models."

"No," he said. "That was one guy."

"Lust crops up," I said. "Can't keep it down."

"That's not what that story means," he said. "It's about arrogance and delusion, not lust. He could have used condoms."

"Right," I said. "Sure. You'll be like him. You'll see."

He reddened then. I'd forgotten that his HIV status might be positive, for all I knew, which did deepen the insult. He shook his head at me. "Oh, Duncan," he said, sourly.

On the night of the concert, I dressed very nicely. I wore a slate-blue shirt, a beautiful celadon tie that Andre had once given me, a stone-gray sports jacket. I hadn't looked that good in years. I sat with some other people from work in a chilly section of the orchestra seats. The string quartet was first, playing a stodgy piece badly. I really did not hear anything until Carl walked onstage to sing Jonathan's songs. He looked pale as marble, an angel with a shimmering crewcut.

He had a few intonation problems at first but sounded lovely and sure once he got going. Jonathan had written him easy music, except for a few jagged rhythm changes. *"Viver ardendo e non sentire il male,"* he sang. "To live burning and not to feel the pain." Wasn't it enough that I suffered at home? Did I have to come here and hear my beloved wail about the trials of the rejected? I wanted to shout in protest. I should not have come, I saw. Who would have cared if I hadn't come?

Then my protest and exasperation fused with the plaint of the songs, with their familiar trouble, and I had a bluesy ache in my chest that was oddly close to solace. I felt the honor of my longing. This idea did quite a lot for me. My situation, ludicrous as it was, at least lost the taint of humiliation.

When the songs were over, I was surprised when the applause did not go on for hours, although people seemed to have liked the pieces well enough. I was still in a faint trance when the concert broke for intermission. I stayed alone in my seat while the others milled around. The second half was a woodwind quartet I had never liked, and they did three numbers. When they were finally done, I moved through the crowd and found Carl in the lobby, surrounded by people clasping him in congratulation. *"Bravissimo,"* I said to him. "Really." He gave me a sudden, broad smile—praise from me probably did mean something to him—but he was busy thanking people.

I stayed around long enough to get pulled along with a group that went out for drinks afterward. I did not ask if I could come, and perhaps I wasn't welcome, but no one said so. We sat at a big round table in a bar with peach-tinted walls. The accompanist, whose playing hadn't been as bad as I'd feared, kept leaning toward Carl with an excited attention that looked like a crush to me.

Carl himself was busy introducing everyone to a slick young giant of a man who turned out to be the chef from his Surviving Partners Group. "My very good friend," Carl called him. "Duncan, you should talk to Larry about his food. You're the one who'll really appreciate what he does."

"Oh, I will?" I said.

"*I* like food," someone else at the table said. "I like it all the time."

I was about to say, "Cooks who are fans of themselves tend to show it," but then I didn't. I decided to shut up, for a change. There was no point to my baiting anyone at the table just for fun, in front of Carl. No point at all now.

But it was hard for me. I stayed sullenly quiet for a while, sulking and leaning back in my chair. When Chef Larry told a funny story about his poultry supplier, I didn't laugh. When Carl talked about a production of *Wozzeck* that he was about to go on tour with, all through Canada, from Quebec to Vancouver, I didn't ask when he was leaving or when he was coming back. I didn't say a word. But then when the pianist said he had been practicing too much in a cold room, and he complained of stiffness in his elbow, I gave him a very good exercise he could do at home. I explained it without sarcasm or snottiness or condescension. I was at my all-time nicest, for Carl's sake, for Carl's benefit. I don't know that he, or anyone, noticed.

. . .

Carl went on tour for six months, as I discovered from his phone machine when I called him later. It didn't surprise me that he hadn't said good-bye—I was probably someone that he wanted out of his life. Still, I dreamed of his return. How could I not? When he came back, I would tell him how I had begun to think of myself as a celibate, too, that I had moved toward a different respect for that as a way to be, and perhaps we could be friends now on a new basis. It made me happy to think of our new comradeship, his easy and constant company, his profile next to me at operas and plays. But I knew, even as I imagined our lively and natural conversations on topics of real interest to both of us, that my reasoning was insincere, only a ruse to win Carl to me in whatever way I could.

But since I could not talk to Carl, who was off singing to the Canadians, I was left with my own recitation of why I treasured austerity running in a loop through my mind. I was the captive audience for what was meant to disarm Carl. This was not the worst speech to be trapped with. It made the tasks I did in solitude—my exercises, my errands—seem finer.

The exercises were a particular annoyance to me. I had done exercises all my life (except for some goofing off during the booking-agency years), but now I had arthritis, plague of old athletes and dancers, in my knees and just starting in my hips. All that hopping and turning and high-kicking had been hard on the cartilage. I had to go through a full range of motion every day to keep the joints flexible, which they did not want to be any-more. Some of this hurt, and I hated being a sloppy mover. But now, swinging my leg to the side, I felt less disgraced by it. My routine, per-formed alone in my bare bedroom, had its merit and order. An hour in the morning and stretches at night. I had my privacy and my discipline.

Every Tuesday evening I went to a guy named Fernando for bodywork. I lay on my stomach while he bent my knees and hooked his thumbs into my muscles. The word "ouch" did not impress him. He had been a dancer once, too. "Stay skinny, that's important," he said. "Good for arthritis, good for your sex life."

"Good for what? I can't remember what that is."

"You can remember, Dunc. You're not that old." Free flirting came with his massages.

"I don't know," I said. "I like my quiet. A life of abstaining isn't as bad as people think."

"So they tell me," Fernando said. "I do hear that."

"See?" I said. "There's a lot of it going around. It's an idea whose time has come."

"For some. Maybe."

"I think I'm happier. Do you believe that?"

"Yes," he said. "That I believe."

I had never been able to throw away the program from Carl's concert, and it lay on a small table near the door, where I saw it whenever I came in or went out. I would read over his name with a ripple of intimate recognition. A ripple or a pang, depending on my mood. The very casualness of its placement on the table pleased me.

I knew from the message on Carl's phone machine that he was returning from Canada at the end of September. Once he was home, I would call him, and at the very least there would be friendliness between us. The wait seemed very long. Thirty days hath September, and in the last week I went to movies every night to keep busy. I saw too many bad, raucous comedies and bloody cop movies. The only thing I liked was a biopic about neurotic artists in the twenties.

When I came out of it into the lobby, there was a crush getting to the doors, and a man in front of me said, "No one pushes like this in Toronto." I took it as a good omen to hear some word in the air about Canada. The man who spoke was not bad-looking, either, nicely muscled in his T-shirt, and he held another man by the elbow to keep from getting dragged away by the crowd. It took me a second before I saw that the other man was Carl. His neck was sunburned, and he had let his hair grow longer.

And Carl saw me. "Hey! Hello!" he said.

He acted perfectly happy to see me. Once we were all out on the street, he introduced me to his companion. Josh, the man's name was, and they had met backstage in Windsor, Ontario.

"And then what could I do? I just packed up and went with him on the rest of the tour," Josh said. "I have heard *Wozzeck* performed more times than any other human being on the planet. Berg is not that easy on the ears, either."

"I like him," I said.

"It was great to have company on the road," Carl said. "You know how the road gets. You and I talked about that."

"Yes," I said.

"I had fun hanging out with the tour," Josh said.

"Are you back here for good?" I said.

"We're looking for a bigger apartment," Josh said. "I like Queens, though. It's not how I thought it would be."

"Some people like Queens," I said. "Certain timid types like Queens."

"Don't mind Duncan," Carl said.

"We'll invite you over when we get settled in," Josh said.

"Whenever that is," I said.

On the subway ride home I was too angry to sit still. All those sweet-faced declarations, and look how long Carl had lasted as a holy soldier of celibacy. I felt that he had tricked me and that he'd had the last laugh in a way that made me writhe. *A respected behavior,* my foot. And I had been ready to tread the same path. I who had never taken the high road in my life.

When I got back to my apartment, I went to the phone and dialed his number. I wanted to ask him: Don't you feel like a fucking hypocrite? Do you know what a pretentious little jerk you are? The two of them weren't back yet, of course. They were probably at the subway station still waiting for the N train to Queens. The phone machine said: Carl and Josh aren't home right now.

I breathed heavily on the message tape for a minute, just to leave something spooky for them to listen to. And what would Carl have said to me, anyway, if I had been able to hammer away at him with hostile questions? *I took my chance when it was offered. Anyone would do the same.* There was nothing else to say.

I had a shot of bourbon, which did not calm me down. It made me want to kick something, but I wasn't ready to throw out my knee from an action that stupid. I had more bourbon, but I might as well have been drinking water. I sat there with my hand pressed against my chest, the way a dog paws its snout if it has a toothache.

I understood, after a while, that there was nothing to do but go to bed. I got out of my clothes, and I went through the set of stretches I always did before sleeping. I felt confused, because for so many months these had been like a secret proof that I was worthy of Carl. I had been consoled and uplifted by the flavor of his ideas mixed in with them.

. . .

Stress was bad for my bones, and I woke up very stiff. My knee locked when I tried to get out of bed. *Look what love has done to me.* I felt like a ham actor playing an old man. I had a hangover, too, and it was still very early in the morning. I wanted to phone Carl, but in disguise as something menacing, a growling wolf or a hissing reptile. I was good at making different sounds. Let him be terrified, just for a second. But then he would know who it was. He would say my name, and I would keep growling or hissing. Duncan, he would say, is that you? Stop, please. Ssssss, I would say. Ssssss.

I was too old to do that, too old for that shit. Instead I ate my simple breakfast and had my simple bath and went out to do my simple errands. A plain and forthright man. I was so calm at the supermarket (who ever heard of someone with a hangover being calm while waiting in line?) that I wondered if the attitude I had developed in Carl's absence was now going to stay with me and be my support.

Perhaps I was going to beat him at his own game (or what had been his game) and become so self-contained that I never spoke to anyone. I could work at my job without much more than nods and signals. I could move through the streets and be perfectly silent, quiet as any monk with a vow. Then Carl would know just who understood the beauty of a principled life.

Oh, in the Middle Ages someone like me might have been a monk, one of the harsh and wily ones, but dutiful. I could be a monk now, old as I was. (I had been raised a Catholic, although not raised well.) I could take orders the way forsaken young women used to, when they were jilted by lying men and wanted only to take themselves out of the world.

I don't know why these thoughts were such a great comfort to me while I waited at the supermarket with my cart of bachelor supplies. But I got through the day, and the rest of the weekend, without doing anything rash. At work on Monday I went about my business in my usual curmudgeonly way. I was in pain, but I wasn't a roiling cauldron. I thought that once the worst of getting over Carl was done, his influence would linger in this elevated feeling about aloneness, just as Andre had left me with a taste for certain music, for Bill Evans and early Coltrane. I was doing well at the moment, better than I would have thought.

.   .   .

A month later I knew differently. I was tormented by longings for Carl night and day. I hardly saw anything around me—sunlight hitting the windows of a building, a man sitting on a park bench, a kid walking in time to his boom box—without superimposing on it the remembrance of Carl and things he had said to me, the most ordinary things. In Sunday school when I was a boy, one of the sisters had told us that the Benedictine rule said to "pray always." I had a good understanding now of how such a thing was possible.

This can't go on, I would say to myself (how many billions of people have said that?), but it went on for a long time, for months and months. Sometimes I called Carl's apartment, to see if the machine still announced he was living with that twinkie from Canada, but it always did. Fernando the masseur told me that the only way to get over him was to find someone new. I picked up a man in a bar who wanted money to be with me, and that made me feel much worse.

Since I had not really known Carl that well, after a year his face did begin to lose its vividness in my mind—I had only a few shreds of encounters to hold on to. But it would not be true to say I forgot him. He was like a hum that was always in my ears. He was something that was not going to go away.

I never thought I would end up the sort of person who hoarded some cruddy Xeroxed program as if it were an artifact from Tut's tomb. As if it were my job to keep the faith. I had become a fool for love, after all. You could say this served me right, but it wasn't the worst thing that might have happened to me. Not by a long shot. No, I was better for it. I understood a number of things I hadn't had a clue about before. Why Madame Butterfly believed Pinkerton was coming back. Why Catherine's grave was dug up by Heathcliff. The devotion of these years improved me, and it burnt off some of the dross. I was less quarrelsome with other people and clearer with myself. My longing stayed with me, no matter what. Who could have known I was going to be so constant? It wasn't at all what I expected, and I had some work getting used to it.

Evan S. Connell

Election Eve

from *The Threepenny Review*

Proctor Cyril Bemis, emeritus C.E.O. of the securities firm that
bore his name—Proctor Bemis, grossly fat, not yet altogether bald,
cheerful when undisturbed by gout, sat beside the fire as a fat man likes to
sit with fingers laced across his belly, jowls at rest, and thought about
Costa Rica while his wife sorted the mail. He thought he would enjoy a
visit to Costa Rica. Sunshine, gentle waves lapping sugar-white beaches,
palm fronds dipping in the breeze, carioca music or whatever it was, pretty
girls smearing oil on their legs, deep-sea fishing, rum, ocean-fresh lob-
ster—oh yes, Mr. Bemis thought, twirling his thumbs on his belly. No
drizzly, threatening overcast. No winter storm watch. No schoolboys in
black trenchcoats gunning down classmates. No lunatics blowing up fed-
eral buildings. No hillbilly militia. No politicians braying platitudes.
Costa Rica ought to be just fine, yes indeed. He dropped one hand into
the silver bowl of cashews, scooped up a handful, and tossed them into his
mouth.

How many people want money? he asked.

His wife looked at him over the top of her spectacles and he thought
she was going to say something about the cashews. Then she turned
through the envelopes.

Democratic National Committee, addressed to you. HOPE. CARE.
Bread for the World. Alligator Refuge. I think that's all, except bills.

How many bills?

One, two, three, she said. Three. No, here's another.

My God, said Mr. Bemis.

Here's a note from Robin. I do hope they're enjoying the trip. Let's see, what else? This looks like an invitation from the Wibbles.

He watched her open the envelope. I don't want to go, he said.

Now isn't this tricky! A masquerade party the night before election. They'll have presidential masks. George Washington. Lincoln. Eisenhower. Nixon. Jimmy Carter, who wasn't one of my favorites. Harry Truman. Gerald Ford. You can take your choice.

No, Mr. Bemis said. No.

You could be Grover Cleveland. He weighed three hundred pounds.

I don't weigh three hundred, Mr. Bemis said. I won't go. Absolutely not.

She opened the envelope from their daughter. Well, my goodness! Mark won a prize at a carnival.

What did he win?

A statue of Donald Duck. He loves it. Melanie skinned her elbow. Ed has a touch of flu. Oh, my word! Somebody broke into their car and stole the radio. They'll need to see the insurance company. Otherwise, everything's fine.

I'm glad they're having a good time, Mr. Bemis said. Now listen, Marguerite. I am seventy-three years old. My knees hurt. My back hurts. I don't want to stand around listening to Thornton and Stu and Betsy and Cliff and all the rest. I know their opinions on everything from school vouchers to nuclear bombs. Let's go to Costa Rica.

You were seventy-five last March. I'm going to phone Renée and tell her we'll be delighted.

I will throw up, Mr. Bemis said. I will kick their damn Siamese cat.

Ooma isn't Siamese. She's Persian. She's just adorable. And you needn't have a fit. The party isn't for another month, three weeks from Monday.

Monday? Mr. Bemis asked with dismay. That's football night. I think the Chiefs and Broncos are playing.

I'll be right back, she said.

Mr. Bemis threw a cashew into the fireplace and wondered how he might talk her out of it. He remembered going to costume parties when he was a child. He had worn a red devil mask and remembered looking through the eye holes. Witches, goblins, clowns, all sorts of games—pin-the-tail-on-the-donkey, blindman's-buff, spin-the-bottle—little girls shriek-ing, balloons popping, parents watching, candied apples, licorice whips, paper hats, ice cream. It had been fun. However, those days were gone. I don't want to bump into Charlie Hochstadt wearing a Reagan mask, he thought. Lord, what have I done to deserve this?

Reagan. Mr. Bemis threw another cashew at the fire. Why hadn't the man been dragged out of office by the heels? Ollie North funneling weapons to the Contras from the White House basement but El Presi-dente knew nothing about it. Smacking his lips when he was questioned, pretending to think. Let me see, now, that must have been some time back, some time ago. Smack. Yes, sir, a while ago. Smack. Well, now, I'm afraid I don't quite recall.

Mr. Bemis grunted and opened the newspaper. Oil prices rising. Elec-tricians vote to strike. Light planes collide. Drought in Oklahoma. Post office worker shot dead. Charlton Heston looking less and less like Moses, more like Madame Tussaud's lover. Another religious cult swallows poi-son. Mutual funds merge.

He glanced up when his wife returned from the telephone.

Renée and I had the most delightful chat. Everyone is excited. It's going to be gobs of fun.

Somebody will put on a Truman mask and play the piano, Mr. Bemis said. Somebody will be FDR and wave a cigarette holder. Some jackass will do Nixon, hunch the shoulders and give us that V sign. Let's go to Costa Rica. Call that nice young woman at the travel agency and book us a flight.

I cannot bear it when you behave like this, she said. Will you please stop whining.

I only whine if there's a reason, Mr. Bemis said. I'm not as fat as Grover Cleveland.

Stop eating those cashews. All you get from now on is grapefruit juice.

Mr. Bemis glared at his left foot, which had begun to ache. He thought about the palm trees and sandy beaches and pretty girls in bathing suits. He looked out the window. It was raining, almost snowing.

As they were being chauffeured to the party on election eve he remem-bered how much he despised Reagan. The man had spent the war in Hol-lywood and never heard a live bullet but he could not stop saluting. He saluted and saluted and saluted. He would snap off that Hollywood salute to a flagpole or a fireplug. He would salute a dachshund if there was a photographer nearby.

Proctor, stop that, his wife said.

Stop what? he asked.

You're grumbling.

I'll keep it to myself, he said.

How long have we been married?

Mr. Bemis thought about this. Why do you want to know?

I know perfectly well. But even now, after so many years, I cannot for the life of me understand you. At times you might as well be a complete stranger. She leaned forward. Phillips, do you have trouble seeing the road?

Phillips answered in his pleasantly neutral voice. No, Madam.

You will be careful, won't you?

Phillips replied that he would be careful.

Mr. Bemis watched snowflakes dissolve on the window and thought about trying to explain, but it would be difficult. She had voted for Reagan. She voted for Bush and Dole and Nixon. If she had been old enough she would have voted for Landon and Hoover and the Whigs. She hated Kennedys, all Kennedys, including wives and fifth cousins, and thought they contaminated whatever they touched. She disapproved of modern art and welfare and foreign aid. She did not like immigrants. She subscribed to newsletters warning that liberals had weakened the armed forces. The United States could be destroyed at any moment. Crazed, malignant letters oozing poison. Absurd theories. Libelous charges. Implausible conspiracies. Rhetorical questions. Secret societies. Jewish bankers. Communist armies in Montana. Letters concocted of hate and fear. Doomsday letters. Nourishment for the paranoid.

We'll have oodles of fun, she said, patting him on the knee. Just you wait.

I do not intend to wear a mask, he said. I like who I am.

Renée told me that several husbands objected. You can be yourself. I wouldn't expect anything else.

What about food?

There'll be a nice buffet.

Itty-bitty pinkie sandwiches and cheese dip, Mr. Bemis said. I wish we were going to Costa Rica.

However, the Wibble buffet was sumptuous, imperial, a whopping tribute to an exemplary bourgeois life. Mr. Bemis gazed with satisfaction at the roast beef, sliced breasts of duck, venison, platoons of shrimp, a giant salmon, lamb chops sprinkled with herbs, prosciutto, crisp little sausages, and more. Rosy red tomatoes stuffed with something creamy. Butterfly pasta. Mushrooms. Mr. Bemis gazed at the beautiful mushrooms. Asparagus points, juicy pickles, gargantuan black olives. Nor was that all, oh no. Desserts. An absolute regiment of alluring desserts. Lemon tart. Mince pie topped with hard sauce. Blue and white cheeses. Chocolate mousse. Peaches. Pears. Melons. Petits fours. Nuts. Strawberries. A silver compote of mints. Fancy bonbons individually wrapped in gold foil. Nor was that all. Mr. Bemis clasped his hands.

Good to see you! boomed a familiar voice. Mighty good! I am counting on your vote, sir!

There stood Quint Huckleby disguised as Abe Lincoln.

Hello, Quint, said Mr. Bemis.

Lincoln is the name, sir. Abraham Lincoln. May I take this opportunity to remind you that our great nation stands at a crossroads. Tomorrow we decide. Shall we permit ourselves to be hornswoggled? Or do we fulfill our grand and glorious destiny with the Grand Old Party? Should I be fortunate enough to earn the confidence of the American public I shall propose to Congress that we chase those Democrat scalawags out of town. Tar and feathers, sir! That's the ticket!

Huckleby shuffled into the crowd, bowing to ladies, clapping men on the shoulder.

Mr. Bemis looked around and saw Marguerite chatting with the Vandenhaags. He looked again at the buffet. An olive, perhaps? One or two little sausages? What harm would there be in a slice of duck?

He noticed Speed Voelker loading a plate. Voelker never seemed to change. Year after year a bulky, menacing presence in a tailored pin-striped suit. Broken nose. Massive, sloping shoulders. Neck like a tree stump. Diamond ring. Hair slicked back like a hoodlum in some gangster film. Big as a water buffalo.

I hear you and Dodie went to Europe, Mr. Bemis said.

Voelker nodded. The whole shebang. Tower of London. Norway. Copenhagen. Swiss Alps. Berlin. Venetian gondolas. You name it. Europe costs like the elephant these days.

Uncle Sam gave me a tour, Mr. Bemis said. Didn't cost a cent. France, Belgium, Rhineland. Mostly on foot.

Voelker grinned. I was a lieutenant in Patton's outfit. Like to froze my nuts off. Mud, rain, C rations, bugs. I saw that old fart once, close enough to touch.

I saw Ike, Mr. Bemis said. He drove by in a Jeep.

McCarthy deserved a medal. Ike didn't do squat about those Commies at State.

Yankee Doodle and all, Mr. Bemis thought.

Voelker pointed his fork at the dessert table. Eisenhower was reaching for a chocolate mousse.

He ought to be here. Straighten out the lefties.

They watched Eisenhower pick up a handful of bonbons.

Tomorrow we kick butt. Dump the goddam liberals. They ought to move to Russia if they don't like the U.S.A.

Enemy headquarters, Mr. Bemis thought. He watched Voelker stab a slice of beef and tried to remember how long they had been acquainted. Norman Voelker. Star athlete. Captain of the high school football team. Honor roll. Class president. Speed to his friends. And what was I? Corridor guide. Nothing else after my name in the yearbook. I didn't know how to catch a football and if I tried to jump a hurdle I'd have broken my neck. He never spoke to me. Not once. Not once in four years did he say hello. Now here we are, high-priced attorney and ex-stockbroker, members of the same country club, almost equal. Almost. Not quite.

Jerry, Voelker said.

And there he stood, jaw protruding, vacuous, amiable, shaking hands with Lucy Waldrop.

He played at Michigan. Pretty good lineman.

Mr. Bemis munched a spear of asparagus and thought about Ford pardoning Nixon. Twenty-five flunkies went to jail, maybe twenty-six, but not Tricky Dick. Everybody thought the republic would collapse if Richard Milhous wore prison stripes. In fact, the republic would be better off if Nixon had spent a couple of decades mumbling and raving in the jug. No man is above the law, we told ourselves. What a lie. The time has come to put this matter behind us, declared his faithful subordinate who by the grace of God and a terrified Congress inherited the office.

Those eighteen minutes of tape. What skulduggery did they preserve? Jimmy Hoffa. Mr. Nixon, high priest of law and order, scourge of corrupt unions, pardoned Jimmy Hoffa, who strolled out of prison and dropped from sight as if he had walked the plank. Was he squashed inside an old Chevrolet? Why did Mr. Nixon intervene? Rosemary Woods deserved a medal for loyalty, if nothing else, trying to demonstrate how she accidentally erased those eighteen minutes, almost twisted her back out of joint. Meanwhile the world's greatest investigative body, the FBI, couldn't figure out what happened.

Mr. Bemis grunted, heard himself make some disrespectful remark and observed Voelker light up with rage.

Norman! Marguerite exclaimed. What a pleasure! It's been ages! You look marvelous! Ida Mae tells me that you and Dodie treated yourselves to the grand tour. That must have been a thrill. Did you see the fountains of Rome? Proctor and I are so jealous.

She went on talking while Mr. Bemis considered the situation. People were gathering around Voelker. They wanted to be seen chatting with him. That being so, why not slip away to the buffet? Nobody would notice. Why not two or three of those tasty little shrimp? Prosciutto? Of course. Mushrooms? Yes, indeed. Another pickle? Maybe a soupçon of pasta?

He found himself at the table. He spoke cheerfully to the Armacosts, recommended the mushrooms. He said hello to Woody Schenk, discussed the Wyandotte Hills Country Club renovation. He nodded to Virginia Tyler, whom he did not like very much, spread anchovy paste on five crackers, reached for some olives, and moved along. He walked around the table for another slice of duck. Then he paused.

Missouri Waltz, he said.

Sure enough, Harry was thumping the piano. Beside him stood Jimmy Carter theatrically beating time.

He thought about Jimmy's struggle with the rabbit. Nobody except Bosch or maybe Lewis Carroll could have dreamed it up—March hare bent upon murder swimming crazily toward the President, planning to bite his ankle. Jimmy in that canoe flailing away with a paddle. The rabbit finished him. Inflation got out of control, which was serious. And that hostage fiasco, American helicopters on a cloak-and-dagger rescue mission lurching around the desert like injured bats, that was humiliating. But the rabbit did him in. The President fighting a loony rabbit, that was too much.

Nancy Reagan should have been there, he thought as he slipped a cracker into his mouth. The newspapers said she carried a pistol, itty-bitty derringer or some such. Whap! No more bunny. Mr. Bemis stopped chewing. Why did she carry a pistol? He tried to remember if she had been in any of Reagan's films, maybe the dance hall girl in some Wild West horse opera. What could happen in the White House? He imagined her leading a gaggle of tourists. They pause to admire a portrait of John Adams when out pops the masked intruder from behind a marble bust of Spiro Agnew. Stick 'em up! Your purse or your life! But the First Lady is prepared. Not so fast, young fellow! Just you wait till I find my derringer. Let's see. Kleenex, aspirin, nail file, sunglasses, eye shadow, lipstick, mascara, brush, comb, tweezers, cold cream, lotion, scissors, hair spray, compact—I know it's here someplace.

He thought about Charlton Heston brandishing an eighteenth-century musket for the benefit of photographers and gung-ho patriots. Moses defending life, liberty, and his Beverly Hills mansion from the redcoats. Why not an assault rifle? Why not wave a Saturday Night Special?

I do believe, murmured a voice from the past, I know this handsome dog.

Mr. Bemis turned around and there beneath a ragged brown toupee resembling a smashed bird nest, decades older than when last seen, was Howie—the same Howie Price-Dodge who got so drunk he tried to climb the Spanish-American War memorial and served heroically in the OSS and married a Chicago stripper and demolished the family fortune.

Get yourself a plate and let's talk, Mr. Bemis said. In fact, I'll join you.

Howie explained that during the Vietnam War he went back into service. He had been a liaison officer stationed at the Pentagon. He knew McNamara. He attended high-level briefings. He shuttled between Washington and Saigon and learned quite a bit. He knew Westmoreland. He had ridden in helicopters while enemy soldiers were interrogated and saw them pushed out.

This world is no place for idealists, he said.

On the contrary, said Mr. Bemis.

Howie squinted, adjusted his toupee, and went on talking while Mr. Bemis thought about the days when they agreed upon almost everything from politics to women to beer. It was strange that so much time had gone by. He looked around the room at familiar faces and it occurred to him that this was where he belonged. Yes, he thought, I'm one of these people. I've lived a solid Republican life. I earned money the good old-fashioned way selling stocks and bonds, lots of money. I joined the best country club. Marguerite and I have a couple of fancy cars and a very expensive home. I drove myself to the office for at least a hundred years while Marguerite took care of everything else. We've done our work, toted that bale. We deserve what we have. Yes, I belong here. The trouble is, I feel like an Eskimo.

Howie was explaining that America could have won the war if it hadn't been for draft dodgers and the liberal media. And while Mr. Bemis listened to Howie justify Vietnam he remembered the ugliness. Even now, after all this time, it festered like the Nixon pardon, provoking arguments, refusing to heal. The flesh of the nation was raw. The photograph of that naked child seared by napalm running toward the camera screaming in agony, that image would not fade. And he reflected that he had frequently touted E. I. Du Pont, which manufactured napalm. Du Pont, as everyone knew, was a substantial corporation with good earnings, a secure dividend, and offered the likelihood of capital appreciation. A dollar invested with Du Pont was a dollar prudently invested.

Mr. Bemis examined his plate. Celery. Two olives. One radish. Not much. Howie was interpreting the disaster, explaining why the security of the United States depended upon Southeast Asia. Mr. Bemis munched an olive and looked around. Next to a flattering oil portrait of Cope Wibble in a huge gold frame stood Emmajane Kathren, Democrat, chatting with the Altschulers while holding a shrimp impaled on a toothpick. Beneath the glowing chandelier stood Monte and Lorraine Fordyce, Democrats both, listening to Joslyn Upshaw. We're not many, he thought. Oh, not many. What's to become of us? Half a century from now will we be extinct? And as he considered this it did not seem implausible.

Is that Speed? Howie asked.

Mr. Bemis nodded. Voelker was holding DeWitt Simms firmly by one elbow while talking to his wife.

Lord God, Howie said, I'll never forget the way he flattened that Rockhurst defensive back. Everybody in the bleachers whooping, then you could hear a pin drop. What was that kid's name?

It happened sixty years ago, Mr. Bemis said. McNabb, McNee, McGee, one of those names.

Paralyzed, Howie said. Just a kid. Hell of a note. I still see that ambulance on the field.

They watched Simms try to pull away. Voelker ignored him.

Built like a piano. Give him the ball and Katie bar the door.

Harry Truman was plunking out "Swanee River." A woman laughed insanely. Voelker—arrogant as a Babylonian king—held Simms captive, demeaning the man in front of his wife. A Texas voice boasted about upholding law and order with a noose. Two masks collided and all at once it seemed to Mr. Bemis that he had entered a madhouse where the inmates were performing a macabre dance.

Voelker approached casually but rapidly, sapphire-blue eyes fixed on Howie. Almost at once they were discussing Vietnam, why it was necessary, how the war could have been won.

Voelker gripped Mr. Bemis by the elbow. What about you, sport? Tell us what you think. Did you support our troops?

I mistrusted the government, Mr. Bemis said.

Tell us about it, soldier. We want to know what you think.

You want to know what I think? I remember how Ike tiptoed into that swamp and Kennedy followed. The best and brightest had no more sense than Hogan's goat. And I remember LBJ plunging ahead like a goddamn rhinoceros. I remember Nixon after everybody got sick of the war telling us he had a secret plan for ending it. He told us delicate negotiations were under way. My grandfather's banana. Nixon kept it going past election day because he wanted another term in office. You want my opinion, Lieutenant? I didn't salute.

Mr. Bemis jerked his arm away from Voelker.

He had addressed the office staff on various occasions, but this was different. It occurred to him that he should have chosen public life. He saw himself on the floor of the Senate addressing misguided colleagues, instructing, ridiculing, exhorting, convincing. Persuasive arguments came to mind, burning rhetoric, soaring imagery.

No doubt you gentlemen recall the domino theory. No doubt you recall the days when half the citizens of this country thought we should turn Hanoi into a parking lot because if we didn't stop the Communists over there we'd have to stop them on the beaches of Hawaii. Do you remember when schoolchildren were taught to crouch underneath their desks? Keep away from windows. Pull down the shades. Do you recall the backyard bomb shelter? Of course you do. We were advised to dig holes in the ground. Furnish the hole with toilet paper, matches, bottled water, spinach, dehydrated beef, Graham crackers. Newspaper delivery may be suspended. Magazines and phonograph records may help to pass the time. Moonstruck madness, gentlemen, if I might borrow a phrase from the great John Milton.

Mr. Bemis discovered that he had an audience. People were staring. Obviously they wished to know more.

Ladies and gentlemen, while destitute citizens rummage through garbage cans and prowl the streets, what does the government do? It sheathes the Pentagon in gold. I submit to you that we could at this moment vaporize whatever creeps, crawls, flies, walks, hops, slithers, or jumps. I submit to you that we could do this thirty times over. Meanwhile, Republicans wring their hands, claiming we are defenseless, ill prepared, at the mercy of two-bit tyrants. In fact, no eight countries on earth allocate as much to the splendid science of war as we do, yet conservatives argue that we need a Maginot Line in the sky. As Mr. Reagan explained it, a missile shield will protect us from nuclear attack just as a roof protects a house from rain. The simplicity of such logic astounds us, but let it pass. Will a magic roof suffice? Of course not. We are surrounded by godless enemies from Zamboanga to Uttar Pradesh.

Mr. Bemis realized that his voice had risen. He patted his brow with a handkerchief.

May I remind you that when Isaac Newton was president of the Royal Society he caused a newly designed cannon to be rejected. Why? Because, Sir Isaac said, it was a diabolic instrument meant only for mass killing. Our culture, ladies and gentlemen, is a culture of death.

What do people in other countries think of us? he asked. How do they regard us?

This was a provocative question so he paused significantly before continuing.

They see a nation steeped in righteousness where guns are as easy to buy as lollipops. A nation that executes criminals without losing a drop of blood. A nation of lecherous hypocritical preachers with the brains of pterodactyls and politicians who would sell their daughters for a vote. But I digress. Let me say a few words about our Teflon President. He informed us that pollution is caused by trees. Many of us did not realize that. He told us that a Nicaraguan army could march from Managua to Harlingen,

Texas, in two days. Quite a march, yes, indeed. Honduras, El Salvador, Guatemala, Mexico. And once across the Rio Grande what would these Nicaraguan Communists do? Burn the Harlingen County Courthouse?

Folks, I'm just getting started. Dutch opened his presidential campaign in Philadelphia, Mississippi. He did that for a reason. He went to that town where three civil rights workers were lynched and declared that he stood for states' rights. Every good ol' boy from Tallahassee to Kalamazoo got the message. Hey, the big guy says it's okay.

Nor should we forget those Marines in Beirut. The Joint Chiefs advised pulling out of Lebanon. Mr. Reagan knew better. What happened? Some Lebanese kid drove up to Marine headquarters in a truck loaded with TNT. Two hundred and forty-one dead Marines.

It occurred to Mr. Bemis that he might have talked long enough, but there was so much to be said.

Ronald Reagan attempted to overthrow the elected government of another country and what did Congress do? Renamed the airport in his honor. Fifty years from now people will wonder what kind of dope we were smoking. Ladies and gentlemen, the emperor has no clothes.

Mr. Bemis took a deep breath. He felt encouraged. People were attentive.

He heard himself speak of George Bush whose nose kept growing— longer, longer, and longer. He spoke of the oil in Kuwait, of April Glaspie. He spoke of Jesse Helms, of Joseph McCarthy, J. Parnell Thomas. He pointed a finger while speaking of the National Rifle Association. Ladies and gentlemen, he said, some things about this country turn my innards upside down. Politicians claim they trust the judgment of ordinary people. Well, sir, I do not. Athenian citizens condemned Socrates to death. So much for the perspicacity of John Q. Public. Did I mention Roman Hruska?

He noticed that his audience was dwindling. He looked around for his wife. There she stood, her face a deathly mask, arms crossed.

Are you satisfied? she asked. Dodie and Norman left in a huff. Norman was livid.

Mr. Bemis felt tired. It was late and his knees ached. He wanted to go home. He saw that it was snowing and wondered if they might have trouble on the Sycamore hill.

All at once people stopped talking because somebody outside had fired a gun. Several men walked uneasily toward the windows.

On the way home Marguerite suddenly threw up both hands like an opera singer. I do not believe, she said, enunciating each word, that ever in my life have I felt so embarrassed and ashamed.

I thought I did quite well, said Mr. Bemis.

Proctor, what in the name of sense? What on earth? I cannot imagine what got into you. Oh, I could simply expire.

It just happened, he said. It felt good.

That speech was utterly incomprehensible. April Glaspie! J. Parnell Thomas! Nobody had the faintest idea what you were talking about.

I did, said Mr. Bemis.

Roman Hruska! I haven't heard that name in fifty years.

I didn't like him, Mr. Bemis said. There were a lot of people I didn't get around to. J. Edgar Hoover. Thurmond. Rusk. Laird. I could think of plenty.

Proctor, do you realize what you've done? We won't be on anyone's guest list. Never again. Never! Never! Never!

That wouldn't be the end of the world, said Mr. Bemis.

She put one hand to her forehead. Oh, this has been a perfect nightmare! I can just see Eunice Hupp telling everyone under the sun. And let there be no mistake, Proctor, I certainly want the United Nations out of our country. Foreigners have no business telling us what to do. If those foreign bankers get their way they'll take every cent we have. Every last cent. Furthermore, you know quite well that the Trilateral Commission is bent on enslaving America.

We've gone through this a hundred times, said Mr. Bemis.

I think I'm going to cry. It was such a nice party. Socrates! I have not the remotest idea what goes on inside your head. There are times when I think I married an alien.

That's interesting, Mr. Bemis said. That hadn't occurred to me.

Everybody was having so much fun. I'm just sick. Honestly, I wanted to sink through the floor. Phillips, she said, raising her voice, are you able to see the road?

Yes, Madam, Phillips replied.

It looks awfully snowy. Shouldn't we take Leimert?

I believe we can make it up Sycamore, Phillips replied in the same neutral voice. We could take Leimert if you prefer.

Mr. Bemis grinned. Phillips didn't want to lose his job. Who are you pulling for? he asked. The elephant or the jackass?

In tomorrow's election, sir? Both candidates seem qualified.

He's afraid I'll fire him, Mr. Bemis thought. I wish he'd speak up. All of us had better speak up.

Phillips looked straight ahead, gloved hands on the wheel, attending to business.

I know who I'm voting for, Mrs. Bemis said. I am unbearably tired of scandal. One thing after another. It's time we restored decency to government.

Mr. Bemis considered mentioning Nixon, but that was a long-dead horse. Decency in government. What an oxymoron. Both candidates seem qualified. Ha! One of them can't remember how to button his shirt and the other would lick dirt from a voter's boots.

As he reflected upon the evening he felt pleased with himself. I blew that party to smithereens, he thought. Hoisted the Jolly Roger—not that it will do any good. And the shot. Sooner or later everybody will find out that Speed blasted a snowdrift or a tree or punched a hole in the sky. Nobody will be able to make sense of it. Ha!

What a blessing Ronald Reagan wasn't there, she said as they waited for a traffic light.

That fake, Mr. Bemis said. I needed another twenty minutes.

Ronald Reagan was a President we could admire and trust. He won the Cold War and cut taxes and set us on the road to prosperity. He made us feel good about ourselves and he brought back morning to America when many people thought we were on the verge of night. Those tax-and-spend Democrats want to give our money to black people.

She heard that on the radio, Mr. Bemis thought. Some right-wing gasbag. She believes whatever they say. She's a true believer and she's terrified. She gets up in the middle of the night to pray.

I just hope the Republicans win, she said.

Mr. Bemis folded his hands across his belly and considered the invasion of Grenada. A sleepy tourist island near Venezuela. Reagan ordered the attack without consulting Congress, probably without consulting anybody except Nancy's astrologer. Why? Because the prime minister was liberal and the airport runway was being extended. Soviet bombers would be able to land and refuel en route to the United States. True enough, if they flew the wrong direction a couple of thousand miles. Reagan never looked at a map in his life. If he did, he couldn't understand all those numbers and squiggly lines. So what happened? U.S. Navy planes bombed the

Grenada mental hospital. They didn't mean to bomb a hospital but they did. An international court of justice at The Hague condemned Reagan. Nobody cared. Millions want his face on the ten-dollar bill. Millions want him on Rushmore. All right, there's room enough if we get rid of Lincoln.

People forget, he said. They ought to be reminded.

You certainly don't forget. And I do not wish to be reminded of anything else. I have heard more than enough, Proctor. More than enough.

She had almost divorced him because of Vietnam so he decided to keep quiet. He thought about Howie, who seemed a bit uncomfortable with himself. Years at the Pentagon. Policy wonks. Alice in Wonderland briefings. Light at the end of the tunnel. Somewhere along the way they got him.

Now what are you grumbling about? she asked.

I wasn't, he said.

I thought you would never stop eating. I was so humiliated. You made four trips to the buffet.

Three, Mr. Bemis said, holding up three fingers.

Eunice Hupp was watching me while you made a fool of yourself. Oh, Proctor, how could you do such a thing? I'll never live it down.

I took one small step for mankind, said Mr. Bemis.

I do not understand what possesses you. We have so much to be thankful for. We have a nice home in the loveliest neighborhood. We have everything we could possibly want. Everything.

She was right, of course. And yet, he thought, she's wrong. Is there anything I want, he asked himself, that I don't have? I don't know. I'm a success. I ought to feel satisfied.

Phillips drove carefully up the Sycamore hill. Streetlights through falling snow reminded Mr. Bemis of a village in France when he had been a private in the Army. He tried to recall the name of the village but it was gone. He touched the window with one finger. The glass was warmer than he expected and the snow was turning to slush. He wondered how he could be seventy-five years old when he had been a young soldier just yesterday.

Marguerite, he said, I'm hungry.

What little of her face could be seen above the collar of the fur coat proved that he had not been forgiven.

You are imagining, she said. You couldn't conceivably be hungry.

That was an hour ago, he said. What's in the fridge?

She refused to answer.

He thought affectionately of the buffet—gorgeous black olives, anchovy crackers, lamb chops, venison, duck, salmon, lemon tart—and heard a familiar rumble in his stomach. He considered the evening while Phillips drove them homeward and something from Aristophanes sifted like a snowflake through the years. What heaps of things have bitten me to the heart! A small few pleased me, very few.

That was not the whole of it, but he could not remember what came next. For now, that was enough.

Tim Johnston

Irish Girl

from *DoubleTake*

THE WAY it began, the way he'd remember it many years later, was a
kick to the leg.

He was under the kitchen table playing with army men and somebody
kicked him. Not too hard but not too soft, either.

William.

He turned and scowled at corduroys and tube socks, all he could see of
his brother. "What?"

"They're waiting for you," William said in an odd voice. "In their bedroom."

And then he walked away.

Before that, of course, were things Charlie didn't know much about, being
eight. He didn't know about Nixon's decision to send troops into Cambo-
dia, or how that led to the shootings at Kent State, or how that led, in
turn, to the smashed shop windows in his own hometown. He did know a
little about the thirteen boys from the agricultural college arrested for riot-
ing, because his father had been their lawyer. But he didn't know how the
trial, which had made the news every night for two weeks, spreading his
father's name across the state like goldenrod, had given his father the idea
to run for office. He didn't know what the Iowa House of Representatives
was, or what people did with all those leaflets he left on their porches, or

what it meant to win by a landslide. And he didn't know his father was still riding the high of victory when he decided, a few days before leaving for the state capitol, to have The Talk.

He didn't know that's where William had just come from, he only knew he'd been under the kitchen table, playing with army men, when his brother kicked him.

It was true: his parents were waiting for him, sitting on the edge of their bed and beaming at him with wet eyes. His father sat him down and explained what adopted meant even though Charlie already knew from school; when you picked on the adopted kid he'd fight and say it was a lie, as if being adopted was the worst thing ever, worse than having no dad at all. Charlie stared at the floor and felt sick to his stomach, waiting for his parents to tell him he was adopted, too. Finally, he had to ask.·

His father leaned forward. He was a big man to begin with and when he leaned forward you couldn't see anything else, he was it. "Would you be sad if you were?" his father asked.

Charlie knew what his father wanted to hear—that Charlie wouldn't give a dog's fart because he still had the best parents in the world, who would love him forever.

But all he could do was shrug.

"Well," his father said at last. "You're not adopted, Charlie. You came from your mom and me." He put his hands on Charlie's shoulders. "But that doesn't mean we love you any more or any less than William, or that he's not your real brother. You understand? You boys will be brothers for-ever."

Charlie understood, but he was so happy not to be adopted he wanted to spread the news, he wanted to put it on a leaflet and hit every porch in the world.

That night, Charlie sat down to dinner like a kid moving underwater, trying to look normal. William was still in the room the boys shared, no light showing under the door. A January wind was in the seams of the back door, moaning eerily. The house, the whole neighborhood, kept its back to open farmland and bore the first, hardest blows of weather. In the spring, the air was soaked in the smell of soil and manure, and at night you heard the cows bawl, and the horn of the freight trains was to warn them, William said, to stay off the tracks or else.

Charlie pushed beans around on his plate and hated himself for being glad he wasn't adopted. He told himself that if anyone ever teased the adopted kid at school again he'd help him fight, he swore to God he would.

"Hey, baby," his mother said, and his father lowered his cup of coffee.

Charlie turned and there was William, hands in his pockets, squinting in the light. He stared at them, and for a second it looked like he might turn and leave, and that's when Charlie moved. Jumped up and ran to him, locked his arms around him so tightly it was hard for William to get his hands out of his pockets. Finally he did, wiggled them out from under Charlie's grip, and got his fingers around Charlie's biceps and moved him, just so, aside. "Lay off, willya?" he said. "I'm hungry."

And that was that. The boys sat down, and Charlie didn't whimper or even rub at the matching dents of pain in his arms where William had sunk his thumbs to the bone.

Their father bought a second car for his trips to Des Moines, a green Cougar convertible, and one Sunday early in his term he took William and Charlie with him to show them where he sat in the session chamber, and they spent the night with him in the cramped, untidy trailer he rented near the interstate.

"You think he likes this place more than home?" Charlie asked William that night. Their father had gone to meet someone, and William had his legs stretched out on a nappy brown sofa, studying the pages of a *Playboy* he'd found under the cushions. The trailer smelled like the inside of leather shoes and shower mildew and old pizza boxes, and Charlie could feel the hum of tractor-trailers through a stiff layer of carpet.

"Shit, Charlie," his brother replied, rising and heading for the toilet. "Wouldn't you?"

Their father was home for Christmas but then didn't return for months, and Charlie's mother told them that it was because he was writing bills and had to work extra hard to get them made into laws. William just stared at her, the same look on his face that always let Charlie know he'd said something really stupid, then walked away. He'd stopped cutting his hair and had begun to smell like cigarettes and car engines. At night when he came in, he'd crash into his bed with superhero exhaustion, as if he'd been pushed to the very limit of his powers. In the mornings Charlie watched him plod across the room in his underwear, his boner out before him like the nose of a German shepherd, and felt so puny he wanted to scream. He checked himself daily for signs of growth, but nothing changed, and he worried that something was wrong with him and that when William was a full-grown man, he would still be the hairless little nothing he was right then.

William was right about their father preferring a smelly trailer to home, because when his two-year term was over and he went back to his law practice, he moved into another one in their hometown. He picked the boys up on Fridays in the Cougar and the three of them ate pizza and went out for breakfast and saw matinees and sat around the trailer watching TV until Sunday afternoon, when their father would let William, who by now had a driver's permit, drive them back to the house.

During the week, when Charlie got home from school he'd find William and his friends strewn in front of the TV like dead men, drinking Cokes and licking potato chip grease from their fingers. The boys called William Billy, and Charlie knew they had all cut school early, if they'd gone at all. William made sure to clear them out by the time their mother got home, but she could count Cokes and read the air with her nose, and she and William would both start yelling and Charlie would shut himself in his room until he heard the front door slam and he knew William had gone out again.

One night, when she tried to keep William home for dinner, he told her to get off his back and she slapped him. Her handprint spread like a warning light over his face, and for a second Charlie thought he was going to slap her back. "Bitch," he said, and she took a step back like he'd gone ahead and done it. Then he left, and the word "adopted" rose in Charlie's throat like vomit, and he wanted to remind her that's what William was and why he said it, because no real son, no flesh-and-blood son, would ever call his mother that name.

Later that night, Charlie got up to pee and heard her on the phone. She said "Mason," their father's name, with a wobble in her throat, and when he came to get the boys the following Friday, William brought along two pillowcases full of clothes.

.   .   .

Charlie didn't miss William until the spring, when he began to hear the cows at night and the moaning trains and he'd remember how he used to sit on William's bed with a flashlight while William made up stories about a gang of killers, whacked-out hippies forever hopping off trains and shooting people. Somehow the hippies always made their way across the fields right up to the living room window where Mason and Connie Whitford sat watching the news of the killing spree. When he told his stories, William's eyes grew brilliant, super-blue, and they lit up a place where he and Charlie were equals, where they snapped into action at the exact same moment and they never failed.

That April, after a month with William, Mason gave up trailers for good. He bought a house, a big old one in the middle of town, and when Charlie arrived for his first weekend he was amazed to learn that the upstairs bedroom with the new bed and the matching dresser and desk and the three windows was all for him. William had his own room on the other side of the wall and Mason's was at the far end of the hall and had its own bathroom. Downstairs, you could reach full speed running from one end of the house to the other, and below that was a basement with a pool table the previous owner had left behind.

His first night in the new house Charlie lay awake for hours, getting used to the shadows of the room and the drone of traffic outside his window. He was finally drifting off when the horn of a freight train, a single short blast, punched through and jerked him back. Warning bells rang in the streets and the horn sounded again, louder this time, so loud he was sure the train was heading right for the house. But the next blast of the horn was weaker, a deflating balloon, and he heard the clacking of the wheels on the rails and it calmed his heart, that rhythm, and he slept.

Mason came downstairs the next night stinking of Brut aftershave and wearing blue jeans that made Charlie laugh. He was going out to dinner with a friend, he told them, and William was in charge.

William stared at the TV. The Six Million Dollar Man was jumping a wall.

"William," his father said.

"Yeah?"

"I said you're going to be in charge for a few hours. Can you handle that?"

"No sweat."

Charlie watched his father standing there squeezing his car keys in his fist, his eyes dark, and for the first time in his life Charlie actually wanted him to go, to leave them alone.

Finally, with a pat to Charlie's head, he did.

"Who's his friend?" Charlie asked when their father was gone.

"What day of the week is it?"

Charlie told him but William just smirked and lit a Camel.

"Dad lets you smoke?"

"Fuck, no." He got up and moved to the open window. "Dad's a fascist."

"What's that?"

"He's the guy who ends up full of bullet holes with old ladies pissing on him in the town square."

Charlie chewed an already raw fingernail. He couldn't believe the things a sixteen-year-old knew, especially one who never went to school.

William eyed him. "You gonna narc on me?"

Charlie shook his head and William took a studious drag on the cigarette. "How 'bout if I split for a while? You gonna be cool with that?"

"If you take me with you."

"Not a chance."

A car horn honked loudly, once, and William flicked his cigarette out the window. Charlie jumped up, but William put a hand on his shoulder, sunk his thumb into the flesh above his collarbone. "I can count on you, Charlie, can't I?" The pressure made Charlie feel like a puppet, like William could make his legs buckle with just the right kind of squeeze.

"Yes," he said, refusing to squirm.

"Promise to God and hope to die?"

"Yes."

William let go. "Outstanding," he said, then he left, banging the screen door behind him. Charlie watched him climb behind the wheel of a Chevy Impala the color of an army tank. A girl with straight red hair mashed her lips against his for a full minute, her fingers deep in his hair, before he finally gunned the engine and backed out of the drive, leaving tracks.

Two hours later Mason called, and Charlie picked up.

Something was coming down the hallway, fast and loud in the middle of the night.

His bed shook and wood exploded and Charlie flattened himself against the mattress, ready for the floor to drop out from under him. "Get up!" his father yelled.

Not at Charlie. At William, on the other side of the wall. He was in William's room. He'd kicked in the door.

"What for?" William tried to sound tough.

"Because I told you to."

"Christ, Dad. Can't it—"

Bedsprings creaked and something hit the floor, and Charlie heard footsteps like two giant kids practicing a dance. "Get! Up!" Mason yelled. "Get up when I tell you!" The dance thudded out into the hall and something, an elbow or a head, bounced against Charlie's door. "Open the door when I tell you," his father said. "Watch your brother when I tell you."

"He can watch himself! He's not a baby!"

"I don't care."

They moved down the hall, and Charlie heard William grunt and his father bark back, "Don't you—don't you even try it," and Charlie's bed picked up the shock waves of William slamming into a wall. "Whattaya gonna do, *Dad*?" William's voice rose and came apart. "Gonna hit me? Go ahead! Hit me! Hit me, *Dad*!"

"Don't test me, William, I warn you."

And then the dance moved on, in bursts and thuds, down the stairs and all the way to the opposite end of the house, where it either stopped or merely ceased to distinguish itself, at that distance, from Charlie's banging heart.

In the morning, Charlie made an inspection of the door. The jamb was split vertically, and a shard of it lay in the middle of William's room, the brass strike plate still attached and looking stunned, like a mouth knocked from a face.

Charlie spent the rest of the day pretending to read comic books or watch TV, waiting to see William. But he never showed up, and Charlie went back to his mother's thinking William had stayed away because of him—that he never wanted to see Charlie's ugly little narc face again.

He didn't see him again until the following Saturday afternoon. Mason was in the middle of a trial and had gone to the office, so Charlie was alone in the house when William walked in and slugged him in the shoulder. Charlie raised his arms, expecting more, but William was grinning.

"Get your shoes, Charlie Horse."

Outside, Charlie saw the tank-colored Chevy and stopped short. Blood filled his chest. He couldn't breathe right.

"What's with you?" William worked up a gob of spit, sent it flying. "Look," he said. "I promise you'll be back before he ever knows you were gone. OK?"

The car was full of big teenagers with long hair and army jackets like William's—and the girl Charlie had seen before with the straight red hair. She and one of the boys shifted to let William behind the wheel, and two boys in back made room for Charlie. "Fuckin' A!" a boy with great shining pimples said. "Fresh troops!" He blew smoke in Charlie's face that didn't smell like cigarettes. Charlie coughed, and the girl craned around and stunned him with white teeth and the biggest, greenest eyes he'd ever seen. She looked right at him and kept smiling and said, "Happy birthday, Charlie."

The girl's name was Colleen and she was a Foosball wizard. Three times during the game she held the ball in place with one of her men while she put her hand over Charlie's and moved his men just so. Then, with a snap of her wrist he couldn't even see, she scored on William and the boy with pimples. William laughed, but the boy with pimples called her a cheater and she told him to grow up, dickweed. The boy glared at Charlie and asked William, out of the side of his mouth as if Charlie wouldn't hear him that way, "He retarded, or what?"

William stared hard at the boy, then gave Charlie a grin. "You retarded, Charlie?"

Charlie was still floating from Colleen's hand on his, and he couldn't imagine any idiot thing a dickweed with pimples could say to bring him down, so he just shook his head.

"He don't say much, do he," the boy said, and William said, "No, he don't. But he's thinking, man. He thinks more in a day than you do in a year."

"Right," the boy said, and Colleen snapped her wrist and the ball disappeared with a bang.

When it was time to go, William had to drag Charlie from the pinball machines, but Charlie was twelve, too old to make a scene, so he jammed his hands in his pockets and tried to look bored. William hooked an arm around Colleen and dropped his hand on her breast for a quick, secret squeeze. "Back in a flash," he told her. She smiled at Charlie and it was too much, he had to look away.

William drove fast, a grim expression on his face, and when they came to the railroad tracks he locked up the brakes and pounded the steering wheel so hard Charlie couldn't believe it didn't crack. They were at the end of a line of cars waiting for a train to pass. The central hub of the Rock Island Railway was not far away, and the people who lived here, it sometimes seemed, lived in the spaces between its lines like prisoners. Freighters plowed through day and night, trains without head or tail, and there was nothing you could do but sit and wait.

William jammed the Chevy into Park and thumbed in the electric lighter. He pushed his hair back from his face, lit a Camel, and dropped the pack on the seat. Charlie breathed in the first cloud of smoke, always the best-smelling one, and picked up the pack. William didn't seem to notice or care as Charlie pulled out one of the Camels with his lips, the way William did. And he didn't budge when Charlie pushed in the electric lighter. But when the lighter popped and Charlie steered the red coil toward the tip of the Camel, his brother reached over and plucked the cigarette from his mouth.

"You gotta do everything I do? You want Mason breaking down your door at two A.M.?"

Charlie recalled that night and was disgusted with himself—cowering in his room like a pussy while William got the crap beaten out of him, all because Charlie hadn't been smart enough, or brave enough, to come up with a lie on the phone.

He'd tell him he was sorry, he decided. Right now.

He'd tell him before that red boxcar crossed the road. . . .

Before the end of the train . . .

But he didn't, and the red lights stopped flashing and the Chevy was moving again and Charlie watched his chance slip away with the caboose.

William whipped into the driveway and braked at the last second, just shy of Mason's Cougar. He shifted into Reverse and tossed Charlie a salute. "Happy birthday, man."

"You're not coming in?"

"Naw. I gotta go get those losers."

Charlie gripped his left hand in his right, remembering the Foosball game. His heart would not slow down.

"I like the girl," he said.

"Colleen?"

He turned and William smiled and Charlie saw a light in his eyes he hadn't seen in so long he'd forgotten it even existed.

"You know what her name means?" William asked.

It was the light, Charlie realized, from the nights when they shared a room and William told stories and they had no idea that one of them was adopted.

"What's it mean?" he asked.

William took a deep drag on the cigarette and stared out the windshield. "Means *Irish girl.*"

Mason was in the kitchen, leaning against the counter with his hands in his pockets, jingling change and keys. "Where'd he take you?" he said quietly.

Charlie glanced into the dining room and saw a chocolate bakery cake with unlit candles and a small pile of gifts on the table. "Nowhere."

"Nowhere?"

He shrugged and felt a wet heat in his armpits, a weakness in his legs that told him what a terrible thing he was about to do. But he did it anyway, and for no good reason except that he hadn't been able to do it the night he should've.

"We went to the movies," he lied. "It was my birthday present." He took a step toward the stairs, but Mason grabbed his arm, pulled him back into the kitchen.

"Don't you walk away from me."

"Let me go!" Charlie wasn't afraid, exactly, his father had never hit him his whole life, but he wanted out of that grip before the tears came and ruined everything.

"You reek of smoke, Charlie. You reek of smoke and pot. Were you smoking pot in that car?"

"What?"

"Did you smoke anything with William?"

"No!"

"Don't you lie to me."

"I'm not!"

Mason had a hold of both arms now, squeezing to the bone, and he was shaking him, a low, rapid jerking that seemed beyond his control. Charlie watched his father's face redden and saw the look in his eyes and thought he was maybe having a heart attack. "Dad," he said. "Dad!" He grabbed his father's wrists and squeezed but his father just held on, staring at him so intensely, so strangely, that Charlie would wonder later if it wasn't at that exact second that William tried to beat the train.

For this to be true he'd have to have driven very fast after dropping Charlie off, in a rush to get back to his friends, back to Colleen, or maybe the light was in his eyes and he drove the only way he knew how when he felt like that, like a man from another planet, like a superhero. Charlie sees him flicking his Camel out the window and gripping the wheel in both hands. He sees his boot stomp the gas pedal and the muscles of his jaw grow hard as the Chevy leaps, and he sees his eyes, the light, the flash of blue wonder, the moment he knows he's not going to make it.

Everything after that seems to happen through a cracked window, with Charlie standing outside looking in. There's the police in the house, led there by a driver's license. There's the drive across town and the sound Charlie can hear, sitting in the Cougar in the driveway, of his mother at the kitchen table, her cry a piercing thing, a teapot beginning to boil, a January wind. There's the funeral and William's friends in their cheap ties and army jackets sulking like war buddies. And there's Colleen, wrapping her arms around Charlie so fiercely, so hungrily that he knows she doesn't know—that she believes Charlie is a true brother, a living blood link to the body in the coffin.

And after that there's just the long withering summer, the weekends with his father, the two of them going out for meals, going to movies, taking long drives at night with the top down. One Saturday, a carpenter comes, an old guy who gets Charlie to help him carry his tools up the stairs and hand him the things he asks for, and when they're done, William's door looks good as new, the brass strike plate, that shocked little mouth, back in place. At the end of the summer, the house is sold and Charlie moves in with Mason for the school year, into a two-bedroom house close to Charlie's new school, and they begin to eat at home in the evenings and Mason begins a new trial and Charlie learns that a pretty girl at school likes him—and still.

Still it's the same town, and when they go somewhere in the Cougar, no matter what streets they take or how they time it, they end up stuck before a passing train. When this happens they don't talk and they don't look at each other, though Charlie would like to know what his father is thinking, if he's thinking about the night he kicked down William's door, or something better, like teaching him to ride a bike, or maybe the day they brought him home, their new son. If his father asked him, Charlie would try to describe the last time he saw William—the look in his eyes, the blue light, the wild secret rush when William said the words "Irish girl."

But his father doesn't ask and the train is a long one, and so they sit there, having no choice, and watch for its end.

Tim O'Brien

What Went Wrong

from *Esquire*

O N THE last day of July 1969, David Todd arrived at the Hubert H.
Humphrey VA Hospital just outside Minneapolis. His right leg had
been amputated in Japan.

His left leg was in dispute. Over the next three and a half weeks, off and
on, a number of meditative, glutinous-sounding voices discussed the possibility of another amputation, the pros and cons. David himself was too
far gone to care. He was back at a narrow, fast-moving river called the
Song Tra Ky, conferring with angels, watching a colony of ants consume
his feet. Fascinating, he decided. Feet to food. The morphine took him to
places he had never visited before, black holes and white dwarfs, ancient
cemeteries, the walls of Troy, a ditch outside Tu Cung, the gaudy bedroom
of a corrupt, complacent, leg-eating, gone-in-the-teeth Cleopatra. He witnessed his own decorous conception. He played shortstop for the '27 Yan-
kees. He was there in Sugamo Prison, a few minutes past midnight on
December 22, 1948, looking on as Hideki Tojo dropped out of time
through a squeaky gallows trapdoor. He bossed mules for Wellington. He
scrubbed the ovens at Dachau, rode point at Washita, sat in on LBJ's war
briefings, attended a mediocre comedy at Ford's Theatre, listened to the
insane blather of Hector Ortiz's transistor radio. At one point, near the
end of his first week in the hospital, David took vaporous note of Marla
Dempsey leaning over him, her lips poised in concern, her eyes filled with

something just short of love. His own imagination, he reasoned. Or maybe not. Either way, when Marla smiled and kissed his forehead, or seemed to, David screamed. He couldn't help it: there was pain in the most delicate touch, in the simplest sound or passing image.

He started to apologize, to sit up, but Marla was no longer present. Nor was David, entirely. He could hear the Song Tra Ky bubbling nearby. He could smell dead friends and mildew and his own rotting feet.

Days later, in a moment of narcotic clarity, Marla Dempsey appeared again. She murmured endearments. She promised to be true. When she vanished, however, someone issued a chuckle from deep in the hospital ethers. "Relax, my friend, it ain't what you think. You're alive, big fella, just like I swore, but from here on, that's basically the whole shitty shebang. Gotta be dead-flat honest. One of the rules, right? This honesty thing, Davy, it drives me nuts. Bureaucracy up the bazoo. Boss lets me exaggerate all I want, wax eloquent, but I don't get to tell no fibs. Real temptation, too. Hate to break hearts." A ghost, or an angel, or just an inner voice named Johnny Ever clicked his tongue in false exasperation. "Anyhow, here's the scoop. What the lady feels right now—Miss Marla, that is—what she feels is real extra sad. Not much else. Maybe some guilt tossed in, which is why she's gonna marry your ass. Pure pity, man. I seen it plenty times before. Eva Braun, Dale Evans." He chuckled again. "Giddyap, cripple."

David was released from the hospital on Christmas Day, 1969. He and Marla were married in the Darton Hall College chapel on New Year's Eve, a few friends, nothing elaborate. "I'll try hard," Marla told him during their honeymoon in Miami, on a crowded white beach behind the hotel. "The thing is, you need to know how scared I am. My whole life, David, I never thought I'd end up married, not to anybody, and I have to admit it's a strange feeling." She paused. Her eyes were hidden behind sunglasses. "You know me, David. I'm not a welcome-home-honey housewife. I'll need room. Time to be myself."

"Fine," David said. "I just hope it isn't charity."

Marla turned toward him.

"My leg," said David. "Ex-leg. I'm not looking for pity."

"That's absurd."

"Is it?"

"Yes," Marla said. "It's our honeymoon, isn't it?"

David looked away.

He was tempted to spend the next few minutes discussing morphine and shot feet and a certain cocksure angel wired into the silver-hot center of the universe. Instead, he shrugged. He covered his prosthesis with a towel and stared down the beach at a group of college-age kids playing volleyball. They were drunk. They were happy. They were ignorant. They had their legs. They did not hear voices in their sleep, nor have access to the appalling drift of things to come.

He looked back at Marla.

"Sorry," he said. "But you'd tell me, right? If you just felt pity for me?"

"David, I do feel pity. Losing your leg, all those baseball dreams. It's ghastly. Not to mention incredibly stupid. The war, I mean, not you. How it's wrecked things for so many people. Honestly, I'd be a moron not to feel angry and sick about it. Even some pity. But that's not why we're married."

"Except you're not sure?"

"I didn't say that. I said I was scared."

"Which sounds unsure."

There was a moment of severe silence. Marla pulled off her sunglasses, rubbed her eyes, sighed, and glanced down at her wedding ring as if it were something she'd picked up off the beach. "David, you're precious to me," she said. "True, I'm not the beaming bride. That's not the person you married. A hard thing to explain. I don't understand what it is or where it came from, but there's something inside me that's just totally alone, totally private. Like a rainy day that goes on and on."

David nodded and said, "Fine, then."

"Not fine," said Marla. "But the truth. I won't lie about it."

Then she rose to her feet, tossed her sunglasses aside, waded into the Atlantic, dove under, and spent thirty seconds of her honeymoon near the bottom, remorseful and frightened, exploring her life, telling herself she should never have gotten married, not in a thousand years, and certainly not to a decent, loving man like David Todd.

In the autumn of her junior year at Darton Hall, while dating David, Marla Dempsey began an affair with a former high school teacher, a married man. The romance lasted just over a month, not long by some measures, a light-year by others. During those four weeks in 1967, Marla seemed to float from spot to spot in a great sparkling bubble. She found herself shopping for sexy clothes—lace panties, see-through negligees—things she'd once despised and ridiculed.

People noticed the change. David, too.

"Query," he said one morning. "Where's Marla these days?"

His tone was cheerful. His eyes showed concern. For a time Marla said nothing, considering her options, and then said, "On vacation, I guess. A brain resort."

In mid-October the affair ended in the parking lot of Marla's dorm. Lovely day. Antique red Cadillac. Engine idling, windows open to the autumn air. The high school teacher, a blond, dark-eyed, poisonously handsome specimen named Jim Anderson, explained the dynamic to her. His voice was slow and condescending, as if he were teaching phonics to a class of dimwits. He talked about guilt and insomnia and issues of honor.

Maybe in another life, he said.

Maybe if x ever happened to intersect with an unlikely y.

"I follow you perfectly," said Marla.

She got out of the car, went up to her room, sat on the floor, filed her nails, dialed David's number, hung up after two rings, screamed an obscenity, changed into shorts and sneakers, and jogged three miles to the teacher's house in a middle-class suburb of St. Paul. The antique Cadillac was parked in the driveway. Nearby, under clear plastic, was what appeared to be a brand-new baby stroller.

Just before dusk Marla rang the doorbell.

Why she was there, or what she expected, was unclear to her, and when Jim Anderson's wife opened the door, Marla found herself unable to think or speak. The woman was an emaciated, brittle-looking creature, thirty-five or so, her reddish-brown hair arranged in a pair of pigtails secured by rubber bands. She wore faded blue jeans, a yellow gauze blouse loose at the waist. In her left hand she gripped a plastic spatula. A TV set blared at full volume in the room behind her: the evening news, trouble in Asia. Dense odors of broccoli and frying pork chops swamped the doorway. These details—the spatula, the pigtails, the smells, the evening news—would remain with Marla Dempsey forever.

The woman seemed to nod.

There was an instant of silence, succeeded by a dull explosion on the TV, succeeded by the sound of a flushing toilet.

Jim Anderson's wife stepped back and used her free hand to tug at one of the pigtails. "Aren't we cute?" she said. Her voice was matter-of-fact. "Awful young to be a husband fucker."

Marla had nothing to say. But she now realized that this woman's sad, unsurprised, washed-out face offered exactly what she'd needed, everything she'd run three miles for, which was to know that she would never be forgiven.

After the honeymoon, David and Marla rented a cheap two-bedroom house in St. Paul, walking distance from the college. Money was a problem. David's disability checks helped a little, but still they needed a bed and a sofa and hot water and something to eat. They had student loans to repay. Their parents could contribute almost nothing.

After some discussion, Marla postponed graduate school and went to work as a paralegal in downtown Minneapolis, which seemed fine at first, but which in the end amounted to little more than a poorly paid, coffee-fetching go-fership. She was advised to widen her smile, shorten her skirts.

It was 1970.

Through their first month of marriage, David continued with his rehab, four hours a day, six days a week, learning to use escalators and climb stairs and navigate slippery surfaces with the aid of a mahogany cane. Progress was slow. Sometimes his stump felt as if it were plugged into an electrical outlet; other times he'd find himself scratching at thin air where his shin or ankle used to be. In a physical sense, David knew he'd make it. His head was something else. At night, often for hours, he lay awake listening to the accusatory chatter of dead friends, Kaz Maples and Buddy Pond and Alvin Campbell and all the others. He watched Doc Paladino get sucked away into the tall, dry grass along the Song Tra Ky. "Man, I told you," Johnny Ever whispered. "All them poor shot-to-shit buddies of yours, they got scads of time on their hands. Eons, you could say. Just harps and halos and virgin-ass angels. Nothin' much to do except talk their guts out." Johnny paused to admire his own gift of gab. "No offense, Davy, but I'll tell you one more thing. Them dudes got long memories. We're talking forever. And I fear they ain't gonna let you forget neither. Survivor guilt, it's a bitch. Killed Custer's horse. Would've killed Custer."

In late April of 1970 David took a part-time job refinishing furniture. The work brought in some cash, boosted his morale, made him feel a little more whole. He was good at it. After two months he opened up his own shop in the garage, building customized cabinets and a few finely made desks and dining tables. The business prospered, and near the end of the summer David expanded his operation into a closed-down gas station off Snelling Avenue. He hung up a handmade sign and hired a helper. "You should be proud," Marla said, and in many ways David was. Carpentry was not baseball, not the majors, but it was something he enjoyed. He liked the feel of tools in his hands. He liked the scent of good wood, the satisfaction of coming up with tidy solutions to problems of geometry. Also, the work helped to push away the voices, kept his mind off the Song Tra Ky.

A week before Christmas he built a delicate black-walnut nightstand as a gift for Marla. While he sanded and stained and oiled, humming to himself, David daydreamed about the big leagues. He had his legs. He was quick on the pivot. He was happily married. He would stay that way. The prophecies were bullshit, nothing but smoke, and Johnny Ever was one more blowhard with a microphone.

From the start, in too many ways, Marla and David were uncomfortable in the marriage. Distracted and wary. Always on edge. Sometimes frightened.

On her part, Marla could never eradicate the high school teacher from her thoughts. The man lounged in her head as if he'd taken up residence inside her, uninvited, sharing her pillow at night, pulling up a chair at meals. Marla missed him. And she missed the happy, wildly infatuated young woman of 1967, bowled-over-Marla, girl-Marla, the Marla Dempsey who for a few incredible weeks had floated around campus in a bubble. Now the black days were back. Not despair exactly, not even unhappiness. Just that familiar old passivity, a cool and listless neutrality of spirit. Nothing moved her. Nothing hurt. She felt sealed off from things: from pain, from joy, from her own emotions. No big ups. No miserable downs. At times, Marla thought, it was as if she'd been pumped full of some powerful drug, Valium or a handful of those new knock-you-dead sleeping pills.

She could move through an entire day, sometimes a week, without once laughing. Sex was fine, never more than fine. Life was good, never more than good. Still, as if to balance things out, her daily routine had a sumptuous tranquillity, the sort of peace that attends a solid marriage to a solid man like David Todd. And the last thing Marla wanted was to hurt him. Which meant faking things.

"What a beautiful, beautiful nightstand," she told him on Christmas morning, 1970.

She grinned furiously.

"I'm blown away," she said. "Just so happy."

In 1973 they bought a house in Bloomington, not far from Met Stadium, and on summer nights, after work, they'd often make the nine-minute drive to take in a Twins game. David would keep a meticulous box score, frowning into a pair of binoculars, analyzing plays or situations that caught his attention. Most of it meant nothing to Marla.

To pass time, she would offer her own commentary on what she called the "team costumes," evaluating fashion issues, chattering about cut and color. She liked the bright stadium lights, the seventh-inning stretch, the smells of beer and popcorn. The game itself remained a mystery to her. Even after David's lectures, all his charts and diagrams, Marla still had no idea about the function of a bunt, or why anyone in his right mind would want to execute a hit-and-run. "If you ask me," she'd tell him, "the whole thing sounds pretty shady, pretty crooked." In a way she was kidding, in a way she wasn't, but it was nice to see a smile come to David's lips, to watch him laugh and shake his head and explain all over again.

Early on, Marla worried that these nights at the ballpark might undo the whole rehab process, send him over some wartime edge, but the effect on David was clearly the opposite. Almost always, his mood would soften. The tension would drain from his eyes, flushing away the war, and at night he didn't talk so often in his sleep—not with the same rage and violence. More than anything, it was the late-hour babble that alarmed and sometimes terrified Marla.

She dreaded bedtime. She dreaded the end of baseball season.

In mid-February of 1975, Marla carried a tape recorder into the bedroom, put it on her dresser, and hit the record button.

At breakfast the next morning, she played the cassette for David.

"That voice," she said. "Who is it?"

David didn't look at her. He pushed to his feet, went to the sink, rinsed his cereal bowl, and poured himself a cup of coffee. He kept his back turned.

"This scares me," she said. "That voice. It's you, but it's not you. All the swearing. Whoever it is, I feel like he's dangerous."

"Dangerous?"

"Like he could hurt somebody."

David swung around toward her. For a few seconds his expression went thoughtful.

"Right," he said. "I suppose he could."

"Who?"

"I'm not sure who. Nightmares. Let's try to forget it."

"David, did you listen to the tape? How do I forget? Tell me how."

"I don't know how."

"So that's it? Don't talk about it, don't look at me? I mean, God, let's just play the tape again, have a laugh, pretend it's the comedy hour. Chalk it up to dreamland. Rub it out."

"Hey, stop." David jabbed a finger at her. His voice rose from deep in his chest, from the darkness inside him, a ravening, suddenly brutal sound. "You don't understand. Nothing. And if I tried to explain, if I started to explain—" He shook his head hard, reached down, pulled up his right pant leg, and rapped his knuckles against the prosthesis. "See that? Chop off a leg, baby. Watch sixteen guys die. Smell the rot. See if you don't cuss in your sleep."

"I wasn't criticizing, David. I was trying—"

"Trying what? To talk?"

"Yes."

He dropped the pant leg, took a jerky half step toward her. Something changed in his face., "Excellent," he said. "Let's talk about Cadillacs. Baby strollers. One leg, honey, but I'm all ears."

Marla looked at him. Outside, an ambulance or police car went by, its siren at high emergency, and in those miserable moments it occurred to Marla that the world was indifferent to all of this, deaf to betrayal and deceit and petty passion.

David's lips curled into a skewed smile she'd never seen before. "Cat got your tongue? Maybe we should rev up that tape recorder. Capture the silence."

"You knew," she said.

"Day one. Lace panties. I'm not an idiot."

"And you never said anything."

He made a contemptuous spitting sound. "What's to say? 'Pretty-please love me'?"

"David."

"Hard to find words, isn't it?"

He took the cassette out of the tape recorder, tossed it in the garbage.

"Ex-teachers, what's a guy to do?" he said. "Thought to myself, Hey, give it time, she'll come around. Leg or no leg. So I wait. Five years, three people. You, me, Mr. Teacher. Eat dinner together. Group sex. Christ, I'd watch you sometimes, sailing away to fantasyland, wherever the fuck you'd go." He laughed. "Robot wife. Makes a guy wonder who the cripple is."

He put his coffee cup in the sink, turned on the water, and then stared at the faucet. He seemed dazed, unfixed to the world. "Writing on the wall. Knew all along."

"Ridiculous," Marla said. "Nobody knows that."

"Yeah, well. In the stars."

"You're saying we're finished?"

He didn't answer.

Marla waited a moment, then went over to him and put a hand on his arm. "I know it's not enough, but I tried hard. That's the truth. Sometimes, though, it felt like you'd already decided everything. Who I was. What I wanted. Almost like you needed to drive me away."

"I'm the villain?"

"No. But people get what they imagine."

David raised his eyebrows, mocking. "Pigtails? Baby strollers?"

"Not that."

"What about the cool Caddy?"

Marla took her hand from his arm. She had the sensation of talking to a new person, someone who'd put on David's face for a Halloween party. "I love you," she said quietly. "But when you suppose from the start that everything's fake and rotten and doomed. . . . Then it is doomed. That's how I've felt for years, like you wanted me to hurt you." She stopped. Something struck her as wrong. "Pigtails? Where did that come from?"

David made a casual motion with the palms of his hands.

"Little birdie," he said.

"That's not an answer."

"But good enough."

For several seconds David looked at her, sadly, but also maliciously, and then he grinned and glanced at the water faucet, where Johnny Ever waited. "What a bitch. Give it time, she's out of here. Ta-ta. Gone as Goebbels. Believe me, partner, we're talkin' history here. Future, too. Cooked goose. Roasted romance."

Marla said, "What?"

The marriage lasted four more years. Both Marla and David did what they could to keep it alive, to work toward some condensed version of happiness, and for periods of time they made themselves believe that whatever they had together—the bond, the covenant—might still be salvageable. They didn't quit. Twice a month, David went to see a VA psychiatrist, a woman his own age, also a veteran of the sixties, with whom he would share a couple of joints and vigorous assurances that Johnny Ever was no angel, no devil, no ghost, no middleman; that, in fact, the man at the microphone was none other than David himself. This made sense. In a way, somewhere inside him, he'd known all along. He slept better. His dreams went foggy and bland. Only rarely did he hear the murderous drone of the Song Tra Ky.

With Marla, he'd come to an accommodation. Tacitly, as if silence could obliterate pain, they avoided conversations that might wander toward Marla's teacher or David's ordeal at the river. Neither of them asked questions. Neither of them volunteered anything. In 1976, Marla quit her paralegal job and began graduate studies in art history at the University of Minnesota. David's furniture business flourished. On the surface, and sometimes beneath, their lives moved along smoothly enough. They had sex three or four times a month, whenever the pressures accumulated. They ate meals in front of the TV, chatted amiably, laughed sometimes, took vacations, planned an addition to their house, visited with friends, gave up cigarettes, started again, celebrated birthdays and anniversaries, listened to music, bought a new Chevrolet, took up yoga, realized none of it was sufficient.

By early 1978 the calm had become excruciating. They never fought, which was like fighting. Acts of kindness had the bite of bribery.

Yet even then they kept trying.

They put x's and o's at the bottom of their grocery lists. They signed up for ballroom dance lessons. In mid-December of 1978, about a year before the end, they began attending services at a Quaker meetinghouse in St. Paul, where silence was the rule, and where they would sit side by side on sturdy oak benches, exhausted skeptics in search of a miracle. "Man, you just plain don't pay attention," Johnny Ever would whisper. "All this wasted effort, it's like watchin' some poor bastard try to breathe underwater. Go ahead, hyperventilate like the dickens, nature just don't work like that. The woman's fadin' fast, Dave. Them gray eyes, that out-of-here stare. Blind man could see it." Sometimes Johnny would sigh, other times he'd chortle. "An' this church shit, Davy. I'll tell you right now, it didn't do jack for ol' Bonhoeffer. Your Nam buddies, either. Should've heard 'em— 'Dear God, dear God!'—real impressive, except all they ever got for it was hoarse, then dead. See, there's good news, bad news. Bad news: you're gonna end up munchin' your heart out. Good news: everybody dies. Face it now, face it later. I'm church."

In those moments, when the inner dialogue went loopy, David realized he was talking to himself, though it didn't quite seem that way. He'd reach for Marla's hand and grip it hard and wait for something in return, a little pressure, the slightest heat.

"Whoa, Nellie," Johnny would mutter. "You're a scrapper, kid."

Marla met a man in the spring of 1979. She thought it might be love: a younger man, a trader of stocks, a rider of motorcycles, no rivers bubbling through his dreams.

She confessed to David on Christmas Day.

A despicable thing, Marla knew, but the alternative was worse.

She slipped out of bed well before daylight. She went to the kitchen, gazed out the window at a neighbor's Christmas lights, returned to the bedroom, lay down beside David, waited for him to wake up, and then moistened her lips and told him.

David put his face in the pillow. Marla got dressed.

There was no sound.

A light snow was falling.

Marla picked up the phone and called her lover and asked him to wait for her down the street. A moment later, as she was hanging up, the thought arose that for David Todd there would never again be another Christmas.

She had some orange juice, half a muffin.

She packed a small knapsack.

At daybreak, she went out the front door and looked down the street to where a black and red Harley waited in the snow.

"The truth is," said Johnny Ever, "I'm not a bad guy. Not a good guy, either, but give me credit. Big John, he deserves one of them blue ribbons in the tell-it-like-it-is contest. Good or bad, up or down, I calls 'em exactly like I sees 'em: broken heart, side pocket. Not much fun. Everybody blames the messenger. No justice in this world, damn little in the after-world." Johnny sighed. "Got my condolences, man. Heartfelt, et cetera." He sighed again, deeper. "Now comes the tough part."

They divorced in April 1980. The house was sold for a good deal of money, which they split down the middle, and after a month Marla moved with her stockbroker to Chicago, where she taught art history to business majors, remarried, got pregnant, miscarried, grew restless, grew bored, went through a difficult second divorce, and then found herself back in the blues, alone, not quite happy, not quite miserable, which seemed to her the only way to be.

David took up for a while with his psychiatrist. It lasted six weeks. "You can do better," Johnny said. "Fact is, I'm surprised you even considered it. Just some New Age, doped-up mind meddler. Total pagan, too. Know-it-all. Claims I'm a figment. I mean, seriously, the broad's in for a shock when she finds out what I got waitin' on her down the pike." David didn't speak. He had learned to tune out this chatter, to recognize its origins in his own heart and to let it go at that.

In many ways, he now realized, Marla had been right. He'd believed in his own vision of things, and in the end, to a greater or lesser degree, the belief had birthed the facts. He would miss her forever. He would never quit hoping. He would drink too much, smoke too much, care too little about the consequences. He would never remarry. To his last day, and per-haps beyond, he would regret his own failure of nerve, which was also a failure of imagination, the inability to divine a happy ending.

In 1987 Marla returned to the Twin Cities. David met her at the airport. He helped her find an apartment, loaned her a sofa bed and some dishes.

"I hope it's not charity," Marla said.

"It's fondness," said David.

They remained friends.

Once or twice a year, they'd meet in one of the bars near Darton Hall, talking over their lives, wishing each other well. At college reunions they were inseparable.

They held hands and drank together and sometimes slept together. Absently, as if nothing had ever changed, David would sometimes find himself twirling a strand of Marla's hair around his finger, or stroking the small of her back as he talked baseball with an ex-teammate. And for Marla it was the same. A kind of repose. A perfect fit. They seemed destined for each other. They seemed in love. People who knew them well, even some who didn't, would often wonder what went wrong.

Chimamanda Ngozi Adichie

The American Embassy

from *Prism International*

S HE STOOD in line outside the American embassy in Lagos, staring straight ahead, unfolding her arms only to wipe an occasional tear before it crawled down her cheek. She was the forty-eighth person in the line of about two hundred that trailed from the closed gates of the American embassy all the way past the smaller vine-encrusted gates of the Czech embassy. She did not notice the newspaper vendors who blew whistles in her ear and pushed *The Guardian, The New Nigeria,* and *The Vanguard* in her face at the same time. Or the beggars who held out enamel plates, or the ice-cream bicycles that honked. When the man standing behind her tapped her on the back and asked, "Do you have change, *abeg,* two tens for twenty naira?" she started. She stared at him for a while, to focus, to remember where she was, before she shook her head and said, "No."

The air around her hung heavy with moist heat and buzzing flies and anxiety. It weighed on her head, made it difficult to keep her mind blank. To keep her mind as blank as possible was the only way to keep her sanity, Doctor Balogun had said yesterday. He had refused to give her any more tranquilizers because she needed to be alert for the visa interview. To keep her mind blank was easy enough to say, as though it were in her power, as though she invited those images of Nnamdi's plump body crumpling before her, the splash on his chest so red she wanted to laugh and tell him not to play with the palm oil in the kitchen. Not that he could even reach up to the shelf where she kept oils and spices, not that he could unscrew the cap on the plastic bottle of palm oil. He was only three years old.

The man behind her tapped her again. She jerked around and nearly screamed from the sharp pain that ran down her back. Twisted muscle, Doctor Balogun had said, his face awed that she had sustained nothing serious after jumping down from the balcony.

"See what that *yeye* soldier is doing there," the man behind her said, pointing.

She turned to look across the street, moving her neck slowly. A soldier was flogging a bespectacled man with a long whip that curled in the air before it landed on the man's body. A small crowd had gathered. The whip landed on the man's face, or his neck—she wasn't sure because the man was raising his hands as if to ward off the whip. She saw his glasses slip off and fall. She saw the angry heel of the soldier's boot squash the plastic frames, the tinted lenses.

"These soldiers think they are Fulani nomads and people here are their *muturu* cattle," the man behind her said.

He was wondering what was wrong with her, she knew, why she did not talk to anybody in line, why she let the flies perch on her hair without swiping at them, why her arms were so resolutely folded. Everybody in the visa line had become familiar from sharing the same unpleasant experience. They had all woken up close to midnight—for those who had slept at all—to get to the American embassy early enough to join the struggle to get in the visa line. They had all dodged the soldiers' swinging whips as they were herded back and forth like wayward cattle before the line was finally formed. They were all afraid that the American embassy might decide not to open its gates today, and they would have to do it all over again the day after tomorrow, because the embassy did not open on Wednesdays.

"Look at his face *sef*, the whip cut his face," the man behind her said.

She did not look because she knew the blood would be bright red, like fresh palm oil. Instead she looked up Eleke Crescent—a winding street, much like other streets in the posh Victoria Island section of Lagos, lined by embassies with lush lawns—at the crowds of people. A breathing sidewalk. A market really, that sprang up during embassy hours and disappeared when the embassy closed.

There was the chair rental outfit where the stacks of white plastic chairs—one hundred naira for an hour—decreased fast. There were the wooden boards propped on cement blocks, colorfully displaying sweets and mangoes and oranges. There were the young people who cushioned cigarette-filled trays on their heads with rolls of cloth. There were the blind beggars and their children, alternating praise chants in English, Yoruba, Arabic, Igbo, Hausa, when somebody put money in their plates.

And there was, of course, the makeshift photo studio. A tall man standing beside a tripod, holding up a chalk-written sign that read *Excellent One Hour Photos, Correct American Visa Specifications.* She'd had her passport photo taken there, sitting on a rickety stool, and she hadn't been surprised that it came out grainy, with her face much lighter-skinned. But then, she'd had no choice, she couldn't have taken the photo earlier.

Yesterday, she buried her child in Ikoyi cemetery and spent the day surrounded by friends she did not remember now. The day before, she drove her husband in the boot of their Peugeot 504 station wagon to the home of his friend, who smuggled him out of the country. And the day before that, she didn't need to take a passport photo. Her life was normal, and she drove back from her elementary school teacher job singing along with Majek Fashek on the radio. If one of those fortune-tellers who tapped on car windows in Lagos traffic to hawk a future-telling for ten naira told her she would have to run away to America in two days, she would have laughed. Perhaps even paid the fortune-teller ten naira extra for a wild imagination.

"See how the people are pleading with the soldier," the man behind her said. "Our people have become too used to pleading with soldiers."

She wished he would shut up. It was his talking that made it even harder to keep her mind blank, free of Nnamdi. She looked across the street again: the soldier was walking away now, and even from this distance she could see the superior glower on his face. The glower of a grown man who could flog another grown man if he wanted to. Was she imagining it or was it the same glower one of the men had had two nights ago when they'd broken the back door open and barged in?

Where is your husband? Where is he? They tore open the wardrobes in the two rooms, even the drawers—she wished she had told them that her husband was over six feet tall, that he could not possibly hide in a drawer. Three men in black trousers. They smelled of alcohol and pepper soup, and much later, as she held Nnamdi's still body, she knew that she would never eat pepper soup again.

Where has your husband gone? Where? They pressed the gun to her head, and she said, "I don't know, he just left yesterday," standing still even though the warm urine trickled down her legs.

One of them, the one with the green beret who smelled the most like alcohol, had eyes that blazed red. He shouted the most, kicked at the TV set, shredded some papers on the table—tests she had been correcting. *You know about the story your husband wrote? You know he is a liar? You know people like him should be in jail because they cause trouble, because they don't want Nigeria to move forward?*

He sat down on the sofa, where her husband sat to watch the night news, and pulled her atop him, grabbed her left breast. *Fine Woman, why you marry a troublemaker?* She felt his sickening hardness, smelt the fermentation on his breath and held her breath to keep the vomit back.

Leave her alone, the other one said. The one with the white mole on his chin like a fruit seed. *Let's go.*

She got up from the sofa and the man in the green beret, still seated, slapped her buttocks. Nnamdi started to cry, to run to her. The man was laughing, saying how soft her breast was, waving his gun. Nnamdi was screaming now, he never screamed when he cried, he was not that kind of child. Then the gun went off and the palm oil splash appeared on Nnamdi's chest.

"See oranges here," the man in line behind her said, offering her a plastic bag of six peeled oranges. She had not noticed him buy them.

She shook her head. "Thank you."

"Take one. I noticed that you have not eaten anything since morning."

She looked at his face then, for the first time. A complexion the color of roasted groundnuts, too smooth for a man. He sounded educated, even though he laced his speech with pidgin English. Polite of him, because pidgin English was the leveler—it was what both people who had not gone to school and people who were scholars could understand.

"No, thank you," she said. She shook her head again. The pain was still there, somewhere between her eyes. It was as if jumping from the balcony had dislodged something inside her head so that it now rattled painfully. Jumping had not been her only choice, she knew, she could have climbed onto the mango tree whose branch reached across the balcony, she could have dashed down the stairs.

The men had been arguing so loudly that they blocked out reality, and she'd believed for a moment that maybe the popping sound had not been the man's gun, maybe it had been the kind of sneaky thunder that came at the beginning of Harmattan, maybe the red splash really was palm oil, and Nnamdi had gotten into it somehow.

Then their words pulled her back, as she stood, frozen. *It was an accident. What do you mean? You think she will tell people it was an accident? Is this what Oga asked us to do? A small child! We will have to take out the mother. No. Yes. She will tell all but if we take her, nobody to tell. No. Yes.*

She dashed toward the balcony then, tore through the mosquito netting and was out the door she had left open because of the steamy evening air. Later, after she heard the roar of the Jeep driving away, she went upstairs smelling of the rotten plantains in the dustbin where she had crawled in. She held Nnamdi's body, placed her cheek to his quiet chest. And realized that she had never felt so ashamed. She had failed him.

"You are anxious about the visa interview, *abi*?" the man behind her asked.

She shrugged, gently, so as not to hurt her shoulders, and forced a vacant smile.

"I am anxious too, but just make sure to look the interviewer in the eye as you answer the questions. Even if you make a mistake, don't correct yourself, they will assume you are lying, *sha*. I have many friends they have refused, for small-small reason."

She looked away from the man, from his earnest eyes, from his words—which were intended to be helpful, but which consumed her with a fierce anger. He sounded like the voices that had been around her: people who had helped with Nnamdi's funeral, who had brought her to the embassy, who had helped with her husband's escape. The familiar voices of people she could no longer remember.

Look the visa person in the eye, the voices had said. Don't falter, tell them all about Nnamdi, what he was like, but don't overdo it because every day people lie to them to get asylum visas, about dead relatives that were never even born. Make Nnamdi real. Cry. It was as though they were telling her the rules for talking to God.

"They don't give our people immigrant visas anymore, unless the person is rich by American standards. But I hear people from European countries have no problems getting visas. Are you applying for an immigrant visa or a visitor's?" the man asked.

"Asylum." She did not look at his face. Rather, she felt his surprise.

"Asylum? That will be hard to prove."

She wondered if he read *The New Nigeria*, if he knew about her husband. Everyone supportive of the pro-democracy press knew about her husband, knew how daring he was, how he had written that story almost four years ago about the people who pushed cocaine for the Head of State. Soldiers had carted away the entire print run of that edition in a black truck. But still photocopies got out somehow and circulated throughout Lagos, ended up pasted on the walls of bridges next to posters announcing church crusades and just-released movies.

The soldiers had detained her husband for a week, had broken the skin on his forehead with the end of a gun and even now he had the scar, the shape of an L. She had been pregnant then, and he was so scared she would lose the baby from worry that he stopped writing for the paper and accepted a temporary lecturer position at the University of Lagos until Nnamdi was born. She didn't worry too much during that period, though, even when the Democratic Coalition secretary—an acquaintance of her husband's—was shot dead in his car. There was something invincible about her husband, about his square shoulders and cynical eyes and laughing mouth.

And even with his last story that listed forty-five names of people killed on the orders of the Head of State, she had not worried that much either. Maybe they would close the paper down. Maybe they would lock him up for a few days. But it would all blow over. It was not as though Nigerians did not know about disappearances, about people thrown in the Atlantic, about hasty graves spread with lye so the bodies would decompose fast. But only a day after the paper came out, BBC Africa carried the story on the news, and interviewed an exiled Nigerian professor of politics who said her husband deserved a Human Rights award. *He fights repression with the pen, he gives a voice to the voiceless, he makes the world know.* Those words angered her now, filled her with an emotion so fierce it was numbing. Just like the advice for talking to God at the American embassy angered her.

Her husband had tried to hide his nervousness from her, that the story had become so big. But that evening, after someone called him anonymously, he no longer hid his fear, he let her see his shaking hands. He got anonymous calls all the time—he was that kind of journalist, the kind that cultivated friendships along the way. The Head of State was personally furious, the caller told him. Soldiers were on their way to arrest him. The word was it would be the last arrest, he would never come back.

Her husband climbed into the boot of the car minutes after the call, so that, if the soldiers asked, the gatemen could honestly say they did not know when her husband had left. She quickly sprinkled water in the boot, even though he told her to hurry, because she felt somehow that a wet boot would be cooler, that he would breathe better. She drove him to his co-editor's house. The next day, he called her from Togo; the co-editor had contacts who had sneaked him over the border. He had a valid visa to America; America was the best bet for now, until things blew over. She told him not to worry, she and Nnamdi would be fine, she would apply for a visa at the end of the school term, in three weeks, and they would join him in America.

That night, Nnamdi was restless and she let him stay up and play with his toy car while she corrected papers at the dining table. When the three men burst in through the kitchen door, she wished she had insisted that Nnamdi go to bed. If only.

"Many people apply for asylum visa and don't get it," the man behind her was saying. Loudly. Perhaps he had been talking all the while.

"Do you read *The New Nigeria*?" she asked suddenly. She did not turn to face the man; instead she watched the couple in front of her buy mangoes that drew flies and packets of biscuits that crackled as they opened them.

"Yes. Why? Do you want to buy it? The vendors may still have some copies."

"No. I was just asking."

"It's a really good paper. Those two editors, they are the kind of people Nigeria needs. They risk their lives every week to tell us the truth. Brave men."

"Is that what bravery is?" She turned to face him, to look into his eyes.

"Yes, of course. Not all of us can do it." He gave her a long look, righteous and suspicious, as though he was wondering if maybe she was a government apologist, one of those people who criticized the pro-democracy movement, who maintained that only a military government would work in Nigeria.

She turned away from him. Her back was throbbing now and puddles of sweat had settled wetly under her breasts. He didn't know that she was not an apologist or a democracy activist. He didn't know that she was nothing. She had not always been nothing, though. She had once been a woman who yearned for a child, who saw a string of fertility specialists, who was grateful to hear she could have one. One chance. One child.

She watched the beggars make their rounds of the visa line and the crowd on the street, over and over. Rangy men in grimy long tunics who fingered prayer beads and quoted the Koran; women with jaundiced eyes who had sickly babies tied to their backs with threadbare cloth; a blind couple led by their daughter, blue medals of the Blessed Virgin Mary hanging around their tattered collars.

She motioned to the blind couple and fumbled in her bag for a twenty-naira note. When she put it in the bowl, they chanted, "God bless you, you will have money, you will have good husband, you will have good job," in pidgin English and then in Igbo and Yoruba.

She watched them walk away and unfolded her arms to wipe away a tear. They had not told her, "You will have many strong children." She had heard them tell that to the woman in front of the line.

The embassy gates swung open and a man in a brown uniform shouted, "First fifty on the line, come in and fill the forms. All the rest, come back another day. The embassy can attend to only fifty today."

"We are lucky, *abi*," the man behind her said.

She watched the visa interviewer behind the cold glass screen, the way limp blond hair grazed the folded neck, the way green eyes peered at her papers above silver frames as though the glasses were unnecessary.

"Can you go through your story again, Ma'am? You haven't given me any details," the visa interviewer said with an encouraging smile.

She looked away for a moment, sideways at a woman in a bright blue *abada* wrapper who leaned close to the glass screen, reverently, as though praying to the visa interviewer behind. She would die gladly at the hands of the man with the mole, or the one with the beret, or the other nondescript one before she said a word about Nnamdi to her interviewer, or to anybody at the American embassy. Before she hawked Nnamdi for a visa to safety.

Her son had been killed, that was all she would say. Killed. Nothing about how his laughter started somehow above his head, bubbly and frothy. How he called sweets and biscuits "breadie-breadie." How he grasped her neck tight when she held him. How her husband said that he would be an artist, because he didn't try to build with his LEGO blocks, he arranged them, side by side, alternating colors. They did not deserve to know.

"Ma'am? You say it was the government?" the visa interviewer asked.

It was not the government. Government was such a big label, it was freeing, it gave people room to maneuver and excuse and re-blame. It was three men. Three men like her husband or her brother, or the man who taught the class next to hers, or the man behind her in the visa line. Three men.

"Yes. They were government agents," she said.

"Can you prove it? Do you have any evidence to show that?"

"Yes. But I buried it yesterday. My son's body."

"Ma'am, I am sorry about your son. I can't imagine the pain of losing a child," the visa interviewer said, shaking her head slowly. "But I need some evidence that you know it was the government. There is fighting going on between tribes, there are private assassinations. I need some evidence of the government's involvement, and I need some evidence that you will be in danger if you stay on in Nigeria."

She looked at the faded pink lips, moving to show tiny teeth. Faded pink lips in a freckled, insulated face. A face that cared about her in a way that was deep yet shallow, in a way that was generic. A face that she might convince to grant her a visa if she said more, if she unfolded her arms, talked about her husband, about Nnamdi, perhaps cried.

"He was three years old," she said.

"Ma'am, please, I want to help you. You have to help me help you. You need to be more detailed."

She had the sudden urge to ask the visa interviewer if the stories in *The New Nigeria* were worth the life of a child. If what her husband did was really bravery or plain foolhardiness. But she didn't. She doubted that the visa interviewer knew about pro-democracy newspapers. She doubted the visa interviewer knew about the long tired lines outside the embassy gates in cordoned-off areas with no shade where the furious sun caused friendships and headaches and despair.

"Ma'am? The United States offers a new life to victims of political persecution but there needs to be proof. . . ."

A new life. She wanted to plant *ixora* flowers in Ikoyi cemetery, the kind whose needle-thin stalks she had sucked as a child. One plant would do—his plot was so small. When it bloomed, and the flowers welcomed bees, she wanted to pluck and suck at them while squatting in the dirt. And afterwards, she wanted to arrange the sucked flowers side by side, like Nnamdi had done with his LEGO blocks. That was the new life she wanted.

"Ma'am? Ma'am?"

Was she imagining it or was the sympathy draining from the visa interviewer's face? She saw the swift way the woman pushed her corn-colored hair back even though it did not disturb her, it stayed quiet on her neck framing a pale face.

Her future rested on that face. A face that did not understand her, that probably did not cook with palm oil or know that palm oil, when fresh, was a bright bright red and, when not fresh, congealed to a lumpy orange.

She turned slowly and headed for the door.

"Ma'am?" she heard the interviewer's voice behind her. "If you choose to leave now, you will have to re-apply for another interview."

She didn't turn. She walked out of the American embassy, past the beggars who still made their rounds with enamel bowls held outstretched, and got into her car.

William Kittredge

Kissing

from *Idaho Review*

WHEN THEY were young they'd walk out on early springtime mornings, into the vast greening and endless Kansas wheat fields his family had been accumulating through generations, since coming from Russia in the 1870s. They would burrow out of sight in one of the gullies, spread a blanket and oil up. "Let's just work at it," Jennie would say. Her face would glisten with sweat. She'd say it out loud. "Fucking." She'd grin.

Decades later, over martinis, Billy said he'd once thought Jennie hung the sun. "Once?" Jennie said. She found a sort of terrific Japanese restaurant in Kansas City, and they feasted on what she called purity, sashimi and Bombay martinis.

Even if that evening didn't cure the boredom, Jennie said, they shouldn't quit on romance. The next spring, as they were driving in southern France, the discovery of prehistoric painted caverns in the gorge of the Ardèche River was announced. Billy read about it in the English-language *Herald Tribune* while they were eating breakfast on the square in Avignon. "Lions," Billy said. "They've never found paintings of lions before."

But no one would even tell them, when they went to the Ardèche, where the caves were located. So they went to see the nearby site of a famous atrocity, a stone village which had been abandoned after the Nazis had shot all the inhabitants, children included, when they were forced to withdraw from southern France. Wildflowers were blooming, blue and orange. Jennie wouldn't get out of their rented Peugeot.

Near Lascaux, the most famous of the painted caverns, no longer open to the public, Jennie consented to let Billy lead her out to an available cave, called Font-de-Gaume. "This," Billy said, "will be the actual thing."

They went in the early morning. The young Frenchwoman who led them to the cave wore a golden silk blouse, silver beads, and black-and-white Nike shoes like the grade-school kids wore in Kansas City. After weaving along a trail through knee-high grass across a flowering meadow, they came around a grove of trees to face a plywood doorway into a limestone cliff.

The stone cavern was like a trail, cool and narrow, undulating and absolutely dark except for a light carried by the woman leading them. Billy whispered that his hands were shaking. "Like going into an animal," Jennie said. Their leader shone her light on a line of buffalo painted on the bulging limestone above their heads, and reindeer with great sweeping antlers, creatures meandering toward the entrance as if they might escape into the sunlight and the good grazing down by the river.

The young Frenchwoman was holding her light in a way designed to illuminate curling etched lines connected to reddish strokes of ancient paint. "Reindeer," she said to Jennie, speaking English in her French way. "Kissing," Jennie said.

The doe, it had to be the doe because she didn't have antlers, was on her knees facing the interior of the cave. The male was bent to her, licking at her, both their tongues reaching to one another. The sweeps of paint were his antlers. All the rest was cut into the stone itself, etched in tiny incised lines. "They're kissing," Jennie said. She took Billy's hand.

God in heaven, Billy thought, this is pathetic. He began trying to think about lunch, some of that perfect soup, and goose-liver pâté. And, fuck it, he thought, this time a bottle of fifty-dollar wine. But by noontime he was asleep in a bedroom overlooking the river, and Jennie was on the side porch in the heat, face up, naked and sunning her entire body.

William Trevor

Sacred Statues

from *The New Yorker*

T HEY WOULD manage, Nuala had always said when there had been family difficulties before. Each time it was she who saw the family through; her faith in Corry, her calmness in adversity, her stubborn optimism were the strengths she brought to the marriage.

"Would you try Mrs. Falloway?" she suggested when, more seriously than ever in the past, their indigence threatened to defeat them. It was a last resort, the best that desperation could do. "Wouldn't you, Corry?"

Corry said nothing and Nuala watched him feeling ashamed, as he had begun to these last few weeks. It wouldn't be asking much of Mrs. Falloway, she said. Tiding them over for a year while he learnt the way of it in the stoneyard wouldn't be much; and after that he'd be back on wages. The chance in the stoneyard was made for him; didn't O'Flynn say it himself?

"I couldn't go near Mrs. Falloway. I couldn't at all."

"Only to put it to her, Corry. Only to say out what's the truth."

"It came to nothing, what she was doing that time. Why'd she be interested in us now?"

"All she saw in you'll be lost if we don't get assistance, Corry. Why wouldn't she still take an interest?"

"It's all in the past, that."

"I know, I know."

"I'd be embarrassed going over there."

"Don't I know that, too, Corry?"

"There's work going on the roads."

"You're not a roadworker, Corry."

"There's things we have to do."

Deliberately Nuala let a silence gather, and Corry broke it, as she knew he would.

"I'd be a day going over there," he said and might have added that there'd be the bus fare and something to pay for the loan of a bicycle in Carrick, but he didn't.

"A day won't hurt, Corry."

They were a couple of the same age, thirty-one, who'd known one another since childhood: Corry tall and bony, Nuala plumper and smaller, with a round, uncomplicated face, her fair hair cut shorter than it had been when she'd first become a wife. The youngest of their children, a girl, took after her in appearance; the boys were both as lean and gangling as their father.

"You always did your best, Corry." The statement hung there, concluding their conversation, necessary because it was true, its repetition softening the crisis in their lives.

Corry's workshop was a shed, all his saints in a row on a shelf he had put up. Beneath them were his Madonnas, his John the Baptist, and a single Crucifixion. His Stations were there, too, propped against the rough concrete wall. Limewood and ash the woods were, apple and holly and box, oak that had come from a creamery paddle.

When the children left the house in the mornings, to be picked up at Quirke's crossroads and driven on to school, when Corry was out looking for work on a farm, Nuala often took pride in her husband's gift; and in the quiet of his workshop she often wondered how it would have been between them if he did not possess it, how she would feel about him if he'd been the master in a school or a counter hand in one of the shops in Carrick, or permanently on a farm.

Corry's saints had become her friends, Nuala sometimes thought, statues brought to life for her, a source of sympathy, and consolation when that was necessary. "And Jesus Fell the Second Time" were the words beneath the Station that was her favorite. Neither saints nor Stations belonged in a concrete shed, any more than the figures of the Virgin did,

or any of the other carvings. They belonged in the places they'd been created for, the inspiration of their making becoming there the inspiration of
prayer. Nuala was certain that this was meant to be, that in receiving his
gift Corry had been entrusted with seeing that this came about. "You were
meant for other times, Corry," a priest had remarked to him once, but not
unkindly or dismissively, as if recognizing that even if the present times
were different from those he spoke of, Corry would persevere. A waste of
himself, it would be otherwise, a waste of the person he was.

Nuala closed the shed door behind her. She fed her hens and then
walked through the vegetable patch she cultivated herself.

Mrs. Falloway would understand: she had before, she would again. The
living that Corry's gift failed to make for him would come naturally when
he had mastered the craft of cutting letters on headstones in O'Flynn's
yard. The headstones were a different kind of thing from his sacred statues
but they'd be enough to bring his skill to people's notice, to the notice of
bishops and priests as well as anyone else's. Sooner or later everyone did
business in a stoneyard; when he'd come to the house to make the offer
O'Flynn had said that, too.

In the field beyond Nuala's vegetable garden the tethered goat jerked
up its head and stared at her. She loosened the chain on the tether post and
watched while the goat pawed at the new grass before eating it. The fresh,
cool air was sharp on her face and for a moment, in spite of the trouble,
she was happy. At least this place was theirs: the field, the garden, the
small, remote house that she and Corry had come to when Mrs. Falloway
lent them the asking price, so certain was she that Corry would one day be
a credit to her. While still savoring this moment of elation, Nuala felt it
slipping away. Naturally, it was possible that Corry would not succeed in
the mission she had sent him on: optimist or not, she was still close to the
reality of things. In the night she had struggled with that, wondering how
she should prepare him, and herself, for the ill fortune of his coming back
empty-handed. It was then that she had remembered the Rynnes. They'd
come into her thoughts as she imagined an inspiration came to Corry; not
that he ever talked like that, but still she felt she knew. She had lain awake
going over what had occurred to her, rejecting it because it upset her,
because it shocked her even to have thought of it. She prayed that Mrs.
Falloway would be generous, as she had been before.

. . .

When Corry reached the crossroads he waited at the petrol pumps for the bus to Carrick. It was late but it didn't matter, since Mrs. Falloway didn't know he was coming. On the way down from the house he'd considered trying to telephone, to put it to her if she was still there what Nuala had put to him, to save himself the expense of the journey. But when first she'd brought the subject up Nuala had said that this wasn't something that could be talked about on the phone even if he managed to find out Mrs. Falloway's number, which he hadn't known in the past.

In Carrick, at Hosey's bicycle shop, he waited while the tires of an old Raleigh were pumped up for him. New batteries were put in the lamp in case he returned after dark, although he kept assuring young Hosey that it wouldn't be possible to be away for so long: the bus back was at three.

It was seven miles to Mountroche House, mostly on a flat bog road bounded by neither ditches nor fencing. Corry remembered it from the time he and Nuala had lived in Carrick, when he'd worked in the Riordans' joinery business and they'd had lodgings in an upstairs room at her mother's. It was then that he began to carve his statues, his instinctive artistry impressing the Riordan brothers, and Mrs. Falloway when the time came. It surprised Corry himself, for he hadn't known it was there.

Those times, the first few years of marriage, cheered him as he rode swiftly on. It could be that Nuala was right, that Mrs. Falloway would be pleased to see him, that she'd understand why they hadn't been able to pay anything back. Nuala had a way of making good things happen, Corry believed; she told you what they might be and then you tried for them.

The flatness of the bog, and the road that went with it, gave way eventually to hills; hedges and trees began. Mountroche House was at the end of an unkempt avenue that continued for another three-quarters of a mile. He had to wheel the bicycle for most of it.

The Rynnes lived in a gray, pebble-dashed bungalow at the crossroads, close to the petrol pumps they operated, across the main road from Quirke's Supervalu. They were well-to-do; besides the petrol business, there was Rynne's insurance agency, which he conducted from the bungalow. His wife attended to the custom at the pumps.

When Nuala rang the doorbell the Rynnes answered it together. They had a way of doing that when both of them were in; and they had a way of conducting their visitors no further than the hall until the purpose of the interruption was established. An insurance matter was usually enough to permit further access.

"I was passing by," Nuala said, "on my way to the Supervalu."

The Rynnes nodded. Their similar elongated features suggested that they might be brother and sister rather than man and wife. They both wore glasses, Rynne's dark-rimmed and serious, his wife's light and pale. They were a childless couple.

"Is it insurance, Nuala?" Rynne inquired.

She shook her head. She'd just looked in, she said, to see how they were getting on. "We often mention you," she said, taking a liberty with the facts.

"Arrah, we're not bad at all," Rynne said. "All right, would you say, Etty?"

"Oh, I would, I would."

The telephone rang and Rynne went to answer it. Nuala could hear him saying he was up to his eyes this morning. "Would tomorrow do?" he suggested. "Would I come up in the evening?"

"I'm sorry, Etty. You're busy."

"It's only I'm typing his proposals. God, it takes your time, and the pumps going too! Twenty-six blooming pages, every one of them!"

In spite of its plaintive note, it was cheerful talk, relegating to its place beneath the surface what had been disguised when Rynne said they were all right; neither Etty Rynne's failure to become pregnant nor the emotional toll it had taken of both husband and wife was ever mentioned by them, but the fact and its consequences were well known in the neighborhood. It was even said that dishearteningly fruitless inquiries had been made regarding the possibility of adoption.

"Goodbye so, Etty." Nuala smiled and nodded before she left, the sympathy of a mother in her eyes. She would have liked to commiserate, but spoken words would have been tactless.

"You're all well above, Nuala?"

"We are."

"Tell Corry I was asking for him."

"I will of course."

Nuala wheeled her bicycle across the road and propped it against the side wall of Quirke's Supervalu. While she was shopping—searching for the cheap lines with a sell-by date due, bundling the few items she could afford into a wire basket—she thought about the Rynnes. She saw them almost as visibly as she had ten minutes ago seen the faraway, sorrowful look in Etty's pale-brown eyes; she heard the unvoiced disappointment that, in both husband and wife, dwindled into weariness. They had given up already, not knowing that they needn't yet; all that, again, passed through Nuala's reflections.

She went on thinking about the Rynnes as she rode away from the crossroads, up the long hill to her house. They were decent people, tied into themselves only because of their childlessness, because of what the longing had done to them. She remembered them as they'd been when first they'd married, the winter card parties they invited people to, Etty like a fashion plate for each occasion, the stories Rynne brought back from his business travels.

"Would it be wrong?" Nuala whispered to herself, since there was no one there to hear. "Would it be against God?"

Unhooking her shopping bags from the handlebars when she reached the house, she asked herself the same questions again, her voice loud now in the stillness. If Corry did well with Mrs. Falloway, there wouldn't be a need to wonder if it would be wrong. There wouldn't even be a need— when years had gone by and they looked back to the bad time there'd been—to mention to Corry what had come into her mind. If Mrs. Falloway came up trumps you'd make yourself forget it, which was something that could be done if you tried.

It was a white house, for the most part, though gray and green in places where the color wash was affected. Roches had lived at Mountroche for generations, until the family came to an end in the nineteen-fifties; Mrs. Falloway had bought it cheaply after it had been empty for seventeen years.

Corry heard the bell jangling in the depths, but no one answered the summons. On the bus and as he rode across the bog he had worried in case Mrs. Falloway had gone, in case years ago she had returned to England; when he jerked the bellpull for the third time he worried again. Then there was a sound somewhere above which he stood. A window opened and Mrs. Falloway's voice called down.

"Mrs. Falloway?" He stepped backward onto the gravel in order to look up. "Mrs. Falloway?"

"Yes, it's me. Hullo."

"Hullo, Mrs. Falloway."

He wouldn't have recognized her and wondered if she recognized him after so long. He said who he was.

"Oh, of course," Mrs. Falloway said. "Wait a minute for me."

When she opened her hall door she was welcoming. She smiled and held a hand out. "Come on, come in."

They passed through a shabby hall and sat in a drawing room that smelt of must. The cold ashes of a fire were partly covered with dead hydrangeas, deposited there from a vase. The room seemed choked with what littered its surfaces: newspapers and magazines, drawings, books face downward as if to mark a place, empty fruit punnets, bric-a-brac in various stages of repair, a summer hat, a pile of clothes beside a workbasket.

"You've come on a bicycle, Corry?" Mrs. Falloway said.

"Only from Carrick. I got the bus to Carrick."

"My dear, you must be exhausted. Let me give you tea at the very least."

Mrs. Falloway was gone for nearly twenty minutes, causing Corry some agitation when he thought of the three-o'clock bus. He and Nuala had sat waiting in this room when they'd come to the house the first time, after Corry got the letter. They'd sat together on the sofa that was a receptacle for oddments now; the room had been tidier then, Mrs. Falloway had been brisker. She'd talked all the time, full of her plans, a table laid in the big bow window to which she brought corned beef and salad, and toast that was moist with the butter she'd spread, and Kia-Ora orange, and tea and fruitcake.

"Not much, I'm afraid," she said now, returning with a plate of biscuits, and cups and saucers and a teapot. The biscuits were decorated with a pink mush of marshmallow and raspberry jam.

Corry was glad of the tea, which was strong and hot. The biscuit he took had gone soft, but even so he liked it. Once in a while Nuala bought the same kind for the children.

"What a lovely surprise!" Mrs. Falloway said.

"I wondered were you still here."

"I'm here forever now, I think."

A dismal look had crept into her face, as if she knew why he had come. If she'd thought about it, she would have guessed long ago about the plight they were in. He wasn't here to say it was her fault; he hoped she didn't think that, because of course it wasn't. All the blame was his.

"I'm sorry we didn't manage to pay anything back," he said.

"You weren't expected to, Corry."

She was a tall woman, seeming fragile now. When she was younger her appearance had been almost intimidating: determination had influenced the set of her features and seemed to be there again in her wide mouth and saucer eyes, in her large hands as they gestured for attention. Swiftly her smile had become stern or insistent; now it was vaguely beseeching; her piled-up hair, which Corry remembered as black with a few strands of gray, had no black left in it. There was a tattered look about her that went with the room they were in.

"You have children now, Corry?"

"We have three. Two boys and a girl."

"You're finding work?"

He shook his head. "It never got going," he said. "All that."

"I'm sorry, Corry."

Soon after Mrs. Falloway bought Mountroche House and came to live there she had attended the funeral of the elderly widow who'd been the occupant of the Mountroche gate lodge. Being, as she put it, a black Protestant from England, who had never, until then, entered an Irish Catholic church, she had not before been exposed to such a profusion of plaster statues as at that funeral Mass. *I hope you do not consider it interference from an outsider,* she wrote in her first letter to Bishop Walshe, *but it is impossible not to be aware of the opportunity there is for young craftsmen and artists.* With time on her hands, she roved Bishop Walshe's diocese in her Morris Minor, taking photographs of grottoes that featured solitary Virgin Marys or Pietàs, or towering Crucifixions. How refreshing it would be, she said enthusiastically to Bishop Walshe when eventually she visited him, to see the art of the great high crosses of Ireland brought into the modern Church, to see Nativities and Annunciations in stained glass, to have old lecterns and altar furniture replaced with contemporary forms. She left behind in the Bishop's hall a selection of postcards she had obtained from Italy, reproductions of the bas-reliefs of Mino da Fiesole and details from the pulpit in Siena Cathedral. When she had compiled a list of craftsmen, she wrote to all of them and visited those who lived within a reasonable distance of Mountroche House. To numerous priests and bishops she explained that what was necessary was to bring wealth and talent together; but for the most part she met with opposition and indifference. Several bishops wrote back crossly, requesting her not to approach them again.

Breaking in half another biscuit, Corry remembered the letter he had received himself. "Will you look at this!" he had exclaimed the morning it arrived. Since he had begun to carve figures in his spare time at the joinery he had been aware of a vocation, of wishing to make a living in this particular way, and Mrs. Falloway's letter reflected entirely what he felt: that the church art with which he was familiar was of poor quality. Who on earth is she? he wondered in bewilderment when he'd read the letter through several times. Less than a week later Mrs. Falloway came to introduce herself.

"I've always been awfully sorry," she repeated now. "Sorrier than I can say."

"Ah, well."

When it was all over, all her efforts made, her project abandoned, Mrs. Falloway had written in defeat to a friend of her distant school days. *Well, yes, I am giving up the struggle. There is a long story to tell, which must wait until next you come for a few summer weeks. Enough to say, that everything has changed in holy Ireland.* Mrs. Falloway spoke of that to Corry now, of her feelings at the time, which she had not expressed to him before. The Church had had enough on its hands, was how she put it; the appearance of things seemed trivial compared with the falling away of congregations and the tide of secular attack. Without knowing it, she had chosen a bad time.

"It was guilt when I gave you that poor little house, Corry. I'd misled you with my certainties that weren't certainties at all. A galumphing English-woman!"

"Ah no, no."

"Ah yes, I'm afraid. I should have restrained you, not urged you to give up your employment in the joinery."

"I wanted to."

"You're hard up now?"

"We are a bit, to tell the truth."

"Is that why you've come over?"

"Well, it is."

She shook her head. There was another pause and then she said, "I'm hard up myself, as things are."

"I'm sorry about that."

"Are you in a bad way, Corry?"

"O'Flynn'll give me a place in the stoneyard at Guileen. He's keen because I'd learn the stone quickly, the knowledge I have with the wood. It's not like he'd be taking on a full apprentice. It's not like the delay there'd be until some young fellow'd get the hang of it."

"You'd be lettering gravestones?"

"I would. He'd put me on wages after a twelvemonth. The only thing is, I'd be the twelvemonth without a penny. I do a few days on a farm here and there if there's anything going, but I'd have to give that up."

"The stoneyard seems the answer then."

"I'd be in touch with anyone who'd maybe be interested in the statues. I'd have them by me in the yard. A priest or a bishop still looking for something would maybe hear tell I could do a Stations. O'Flynn said that to Nuala."

They went on talking. Mrs. Falloway poured out more tea. She pressed Corry to have another biscuit.

"I'd have the wages steady behind me," Corry said, "once we managed the year. I'd ride over to Guileen every morning on the bike we have, no problem at all."

"I haven't money, Corry."

There was a quietness in the room then, neither of them saying anything, but Corry didn't go at once. After a few moments they talked about the time in the past. Mrs. Falloway offered to cook something, but Corry said no. He stood up as he did so, explaining about the three-o'clock bus.

At the hall door Mrs. Falloway again said she was sorry, and Corry shook his head.

"Nuala's tried for work herself only there's nothing doing. There's another baby coming," Corry said, feeling he should pass that on also.

When Nuala heard, she said it had been a forlorn hope anyway, and when Corry described the state of Mountroche House she felt sorry for Mrs. Falloway, whose belief in Corry had always seemed to Nuala to be a confirmation of the sacred nature of his gift, as if Mrs. Falloway had been sent into their lives to offer that encouragement. Even though her project had failed, it was hardly by chance that she had come to live only fourteen miles from Carrick at a time when Corry was employed in the Riordans' joinery; and hardly by chance that she'd become determined in her intentions when she saw the first of his saints. He'd made the little figure of St. Brigid for Father Ryan to set in the niche in St. Brigid's parish hall even though Father Ryan couldn't pay him anything for it. Whenever Nuala was in Carrick she called in at the parish hall to look again at it, remembering her amazement—similar to Mrs. Falloway's—when she'd first seen it. "He has a right way with a chisel," O'Flynn said when he'd made his offer of employment in the stoneyard. "I don't know did I ever see better." For Nuala it was all of a piece—the first of the saints, and Mrs. Falloway coming to live nearby, and O'Flynn's offer when they'd nearly given up hope. She could feel it in her bones that that was how it was.

"Rest yourself," she urged Corry in the kitchen, "while I'll get the tea."

"They all right?"

The children were out playing in the back field, she said; they'd been no trouble since they'd come in. She spread out rashers of streaky bacon on the pan that was warming on the stove. She'd gone down to the Supervalu, she said, and Corry told her how he'd nearly missed the bus back.

"He was drawing away. I had to stop him."

"I shouldn't have sent you over on that awful old trek, Corry."

"Ah no, no. To tell you the truth, it was good to see her. Except she was a bit shook."

He talked about the journey on the bus, the people on it when he was coming back. Nuala didn't mention the Rynnes.

"Glory be to God!" Etty Rynne exclaimed. She felt shaky so she sat down, on a chair by the hall stand. "I don't think I understood you," she said, although she knew she had. She listened, not wanting to, when Nuala went into it. "It'd be April," Nuala said and repeated the sum of money she had mentioned already. Late April, she thought, maybe just into May. She'd never been early, she said.

"Himself would say it was against the law, Nuala. I'd wonder was it myself."

The daylight in the hall had blurs of blue and pink in it from the colored panes on either side of the front door. It was a dim, soft light because of that, and while she tried to gather her thoughts together Etty Rynne found herself thinking that its cloudiness was suitable for the conversation that was being conducted—neither of them able to see the other's face clearly, her own incomprehension.

"It would be confidential between us," Nuala said, "that there was money."

Not meaning to, and in a whisper, Etty Rynne repeated that. A secret was what was meant: a secret kept forever between the four of them, a secret that was begun already because Nuala had waited for the car to drive off, maybe watching from the Supervalu's windows. She'd have seen him walking out of the bungalow; when the car had gone she'd have crossed the road.

"Listen to me, Etty."

Corry's statues came into what Nuala said, the wooden figures he made, the Blessed Virgin and the saints, St. Brigid in the St. Brigid's Hall in Carrick. And Nuala trying for work in the Supervalu and anywhere she could think of came into it. With the baby due she'd be tied down, but she'd have managed somehow if there was work, only there wasn't. How Corry had drawn a blank with a woman whose name was unfamiliar came into it. And O'Flynn who had the stoneyard at Guileen did.

"O'Flynn has his insurances with us." For a moment in her mind's eye Etty Rynne saw the bulky gray-haired stonemason, who always dropped the premiums in himself in case they went astray, who afterward drew his Peugeot pickup in at the pumps for a fill-up. It was a relief when all that flickered in Etty Rynne's memory, after the shock that had left her weak in the legs and wanting to gasp and not being able to.

"It's a long time since you put the room ready, Etty."

"Did I show it to you?"

"You did one time."

She used to show it to people, the small room at the back of the bungalow that she'd painted a bright buttercup shade, the door and windowsills in white gloss.

"It's still the same," she said.

"That's what I was thinking."

She'd made the curtains herself, blue that matched the carpet, dolls playing ring-a-roses on them. They'd never bought furniture for the little room. Tempting Providence it would be, he said.

"There'd be no deception," Nuala said. "No lie, nothing like that. Only the money side kept out of it."

Etty nodded. Like a dream, it was disordered and peculiar: the ring at the door and Nuala smiling there, and standing in the hall with Nuala and having to sit down, her face going red and then the blood draining out of it when Nuala asked if she had savings in the bank or in a credit society, and mentioning the sum that would be enough.

"I couldn't take your baby off of you, Nuala."

"I wouldn't be deprived. I'd have another one, maybe two or three. A bit of time gone by and people would understand."

"Oh God, I doubt they would."

"It isn't against the law, Etty. No way."

"I couldn't. I never could." Pregnancy made you fanciful sometimes and she wondered if it was that that had got at Nuala. She didn't say it in case it made things worse. Slowly she shook her head. "God, I couldn't," she said again.

"Nowadays if a man and woman can't have a baby there's things can be done."

"I know, I know."

"Nowadays—"

"I couldn't do what you're saying, Nuala."

"Is it the money?"

"It's everything, Nuala. It's what people'd say. He'd blow his head off if he knew what you're after suggesting. It would bring down the business, he'd say. Nobody'd come near us."

"People—"

"They'd never come round to it, Nuala."

A silence came, and the silence was worse than the talk. Then Nuala said, "Would we sit down to a cup of coffee?"

"God, I'm sorry. Of course we will."

She could feel sweat on the sides of her body and on her neck and her forehead. The palms of her hands were cold. She stood up and it was better than before.

"I didn't mean to upset you, Etty."

"Come into the kitchen."

Filling the kettle, spooning Nescafé into two cups, pouring in milk, Etty Rynne felt her jittery unease beginning to recede, leaving her with stark astonishment. She knew Nuala well. She'd known her since they were six, when first they'd been at school together. There had never been any sign whatsoever of stuff like this: Nuala was what she looked like, down-to-earth and sensible, both feet on the ground.

"The pregnancy? Would it be that, Nuala?"

"It's no different from the others. It's just that I thought of the way things are with you. And with Corry, talking about going to work on the roads."

Two troubles, Etty Rynne heard then, and something good drawn out of them when you'd put them together. That's all it was, Nuala said; no more than that.

"What you said will never go outside these four walls," Etty Rynne promised. "Nor mentioned within them, either." It was a woman's thing, whatever it was. Wild horses wouldn't drag the conversation they'd had out of her. "Didn't you mean well? Don't I know you did?"

The coffee calmed their two different moods. They walked through the narrow hall together and a cold breeze blew in when the front door was opened. A car drew up at the petrol pumps and Etty Rynne hurried to attend to it. She waved when Nuala rode away from the crossroads on the bicycle she shared with her husband.

"It's how it is," Corry said when he rejected O'Flynn's offer of a place in the stoneyard, and he said it again when he agreed to work on the roads.

Stubbornly, Nuala considered that it needn't be how it was. It was ridiculous that there should live within a mile of one another a barren wife and a statue maker robbed by adverse circumstances of his purpose in God's world. It was stupid and silly and perverse, when all that had to be done was to take savings out of a bank. The buttercup-yellow room so lovingly prepared would never now be occupied. In the tarmac surfaces he laid on roads Corry would see the visions he had betrayed.

Nuala nursed her anger, keeping it to herself. She went about her tasks, collecting eggs from where her hens had laid, preparing food, kneading dough for the bread she made every second day; and all the time her anger nagged. It surely was not too terrible a sin, too redolent of insidious presumption, that people should impose an order of their own on what they were given? Had she been clumsy in her manner of putting it to Etty Rynne? Or wrong not to have revealed her intentions to Corry, in the hope that, with thought, he would have accepted the sense of them? But doubt spread then; Corry never would have. No matter how it had been put, Etty Rynne would have been terrified.

Corry bought new boots before he went to work on the roads. They were doing a job on the quarry boreen, he said, resurfacing it because of the complaints there'd been from the lorry drivers. A protective cape was supplied to him in case there'd be rain.

On the night before his new work began Nuala watched him applying waterproof stuff to the boots and rubbing it in. They were useless without it, he'd been told. He took it all in his stride.

"Things happen differently," he said, as if something in Nuala's demeanor allowed him to sense her melancholy. "We're never in charge."

She didn't argue; there was no point in argument. She might have confessed instead that she had frightened Etty Rynne; she might have tried to explain that her wild talk had been an effort to make something good out of what there was, as so often she had seen the spread of angels' wings emerging from roughly sawn wood. But all that was too difficult, so Nuala said nothing.

Her anger was still merciless when that day ended; and through the dark of the night she felt herself oppressed by it and bleakly prayed, waiting for a response that did not come. She reached out in the morning dusk to hold for a moment her husband's hand. Had he woken she would have told him all she had kept to herself, unable now to be silent.

But it was Corry's day that was beginning, and it was he who needed sympathy and support. Making breakfast for him and for her children, Nuala gave him both as best she could, banishing from her mood all outward traces of what she knew would always now be private. When the house was empty again but for herself, she washed up the morning's dishes and tidied the kitchen as she liked to have it. She damped the fire down in the stove. Outside, she fed her hens.

In Corry's workshop she remained longer than she usually did on her morning visit to the saints who had become her friends: St. Lawrence with his gridiron, St. Gabriel the messenger, St. Clare of Assisi, St. Thomas the Apostle and blind St. Lucy, St. Catherine, St. Agnes. Corry had made them live for her and she felt the first faint slipping away of her anger as they returned her gaze with undisturbed tranquillity. Touched by it, lost in its peace, she sensed their resignation, too. The world, not she, had failed.

Molly Giles

Two Words

from *Missouri Review*

R OY GOT up at five to start cooking for the firemen. He had been getting up at dawn for weeks now anyway, ever since the last seizure, but usually he just read his affirmations and practiced tai chi in front of the turned-off television set. Today he wanted to talk. He couldn't wake Jill; she needed her sleep, and as their marriage counselor had pointed out, she also needed plain and simple "time out" because Roy (and Roy knew this and was sorry) was driving her crazy. So Roy slipped out of bed and went to his daughter's room. Baby Tess lifted her arms and allowed herself to be carried to the kitchen, but she squirmed and covered her ears with her blanket the minute he opened his mouth, so Roy had no choice but to address God as he understood Him.

Or Her. For Roy's God was a girl, about twelve years old, slim and lazy with lit, dewy eyes and sharp little teeth. She could be generous and fond one minute and casually vicious the next. He had felt Her sour breath on his neck since his childhood but only named Her God and honored Her as such since the diagnosis of his brain tumor six months ago. By trial and error he had also discovered, at about the same time, that the best way to treat Her was with extravagant respect. No matter how badly She herself behaved, She expected good manners from him. She especially liked to be thanked.

Thank You, God, he said silently, sitting naked on the kitchen floor among the tumbled cookbooks with his palms turned up and his closed eyelids jumping as fast as his pulse, *for all the people I've known who are up there with You now, including* (he counted) *mother, father, stepmother one, stepmother two and Leslie, poor Leslie. May they be filled with lovingkindness. And in the meantime, thank You for keeping me away from them and letting me live with these beloved strangers down here a while longer. Thank You for the Zen Center, the Positive Center, WellSpring and Esalen. Thank You for chemo and radiation and antidepressants and aspirin and medical insurance. Thank You for all the doctors, even the last one.* He paused and passed one hand over his bald head, pleased as always by the plush resilience of skin over skull. *Thank You for giving me a nice round head. Thank You for making it the color of mozzarella.* Thinking of mozzarella made him remember the lasagna he had promised the firemen. *Thank You,* he finished, palms tingling, eyelids twitching, Baby Tess poking at the dragonfly tattoo on his thigh, *for helping me find the right recipe.*

He had spent the day before at the library, going through cookbooks. He had explained to the librarians that he wanted a recipe that was saucy and cheesy and rich, and it was astonishing both to him and the two helpful women how many so-called good cookbooks called for low-fat cottage cheese in place of ricotta, yogurt in place of white sauce, ground turkey or even sliced zucchini in place of sausage and beef. Some chefs used no salt; others relied on oregano only, and none gave directions for making the noodles from scratch. He had no luck finding the recipe he'd used as a boy, working alone in his father's bachelor apartment, but Martha Stewart, of all people, had a cookbook that offered a passable compromise, and if he combined it with recipes from four other books, he knew he'd have a killer dish, fit for firemen.

"Roy!" Jill said, coming into the kitchen. "What are you doing?" She stopped. The marriage counselor had told her not to assign blame. "Are you all right?" she asked, her voice intent on softening.

"I'm fine." Roy opened his eyes, flexed his palms and smiled. He always smiled when he saw Jill. She was so pretty and young and quick. Her eyes matched the blue of her bathrobe, the blue of the ribbon around her long, drooping ponytail. She was the best thing that had ever happened to him; he told her that all the time, and at first she used to chime in and say, *No, you* are the best thing that had ever happened to *me,* but she didn't say that anymore. "I knew there would be problems," Jill had told the counselor.

Last week? The week before? "I mean, he's ten years older and widowed and had a baby, but I never thought there would be problems like this. I never imagined this."

Who could? First the trouble with his balance. Then the memory loops. Handwriting shot. Headaches like train wrecks. "And now," Jill had said, "I have two children. Two children and I've never even been pregnant!" She'd started to laugh, but then she burst into tears and Roy had sunk into a ball, right there on the counselor's carpet, curled up, hugging his ankles, rocking back and forth, crying too, so sorry he'd done this to her, so sorry! Until at last she reached down and said, "It's all right." But it wasn't. It couldn't be. What had he cooked for poor Jill on their first date? Wild duck? Caviar risotto?

Thinking of food made him jiggle Baby Tess off his thigh and hand her to Jill, who cupped her up incompetently and stood there looking at him. Beauties, both of them. "I'm a lucky man," he said as Jill carried Baby Tess back to her crib. He stood, waited until the dizziness sank and he was sure he was not going to keel over, then tied an apron over his bare belly, found his reading glasses by the phone and opened the cookbooks to their marked places. Make the noodles first. Then the three sauces. Assemble. For dessert, good vanilla ice cream, fresh strawberries and the same chocolate-chip cookies he'd made for the boy after his first seizure, when he'd writhed in the rain in the middle of the street until the delivery van braked for him. He could still hear the boy's high, astounded voice. *You're fucking lucky to be alive, man. You're a miracle man.* And he was. Nothing but a bruised hip from that one. And other miracles followed. A dislocated shoulder from a fall in the shower had been fixed with one good whack from the chiropractor. A tumble off the roof that should have broken his neck only banged up one knee. Jill had yanked his arm back in time from the garbage disposal. God had screamed, "Truck!" in his ear the last day he'd driven. He'd swerved off the road, and though he'd cut his eyebrow on the steering wheel there was no mark now. Odd, the parts of the body that decided to heal, while the tumor wavered, shrinking and then swelling again, capricious. Five years, one doctor had said. Five minutes, the last one had said.

He shook out his morning dose of deadly meds, swallowed them down with Willard's Water, and began to measure out flour for the pasta. After a while, excited by the elasticity of the dough beneath his hands as he kneaded, he forgot his promise to be quiet if he got up early, opened his mouth and started to sing.

Jill heard him, but she wasn't mad. She smiled when she came back in to make coffee, a slight smile, not granting much, but enough to let him know that the sight of a bald man draping noodles to dry over the backs of kitchen chairs dressed in nothing but an apron and a tattoo while singing "You Are the Sunshine of My Life" was all right, was fine, was funny, was sweet. She had not smiled at all last month—was it last month? month before?—when he'd risen at dawn to rearrange the living room. She had not liked the feng shui; he'd had to put everything back. She'd been upset when he'd cut the plum tree down—it almost fell on the house—and after he'd pulled up the carpet to expose the genuine, if battered, parquet underneath, she'd forbidden him to refinish the floors. But since the last seizure, on the hiking trail, she'd been gentler. And now, as she opened the refrigerator for milk, saw the packages of ground beef and Italian sausage he'd forgotten to add to the tomato sauce, she was almost as upset for him as he was for himself.

"I want the firemen to like us," Roy explained, fighting tears as he sautéed more garlic and added the meat. He leaned over the flaming pan and tried to kiss Jill on the cheek. She gasped and reached for the handle in time. "I want them to *like you*," he added, chastised, moving back as she waved him toward a chair. "I want one of them to like you a lot."

"You're not making sense," Jill sighed.

She said that often.

But she was wrong.

"You can't really be mad at him." He heard her on the phone later that day as he was painting Baby Tess's toenails. She'd wanted blue. "It's the medication he's on. They change it every week. They don't know what they're doing." He blew on Baby Tess's toes until they were dry, then fitted one fat foot into a new red sandal.

"Ready to walk to the store?" he asked.

"No," Baby Tess said. "Store."

He looked into her fierce eyes. "You are just like your mother," he revealed. Baby Tess, who had never known Leslie and thought Jill was her mother, raised a fist, and he kissed it.

"I'll say one thing about those firemen," Jill paused. He could actually hear her lick her lips across the length of the room. "Eye candy. Total eye candy."

Good, Roy thought. He smiled as he fitted the second sandal onto Baby Tess's foot. So Jill had noticed after all. He just hoped she'd notice the right one. Two of the firemen had given him CPR, two others had carried him down the trail on a stretcher, but it was the tall, strong one who had stayed with him in the ambulance, soothing Jill in a deep voice, whom he was counting on. Stu. The chief. Roy pulled on his beret and followed Baby Tess to the front door. "'Bye, love," he called. "We're going to the store." Baby Tess opened her mouth to scream. "Park," he amended. "I'll be back in time to make the cookies." Jill, on the phone, giggled throatily, ignoring him. Am I jealous? he wondered. He shut the door and trudged down the driveway. He hoped he wasn't jealous. It was all right for Baby Tess to be like her, but he himself did not want to be like Leslie.

Leslie. His first wife. The one who had died. Leslie's last days had been so miserable that Roy had taken them to heart as life's lesson. No whining for him, no complaining, none of that Why Me—it just made things worse. Who knew why God dumped a bucket of bad luck on one person and slipped a promise ring onto the finger of another? It made no sense. Leslie had had a grotesque life. She'd been orphaned as a baby, abused as a child, abandoned as a teenager. He'd been thrilled by her nervy blond looks and her easy, articulate self-pity. He'd cooked—what had he cooked for Leslie on their wedding night?—rack of lamb in pomegranate sauce? And then, with no warning, she'd been stricken with a debilitating and very rare neurological disease. It was a joke; it was no joke. She was paralyzed. The pregnancy she refused to terminate was a horror; she was blind, crippled, furious. She blamed him; she blamed Baby Tess. She sat in the dark and begged for a gun, over and over, *Just get me a gun, goddam you, do something right for once.* She'd probably be deeply gratified to see what had happened to him now. She'd probably say, *You see? I was right. No one escapes. Not even you, Mister Enabler. Mister How-Can-I-Help-You. Mister Totally Useless.*

He nodded to Mrs. Holst, who lived across the street, and stopped, Baby Tess yanking hard on his hand, to talk to Old Ed, the neighbor on the left, about the new stop sign. Was it a good thing? A bad thing? A good *and* a bad thing? Gypsy, the Brogans' dog, met them at the corner and was soon joined by Marcus, the Kleins' Lab, and Flip, the Legaspis' mutt. "We are leading the dog parade," Roy said to Baby Tess. "They want to go to the park too."

"Store," Baby Tess corrected, but the minute he turned toward the store she steered him toward the park, where he happily spent the next hour pushing her in the swing, throwing sticks for the dogs, digging in the sandbox for China. When he came home, the house smelled like chocolate—Jill had gone ahead and baked the cookies for him—and there was time for a bath and a nap before they drove to the firehouse. There was even time to paint his own toenails blue.

The firemen were waiting at the firehouse door, seven of them, maybe not "eye candy," but good-looking men, nonetheless, better-looking than Roy had been in his prime. Stu, in his crisp white jacket, introduced the others: Scott, Skip, Steve, Stan, Scott Again, and Sam. They ranged in age from twenty-one to about sixty, but they all had thick heads of hair, wide shoulders and open, outdoorsy faces. "I salute you," Roy said, shaking hands. "You are my heroes." Stu laughed politely; he probably heard that all the time, but a few of the other S's gave him strange looks. Roy knew what they saw; a puffed, pale freak with wide-lit eyes, whose life they had saved once and might need to save again soon. Until then, a voter. A homeowner. Proud father of a cute, if clingy, little girl (Baby Tess was clamped around his neck), with a pretty, much younger wife.

Jill had washed her hair and released it from its ponytail so it waved over her shoulders. She was wearing rose perfume and slick brown lipstick. Two of the firemen helped Roy carry the foil-wrapped casseroles, the garlic bread and the salad in from the car. Places were already set at a long table in front of an enormous television set. The baseball game was on, and Jill asked intelligent questions about it. Roy did not care for baseball, but he chuckled attentively as one of the Scotts reported on the inning they had just missed.

Stu gave them a tour of the station before dinner. Jill admired the new computer system while Roy studied the huge county map on the office wall. "This is where you found me," he said, pointing to a dotted hiking trail.

"I won't let him walk there anymore," Jill chimed in, sounding authentically wifely.

"Now I just go to the store and the park," Roy agreed.

"Hospital," Baby Tess offered, lifting her head off his neck, her first word in an hour.

"But we drive him to the hospital, honey," Jill explained to Baby Tess. "He doesn't walk there."

"That would be a long walk," Stu said. Strong chin. Strong back. Ringless. Roy smiled and moved in.

"Jill is a wonderful woman, isn't she?" he said. "Beautiful, the best, and Baby Tess, what a darling. And you know what?" He looked up into Stu's clear, hazel eyes. "They would be all alone now if you hadn't helped me."

"That's our job," the firemen said, all of them, one after the other, looking neither pleased nor puzzled, just matter-of-fact.

"Well, it may be your job," Roy continued at dinner, "but I want to make a toast anyway." He stood and lifted his plastic glass of lemonade to the table. "I'm only sorry this isn't champagne," he began. "Or"—amending that at the sight of the flat, polite looks that met him—"beer." The men relaxed and smiled. He was glad to see they had all helped themselves heartily to lasagna and bread. "It's a crazy thing to bring dinner to the world's greatest cooks—everyone knows firemen are the world's greatest cooks—but I've been cooking since I was eleven. I used to cook for my father after he left my mother—that's how he got women, my father, and what a miserable lot he got, poor guy, he'd bring them back to the apartment and I'd cook for them—you might say my brisket cooked his goose—anyway, I know, honey"—to Jill—"I'll get to it, the thing is, I couldn't think how else to say thank you. I wouldn't be here tonight if it weren't for you guys. You saved my life, and I just wanted you to know how grateful I am. That's it. That's all. Just thank you." He put down his glass and clapped, and Jill and then, surprisingly, Baby Tess clapped with him.

The firemen waited until Stu said, "Sure, no problem," and then they all ate, and the conversation turned to jobs in general, Roy telling them how he thought his old job in sales was probably the reason he had the tumor in the first place—all that getting up and getting dressed and getting out every day when he had never, not once, wanted to, and Stu, smiling at Jill, saying there wasn't a day when he didn't feel happy to go to work, and Jill saying she was lucky to be able to work at home now that Roy needed watching, and one of the S's saying he had once, years ago, thought of being a policeman instead of a fireman.

"Oh, but that's a dirty job," another S said.

"The things you see," another agreed.

"Makes you hate human nature," another said. "Makes you mean."

"Policemen are mean," Roy agreed. "When my wife—my first wife, that is—died, a bunch of policemen came to the house. They . . ." He trailed away, stopped by Jill's curious look. He had never told her about Leslie's death. "They didn't come to help," he finished. He was glad when the S on his left asked about the lasagna recipe. The mention of Martha Stewart silenced everyone; then they recovered to talk of other entrepreneurs, stock tips, day trading, hobbies, sports, fishing, all interlaced with the shy references Roy had become used to about various bizarre illnesses and, as always when talking to other men, hairstyles. No one mentioned baldness, but it had become clear from some clannish laughter at the end of the table that Stan used Grecian Formula and that Skip had a hairpiece. Stu could not bear to have his hair ruffled, and Stan had a special comb no one else was allowed to touch.

"Is this what you do when there aren't any fires to put out?" Jill asked, teasing. "Pick on each other?" The men laughed, blushed, hung their handsome heads. The casseroles and salads went around and around, followed by cookies and ice cream and fruit. No one would let Roy clear, and although Jill tried to do the dishes, the men marched by her one by one and rinsed and loaded their plates into the industrial-size dishwasher. Roy crouched with Baby Tess by a white blackboard on the wall, helping her draw a wall of flames with colored chalk. He heard Jill in the kitchen talking to Stu in the same dramatic, low voice she used at the marriage counselor's. How pretty she looked. How easy it would be. He'd simply invite Stu over to check the firebreak around the house next week. Leave an apricot pie on the counter to cool, make a pot of fresh coffee, and then take Baby Tess on a long walk; they'd go to the park *and* the store.

He straightened, tired. Jill saw his drained face and made their goodbyes. And they left with their clean dishes, everyone waving. "Glad to see us go," Roy said, cheerful, as he sank into his seat in the car. "Now they can be themselves again."

"Oh, I don't think so, honey." Jill drove with both hands on top of the wheel. "I think they had a good time. That fire chief, Stu, told me hardly anyone ever thanks them. And that's a shame."

"It is," Roy agreed. He closed his eyes. His father had never thanked him for his stepmothers. Well, who would? Leslie had never thanked him either. "The thing we don't understand," the policemen kept saying, "is how she managed to kill herself with a gun in the first place. Blind and in a wheelchair? How'd she get a loaded gun?"

It would not have taken much on Leslie's part. She'd had time. He'd left pen and paper beside the revolver. A short note would have done it. Two words. But no. Forget it, Roy thought. It's over and done with. He felt God come down, heard Her hot little giggle, felt Her fingers, sharp and pointy, start to twist his skull as if it were the knob of a disliked doll. His head rose toward Her, light and obedient, a balloon in the night, ascending. *Thank you,* he forced himself to say. *Thank you.*

Alice Munro

Fathers

from *The New Yorker*

O N FRIDAY *morning last, Harvey Ryan Newcombe, a well-known farmer of Shelby Township, lost his life due to electrocution. The funeral was held Monday afternoon from Reavie Brothers Funeral Home and interment was in Bethel Cemetery. Come unto me, all ye that labor and are heavy-laden, and I will give you rest.*

Dahlia Newcombe could not possibly have had anything to do with her father's accident. It had happened when he reached up to turn on a light in a hanging brass socket while standing on the wet floor in a neighbor's stable. He had taken one of his cows there to visit the bull. For some reason that nobody could understand, he was not wearing his rubber boots.

All over the countryside that spring, there was a sound that would soon disappear. Perhaps it would have disappeared already, if it were not for the war. The war meant that the people who had the money to buy tractors could not find any to buy, and the few who already had tractors could not get the fuel to run them. So the farmers were out on the land with their horses for the spring plowing, and from time to time, near and far, you could hear them calling out their commands, in which there would be varying degrees of encouragement, or impatience, or warning. You couldn't hear the exact words, any more than you could make out what the seagulls were saying on their inland flights, or decipher the arguments of crows.

From the tone of voice, though, you could probably tell when the farmers were swearing.

With one man, it was all swearing. It didn't matter which words he was using. He could have been saying "butter and eggs" or "afternoon tea" and the spirit would have been the same. As if he were boiling over with bitter rage, with loathing.

His name was Bunt Newcombe, and he had the first farm on the highway that curved southwest from town. Bunt was probably a nickname given to him at school, for going around with his head lowered, ready to bump and shove anybody aside. A boyish name, when you thought about it, not well matched to his behavior, his reputation as a grown man.

People sometimes wondered what could be the matter with him. He wasn't poor, after all—he had two hundred acres of decent land, and a banked barn with a peaked silo, and a drive shed, and a square red brick house, though the house, like the man himself, had a look of bad temper. There were dark-green blinds pulled most or all of the way down on the windows, no curtains visible, and a scar along the front wall where the porch had been torn away. The front door must, at one time, have opened onto the porch, which no steps had been built to replace; now it opened three feet above weeds and rubble.

Bunt Newcombe was not a drunk. Nor was he a gambler—he was too careful of his money for that. But he was mean in both senses of the word, and he seemed to have been born that way. He mistreated his horses, and it goes without saying that he mistreated his family. In the winter he took his milk cans to town on his sleigh just at that time of the morning when everybody was going to school, and he didn't slow down, as other farmers did, to give you a ride. He picked up the whip instead.

Mrs. Newcombe was never with him, on the sleigh or in the car. She walked to town wearing old-fashioned galoshes even when the weather got warm, and a long drab coat and a scarf over her hair. She mumbled hello but never looked at you, and sometimes turned her head away, not speaking at all. I think she was missing some teeth. That was more common then than now, and it was more common also for people to make plain their state of mind, in their speech and dress and gestures, so that everything about them said, "I know how I should look and behave and nobody can say otherwise," or, "I don't care—things have gone too far with me, and you can think what you like."

Nowadays, Mrs. Newcombe might be seen as a serious case, terminally depressed, and her husband, with his brutish ways, might be looked on with concern and compassion as someone who needed help. In those days, they were just taken as they were and allowed to live out their lives without a thought of intervention—regarded, in fact, as a source of interest and entertainment. Some people were born to make others miserable, and some let themselves in for being made miserable, and that was all there was to it.

The Newcombes had five daughters, then one son. The girls' names were April, Corinne, Gloria, Susannah, and Dahlia. I thought these names fanciful and lovely, and I would have liked the daughters' looks to match them—as if they were the beautiful children of an ogre in a fairy tale. April and Corinne had been gone from home for some time, so I had no way of knowing what they looked like. Gloria was married and had dropped from view, as married girls did. Susannah worked in the hardware store, and she was a stout girl, not at all pretty, but quite normal-looking—not cowed like her mother or brutal like her father.

Dahlia was a couple of years older than I was. She was the first member of the family to go to high school. She was sturdy and handsome, though not my idea of an ogre's daughter, with rippling yellow hair and a sweetly pining expression. Her hair was brown, her shoulders square, her breasts firm and high. She got quite respectable marks and was notably good at games, particularly basketball.

During my first few months of high school, I found myself walking part of the way to school with her. We had lived our lives within shouting distance of each other, you might say, but the school districts were divided in such a way that I had always gone to the town elementary school while the Newcombes had gone to a country school, farther out along the highway. But now that we were both going to the high school we would usually meet where our roads joined, and if either of us saw the other coming we would wait. Walking together did not mean that we became particular friends. It was just that it would have seemed odd to walk singly when we were going the same way and to the same place. I don't know what we talked about. I have an idea that there were long periods of silence, which were not disagreeable.

One morning Dahlia didn't appear, and I went on alone. In the cloakroom at school, she said to me, "I won't be coming in that way from now on, because I'm staying in town now. I'm staying at Gloria's."

And we hardly spoke again until one day in early spring—that time I was talking about, with the trees bare but reddening, and the crows and the seagulls busy, and the farmers hollering to their horses. She caught up to me as we were leaving school. She said, "You going right home?" I said yes, and she started to walk beside me.

I asked her if she was living at home again, and she said, "Nope. Still at Gloria's."

When we had walked a bit farther, she said, "I'm just going along out there to see what's what."

Over the winter, she had shone as the best player on the basketball team, and the team had nearly won the county championship. It gave me a feeling of distinction to be walking with her. She must have started high school with all the business of her family dragging behind her, but now she had been allowed, to an extent, to slip free of that. The independence of spirit, the faith you had to have in your body, to become an athlete won respect and discouraged anybody who would think of tormenting you. She was well dressed, too—she had very few clothes but they were quite all right, not like the matronly hand-me-downs that country girls often wore, or the homemade outfits my mother labored at for me. I remember a red turtleneck sweater she often wore, and a pleated Royal Stewart skirt. Maybe Gloria and Susannah thought of her as the representative and pride of the family and had pooled some of their slight resources to dress her handsomely.

We were out of town before she spoke again.

"I got to keep track of what my old man is up to," she said. "He better not be beating up on Raymond."

Raymond. That was the brother.

"Does he beat up on him?" I said. I felt as if I had to pretend to know less about her family than I—and everybody—actually did.

"Yeah. Some," she said. "Raymond used to get off better than the rest of us, but now he's the only one left, I wonder."

I said, "Did he beat you?" I tried to sound as if I felt this was an everyday and not even very interesting matter.

"Are you kidding?" she said. "Before I got away the last time, it looked like he was going to brain me with the shovel. And I was yelling at him, 'Come on. Come on, let's see you kill me. Then you'll get hung.' Yeah. But then I thought, OK, but I wouldn't get the satisfaction of seeing him.

Hung. I hate him," she said, in the same breezy but formidable tone. "If somebody told me he was drowning in the river, I would go and stand on the bank and cheer."

"What if he takes after you now?"

"I don't mean him to see me. I just mean to spy on him."

When we came to the division of our roads, she said, "Come on with me. I'll show you how I spy."

We walked across the bridge and looked through the cracks between the planks at the high-flowing river.

"In the wintertime, I used to come out after dark and get right up at the kitchen windows, but it stays light too late to do that," she said. "What I wanted was for him to see the boot marks in the snow and know there was somebody had been spying on him and go out of his mind."

I asked whether he had a shotgun.

"Sure," she said. "Same story. Shoots me and gets hung and goes to Hell. Don't worry—he's not going to see us."

Before we were in sight of the Newcombes' buildings, we climbed a bank on the opposite side of the road, where there was a thick growth of sumac bordering a planted windbreak of spruce. When Dahlia, ahead of me, began to walk in a crouch, I did the same. And when she stopped, I stopped.

There was the barn and the barnyard full of cows. I realized, once we had stopped making our own noise among the branches, that we had been hearing them all along. There wasn't enough fresh grass for them to be put out to pasture yet—the low places in the pastures were still mostly under water—but they were let out of the stable to exercise before the evening milking. From behind our screen of sumac, we looked right down at the cows that were jostling each other and blundering around in the muck, complaining of their full udders. Even if we snapped a branch or spoke above a whisper, there would be too much going on over there for anybody to hear us.

Raymond, a boy about ten years old, came around the corner of the barn. He had a stick but he was just tapping the cows' rumps with it, pushing them and saying, "So-boss, so-boss," in an easygoing rhythm and urging them toward the stable door. It was the sort of mixed herd most farms had at that time. A black cow, a rusty-red cow, a pretty golden cow that must have been part Jersey, others splotched brown-and-white and black-and-white in all sorts of combinations. They hadn't been deprived of their horns, which gave them that look of dignity and ferocity that cows have since lost.

A man's voice, Bunt Newcombe's voice, called from the stable. "Hurry up," or "What's the holdup?"

Raymond called back, "OK, OK." His tone did not indicate anything to me, except that he didn't seem scared. But Dahlia said, "Yah. He's givin' him lip. Good for him."

Bunt Newcombe came out of a side door of the stable. He was wearing overalls and a greasy barn smock, and he moved with an odd swing of one leg.

"Bum leg," Dahlia said. "I heard a horse kicked him but I thought it was too good to be true. Too bad it wasn't his head."

He was carrying a pitchfork. But he used it only to pitch manure out of that doorway while the cows were driven in at the other.

Perhaps a son was abhorred less than daughters?

"If I had a gun I could get him now," Dahlia said. "I wouldn't mind. I should do it while I'm still young enough. Then I don't get hung."

"You'd go to jail," I said.

"So what? He runs his own jail. Maybe they'd never catch me."

She couldn't have meant what she was saying. If she had had any such intentions, wouldn't it be crazy of her to tell me about them? I might betray her. I would not intend to, but somebody might get it out of me. Because of the war that was just ending that spring, I often thought about what it would be like to be tortured. How much would I be able to stand? At the dentist's, when he hit a nerve, I had asked myself, If a pain like that went on and on unless I betrayed where my father was hiding with the Resistance, what would I do?

When the cows were all inside and Raymond and his father had shut the stable doors, we walked, still bent, through the sumac and, once out of sight, climbed down to the road. I thought that Dahlia might say now that she had only been kidding about the shooting part, but she didn't. I wondered why she had not said anything about her mother—about being worried for her mother as she had been for Raymond. Then I thought that she probably despised her mother, for what she had put up with and what she had become. You would have to show some spirit to make the grade with Dahlia. I wouldn't have wanted her to know that I was afraid of the horned cows.

We must have said goodbye when she took the route back to town, to Gloria's house, and I turned onto our dead-end road. I kept thinking about whether she could really kill her father. I had a strange idea that she was too young to do it—as if killing somebody were like driving a car or voting or getting married. I also had some idea—though I would not have known how to express it—that killing him wouldn't be any relief to her, hating him having got to be such a habit. She had taken me along with her not to confide in me or because I was anything like an intimate friend—she had just wanted someone to see her hating.

At one time, there had been perhaps a dozen houses on our road. Most were small cheap rental cottages—until you got to our house, which was an ordinary farmhouse on a small farm. And, not so long ago, they had all had people living in them. But when the war jobs had taken those families away, some of the houses had been carted elsewhere to serve as garages or chicken sheds. A couple of those that were left were empty, and the rest were mostly occupied by old people: the old bachelor blacksmith; the couple who used to have a grocery store and still had an Orange Crush sign in their front window; another couple who bootlegged and buried their money, it was said, in quart sealers in the back yard; and the old women who had been left on their own. Mrs. Currie raised dogs that raced about barking insanely all day in a wire pen and at night were taken inside her house, which was partly built into the bank of a hill and must have been very dark and smelly. Mrs. Horne raised flowers, and her tiny house and yard were like an embroidery sampler—clematis vines, rose of Sharon, every sort of phlox and delphinium. Bessie Stewart dressed smartly and went uptown in the afternoons to smoke cigarettes and drink coffee in the Paragon Restaurant. Though unmarried, she was said to have a "friend."

One empty house had belonged, or maybe still belonged, to a Mrs. Eddy. For a short while, years earlier—that is, four or five years before I ever met Dahlia, a long time in my life—some people named Wainwright had lived in that house. They were related to Mrs. Eddy, and she was letting them live there, but she wasn't living with them. She had already been taken away to wherever she was taken.

Mr. and Mrs. Wainwright came from Chicago, where they had both worked as window dressers for a department store. The store had closed down or had decided that it didn't need so many windows dressed—whatever had happened, they had lost their jobs and come here, to live in Mrs. Eddy's house and try to set up a wallpapering business.

They had a daughter, Frances, who was a year younger than I was. She was small and thin and she got out of breath easily, because she had asthma. On my first day in grade five, Mr. Wainwright came out and stopped me on the road, with Frances lagging behind him. He asked me if I would take Frances to school and show her where the grade-four classroom was, and if I would be her friend, because she didn't know anybody yet or where anything was. Frances was all dolled up in a very short checked cotton dress with a flounce around the skirt and a matching hair ribbon.

Soon it became understood that I would walk to school with Frances and walk home with her afterward. We both carried our lunches to school, but as I had not expressly been asked to eat lunch with her I never did. Very few students lived far enough away to eat lunch at the school, but there happened to be one girl in my own class who did. Her name was Wanda Louise Palmer, and her parents owned and lived in the dance hall to the south of town. She and I ate together and formed a friendship of sorts, which was based mostly on avoiding Frances. We ate in the girls' basement, behind a barricade of broken old desks that were heaped up in a corner. As soon as we finished, we'd sneak out and leave the school grounds to walk around the nearby streets or go downtown and look in store windows. Wanda Louise should have been an interesting companion, because of her life at the dance hall, but she was so apt to lose track of what she was telling me (but not to stop talking) that she was actually very boring. All we really had in common was our bond against Frances, and our desperate stifled laughter when we peered through the desks and saw her looking for us. After a while, she didn't do that anymore; she ate her lunch alone.

I would like to think that it was Wanda Louise who pointed her out to our classmates, when we stood in line ready to march into the schoolroom, as the girl we were always trying to avoid. But I could have been the one who did that, and certainly I went along with the joke, and was glad to be on the side of those doing the giggling and excluding. Living on the outskirts of town, as I did, and being easily embarrassed yet a showoff, as I improbably was, I could never stand up for anybody who was being humiliated, never rise above a feeling of relief that it was not me.

The hair ribbons became part of it. Just to go up to Frances and say, "I love your hair ribbon. Where did you get it?" and have her say, in innocent bewilderment, "In Chicago," was a lasting source of glee. For a while, "in Chicago," or just "Chicago," became the answer to everything. "Where did you go after school yesterday?" "Chicago." Or "Where did your sister get her hair waved?" "Oh, in Chicago." Some girls got into fits of laughing that were like hiccups; some feared that they were going to be sick.

How much Frances was aware of, I don't know. She may have thought that there was some special place where girls in my class always went to have lunch. She may not have understood what the giggling was about. She never asked about it.

She tried to hold my hand crossing the street, but I pulled away and told her not to. She said she always used to hold Sadie's hand, when Sadie walked her to school in Chicago. "But that was different," she said. "There aren't any street-cars here."

One day, she offered me a cookie left over from her lunch. I refused, so as not to feel an inconvenient obligation. "Go on," she said. "My mother put it in for you."

Then I understood. Her mother put in this extra cookie, this treat, for me to eat when we had our lunches together. She had never told her mother that I didn't show up at lunchtime and she couldn't find me. She must have been eating the extra cookie herself, but now the dishonesty was bothering her. So every day from then on she offered it, almost at the last minute, as if she were embarrassed, and every day I accepted.

We began to have a little conversation on our walks, starting when we were almost clear of town. We were both interested in movie stars. She had seen far more movies than I had—in Chicago, you could see movies every afternoon, and Sadie used to take her—but I walked past our theater and looked at the stills every time the picture changed, so I knew something about them, too. And I had one movie magazine at home, which a visiting cousin had left. It had pictures of Deanna Durbin's wedding in it, so we talked about that, and about what we wanted our own weddings to be like—the bridal gowns and the bridesmaids' dresses and the flowers and the going-away outfits. The same cousin had given me a present—a "Ziegfeld Girl" cutout book. Frances had seen the "Ziegfeld Girl" movie, and we talked about which Ziegfeld girl we would like to be. She chose Judy Garland because she could sing, and I chose Hedy Lamarr because she was so beautiful.

"My father and mother used to sing in the Light Opera Society," she said. "They sang in *The Pirates of Penzance*."

Lightopra society. Pirazapenzanze. I filed those words away but could not ask what they meant.

If her mother came out to greet us, she might ask if I could come in and play. I always said I had to go straight home.

Shortly before Christmas, Mrs. Wainwright asked me if I could come to have supper the next Sunday. She said it would be a little thank-you party and a farewell party, now that they were going away. I was on the point of saying that I didn't think my mother would let me, but when I heard the word "farewell" I saw the invitation in a different light. The burden of Frances would be lifted, no further obligation would be involved, and no intimacy enforced. Mrs. Wainwright said that she had written a little note to my mother, since they didn't have a phone.

My mother would have liked it better if I had been asked to some town girl's house, but she said yes. She, too, took it into account that the Wainwrights were moving away.

"I don't know what they were thinking of," she said. "Anybody who can afford wallpapering here does it themselves."

"Where are you going?" I asked Frances.

"Burlington."

"Where's that?"

"It's in Canada, too. We're going to stay with my aunt and uncle, but we'll have our own toilet upstairs and our sink and a hot plate. My dad's going to get a better job."

"What doing?"

"I don't know."

Their Christmas tree was in a corner. The front room had only one window, and if they had put the tree there it would have blocked off all the light. It was not a big or well-shaped tree but it was smothered in tinsel, gold and silver beads, and beautiful intricate ornaments. In another corner of the room was a parlor stove, a woodstove, in which the fire seemed to have been recently lit. The air was still cold and heavy with the forest smell of the tree. Neither Mr. nor Mrs. Wainwright was very confident about the fire. First one and then the other kept fiddling with the damper and timidly reaching in with the poker and patting the pipe to see if it was getting hot or, by any chance, too hot. The wind was fierce that day, and sometimes blew the smoke down the chimney.

That was no matter to Frances and me. On a card table set up in the middle of the room there was a Chinese-checker board, ready for two people to play, and a stack of movie magazines. I fell upon them at once. I had never imagined such a feast. It made no difference that they were not new and that some had been looked through so often they were almost falling apart. Frances stood beside my chair, interfering with my pleasure a little by telling me what was just ahead and what was in a magazine I hadn't opened yet. This was obviously her idea and I had to be patient with her—the magazines were her property, and if she had taken it into her head to remove them I would have been more grief-stricken than when my father drowned the kittens I had found in the barn.

Frances was wearing an outfit that could have come out of one of those magazines—a party dress of deep-red velvet with a white lace collar and a black ribbon threaded through the lace. Her mother's dress was exactly the same, and they both had their hair done the same way—a roll in front and long in the back. Frances's hair was thin and fine and, what with her excitement and her jumping around to show me things, the roll was already coming undone.

It was getting dark in the room. There were wires sticking out of the ceiling, but no bulbs. Mrs. Wainwright brought in a lamp with a long cord that plugged into the wall. The light shone through the pale-green glass of a lady's skirt.

"That's Scarlett O'Hara," Frances said. "Daddy and I gave it to Mother for her birthday."

We never got around to the Chinese checkers, and in time the board was removed. We shifted the magazines to the floor. A piece of lace—not a real tablecloth—was laid across the table. Dishes followed. Evidently, Frances and I were to eat in here, by ourselves. Both parents were involved in laying the table—Mrs. Wainwright wearing a fancy apron over her red velvet and Mr. Wainwright in shirtsleeves and a silk-backed vest.

When everything was set up, we were called over. I had expected Mr. Wainwright to leave the serving of the food to his wife—in fact, I had already been very surprised to see him hovering with knives and forks— but now he pulled out our chairs and announced that he was our waiter. When he was that close, I could smell him, and hear his breathing, which sounded eager, like a dog's. His smell was of talcum and lotion, suggesting an innocent intimacy that made me think of a baby's fresh diapers.

"Now, my lovely young ladies," he said. "I am going to bring you some champagne."

He brought a pitcher of lemonade and filled our glasses. I was alarmed, until I took a sip of it—I knew that champagne was an alcoholic drink. We never had such drinks in our house, and neither did anybody I knew. Mr. Wainwright watched me taste it and seemed to guess my feelings.

"Is that all right? Not worried now?" he said. "All satisfactory to your ladyship?"

Then he made a bow.

"Now," he said. "What would you care for, to eat?" He reeled off a list of unfamiliar things—all I recognized was venison, which I certainly had never tasted. The list ended up with sweetbreads. Frances giggled and said, "We'll have sweetbreads, please. And potatoes."

I expected the sweetbreads to be like their name—some sort of bun with jam or brown sugar, but couldn't see why that would come with potatoes. What arrived, however, were small pads of meat wrapped in crisp bacon, and little potatoes with their skins on, which had been rolled in hot butter and crisped in the pan. Also thin sticks of carrot with a slightly candied flavor. Those I could have done without, but I had never eaten potatoes so delicious or meat so tender. All I wished was for Mr. Wainwright to stay in the kitchen instead of hanging around us pouring out lemonade and asking if everything was to our liking.

Dessert was another wonder—a satin vanilla pudding with a sort of lid of golden-brown baked sugar. Tiny cakes to go with it, iced on all sides with very dark, rich chocolate.

When not a lick or a crumb was left, I sat replete. I looked at the fairy-tale tree with the ornaments that could have been miniature castles or angels. Drafts came in around the window and moved the branches a little, causing the showers of tinsel to wave and the ornaments to turn slightly to show new points of light. Full of this rich and delicate food, I seemed to have entered a dream, in which everything I saw was both potent and benign.

I saw the firelight, too, a dull rusty glow up in the pipe, and I said to Frances, without alarm, "I think your pipe's on fire."

She called out in a party spirit, "Pipe's on fire," and in came Mr. Wainwright, who had finally retired to the kitchen, and Mrs. Wainwright close behind him.

Mrs. Wainwright said, "Oh, God, Billy. What do we do?"

Mr. Wainwright said in a squeaky, scared, unfatherly voice, "Close off the draft, I guess."

He did that, then yelped and shook his hand, which must have got burned. Now they both stood and looked at the red pipe, and she said, "There's something you're supposed to put on it. What is it? Baking soda?" She ran to the kitchen and came back with the box of baking soda, saying, "Right on the flames." Mr. Wainwright was still nursing his burned hand, so she wrapped her apron round her own hand and used the stove lifter and scattered the powder on the flames. There was a spitting sound as they began to die down, and smoke rose into the room.

"Girls," she said. "Girls. Maybe you better run outside." She sounded about to break into tears.

I remembered something, from a similar crisis at home.

"You wrap wet towels round the pipe," I said.

"Wet towels," she said. "That sounds like a good idea. Yes." She ran to the kitchen, where we heard her pumping water. Mr. Wainwright followed her, holding his burned hand up in front of his eyes, and both returned with towels dripping. Some were wrapped around the pipe, and as soon as they began to heat up and dry others were put in their place. The room began to smell of burned creosote, and Frances started coughing.

"Get some air," Mr. Wainwright said. It took him a while, with his good hand, to wrench open the unused front door, letting fly the bits of old newspaper and rotten rags that had been stuffed around it. There was a snowdrift outside, a white wave lapping at the room.

"Throw snow on the fire," Frances said, still sounding jubilant between coughs, and she and I picked up armfuls of snow and threw them into the stove. Some hit what was left of the fire and some missed and melted and ran into the puddles that the drip from the towels had already made on the floor.

In the midst of these puddles, the danger over and the room growing frigid, stood Mr. and Mrs. Wainwright with their arms around each other, laughing and commiserating.

"Oh, your poor hand," Mrs. Wainwright said. "And I wasn't the least bit sympathetic about it. I was so afraid the house was going to burn down." She tried to kiss the hand, and he said, "Ouch. Ouch." He had tears in his eyes from the smoke or the pain.

She patted him on the arms and shoulders and down lower, even on his buttocks, saying, "Poor, poor sweet baby," and things of that sort, while he made a pouty face and kissed her with a great smack on the mouth. Then with his good hand he squeezed her behind.

It looked as if this fondling could go on for some time.

"Shut the door, it's freezing," Frances cried, all red from coughing and happy excitement. If she meant for her parents to do this, they took no notice, but went on with the appalling behavior that did not seem to embarrass her or even to be worth her notice. She and I got hold of the door and pushed it against the wind that was whipping up over the drift and blowing more snow into the house.

I did not tell about any of this at home, though the food and the ornaments and the fire were so interesting. There were too many other things that I could not describe and that made me feel off balance, slightly sick, so that somehow I did not like to mention any of it. The way the adults had put themselves at the service of children. The charade of Mr. Wainwright as the waiter, his thick soapy-white hands and pale face and wings of fine glistening light-brown hair. The insistence—the too-closeness—of his soft footsteps in fat plaid slippers. Then the laughing, so inappropriate following a near-disaster. The shameless hands and the smacking kiss. There was a creepy menace about all this, which started with the falsity of corralling me into playing the role of little friend—both of them had called me that—when I was not. Treating me as good and guileless when I was not.

Was this just the menace of love, or of lovingness? If that was what it was, then you would have to say that I had made its acquaintance too late. Such slopping-over of attention made me feel cornered and humiliated, almost as if somebody had taken a peep into my pants. Even the wonderful unfamiliar food was suspect in my memory. The movie magazines alone escaped the taint.

By the end of the Christmas holidays, the Wainwrights' house was empty. The snow was so heavy that year that the kitchen roof caved in. Even then, nobody bothered to pull the house down or put up a "No Trespassing" sign, and for years children—I was among them—poked around in the risky ruins just to see what they could find. People didn't seem to worry then about injuries or liability. No movie magazines came to light.

I did tell about Dahlia. By then, I was an entirely different person, to my own way of thinking, than the girl who had been in the Wainwrights' house. In my early teens, I had become the entertainer around home. I don't mean that I was always trying to make the family laugh—though I did that, too—but that I relayed news and gossip. I told about things that had happened at school or in town. Or I just described the looks or speech of someone I had seen on the street. I had learned how to do this in a way that would not get me rebuked for being sarcastic or vulgar or too smart for my own good. I had mastered a deadpan, almost demure style that could make people laugh even when they thought they shouldn't and which made it hard to tell whether I was innocent or malicious.

That was the way I told about Dahlia's creeping around in the sumac to spy on her father, about her hatred of him and her mention of murder. And that was the way any story about the Newcombes had to be told, not just by me. The undeviating style of Bunt Newcombe's behavior had made him—and his wife—into such caricatures that a story ought to confirm, to everybody's satisfaction, just how thoroughly and faithfully they played out their roles. And now Dahlia, as well, was seen to belong to the picture. The spying, the threats, the melodrama. His coming after her with the shovel. Her notion that if he had killed her he would have been hanged. And that she wouldn't be if she did it while she was still a juvenile.

"Hard to get a court around here to convict her," my father said.

My mother said, "It's a shame."

It seems strange to me now that we could conduct this conversation so easily, without its seeming ever to enter our heads that my father had beaten me, at times, and that I had screamed out not that I wanted to kill him but that I wanted to die. And that this had happened not so long ago—three or four times, I would think, in the years when I was around eleven or twelve. It had happened in between my knowing Frances and my knowing Dahlia. I was being punished, at those times, for some falling-out with my mother, some back talk or intransigence. She would fetch my father from his outside work to deal with me, and I would await his arrival first in balked fury and then in a sickening despair. I felt as if it must be my very self that they were after, my dark and disputatious self that had to be beaten out of me. When my father began to remove his belt—that was what he beat me with—I would begin to scream and plead my case incoherently, in a way that seemed to make him despise me. And, indeed, my behavior then would arouse contempt—it did not show a proud or even a self-respecting nature. I did not care. When the belt was raised—in the second before it descended—there was a moment of terrible revelation. Injustice ruled and detestation was supreme. How could I not find myself howling at such perversion in the universe?

If he were alive now, I am sure my father would say that I exaggerate, that the humiliation he meant to inflict was not so great, that my offenses were perplexing, and whatever other way is there to handle children? I was causing trouble for him and grief for my mother, and I had to be persuaded to change my ways.

And I did. I grew older. I became useful around the house. I learned not to give lip. I found ways to make myself agreeable.

When I was with Dahlia, listening to her, when I was walking home by myself, when I was telling the story to my family, I never once thought to compare my situation with hers. Of course not. We were decent people. My mother, though sometimes distraught at the behavior of her family, did not go into town with snaggly hair or wear floppy rubber galoshes. My father did not swear. He was a man of honor and competence and humor, and he was the parent I sorely wanted to please. I did not hate him, could not consider hating him. Instead, I saw what he hated in me. A shaky arrogance in my nature, something brazen yet cowardly, was what awoke in him this fury.

Shame. The shame of being beaten, and the shame of cringing from the beating. Perpetual shame. Exposure. And something connects this, as I feel it now, with the shame, the queasiness that crept up on me when I heard the padding of Mr. Wainwright's slippered feet and his breathing. There were demands that fathers made that seemed indecent, there were horrid invasions, both sneaky and straightforward. Some that I could tighten my skin against, others that left it raw. All in the hazards of life as a child.

And, as the saying goes, about this matter of what molds or warps us, if it's not one thing it will be another. At least that was a saying of my elders in those days. Mysterious, uncomforting, unaccusing.

Denis Johnson

Train Dreams

from *Paris Review*

I.

I N THE summer of 1917 Robert Grainier took part in an attempt on the life of a Chinese laborer caught, or anyway accused of, stealing from the company stores of the Spokane International Railway in the Idaho Panhandle.

Three of the railroad gang put the thief under restraint and dragged him up the long bank toward the bridge under construction fifty feet above the Moyea River. A rapid singsong streamed from the Chinaman voluminously. He shipped and twisted like a weasel in a sack, lashing backward with his one free fist at the man lugging him by the neck. As this group passed him, Grainier, seeing them in some distress, lent assistance and found himself holding one of the culprit's bare feet. The man facing him, Mr. Sears, of Spokane International's management, held the prisoner almost uselessly by the armpit and was the only one of them, besides the incomprehensible Chinaman, to talk during the hardest part of their labors: "Boys, I'm damned if we ever see the top of this heap!" Then we're hauling him all the way? was the question Grainier wished to ask, but thought it better to save his breath for the struggle. Sears laughed once, his face pale with fatigue and horror. They all went down in the dust and got righted, went down again, the Chinaman speaking in tongues and terrifying the four of them to the point that whatever they may have had in mind at the outset, he was a deader now. Nothing would do but to toss him off the trestle.

They came abreast of the others, a gang of a dozen men pausing in the sun to lean on their tools and wipe at sweat and watch this thing. Grainier held on convulsively to the Chinaman's horny foot, wondering at himself, and the man with the other foot let loose and sat down gasping in the dirt and got himself kicked in the eye before Grainier took charge of the free-flailing limb. "It was just for fun. For fun," the man sitting in the dirt said, and to his confederate there he said, "Come on, Jel Toomis, let's give it up." "I can't let loose," this Mr. Toomis said, "I'm the one's got him by the neck!" and laughed with a gust of confusion passing across his features. "Well, I've got him!" Grainier said, catching both the little demon's feet tighter in his embrace. "I've got the bastard, and I'm your man!"

The party of executioners got to the midst of the last completed span, sixty feet above the rapids, and made every effort to toss the Chinaman over. But he bested them by clinging to their arms and legs, weeping his gibberish, until suddenly he let go and grabbed the beam beneath him with one hand. He kicked free of his captors easily, as they were trying to shed themselves of him anyway, and went over the side, dangling over the gorge and making hand-over-hand out over the river on the skeleton form of the next span. Mr. Toomis's companion rushed over now, balancing on a beam, kicking at the fellow's fingers. The Chinaman dropped from beam to beam like a circus artist downward along the crosshatch structure. A couple of the work gang cheered his escape, while others, though not quite certain why he was being chased, shouted that the villain ought to be stopped. Mr. Sears removed from the holster on his belt a large old four-shot black-powder revolver and took his four, to no effect. By then the Chinaman had vanished.

Hiking to his home after this incident, Grainier detoured two miles to the store at the railroad village of Meadow Creek to get a bottle of Hood's Sarsaparilla for his wife, Gladys, and their infant daughter, Kate. It was hot going up the hill through the woods toward the cabin, and before getting the last mile he stopped and bathed in the river, the Moyea, at a deep place upstream from the village.

It was Saturday night, and in preparation for the evening a number of the railroad gang from Meadow Creek were gathered at the hole, bathing with their clothes on and sitting themselves out on the rocks to dry before the last of the daylight left the canyon. The men left their shoes and boots aside and waded in slowly up to their shoulders, whooping and splashing. Many of the men already sipped whiskey from flasks as they sat shivering after their ablutions. Here and there an arm and hand clutching a shabby hat jutted from the surface while somebody got his head wet. Grainier recognized nobody and stayed off by himself and kept a close eye on his boots and his bottle of sarsaparilla.

Walking home in the falling dark, Grainier almost met the Chinaman everywhere. Chinaman in the road. Chinaman in the woods. Chinaman walking softly, dangling his hands on arms like ropes. Chinaman dancing up out of the creek like a spider.

He gave the Hood's to Gladys. She sat up in bed by the stove, nursing the baby at her breast, down with a case of the salt rheum. She could easily have braved it and done her washing and cut up potatoes and trout for supper, but it was their custom to let her lie up with a bottle or two of the sweet-tasting Hood's tonic when her head ached and her nose stopped, and get a holiday from such chores. Grainier's baby daughter, too, looked rheumy. Her eyes were a bit crusted and the discharge bubbled pendulously at her nostrils while she suckled and snorted at her mother's breast. Kate was four months old, still entirely bald. She did not seem to recognize him. Her little illness wouldn't hurt her as long as she didn't develop a cough out of it.

Now Grainier stood by the table in the single-room cabin and worried. The Chinaman, he was sure, had cursed them powerfully while they dragged him along, and any bad thing might come of it. Though astonished now at the frenzy of the afternoon, baffled by the violence, at how it had carried him away like a seed in a wind, young Grainier still wished they'd gone ahead and killed that Chinaman before he'd cursed them.

He sat on the edge of the bed.

"Thank you, Bob," his wife said.

"Do you like your sarsaparilla?"

"I do. Yes, Bob."

"Do you suppose little Kate can taste it out your teat?"

"Of course she can."

.   .   .

Many nights they heard the northbound Spokane International train as it passed through Meadow Creek, two miles down the valley. Tonight the distant whistle woke him, and he found himself alone in the straw bed.

Gladys was up with Kate, sitting on the bench by the stove, scraping cold boiled oats off the sides of the pot and letting the baby suckle this porridge from the end of her finger.

"How much does she know, do you suppose, Gladys? As much as a dog-pup, do you suppose?"

"A dog-pup can live by its own after the bitch weans it away," Gladys said.

He waited for her to explain what this meant. She often thought ahead of him.

"A man-child couldn't do that way," she said, "just go off and live after it was weaned. A dog knows more than a babe until the babe knows its words. But not just a few words. A dog raised around the house knows some words, too—as many as a baby."

"How many words, Gladys?"

"You know," she said, "the words for its tricks and the things you tell it to do."

"Just say some of the words, Glad." It was dark and he wanted to keep hearing her voice.

"Well, fetch, and come, and sit, and lay, and roll over. Whatever it knows to do, it knows the words."

In the dark he felt his daughter's eyes turned on him like a cornered brute's. It was only his thoughts tricking him, but it poured something cold down his spine. He shuddered and pulled the quilt up to his neck.

All of his life Robert Grainier was able to recall this very moment on this very night.

2.

Forty-one days later, Grainier stood among the railroad gang and watched while the first locomotive crossed the 112-foot interval of air over the sixty-foot-deep gorge, traveling on the bridge they'd made. Mr. Sears stood next to the machine, a single engine, and raised his four-shooter to signal the commencement. At the sound of the gun the engineer tripped the brake and hopped out of the contraption, and the men shouted it on as it trudged very slowly over the tracks and across the Moyea to the other side, where a second man waited to jump aboard and halt it before it ran out of track. The men cheered and whooped. Grainier felt sad. He couldn't think why. He cheered and hollered too. The structure would be called "Eleven-Mile Cutoff Bridge" because it eliminated a long curve around the gorge and through an adjacent pass and saved the Spokane International's having to look after that eleven-mile stretch of rails and ties.

Grainier's experience on the Eleven-Mile Cutoff made him hungry to be around other such massive undertakings, where swarms of men did away with portions of the forest and assembled structures as big as anything going, knitting massive wooden trestles in the air of impassable chasms, always bigger, longer, deeper. He went to northwestern Washington in 1920 to help make repairs on the Robinson Gorge Bridge, the grandest yet. The conceivers of these schemes had managed to bridge a space 208 feet deep and 804 feet wide with a railway capable of supporting an engine and two flatcars of logs. The Robinson Gorge Bridge was nearly thirty years old, wobbly and terrifying—nobody ever rode the cars across, not even the engineer. The brakeman caught it at the other end.

When the repairs were done, Grainier moved higher into the forest with the Simpson Company and worked getting timber out. A system of brief corduroy roads worked all over the area. The rails were meant only for transporting timber out of the forest; it was the job of the forty-some-odd men whom Grainier had joined to get the logs by six-horse teams within cable's reach of the railway landing.

At the landing crouched a giant engine the captain called a donkey, an affair with two tremendous iron drums, one paying out cable and the other winding it in, dragging logs to the landing and sending out the hook simultaneously to the choker, who noosed the next log. The engine was an old wood-burning steam colossus, throbbing and booming and groaning while its vapors roared like a falls, the horses over on the skid road moving gigantically in a kind of silence, their noises erased by the commotion of steam and machinery. From the landing the logs went onto railroad flatcars, and then across the wondrous empty depth of Robinson Gorge and down the mountain to the link with all the railways of the American continent.

Meanwhile Robert Grainier had passed his thirty-fifth birthday. He missed Gladys and Kate, his Li'l Girl and Li'l Li'l Girl, but he'd lived thirty-two years a bachelor before finding a wife, and easily slipped back into a steadying loneliness out here among the countless spruce.

Grainier himself served as a choker—not on the landing, but down in the woods, where sawyers labored in pairs to fell the spruce, limbers worked with axes to get them clean, and buckers cut them into eighteen-foot lengths before the chokers looped them around with cable to be hauled out by the horses. Grainier relished the work, the straining, the heady exhaustion, the deep rest at the end of the day. He liked the grand size of things in the woods, the feeling of being lost and far away, and the sense he had that with so many trees as wardens, no danger could find him. But according to one of the fellows, Arn Peeples, an old man now, formerly a jim-crack sawyer, the trees themselves were killers, and while a good sawyer might judge ninety-nine times correctly how a fall would go, and even by remarkable cuts and wedging tell a fifty-tonner to swing around uphill and light behind him as deftly as a needle, the hundredth time might see him smacked in the face and deader than a rock, just like that. Arn Peeples said he'd once watched a five-ton log jump up startled and fly off the cart and tumble over six horses, killing all six. It was only when you left it alone that a tree might treat you as a friend. After the blade bit in, you had yourself a war.

Cut off from anything else that might trouble them, the gang, numbering sometimes over forty and never fewer than thirty-five men, fought the forest from sunrise until suppertime, felling and bucking the giant spruce into pieces of a barely manageable size, accomplishing labors, Grainier sometimes thought, tantamount to the pyramids, changing the face of the mountainsides, talking little, shouting their communications, living with the sticky feel of pitch in their beards, sweat washing the dust off their long johns and caking it in the creases of their necks and joints, the odor of pitch so think it abraded their throats and stung their eyes, and even overlaid the stink of beasts and manure. At day's end the gang slept nearly where they fell. A few rated cabins. Most stayed in tents: These were ancient affairs patched extensively with burlap, most of them; but their canvas came originally from infantry tents of the Civil War, on the Union side, according to Arn Peeples. He pointed out stains of blood on the fabric. Some of these tents had gone on to house U.S. Cavalry in the Indian campaigns, serving longer, surely, than any they sheltered, so reckoned Arn Peeples.

"Just let me at that hatchet, boys," he liked to say. "When I get to chopping, you'll come to work in the morning and the chips won't yet be settled from yesterday. . . .

"I'm made for this summer logging," said Arn Peeples. "You Minnesota fellers might like to complain about it. I don't get my gears turning smooth till it's over a hundred. I worked on a peak outside Bisbee, Arizona, where we were only eleven or twelve miles from the sun. It was a hundred and sixteen degrees on the thermometer, and every degree was a foot long. And that was in the shade. And there wasn't no shade." He called all his logging comrades "Minnesota fellers." As far as anybody could ascertain, nobody among them had ever laid eyes on Minnesota.

Arn Peeples had come up from the Southwest and claimed to have seen and spoken to the Earp brothers in Tombstone; he described the famous lawmen as "crazy trash." He'd worked in Arizona mines in his youth, then sawed all over logging country for decades, and now he was a frail and shrunken gadabout, always yammering, staying out of the way of hard work, the oldest man in the woods.

His real use was occasional. When a tunnel had to be excavated, he served as the powder monkey, setting charges and blasting his way deeper and deeper into a bluff until he came out the other side, men clearing away the rubble for him after each explosion. He was a superstitious person and did each thing exactly the way he'd done it in the Mule Mountains in south Arizona, in the copper mines.

"I witnessed Mr. John Jacob Warren lose his entire fortune. Drunk and said he could outrun a horse." This might have been true. Arn Peeples wasn't given to lying, at least didn't make claims to know many famous figures, other than the Earps, and, in any case, nobody up here had heard of any John Jacob Warren. "Wagered he could outrun a three-year-old stallion! Stood in the street swaying back and forth with his eyes crossed, that drunk, I mean to say—the richest man in Arizona!—and he took off running with that stallion's butt-end looking at him all the way. Bet the whole Copper Queen Mine. And lost it, too! There's a feller I'd like to gamble with! Of course, he's busted down to his drop-bottoms now, and couldn't make a decent wager."

Sometimes Peeples set a charge, turned the screw to set it off, and got nothing for his trouble. Then a general tension and silence gripped the woods. Men working half a mile away would somehow get an understanding that a dud charge had to be dealt with, and all work stopped. Peeples would empty his pockets of his few valuables—a brass watch, a tin comb, and a silver toothpick—lay them on a stump, and proceed into the darkness of his tunnel without looking back. When he came out and turned his screws again and the dynamite blew with a whomp, the men cheered and a cloud of dust rushed from the tunnel and powdered rock came raining down over everyone.

It looked certain Arn Peeples would exit this world in a puff of smoke with a monstrous noise, but he went out quite differently, hit across the back of his head by a dead branch falling off a tall larch—the kind of snag called a "widowmaker" with just this kind of misfortune in mind. The blow knocked him silly, but he soon came around and seemed fine, complaining only that his spine felt "knotty amongst the knuckles" and "I want to walk suchways—crooked." He had a number of dizzy spells and grew dreamy and forgetful over the course of the next few days, lay up all day Sunday racked with chills and fever, and on Monday morning was found in his bed deceased, with the covers up under his chin and "such a sight of comfort," as the captain said, "that you'd just as soon not disturb him—just lower him down into a great long wide grave, bed and all." Arn Peeples had said a standing tree might be a friend, but it was from just such a tree that his death had descended.

Arn's best friend, Billy, also an old man, but generally wordless, mustered a couple of remarks by the grave mound: "Arn Peeples never cheated a man in his life," he said. "He never stole, not even a stick of candy when he was a small, small boy, and he lived to be pretty old. I guess there's a lesson in there for all of us to be square, and we'll all get along. In Jesus' name, amen." The others said, "Amen." "I wish I could let us all lay off a day," the captain said. "But it's the company, and it's the war." The war in Europe had created a great demand for spruce. An armistice had actually been signed eighteen months before, but the captain believed an armistice to be only a temporary thing until the battles resumed and one side massacred the other to the last man.

That night the men discussed Arn's assets and failings and went over the details of his final hours. Had the injuries to his brain addled him, or was it the fever he'd suddenly come down with? In his delirium he'd shouted mad words—"RIGHT REVEREND RISING ROCKIES!" he'd shouted—"forerunner grub holdup feller! Caution! Caution!"—and called out to the spirits from his past, and said he'd been paid a visit by his sister and his sister's husband, though both, as Billy said he knew for certain, had been many years dead.

Billy's jobs were to keep the double drum's engine watered and lubricated and to watch the cables for wear. This was easy work, old man's work. The outfit's real grease monkey was a boy, twelve-year-old Harold, the captain's son, who moved along before the teams of horses with a bucket of dogfish oil, slathering it across the skids with a swab of burlap to keep the huge logs sliding. One morning, Wednesday morning, just two days after Arn Peeples's death and burial, young Harold himself took a dizzy spell and fell over onto his work, and the horses shied and nearly overturned the load, trying to keep from trampling him. The boy was saved from a mutilated death by the lucky presence of Grainier himself, who happened to be standing aside waiting to cross the skid road and hauled the boy out of the way by the leg of his pants. The captain watched over his son all afternoon, bathing his forehead with springwater. The youth was feverish and crazy, and it was this malady that had laid him out in front of the big animals.

That night old Billy also took a chill and lay pitching from side to side on his cot and steadily raving until well past midnight. Except for his remarks at his friend's graveside, Billy probably hadn't let go of two or three words the whole time the men had known him, but now he kept the nearest ones awake, and those sleeping farther away in the camp later reported hearing from him in their dreams that night, mostly calling out his own name—"Who is it? Who's here?" he called. "Billy? Billy? Is that you, Billy?"

Harold's fever broke, but Billy's lingered. The captain acted like a man full of haunts, wandering the camp and bothering the men, catching one whenever he could and poking his joints, thumbing back his eyelids and prying apart his jaws like a buyer of livestock. "We're finished for the summer," he told the men Friday night as they lined up for supper. He'd calculated each man's payoff—Grainier had sent money home all summer and still had four hundred dollars coming to him.

By Sunday night they had the job shut up and the last logs down the mountain, and six more men had come over with chills. Monday morning the captain gave each of his workers a four-dollar bonus and said, "Get out of this place, boys." By this time Billy, too, had survived the crisis of his illness. But the captain said he feared an influenza epidemic like the one in 1897. He himself had been orphaned then, his entire family of thirteen siblings dead in a single week. Grainier felt pity for his boss. The captain had been a strong leader and a fair one, a blue-eyed, middle-aged man who trafficked little with anybody but his son Harold, and he'd never told anyone he'd grown up without any family.

This was Grainier's first summer in the woods, and the Robinson Gorge was the first of several railroad bridges he worked on. Years later, many decades later, in fact, in 1962 or 1963, he watched young ironworkers on a trestle where U.S. Highway 2 crossed the Moyea River's deepest gorge, every bit as long and deep as the Robinson. The old highway took a long detour to cross at a shallow place; the new highway shot straight across the chasm, several hundred feet above the river. Grainier marveled at the youngsters swiping each other's hard hats and tossing them down onto the safety net thirty or forty feet below, jumping down after them to bounce crazily in the netting, clambering up its strands back to the wooden catwalk. He'd been a regular chimpanzee on the girders himself, but now he couldn't get up on a high stool without feeling just a little queasy. As he watched them, it occurred to him that he'd lived almost eighty years and had seen the world turn and turn.

Some years earlier, in the mid-1950s, Grainier had paid ten cents to view the World's Fattest Man, who rested on a divan in a trailer that took him from town to town. To get the World's Fattest Man onto this divan they'd had to take the trailer's roof off and lower him down with a crane. He weighed in at just over a thousand pounds. There he sat, immense and dripping sweat, with a mustache and goatee and one gold earring like a pirate's, wearing shiny gold short pants and nothing else, his flesh rolling out on either side of him from one end of the divan to the other and spilling over and dangling toward the floor like an arrested waterfall, while out of this big pile of himself poked his head and arms and legs. People waited in line to stand at the open doorway and look in. He told each one to buy a picture of him from a stack by the window there for a dime.

Later in his long life Grainier confused the chronology of the past and felt certain that the day he'd viewed the World's Fattest Man—that evening—was the very same day he stood on Fourth Street in Troy, Montana, twenty-six miles east of the bridge, and looked at a railway car carrying the strange young hillbilly entertainer Elvis Presley. Presley's private train had stopped for some reason, maybe for repairs, here in this little town that didn't even merit its own station. The famous youth had appeared in a window briefly and raised his hand in greeting, but Grainier had come out of the barbershop across the street too late to see this. He'd only had it told to him by the townspeople standing in the late dusk, strung along the street beside the deep bass of the idling diesel, speaking very low if speaking at all, staring into the mystery and grandeur of a boy so high and solitary.

Grainier had also once seen a wonder horse, and a wolf-boy, and he'd flown in the air in a biplane in 1927. He'd started his life story on a train ride he couldn't remember, and ended up standing outside a train with Elvis Presley in it.

3.

When a child, Grainier had been sent by himself to Idaho. From precisely where he'd been sent he didn't know, because his eldest cousin said one thing and his second-eldest another, and he himself couldn't remember. His second-eldest cousin also claimed not to be his cousin at all, while the first said yes, they were cousins—their mother, whom Grainier thought of as his own mother as much as theirs, was actually his aunt, the sister of his father. All three of his cousins agreed Grainier had come on a train. How had he lost his original parents? Nobody ever told him.

When he disembarked in the town of Fry, Idaho, he was six—or possibly seven, as it seemed a long time since his last birthday and he thought he may have missed the date, and couldn't say, anyhow, where it fell. As far as he could ever fix it, he'd been born sometime in 1886, either in Utah or in Canada, and had found his way to his new family on the Great Northern Railroad, the building of which had been completed in 1892. He arrived after several days on the train with his destination pinned to his chest on the back of a store receipt. He'd eaten all of his food the first day of his travels, but various conductors had kept him fed along the way. The whole adventure made him forget things as soon as they happened, and he very soon misplaced this earliest part of his life entirely. His eldest cousin, a girl, said he'd come from northeast Canada and had spoken only French when they'd first seen him, and they'd had to whip the French out of him to get room for the English tongue. The other two cousins, both boys, said he was a Mormon from Utah. At so early an age it never occurred to him to find out from his aunt and uncle who he was. By the time he thought to ask them, many years had passed and they'd long since died, both of them.

His earliest memory was that of standing beside his uncle Robert Grainier the First, standing no higher than the elbow of this smoky-smelling man he'd quickly got to calling Father, in the mud street of Fry within sight of the Kootenai River, observing the mass deportation of a hundred or more Chinese families from the town. Down at the street's end, at the Bonner Lumber Company's railroad yard, men with axes, pistols, and shotguns in their hands stood by saying very little while the strange people clambered onto three flatcars, jabbering like birds and herding their children into the midst of themselves, away from the edges of the open cars. The small, flat-faced men sat on the outside of the three groups, their knees drawn up and their hands locked around their shins, as the train left Fry and headed away to someplace it didn't occur to Grainier to wonder about until decades later, when he was a grown man and had come very near killing a China-man—had wanted to kill him. Most had ended up thirty or so miles west, in Montana, between the towns of Troy and Libby, in a place beside the Kootenai River that came to be called China Basin. By the time Grainier was working on bridges, the community had dispersed, and only a few lived here and there in the area, and nobody was afraid of them anymore.

The Kootenai River flowed past Fry as well. Grainier had patchy memories of a week when the water broke over its banks and flooded the lower portion of Fry. A few of the frailest structures washed away and broke apart downstream. The post office was undermined and carried off, and Grainier remembered being lifted up by somebody, maybe his father, and surfacing above the heads of a large crowd of townspeople to watch the building sail away on the flood. Afterwards some Canadians found the post office stranded on the lowlands one hundred miles downriver in British Columbia.

Robert and his new family lived in town. Only two doors away a bald man, always in a denim oversuit, always hatless—a large man, with very small, strong hands—kept a shop where he mended boots. Sometimes when he was out of sight little Robert or one of his cousins liked to nip in and rake out a gob of beeswax from the mason jar of it on his workbench. The mender used it to wax his thread when he sewed on tough leather, but the children sucked at it like candy.

The mender, for his part, chewed tobacco like many folks. One day he caught the three neighbor children as they passed his door. "Look here," he said. He bent over and expectorated half a mouthful into a glass canning jar nestled up against the leg of his table. He picked up this receptacle and swirled the couple inches of murky spit it held. "You children want a little taste out of this?"

They didn't answer.

"Go ahead and have a drink!—if you think you'd like to," he said.

They didn't answer.

He poured the horrible liquid into his jar of beeswax and glopped it all around with a finger and held the finger out toward their faces and hollered, "Take some anytime you'd like!" He laughed and laughed. He rocked in his chair, wiping his tiny fingers on his denim lap. A vague disappointment shone in his eyes as he looked around and found nobody there to tell about his maneuver.

In 1899 the towns of Fry and Eatonville were combined under the name of Bonners Ferry. Grainier got his reading and numbers at the Bonners Ferry schoolhouse. He was never a scholar, but he learned to decipher writing on a page, and it helped him to get along in the world. In his teens he lived with his eldest cousin, Suzanne, and her family after she married, this following the death of their parents, his aunt and uncle Helen and Robert Grainier.

He quit attending school in his early teens and, without parents to fuss at him, became a layabout. Fishing by himself along the Kootenai one day, just a mile or so upriver from town, he came on an itinerant bum, a "boomer," as his sort was known, holed up among some birches in a sloppy camp, nursing an injured leg. "Come on up here. Please, young feller," the boomer called. "Please—please! I'm cut through the cords of my knee, and I want you to know a few things."

Young Robert wound in his line and laid the pole aside. He climbed the bank and stopped ten feet from where the man sat up against a tree with his legs out straight, barefoot, the left leg resting over a pallet of evergreen limbs. The man's old shoes lay one on either side of him. He was bearded and streaked with dust, and bits of the woods clung to him every-where. "Rest your gaze on a murdered man," he said.

"I ain't even going to ask you to bring me a drink of water," the man said. "I'm dry as boots, but I'm going to die, so I don't think I need any favors." Robert was paralyzed. He had the impression of a mouth hole moving in a stack of leaves and rags and matted brown hair. "I've got just one or two things that must be said, or they'll go to my grave. . . .

"That's right," he said. "I been cut behind the knee by this one feller they call Big-Ear Al. And I have to say, I know he's killed me. That's the first thing. Take that news to your sheriff, son. William Coswell Haley, from St. Louis, Missouri, has been robbed, cut in the leg, and murdered by the boomer they call Big-Ear Al. He snatched my roll of fourteen dollars off me whilst I slept, and he cut the strings back of my knee so's I wouldn't chase after him. My leg's stinking," he said, "because I've laid up here so long the rot's set in. You know how that'll do. That rot will travel till I'm dead right up to my eyes. Till I'm a corpse able to see things. Able to think its thoughts. Then about the fourth day I'll be all the way dead. I don't know what happens to us then—if we can think our thoughts in the grave, or we fly to Heaven, or get taken to the Devil. But here's what I have to say, just in case:

"I am William Coswell Haley, forty-two years old. I was a good man with jobs and prospects in St. Louis, Missouri, until a bit more than four years ago. At that time my niece Susan Haley became about twelve years of age, and, as I was living in my brother's house in those days, I started to get around her in her bed at night. I couldn't sleep—it got that way, I couldn't stop my heart from running and racing—until I'd got up from my pallet and snuck to the girl's room and got around her bed, and just stood there quiet. Well, she never woke. Not even one night when I rustled her covers. Another night I touched her face and she never woke, grabbed at her foot and didn't get a rise. Another night I pulled at her covers, and she was the same as dead. I touched her, lifted her shift, did every little thing I wanted. Every little thing. And she never woke.

"And that got to be my way. Night after night. Every little thing. She never woke.

"Well, I came home one day, and I'd been working at the candle fac-tory, which was an easy job to acquire when a feller had no other. Mostly old gals working there, but they'd take anybody on. When I got to the house, my sister-in-law, Alice Haley, was sitting in the yard on a wet winter's day, sitting on the greasy grass. Just plunked there. Bawling like a baby.

"'What is it, Alice?'

"'My husband's took a stick to our little daughter Susan! My husband's took a stick to her! A stick!'

"'Good God, is she hurt,' I said, 'or is it just her feelings?'

"'Hurt? Hurt?' she cries at me—'My little girl is dead!'

"I didn't even go into the house. Left whatever-all I owned and walked to the railway and got on a flatcar, and I've never been a hundred yards from these train tracks ever since. Been all over the country. Canada, too. Never a hundred yards from these rails and ties.

"Little young Susan had a child in her, is what her mother told me. And her father beat on her to drive that poor child out of her belly. Beat on her till he'd killed her."

For a few minutes the dying man stopped talking. He grabbed at breaths, put his hands to the ground either side of him and seemed to want to shift his posture, but had no strength. He couldn't seem to get a decent breath in his lungs, panting and wheezing. "I'll take that drink of water now." He closed his eyes and ceased struggling for air. When Robert got near, certain the man had died, William Haley spoke without opening his eyes: "Just bring it to me in that old shoe."

4.

The boy never told anyone about William Coswell Haley. Not the sheriff, or his cousin Suzanne, or anyone else. He brought the man one swallow of water in the man's own boot, and left William Haley to die alone. It was the most cowardly and selfish of the many omissions that might have been counted against him in his early years. But maybe the incident affected him in a way nobody could have traced successfully, because Robert Grainier settled in and worked through the rest of his youth as one of the labor pool around town, hiring out to the railroad or to the entrepreneurial families of the area, the Eatons, the Frys, or the Bonners, finding work on the crews pretty well whenever he needed, because he stayed away from drink or anything unseemly and was known as a steady man.

He worked around town right through his twenties—a man of whom it might have been said, but nothing was ever said of him, that he had little to interest him. At thirty-one he still chopped firewood, loaded trucks, served among various gangs formed up by more enterprising men for brief jobs here and there.

Then he met Gladys Olding. One of his cousins, later he couldn't remember which one to thank, took him to church with the Methodists, and there she was, a small girl just across the aisle from him, who sang softly during the hymns in a voice he picked out without any trouble. A session of lemonade and pastries followed the service, and there in the courtyard she introduced herself to him casually, with an easy smile, as if girls did things like that every day, and maybe they did—Robert Grainier didn't know, as Robert Grainier stayed away from girls. Gladys looked much older than her years, having grown up, she explained to him, in a house in a sunny pasture, and having spent too much time in the summer light. Her hands were as rough as any fifty-year-old man's.

They saw each other frequently, Grainier forced, by the nature of their friendship, to seek her out almost always at the Methodist Sunday services and at the Wednesday-night prayer group. When the summer was full on, Grainier took her by the river road to show her the acre he'd acquired on the short bluff above the Moyea. He'd bought it from young Glenwood Fry, who had wanted an automobile and who eventually got one by selling many small parcels of land to other young people. He told her he'd try some gardening here. The nicest place for a cabin lay just down a path from a sparsely overgrown knoll he could easily level by moving around the stones it was composed of. He could clear a bigger area cutting logs for a cabin, and pulling at stumps wouldn't be urgent, as he'd just garden among them, to start. A half-mile path through a thick woods led into a meadow cleared some years back by Willis Grossling, now deceased. Grossling's daughter had said Grainier could graze a few animals there as long as he didn't run a real herd over the place. Anyway he didn't want more than a couple sheep and a couple goats. Maybe a milk cow. Grainier explained all this to Gladys without explaining why he was explaining. He hoped she guessed. He thought she must, because for this outing she'd put on the same dress she usually wore to church.

This was on a hot June day. They'd borrowed a wagon from Gladys's father and brought a picnic in two baskets. They hiked over to Grossling's meadow and waded into it through daisies up to their knees. They put out a blanket beside a seasonal creek trickling over the grass and lay back together. Grainier considered the pasture a beautiful place. Somebody should paint it, he said to Gladys. The buttercups nodded in the breeze and the petals of the daisies trembled. Yet further off, across the field, they seemed stationary.

Gladys said, "Right now I could just about understand everything there is." Grainier knew how seriously she took her church and her Bible, and he thought she might be talking about something in that realm of things. "Well, you see what I like," he said.

"Yes, I do," she said.

"And I see what I like very, very well," he said, and kissed her lips.

"Ow," she said. "You got my mouth flat against my teeth."

"Are you sorry?"

"No. Do it again. But easy does it."

The first kiss plummeted him down a hole and popped him out into a world he thought he could get along in—as if he'd been pulling hard the wrong way and was now turned around headed downstream. They spent the whole afternoon among the daisies kissing. He felt glorious and full of more blood than he was supposed to have in him.

When the sun got too hot, they moved under a lone jack pine in the pasture of jeremy grass, he with his back against the bark and she with her cheek on his shoulder. The white daisies dabbed the field so profusely that it seemed to foam. He wanted to ask for her hand now. He was afraid to ask. She must want him to ask, or surely she wouldn't lie here with him, breathing against his arm, his face against her hair—her hair faintly fragrant of sweat and soap. . . . "Would you care to be my wife, Gladys?" he astonished himself by saying.

"Yes, Bob, I believe I would like it," she said, and she seemed to hold her breath a minute; then he sighed, and both laughed.

When, in the summer of 1920, he came back from the Robinson Gorge job with four hundred dollars in his pocket, riding in a passenger car as far as Coeur d'Alene, Idaho, and then in a wagon up the Panhandle, a fire was consuming the Moyea Valley. He rode through a steadily thickening haze of wood smoke into Booners Ferry and found the little town crowded with residents from along the Moyea River who no longer had any homes.

Grainier searched for his wife and daughter among the folks sheltering in town. Many had nothing to do now but move on, destitute. Nobody had word of his family.

He searched among the crowd of some one hundred or so people camping at the fairgrounds among tiny collections of the remnants of their worldly possessions, random things, dolls and mirrors and bridles, all waterlogged. These had managed to wade down the river and through the conflagration and out the southern side of it. Others, who'd headed north and tried to outrun the flames, had not been heard of since. Grainier questioned everyone, but got no news of his wife and daughter, and he grew increasingly frantic as he witnessed the refugees' strange happiness at having got out alive and their apparent disinterest in the fate of anyone who might have failed to.

The northbound Spokane International was stopped in Bonners and wouldn't move on until the fire was down and a good rain had soaked the Panhandle. Grainier walked the twenty miles out along the Moyea River Road toward his home with a handkerchief tied over his nose and mouth to strain the smoke, stopping to wet it often in the river, passing through a silvery snow of ash. Nothing here was burning. The fire had started on the river's east side not far above the village of Meadow Creek and worked north, crossed the river at a narrow gorge bridged by flaming mammoth spruce trees as they fell, and devoured the valley. Meadow Creek was deserted. He stopped at the railroad platform and drank water from the barrel there and went quickly on without resting. Soon he was passing through a forest of charred, gigantic spears that only a few days past had been evergreens. The world was gray, white, black, and acrid, without a single live animal or plant, no longer burning and yet still full of the warmth and life of the fire. So much ash, so much choking smoke—it was clear to him miles before he reached his home that nothing could be left of it, but he went on anyway, weeping for his wife and daughter, calling, "Kate! Gladys!" over and over. He turned off the road to look in on the homesite of the Andersens, the first one past Meadow Creek. At first he couldn't tell even where the cabin had stood. Their acreage looked like the rest of the valley, burned and silent except for the collective hiss of the very last remnants of combustion. He found their cookstove mounding out of a tall drift of ashes where its iron legs had buckled in the heat. A few of the biggest stones from the chimney lay strewn nearby. Ash had buried the rest.

The farther north he hiked, the louder came the reports of cracking logs and the hiss of burning, until every charred tree around him still gave off smoke. He rounded a bend to hear the roar of the conflagration and see the fire a half mile ahead like a black and red curtain dropped from a night sky. Even from this distance the heat of it stopped him. He collapsed to his knees, sat in the warm ashes through which he'd been wading, and wept.

Ten days later, when the Spokane International was running again, Grainier rode it up into Creston, B.C., and back south again the evening of the same day through the valley that had been his home. The blaze had climbed to the ridges either side of the valley and stalled halfway down the other side of the mountains, according to the reports Grainier had listened to intently. It had gutted the valley along its entire length like a campfire in a ditch. All his life Robert Grainier would remember vividly the burned valley at sundown, the most dreamlike business he'd ever witnessed waking—the brilliant pastels of the last light overhead, some clouds high and white, catching daylight from beyond the valley, others ribbed and gray and pink, the lowest of them rubbing the peaks of Bussard and Queen mountains; and beneath this wondrous sky the black valley, utterly still, the train moving through it making a great noise but unable to wake this dead world.

The news in Creston was terrible. No escapees from the Moyea Valley fire had appeared there.

Grainier stayed at his cousin's home for several weeks, not good for much, sickened by his natural grief and confused by the situation. He understood that he'd lost his wife and little girl, but sometimes the idea stormed over him, positively stormed into his thoughts like an irresistible army, that Gladys and Kate had escaped the fire and that he should look for them everywhere in the world until he found them. Nightmares woke him every night: Gladys came out of the black landscape onto their home-site, dressed in smoking rags and carrying their daughter, and found nothing there, and stood crying in the waste.

In September, thirty days after the fire, Grainier rented a pair of horses and a wagon and set out up the river road carting a heap of supplies, intending to put up shelter on his acre and wait all winter for his family to return. Some might have called it an ill-considered plan, but the experiment had the effect of bringing him to his senses. As soon as he entered the remains he felt his heart's sorrow blackened and purified, as if it were an actual lump of matter from which all the hopeful, crazy thinking was burning away. He drove through a layer of ash deep enough, in some places, that he couldn't make out the roadbed any better than if he'd driven through winter snows. Only the fastest animals and those with wings could have escaped this feasting fire.

After traveling through the waste for several miles, scarcely able to breathe for the reek of it, he quit and turned around and went back to live in town.

Not long after the start of autumn, businessmen from Spokane raised a hotel at the little railroad camp of Meadow Creek. By spring a few dispossessed families had returned to start again in the Moyea Valley. Grainier hadn't thought he'd try it himself, but in May he camped alongside the river, fishing for speckled trout and hunting for a rare and very flavorful mushroom the Canadians called morel, which sprang up on ground disturbed by fire. Progressing north for several days, Grainier found himself within a shout of his old home and climbed the draw by which he and Gladys had habitually found their way to and from the water. He marveled at how many shoots and flowers had sprouted already from the general death.

He climbed to their cabin site and saw no hint, no sign at all of his former life, only a patch of dark ground surrounded by the black spikes of spruce. The cabin was cinders, burned so completely that its ashes had mixed in with a common layer all about and then been tamped down by the snows and washed and dissolved by the thaw.

He found the woodstove lying on its side with its legs curled up under it like a beetle's. He righted it and pried at the handle. The hinges broke away and the door came off. Inside sat a chunk of birch, barely charred. "Gladys!" he said out loud. Everything he'd loved lying ashes around him, but here this thing she'd touched and held.

He poked through the caked mud around the grounds and found almost nothing he could recognize. He scuffed along through the ashes and kicked up one of the spikes he'd used in building the cabin's walls, but couldn't find any others.

He saw no sign of their Bible, either. If the Lord had failed to protect even the book of his own Word, this proved to Grainier that here had come a fire stronger than God.

Come June and July this clearing would be grassy and green. Already foot-tall jack pine sprouted from the ashes, dozens of them. He thought of poor little Kate and talked to himself again out loud: "She never even growed up to a sprout."

Grainier thought he must be very nearly the only creature in this sterile region. But standing in his old homesite, talking out loud, he heard himself answered by wolves on the peaks in the distance, these answered in turn by others, until the whole valley was singing. There were birds about, too, not foraging, maybe, but lighting to rest briefly as they headed across the burn.

Gladys, or her spirit, was palpably near. A feeling overcame him that something belonging to her and the baby, to both of them, lay around here to be claimed. What thing? He believed it might be the chocolates Gladys had bought in a red box, chocolates cupped in white paper. A crazy thought, but he didn't bother to argue with it. Once every week, she and the tyke had sucked one chocolate apiece. Suddenly he could see those white cups scattered all around him. When he looked directly at any one of them, it disappeared.

Toward dark, as Grainier lay by the river in a blanket, his eye caught on a quick thing up above, flying along the river. He looked and saw his wife Gladys's white bonnet sailing past overhead. Just sailing past.

He stayed on for weeks in this camp, waiting, wanting many more such visions as that of the bonnet, and the chocolates—as many as wanted to come to him; and he figured as long as he saw impossible things in this place, and liked them, he might as well be in the habit of talking to himself, too. Many times each day he found himself deflating on a gigantic sigh and saying, "A pretty mean circumstance!" He thought he'd better be up and doing things so as not to sigh quite as much.

Sometimes he thought about Kate, the pretty little tyke, but not frequently. Hers was not such a sad story. She'd hardly been awake, much less alive.

He lived through the summer off dried morel mushrooms and fresh trout cooked up together in butter he bought at the store in Meadow Creek. After a while a dog came along, a little red-haired female. The dog stayed with him, and he stopped talking to himself because he was ashamed to have the animal catch him at it. He bought a canvas tarp and some rope in Meadow Creek, and later he bought a nanny goat and walked her back to his camp, the dog wary and following this newcomer at a distance. He picketed the nanny near his lean-to.

He spent several days along the creek in gorges where the burn wasn't so bad, collecting willow whips from which he wove a crate about two yards square and half as tall. He and the dog walked to Meadow Creek and he bought four hens, also a rooster to keep them in line, and carted them home in a grain sack and cooped them up in the crate. He let them out for a day or two every now and then, penning them frequently so the hens wouldn't lay in secret places, not that there were many places in this destruction even to hide an egg.

The little red dog lived on goat's milk and fish heads and, Grainier supposed, whatever she could catch. She served as decent company when she cared to, but tended to wander for days at a time.

Because the ground was too bare for grazing, he raised his goat on the same laying mash he fed the chickens. This got to be expensive. Following the first frost in September he butchered the goat and jerked most of its meat.

After the second frost of the season, he started strangling and stewing the fowls one by one over the course of a couple of weeks, until he and the dog had eaten them all, the rooster, too. Then he left for Meadow Creek. He had grown no garden and built no structure other than his lean-to.

As he got ready to depart, he discussed the future with his dog. "To keep a dog in town it ain't my nature," he told the animal. "But you seem to me elderly, and I don't think an elderly old dog can make the winter by your lonely up around these hills." He told her he would pay an extra nickel to bring her aboard the train a dozen miles into Bonners Ferry. But this must not have suited her. On the day he gathered his few things to hike down to the platform at Meadow Creek, the little red dog was nowhere to be found, and he left without her.

The abbreviated job a year earlier at Robinson Gorge had given him money enough to last through the winter in Bonners Ferry, but in order to stretch it Grainier worked for twenty cents an hour for a man named Williams who'd contracted with Great Northern to sell them one thousand cords of firewood for two dollars and seventy-five cents each. The steady daylong exertions kept him and seven other men warm through the days, even as the winter turned into the coldest seen in many years. The Kootenai River froze hard enough that one day they watched, from the lot where wagons brought them logs of birch and larch to be sawn and split, a herd of two hundred cattle being driven across the river on the ice. They moved onto the blank white surface and churned up a snowy fog that first lost them in itself, then took in all the world north of the riverbank, and finally rose high enough to hide the sun and sky.

Late that March Grainier returned to his homesite in the Moyea Valley, this time hauling a wagon-load of supplies.

Animals had returned to what was left of the forest. As Grainier drove along in the wagon behind a wide, slow, sand-colored mare, clusters of orange butterflies exploded off the blackish-purple piles of bear-sign and winked and fluttered magically like leaves without trees. More bears than people traveled the muddy road, leaving tracks straight up and down the middle of it; later in the summer they would forage in the low patches of huckleberry he already saw coming back on the blackened hillsides.

At his old campsite by the river he raised his canvas lean-to and went about chopping down five dozen burned spruce, none of them bigger around than his own hat size, acting on the generally acknowledged theory that one man working alone could handle a house log about the circumference of his own head. With the rented horse he got the timber decked in his clearing, then had to return the outfit to the stables in Bonners Ferry and hop the train back to Meadow Creek.

It wasn't until a couple of days later, when he got back to his old home—now his new home—that he noticed what his labors had prevented his seeing: It was full on spring, sunny and beautiful, and the Moyea Valley showed a lot of green against the dark of the burn. The ground about was healing. Fireweed and jack pine stood up about thigh high. A mustard-tinted fog of pine pollen drifted through the valley when the wind came up. If he didn't yank this crop of new ones, his clearing would return to forest.

He built his cabin about eighteen by eighteen, laying out lines, making a foundation of stones in a ditch knee-deep to get down below the frost line, scribing and hewing the logs to keep each one flush against the next, hacking notches, getting his back under the higher ones to lift them into place. In a month he'd raised four walls nearly eight feet in height. The windows and roof he left for later, when he could get some milled lumber. He tossed his canvas over the east end to keep the rain out. No peeling had been required, because the fire had managed that for him. He'd heard that fire-killed trees lasted best, but the cabin stank. He burned heaps of jack pine needles in the middle of the dirt floor trying to change the odor's character, and felt after a while that he'd succeeded.

In early June the red dog appeared, took up residence in a corner, and whelped a brood of four pups that appeared quite wolfish.

Down at the Meadow Creek store he spoke about this development with a Kootenai Indian named Bob. Kootenai Bob was a steady man who had always refused liquor and worked frequently at jobs in town, just as Grainier did, and they'd known each other for many years. Kootenai Bob said that if the dog's pups had come out wolfish, that would be quite strange. The Kootenais had it that only one pair in a wolf den ever made pups—that you couldn't get any of the he-wolves to mate except one, the chief of the wolf tribe. And the she-wolf he chose to bear his litters was the only bitch in the pack who ever came in heat. "And so I tell you," Bob said, "that therefore your wandering dog wouldn't drop a litter of wolves." But what if she'd encountered the wolf pack at just the moment she was coming into heat, Grainier wanted to know—might the king wolf have mounted her then, just for the newness of the experience? "Then perhaps, perhaps," Bob said. "Might be. Might be you've got yourself some dog-of-wolf. Might be you've started your own pack, Robert."

Three of the pups wandered off immediately as the little dog weaned them, but one, a discoordinated male, stayed around and was tolerated by its mother. Grainier felt sure this dog was got of a wolf, but it never even whimpered in reply when the packs in the distance, some as far away as the Selkirks on the British Columbia side, sang at dusk. The creature needed to be taught its nature, Grainier felt. One evening he got down beside it and howled. The little pup only sat on its rump with an inch of pink tongue jutting stupidly from its closed mouth. "You're not growing the direction of your own nature, which is to howl when the others do," he told the mongrel. He stood up straight himself and howled long and sorrowfully over the gorge, and over the low quiet river he could hardly see across this close to nightfall. . . . Nothing from the pup. But often, thereafter, when Grainier heard wolves at dusk, he laid his head back and howled for all he was worth, because it did him good. It flushed out something heavy that tended to collect in his heart, and after an evening's program with his choir of British Columbian wolves he felt warm and buoyant.

He tried telling Kootenai Bob of this development. "Howling, are you?" the Indian said. "There it is for you, then. That's what happens, that's what they say: There's not a wolf alive that can't tame a man."

The pup disappeared before autumn, and Grainier hoped he'd made it across the line to his brothers in Canada, but he had to assume the worst: food for a hawk, or for the coyotes.

Many years later—in 1930—Grainier saw Kootenai Bob on the very day the Indian died. That day Kootenai Bob was drunk for the first time in his life. Some ranch hands visiting from across the line in British Columbia had managed to get him to take a drink by fixing up a jug of shandy, a mixture of lemonade and beer. They'd told him he could drink this with impunity, as the action of the lemon juice would nullify any effect of the beer, and Kootenai Bob had believed them, because the United States was by now more than a decade into Prohibition, and the folks from Canada, where liquor was still allowed, were considered experts when it came to alcohol. Grainier found old Bob sitting on a bench out front of the hotel in Meadow Creek toward evening with his legs wrapped around an eight-quart canning pan full of beer—no sign of lemonade by now—lapping at it like a thirsty mutt. The Indian had been guzzling all afternoon, and he'd pissed himself repeatedly and no longer had the power of speech. Sometime after dark he wandered off and managed to get himself a mile up the tracks, where he lay down unconscious across the ties and was run over by a succession of trains. Four or five came over him, until late next afternoon the gathering multitude of crows prompted someone to investigate. By then Kootenai Bob was strewn for a quarter mile along the right-of-way. Over the next few days his people were seen plying along the blank patch of earth beside the rails, locating whatever little tokens of flesh and bone and cloth the crows had missed and collecting them in brightly, beautifully painted leather pouches, which they must have taken off somewhere and buried with a fitting ceremony.

5.

At just about the time Grainier discovered a rhythm to his seasons—summers in Washington, spring and fall at his cabin, winters boarding in Bonners Ferry—he began to see he couldn't make it last. This was some four years into his residence in the second cabin.

His summer wages gave him enough to live on all year, but he wasn't built for logging. First he became aware how much he needed the winter to rest and mend; then he suspected the winter wasn't long enough to mend him. Both his knees ached. His elbows cracked loudly when he straightened his arms, and something hitched and snapped in his right shoulder when he moved it the wrong way; a general stiffness of his frame worked itself out by halves through most mornings, and he labored like an engine through the afternoons, but he was well past thirty-five years, closer now to forty, and he really wasn't much good in the woods anymore.

When the month of April arrived in 1925, he didn't leave for Washington. These days there was plenty of work in town for anybody willing to get around after it. He felt like staying closer to home, and he'd come into possession of a pair of horses and a wagon—by a sad circumstance, however. The wagon had been owned by Mr. and Mrs. Pinkham, who ran a machine shop on Highway 2. He'd agreed to help their grandson Henry, known as Hank, an enormous youth in his late teens, certainly no older than his early twenties, to load sacks of cornmeal aboard the Pinkhams' wagon, this favor a result of Grainier's having stopped in briefly to get some screws for a saw handle. They'd only loaded the first two sacks when Hank sloughed the third one from his shoulder onto the dirt floor of the barn and said, "I am as dizzy as anything today," sat on the pile of sacks, removed his hat, flopped over sideways, and died.

His grandfather hastened from the house when Grainier called him and went to the boy right away, saying, "Oh. Oh. Oh." He was open-mouthed with uncomprehension. "He's not gone, is he?"

"I don't know, sir. I just couldn't say. He sat down and fell over. I don't even think he said anything to complain," Grainier told him.

"We've got to send you for help," Mr. Pinkham said.

"Where should I go?"

"I've got to get Mother," Pinkham said, looking at Grainier with terror on his face. "She's inside the house."

Grainier remained with the dead boy but didn't look at him while they were alone.

Old Mrs. Pinkham came into the barn flapping her hands and said, "Hank? Hank?" and bent close, taking her grandson's face in her hands. "Are you gone?"

"He's gone, isn't he?" her husband said.

"He's gone! He's gone!"

"He's gone, Pearl."

"God has him now," Mrs. Pinkham said.

"Dear Lord, take this boy to your bosom. . . ."

"You could seen this coming ever since!" the old woman cried.

"His heart wasn't strong," Mr. Pinkham explained. "You could see that about him. We always knew that much."

"His heart was his fate," Mrs. Pinkham said. "You could've looked right at him any time you wanted and seen this."

"Yes," Mr. Pinkham agreed.

"He was that sweet and good," Mrs. Pinkham said. "Still in his youth. Still in his youth!" She stood up angrily and marched from the barn and over to the edge of the roadway—U.S. Highway 2—and stopped.

Grainier had seen people dead, but he'd never seen anybody die. He didn't know what to say or do. He felt he should leave, and he felt he shouldn't leave.

Mr. Pinkham asked Grainier a favor, standing in the shadow of the house while his wife waited in the yard under a wild mixture of clouds and sunshine, looking amazed and, from this distance, as young as a child, and also very beautiful, it seemed to Grainier. "Would you take him down to Helmer's?" Helmer was in charge of the cemetery and, with Smithson the barber's help, often prepared corpses for the ground. "We'll get poor young Hank in the wagon. We'll get him in the wagon, and you'll go ahead and take him for me, won't you? So I can tend to his grandmother. She's gone out of her mind."

Together they wrestled the heavy dead boy aboard the wagon, resorting after much struggle to the use of two long boards. They inclined them against the wagon's bed and flopped the corpse up and over, up and over, until it rested in the conveyance. "Oh—oh—oh—oh—" exclaimed the grandfather with each and every nudge. As for Grainier, he hadn't touched another person in several years, and even apart from the strangeness of this situation, the experience was something to remark on and remember. He giddyapped Pinkham's pair of old mares, and they pulled young dead Hank Pinkham to Helmer's cemetery.

Helmer, too, had a favor to ask of Grainier, once he'd taken the body off his hands. "If you'll deliver a coffin over to the jail in Troy and pick up a load of lumber for me at the yard on Main, then take the lumber to Leona for me, I'll pay you rates for both jobs separate. Two for the price of one. Or come to think of it," he said, "one job for the price of two, that's what it would be, ain't it, sir?"

"I don't mind," Grainier told him.

"I'll give you a nickel for every mile of it."

"I'd have to stop at Pinkham's and bargain a rate from them. I'd need twenty cents a mile before I saw a profit."

"All right then. Ten cents and it's done."

"I'd need a bit more."

"Six dollars entire."

"I'll need a pencil and a paper. I don't know my numbers without a pencil and a paper."

The little undertaker brought him what he needed, and together they decided that six-and-a-half dollars was fair.

For the rest of the fall and even a ways into winter, Grainier leased the pair and wagon from the Pinkhams, boarding the mares with their owners, and kept himself busy as a freighter of sorts. Most of his jobs took him east and west along Highway 2, among the small communities there that had no close access to the railways.

Some of these errands took him down along the Kootenai River, and traveling beside it always brought into his mind the image of William Coswell Haley, the dying boomer. Rather than wearing away, Grainier's regret at not having helped the man had grown much keener as the years had passed. Sometimes he thought also of the Chinese railroad hand he'd almost helped to kill. The thought paralyzed his heart. He was certain the man had taken his revenge by calling down a curse that had incinerated Kate and Gladys. He believed the punishment was too great.

But the hauling itself was better work than any he'd undertaken, a ticket to a kind of show, to an entertainment comprised of the follies and endeavors of his neighbors. Grainier was having the time of his life. He contracted with the Pinkhams to buy the horses and wagon in installments for three hundred dollars.

By the time he'd made this decision, the region had seen over a foot of snow, but he continued a couple of more weeks in the freight business. It didn't seem a particularly bad winter down below, but the higher country had frozen through, and one of Grainier's last jobs was to get up the Yahk River Road to the saloon at the logging village of Sylvanite, in the hills above which a lone prospector had blown himself up in his shack while trying to thaw out frozen dynamite on his stove. The man lay out on the bartop, alive and talking, sipping free whiskey and praising his dog. His dog's going for help had saved him. For half a day the animal had made such a nuisance of himself around the saloon that one of the patrons had finally noosed him and dragged him home and found his master extensively lacerated and raving from exposure in what remained of his shack.

Much that was astonishing was told of the dogs in the Panhandle and along the Kootenai River, tales of rescues, tricks, feats of super-canine intelligence and humanlike understanding. As his last job for that year, Grainier agreed to transport a man from Meadow Creek to Bonners who'd actually been shot by his own dog.

The dog-shot man was a bare acquaintance of Grainier's, a surveyor for Spokane International who came and went in the area, name of Peterson, originally from Virginia. Peterson's boss and comrades might have put him on the train into town the next morning if they'd waited, but they thought he might perish before then, so Grainier hauled him down the Moyea River Road wrapped in a blanket and half sitting up on a load of half a dozen sacks of wood chips bagged up just to make him comfortable.

"Are you feeling like you need anything?" Grainier said at the start.

Grainier thought Peterson had gone to sleep. Or worse. But in a minute the victim answered: "Nope. I'm perfect."

A long thaw had come earlier in the month. The snow was melted out of the ruts. Bare earth showed off in the woods. But now, again, the weather was freezing, and Grainier hoped he wouldn't end up bringing in a corpse dead of the cold.

For the first few miles he didn't talk much to his passenger, because Peterson had a dented head and crazy eye, the result of some mishap in his youth, and he was hard to look at.

Grainier steeled himself to glance once in a while in the man's direction, just to be sure he was alive. As the sun left the valley, Peterson's crazy eye and then his entire face became invisible. If he died now, Grainier probably wouldn't know it until they came into the light of the two gas lamps either side of the doctor's house. After they'd moved along for nearly an hour without conversation, listening only to the creaking of the wagon and the sound of the nearby river and the clop of the mares, it grew dark.

Grainier disliked the eeriness of the shadows, the spindly silhouettes of birch trees, and the clouds strung around the yellow half-moon. It all seemed designed to frighten the child in him. "Sir, are you dead?" he asked Peterson.

"Who? Me? Nope. Alive," said Peterson.

"Well, I was wondering—do you feel as if you might go on?"

"You mean as if I might die?"

"Yessir," Grainier said.

"Nope. Ain't going to die tonight."

"That's good."

"Even better for me, I'd say."

Grainier now felt they'd chatted sufficiently that he might raise a matter of some curiosity to him. "Mrs. Stout, your boss's wife, there. She said your dog shot you."

"Well, she's a very upright lady—to my way of knowing, anyways."

"Yes, I have the same impression of her right around," Grainier said, "and she said your dog shot you."

Peterson was silent a minute. In a bit, he coughed and said, "Do you feel a little warm patch in the air? As if maybe last week's warm weather turned around and might be coming back on us?"

"Not as such to me," Grainier said. "Just holding the warm of the day the way it does before you get around this ridge."

They continued along under the rising moon.

"Anyway," Grainier said.

Peterson didn't respond. Might not have heard.

"Did your dog really shoot you?"

"Yes, he did. My own dog shot me with my own gun. Ouch!" Peterson said, shifting himself gently. "Can you take your team a little more gradual over these ruts, Mister?"

"I don't mind," Grainier said. "But you've got to get your medical attention, or anything could happen to you."

"All right. Go at it like the Pony Express, then, if you want."

"I don't see how a dog shoots a gun."

"Well, he did."

"Did he use a rifle?"

"It weren't a cannon. It weren't a pistol. It were a rifle."

"Well, that's pretty mysterious, Mr. Peterson. How did that happen?"

"It was self-defense."

Grainier waited. A full minute passed, but Peterson stayed silent.

"That just tears it then," Grainier said, quite agitated. "I'm pulling this team up, and you can walk from here, if you want to beat around and around the bush. I'm taking you to town with a hole in you, and I ask a simple question about how your dog shot you, and you have to play like a bunkhouse lout who don't know the answer."

"All right!" Peterson laughed, then groaned with the pain it caused him. "My dog shot me in self-defense. I went to shoot him, at first, because of what Kootenai Bob the Indian said about him, and he slipped the rope. I had him tied for the business we were about to do." Peterson coughed and went quiet a few seconds. "I ain't stalling you now! I just got to get over the hurt a little bit."

"All right. But why did you have Kootenai Bob tied up, and what has Kootenai Bob got to do with this, anyways?"

"Not Kootenai Bob! I had the dog tied up. Kootenai Bob weren't nowhere near this scene I'm relating. He was before."

"But the dog, I say."

"And say I also, the dog. He's the one I ties. He's the one slips the rope, and I couldn't get near him—he'd just back off a step for every step I took in his direction. He knew I had his end in mind, which I decided to do on account of what Kootenai Bob said about him. That dog knew things— because of what happened to him, which is what Kootenai Bob the Indian told me about him—that animal all of a sudden knew things. So I swung the rifle by the barrel and butt-ended that old pup to stop his sass, and wham! I'm sitting on my very own butt-end pretty quick. Then I'm laying back, and the sky is traveling away from me in the wrong direction. Mr. Grainier, I'd been shot! Right here!" Peterson pointed to the bandages around his left shoulder and chest. "By my own dog!"

Peterson continued: "I believe he did it because he'd been confabulating with that wolf-girl person. If she is a person. Or I don't know. A creature is what you can call her, if ever she was created. But there are some creatures on this earth that God didn't create."

"Confabulating?"

"Yes. I let that dog in the house one night last summer because he got so yappy and wouldn't quit. I wanted him right by me where I could beat him with a kindling should he irritate me one more time. Well, next morning he got up the wall and out through the window like a bear clawing up a tree, and he started working that porch, back and forth. Then he started working that yard, back and forth, back and forth, and off he goes, and down to the woods, and I didn't see him for thirteen days. All right. All right—Kootenai Bob stopped by the place one day a while after that. Do you know him? His name is Bobcat such and such, Bobcat Ate a Mountain or one of those rooty-toot Indian names. He wants to beg you for a little money, wants a pinch of snuff, little drink of water, stops around twice in every season or so. Tells me—you can guess what: Tells me the wolf-girl has been spotted around. I showed him my dog and says this animal was gone thirteen days and come back just about wild and hardly knew me. Bob looks him in the face, getting down very close, you see, and says, 'I am goddamned if you hadn't better shoot this dog. I can see the girl's picture on the black of this dog's eyes. This dog has been with wolves, Mr. Peterson. Yes, you better shoot this dog before you get a full moon again, or he'll call that wolf-girl person right into your house, and you'll be meat for wolves, and your blood will be her drink like whiskey.' Do you think I was scared? Well, I was. 'She'll be blood-drunk and running along the roads talking in your own voice, Mr. Peterson,' is what he says to me. 'In your own voice she'll go to the window of every person you did a dirty to, and tell them what you did.' Well, I know about the girl. That wolf-girl was first seen many years back, leading a pack. Stout's cousin visiting from Seattle last Christmas saw her, and he said she had a bloody mess hanging down between her legs."

"A bloody mess?" Grainier asked, terrified in his soul.

"Don't ask me what it was. A bloody mess is all. But Bob the Kootenai feller said some of them want to believe it was the afterbirth or some part of a wolf-child torn out of her womb. You know they believe in Christ."

"What? Who?"

"The Kootenais—in Christ, and angels, devils, and creatures God didn't create, like half-wolves. They believe just about anything funny or witchy or religious they hear about. The Kootenais call animals to be people. 'Coyote-person,' 'Bear-person,' and such a way of talking."

Grainier watched the darkness on the road ahead, afraid of seeing the wolf-girl. "Dear God," he said. "I don't know where I'll get the strength to take this road at night anymore."

"And what do you think?—I can't sleep through the night, myself," Peterson said.

"God'll give me the strength, I guess."

Peterson snorted. "This wolf-girl is a creature God didn't create. She was made out of wolves and a man of unnatural desires. Did you ever get with some boys and jigger yourselves a cow?"

"What!"

"When you was a boy, did you ever get on a stump and love a cow? They all did it over where I'm from. It's not unnatural down around that way."

"Are you saying you could make a baby with a cow, or make a baby with a wolf? You? Me? A person?"

Peterson's voice sounded wet from fear and passion. "I'm saying it gets dark, and the moon gets full, and there's creatures God did not create." He made a strangling sound. "God!—this hole in me hurts when I cough. But I'm glad I don't have to try and sleep through the night, waiting on that wolf-girl and her pack to come after me."

"But did you do like the Indian told you to? Did you shoot your dog?"

"No! He shot me."

"Oh," Grainier said. Mixed up and afraid, he'd entirely forgotten that part of it. He continued to watch the woods on either side, but that night no spawn of unnatural unions showed herself.

For a while the rumors circulated. The sheriff had examined the few witnesses claiming to have seen the creature and had determined them to be frank and sober men. By their accounts, the sheriff judged her to be a female. People feared she'd whelp more hybrid pups, more wolf-people, more monsters who eventually, logically, would attract the lust of the Devil himself and bring down over the region all manner of evil influence. The Kootenais, wedded as they were known to be to pagan and superstitious practice, would fall prey completely to Satan. Before the matter ended, only fire and blood would purge the valley. . . .

But these were the malicious speculations of idle minds, and, when the election season came, the demons of the silver standard and the railroad land snatch took their attention, and the mysteries in the hills around the Moyea Valley were forgotten for a while.

6.

Not four years after his wedding and already a widower, Grainier lived in his lean-to by the river below the site where his home had been. He kept a campfire going as far as he could into the night and often didn't sleep until dawn. He feared his dreams. At first he dreamed of Gladys and Kate. Then only of Gladys. And finally, by the time he'd passed a couple of months in solitary silence, Grainier dreamed only of his campfire, of tending it just as he had before he slept—the silhouette of his hand and the charred length of lodgepole he used as a poker—and was surprised to find it gray ash and butt-ends in the morning, because he'd watched it burn all night in his dreams.

And three years later still, he lived in his second cabin, precisely where the old one had stood. Now he slept soundly through the nights, and often he dreamed of trains, and often of one particular train: He was on it; he could smell the coal smoke; a world went by. And then he was standing in that world as the sound of the train died away. A frail familiarity in these scenes hinted to him that they came from his childhood. Sometimes he woke to hear the sound of the Spokane International fading up the valley and realized he'd been hearing the locomotive as he dreamed.

Just such a dream woke him in December his second winter at the new cabin. The train passed northward until he couldn't hear it anymore. To be a child again in that other world had terrified him, and he couldn't get back to sleep. He stared around the cabin in the dark. By now he'd roofed his home properly, put in windows, equipped it with two benches, a table, a barrel stove. He and the red dog still bedded on a pallet on the floor, but for the most part he'd made as much a home here as he and Gladys and little Kate had ever enjoyed. Maybe it was his understanding of this fact, right now, in the dark, after his nightmare, that called Gladys back to visit him in spirit form. For many minutes before she showed herself, he felt her moving around the place. He detected her presence as unmistakably as he would have sensed the shape of someone blocking the light through a window, even with his eyes closed.

He put his right hand on the little dog stretched beside him. The dog didn't bark or growl, but he felt the hair on her back rise and stiffen as the visitation began to manifest itself visibly in the room, at first only as a quavering illumination, like that from a guttering candle, and then as the shape of a woman. She shimmered, and her light shook. Around her the shadows trembled. And then it was Gladys—nobody else—flickering and false, like a figure in a motion picture.

Gladys didn't speak, but she broadcast what she was feeling: She mourned for her daughter, whom she couldn't find. Without her baby she couldn't go to sleep in Jesus or rest in Abraham's bosom. Her daughter hadn't come across among the spirits, but lingered here in the world of life, a child alone in the burning forest. But the forest isn't burning, he told her. But Gladys couldn't hear. Before his sight she was living again her last moments: The forest burned, and she had only a minute to gather a few things and her baby and run from the cabin as the fire smoked down the hill. Of what she'd snatched up, less and less seemed worthy, and she tossed away clothes and valuables as the heat drove her toward the river. At the lip of the bluff she held only her Bible and her red box of chocolates, each pinned against her with an elbow, and the baby clutched against her chest with both her hands. She stooped and dropped the candy and the heavy book at her feet while she tied the child inside her apron, and then she was able to pick them up again. Needing a hand to steady her along the rocky bluff as they descended, she tossed away the Bible rather than the chocolates. This uncovering of her indifference to God, the Father of All—this was her undoing. Twenty feet above the water she kicked loose a stone, and not a heartbeat later she'd broken her back on the rocks below. Her legs lost all feeling and wouldn't move. She was only able to pluck at the knot across her bodice until the child was free to crawl away and fend for itself, however briefly, along the shore. The water stroked at Gladys until by the very power of its gentleness, it seemed, it lifted her down and claimed her, and she drowned. One by one from eddy pools and from among the rocks, the baby plucked the scattered chocolates. Eighty-foot-long spruce jutting out over the water burned through and fell into the gorge, their clumps of green needles afire and trailing smoke like pyrotechnical snakes, their flaming tops hissing as they hit the river. Gladys floated past it all, no longer in the water but now overhead, seeing everything in the world. The moss on the shingled roof of her home curled and began to smoke faintly. The logs in the walls stressed and popped like large-bore cartridges going off. On the table by the stove a magazine curled, darkened, flamed, spiraled upward, and flew away page by page, burning and circling. The cabin's one glass window shattered, the curtains began to blacken at the hems, the wax melted off the jars of tomatoes, beans, and Canada cherries on a shelf above the steaming kitchen tub. Suddenly all the lamps in the cabin were lit. On the table a metal-lidded jar of salt exploded, and then the whole structure ignited like a match head.

Gladys had seen all of this, and she made it his to know. She'd lost her fortune to death, and lost her child to life. Kate had escaped the fire.

Escaped? Grainier didn't understand this news. Had some family downriver rescued his baby daughter? "But I don't see how they could have done, not unbeknownst to anybody. Such a strange and lucky turn would have made a big story for the newspapers—like it made for the Bible, when it happened to Moses."

He was talking out loud. But where was Gladys to hear him? He sensed her presence no more. The cabin was dark. The dog no longer trembled.

7.

Thereafter, Grainier lived in the cabin, even through the winters. By most Januaries, when the snow had deepened, the valley seemed stopped with a perpetual silence, but as a matter of fact it was often filled with the rumble of trains and the choirs of distant wolves and the nearer mad jibbering of coyotes. Also his own howling, as he'd taken it up as a kind of sport.

The spirit form of his departed wife never reappeared to him. At times he dreamed of her, and dreamed also of the loud flames that had taken her. Usually he woke in the middle of this roaring dream to find himself surrounded by the thunder of the Spokane International going up the valley in the night.

But he wasn't just a lone eccentric bachelor who lived in the woods and howled with the wolves. By his own lights, Grainier had amounted to something. He had a business in the hauling.

He was glad he hadn't married another wife, not that one would have been easy to find, but a Kootenai widow might have been willing. That he'd taken on an acre and a home in the first place he owed to Gladys. He'd felt able to tackle the responsibilities that came with a team and wagon because Gladys stayed in his heart and in his thoughts.

He boarded the mares in town during winters—two elderly logging horses in about the same shape and situation as himself, but smart with the wagon, and more than strong enough. To pay for the outfit he worked in the Washington woods one last summer, very glad to call it his last. Early that season a wild limb knocked his jaw crooked, and he never quite got the left side hooked back properly on its hinge again. It pained him to chew his food, and that accounted more than anything else for his lifelong skinniness. His joints went to pieces. If he reached the wrong way behind him, his right shoulder locked up as dead as a vault door until somebody freed it by putting a foot against his ribs and pulling on his arm. "It takes a great much of pulling," he'd explain to anyone helping him, closing his eyes and entering a darkness of bone torment, "more than that—pull harder— a great deal of pulling now, greater, greater, you just have to pull—" until the big joint unlocked with a sound between a pop and a gulp. His right knee began to wobble sideways out from under him more and more often; it grew dangerous to trust him with the other end of a load. "I'm got so I'm joined up too tricky to pay me," he told his boss one day. He stayed out the job, his only duty tearing down old coolie shacks and salvaging the better lumber, and when that chore was done he went back to Bonners Ferry. He was finished as a woodsman.

He rode the Great Northern to Spokane. With nearly five hundred dollars in his pocket, more than plenty to pay off his team and wagon, he stayed in a room at the Riverside Hotel and visited the county fair, a diversion that lasted only half an hour, because his first decision at the fairgrounds was a wrong one.

In the middle of a field, two men from Alberta had parked an airplane and were offering rides in the sky for four dollars a passenger—quite a hefty asking price, and not many took them up on it. But Grainier had to try. The young pilot—just a kid, twenty or so at the most, a blond boy in a brown oversuit with metal buttons up the front—gave him a pair of goggles to wear and boosted him aboard. "Climb on over. Get something under your butt," the boy said.

Grainier seated himself on a bench behind the pilot's. He was now about six feet off the ground, and already that seemed high enough. The two wings on either side of this device seemed constructed of the frailest stuff. How did it fly when its wings stayed still?—by making its own gale evidently, propelling the air with its propeller, which the other Albertan, the boy's grim father, turned with his hands to get it spinning.

Grainier was aware only of a great astonishment, and then he was high in the sky, while his stomach was somewhere else. It never did catch up with him. He looked down at the fairgrounds as if from a cloud. The earth's surface turned sideways, and he misplaced all sense of up and down. The craft righted itself and began a slow, rackety ascent, winding its way upward like a wagon around a mountain. Except for the churning in his gut, Grainier felt he might be getting accustomed to it all. At this point the pilot looked backward at him, resembling a raccoon in his cap and goggles, shouting and baring his teeth, and then he faced forward. The plane began to plummet like a hawk, steeper and steeper, its engine almost silent, and Grainier's organs pushed back against his spine. He saw the moment with his wife and child as they drank Hood's Sarsaparilla in their little cabin on a summer's night, then another cabin he'd never remembered before, the places of his hidden childhood, a vast golden wheat field, heat shimmering above a road, arms encircling him, and a woman's voice crooning, and all the mysteries of this life were answered. The present world materialized before his eyes as the engine roared and the plane leveled off, circled the fairgrounds once, and returned to earth, landing so abruptly Grainier's throat nearly jumped out of his mouth.

The young pilot helped him overboard. Grainier rolled over the side and slid down the barrel of the fuselage. He tried to steady himself with a hand on a wing, but the wing itself was unsteady. He said, "What was all that durn hollering about?"

"I was telling you, 'This is a nosedive!'"

Grainier shook the fellow's hand, said, "Thank you very much," and left the field.

He sat on the large porch out front of the Riverside Hotel all afternoon until he found an excuse to make his way back up the Panhandle—an excuse in Eddie Sauer, whom he'd known since they were boys in Bonners Ferry and who'd just lost all his summer wages in taverns and bawdy environs and said he'd made up his mind to walk home in shame.

Eddie said, "I was rolled by a whore."

"Rolled! I thought that meant they killed you!"

"No, it don't mean they killed you or anything. I ain't dead. I only wish I was."

Grainier thought Eddie and he must be the same age, but the loose life had put a number of extra years on Eddie. His whiskers were white, and his lips puckered around gums probably nearly toothless. Grainier paid the freight for both of them, and they took the train together in Meadow Creek, where Eddie might get a job on a crew.

After a month on the Meadow Creek rail-and-ties crew, Eddie offered to pay Grainier twenty-five dollars to help him move Claire Thompson, whose husband had passed away the previous summer, from Noxon, Montana, over to Sandpoint, Idaho. Claire herself would pay nothing. Eddie's motives in helping the widow were easily deduced, and he didn't state them. "We'll go by road number 200," he told Grainier, as if there were any other road.

Grainier took his mares and his wagon. Eddie had his sister's husband's Model T Ford. The brother-in-law had cut away the rumble seat and built onto it a flat cargo bed that would have to be loaded judiciously so as not to upend the entire apparatus. Grainier rendezvoused with Eddie early in the morning in Troy, Montana, and headed east to the Bullhead Lake road that would take them south to Noxon, Grainier preceding by half a mile because his horses disliked the automobile, and also seemed to dislike Eddie.

A little German fellow named Heinz ran an automobile filling station on the hill east of Troy, but he, too, had something against Eddie, and refused to sell him gas. Grainier wasn't aware of this problem until Eddie came roaring up behind with his horn squawking and nearly stampeded the horses. "You know, these gals have seen all kinds of commotion," he told Eddie irritably when they'd pulled to the side of the dusty road and he'd walked back to the Ford. "They're used to anything, but they don't like a horn. Don't blast that thing around my mares."

"You'll have to take the wagon back and buy up two or three jugs of fuel," Eddie said. "That old schnitzel-kraut won't even talk to me."

"What'd you do to him?"

"I never did a thing! I swear! He just picks out a few to hate, and I'm on the list."

The old man had a Model T of his own out front of his place. He had its motor's cover hoisted and was half-lost down its throat, it seemed to Grainier, who'd never had much to do with these explosive machines. Grainier asked him, "Do you really know how that motor works inside of there?"

"I know everything." Heinz sputtered and fumed somewhat like an automobile himself, and said, "I'm God!"

Grainier thought about how to answer. Here seemed a conversation that could go no further.

"Then you must know what I'm about to say."

"You want gas for your friend. He's the Devil. You think I sell gas to the Devil?"

"It's me buying it. I'll need fifteen gallons, and jugs for it, too."

"You better give me five dollars."

"I don't mind."

"You're a good fellow," the German said. He was quite a small man. He dragged over a low crate to stand on so he could look straight into Grainier's eyes. "All right. Four dollars."

"You're better off having that feller hate you," Grainier told Eddie when he pulled up next to the Ford with the gasoline in three olive military fuel cans.

"He hates me because his daughter used to whore out of the barbershop in Troy," Eddie said, "and I was one of her happiest customers. She's respectable over in Seattle now," he added, "so why does he hold a grudge?"

They camped overnight in the woods north of Noxon. Grainier slept late, stretched out comfortably in his empty wagon, until Eddie brought him to attention with his Model T's yodeling horn. Eddie had bathed in the creek. He was going hatless for the first time Grainier ever knew about. His hair was wild and mostly gray and a little of it blond. He'd shaved his face and fixed several nicks with plaster. He wore no collar, but he'd tied his neck with a red-and-white necktie that dangled clear down to his crotch. His shirt was the same old one from the Saturday Trade or Discard at the Lutheran church, but he'd scrubbed his ugly working boots, and his clean black pants were starched so stiffly his gait seemed to be affected. This sudden attention to terrain so long neglected constituted a disruption in the natural world, about as much as if the Almighty himself had been hit in the head, and Eddie well knew it. He behaved with a cool, contained hysteria.

"Terrence Naples has took a run at Mrs. Widow," he told Grainier, standing at attention in his starched pants and speaking strangely, moving just his lips so as not to disturb the plaster dabs on his facial wounds, "but I told old Terrence it's going to be my chance now with the lady, or I'll knock him around the county on the twenty-four-hour plan. That's right, I had to threaten him. But it's no idle boast. I'll thrub him till his bags bust. I'm too horrible for the young ones, and she's the only go—unless I'd like a Kootenai gal, or I migrate down to Spokane, or go crawling over to Wallace." Wallace, Idaho, was famous for its brothels and for its whores, an occasional one of whom could be had for keeping house with on her retirement. "And I knew old Claire first, before Terrence ever did," he said. "Yes, in my teens I had a short, miserable spell of religion and taught the

Sunday-school class for tots before services, and she was one of them tots, I think so, anyway. I seem to remember, anyway."

Grainier had known Claire Thompson when she'd been Clair Shook, some years behind him in classes in Bonners Ferry. She'd been a fine young lady whose looks hadn't suffered at all from a little extra weight and her hair's going gray. Claire had worked in Europe as a nurse during the Great War. She'd married quite late and been widowed within a few years. Now she'd sold her home and would rent a house in Sandpoint along the road running up and down the Idaho Panhandle.

The town of Noxon lay on the south side of the Clark Fork River and the widow's house lay on the north, so they didn't get a chance even to stop over at the store for a soda, but pulled up into Claire's front yard and emptied the house and loaded as many of her worldly possessions onto the wagon as the horses would pull, mostly heavy locked trunks, tools, and kitchen gear, heaping the rest aboard the Model T and creating a pile as high up as a man could reach with a hoe, and at the pinnacle two mattresses and two children, also a little dog. By the time Grainier noticed them, the children were too far above him to distinguish their age or sexual type. The work went fast. At noon Claire gave them iced tea and sandwiches of venison and cheese, and they were on the road by one o'clock. The widow herself sat up front next to Eddie with her arm hooked in his, wearing a white scarf over her head and a black dress she must have bought nearly a year ago for mourning, laughing and conversing while her escort tried to steer by one hand. Grainier gave them a good start, but he caught up with them frequently at the top of the long rises, when the auto labored hard and boiled over, Eddie giving it water from gallon jugs the children—boys, it seemed—filled from the river. The caravan moved slowly enough that the children's pup was able to jump down from its perch atop the cargo to chase gophers and nose at their burrows, then clamber up the road bank to a high spot and jump down again between the children, who sat stiff-armed with their feet jutting out in front, hanging on to the tie-downs on either side of them.

At a neighbor's a few hours along they stopped to take on one more item, a two-barreled shotgun Claire Thompson's husband had given as collateral on a loan. Apparently Thompson had failed to pay up, but in honor of his death the neighbor's wife had persuaded her husband to return the old .12 gauge. This Grainier learned after pulling the mares to the side of the road, where they could snatch at grass and guzzle from the neighbor's spring box.

Though Grainier stood very near them, Eddie chose this moment to speak sincerely with the widow. She sat beside him in the auto shaking the gray dust from her head kerchief and wiping her face. "I mean to say," he said—but must have felt this wouldn't do. He opened his door quite suddenly and scrambled out, as flustered as if the auto were sinking in a swamp, and raced around to the passenger's side to stand by the widow.

"The late Mr. Thompson was a fine feller," he told her. He spent a tense minute getting up steam, then went on: "The late Mr. Thompson was a fine feller. Yes."

Claire said, "Yes?"

"Yes. Everybody who knew him tells me he was an excellent feller and also a most . . . excellent feller, you might say. So they say. As far as them who knew him."

"Well, did you know him, Mr. Sauer?"

"Not to talk to. No. He did me a mean bit of business once. . . . But he was a fine feller, I'm saying."

"A mean bit of business, Mr. Sauer?"

"He runned over my goat's picket and broke its neck with his wagon! He was a sonofabitch who'd sooner steal than work, wadn't he? But I mean to say! Will you marry a feller?"

"Which feller do you mean?"

Eddie had trouble getting a reply lined up. Meanwhile, Claire opened her door and pushed him aside, climbing out. She turned her back and stood looking studiously at Grainier's horses.

Eddie came over to Grainier and said to him, "Which feller does she think I mean? This feller! Me!"

Grainier could only shrug, laugh, shake his head.

Eddie stood three feet behind the widow and addressed the back of her: "The feller I mentioned! The one to marry! I'm the feller!"

She turned, took Eddie by the arm, and guided him back to the Ford. "I don't believe you are," she said. "Not the feller for me." She didn't seem upset anymore.

When they traveled on, she sat next to Grainier in his wagon. Grainier was made desperately uncomfortable because he didn't want to get too near the nose of a sensitive women like Claire Shook, now Claire Thompson—his clothes stank. He wanted to apologize for it, but couldn't quite. The widow was silent. He felt compelled to converse. "Well," he said.

"Well what?"

"Well," he said, "that's Eddie for you."

"That's not Eddie for me," she said.

"I suppose," he said.

"In a civilized place, the widows don't have much to say about who they marry. There's too many running around without husbands. But here on the frontier, we're at a premium. We can take who we want, though it's not such a bargain. The trouble is you men are all worn down pretty early in life. Are you going to marry again?"

"No," he said.

"No. You just don't want to work any harder than you do now. Do you?"

"No, I do not."

"Well then, you aren't going to marry again, not ever."

"I was married before," he said, feeling almost required to defend himself, "and I'm more than satisfied with all of everything's been left to me." He did feel as if he was defending himself. But why should he have to? Why did this woman come at him waving her topic of marriage like a big stick? "If you're prowling for a husband," he said, "I can't think of a bigger mistake to make than to get around me."

"I'm in agreement with you," she said. She didn't seem particularly happy or sad to agree. "I wanted to see if your own impression of you matched up with mine is all, Robert."

"Well, then."

"God needs the hermit in the woods as much as He needs the man in the pulpit. Did you ever think about that?"

"I don't believe I am a hermit," Grainier replied, but when the day was over, he went off asking himself, Am I a hermit? Is this what a hermit is?

Eddie became pals with a Kootenai woman who wore her hair in a mop like a cinema vamp and painted her lips sloppy red. When Grainier first saw them together, he couldn't guess how old she was, but she had brown, wrinkled skin. Somewhere she had come into possession of a pair of hexagonal eyeglasses tinted such a deep blue that behind them her eyes were invisible, and it was by no means certain she could see any objects except in the brightest glare. She must have been easy to get along with, because she never spoke. But whenever Eddie engaged in talk she muttered to herself continually, sighed and grunted, even whistled very softly and tunelessly. Grainier would have figured her for mad if she'd been white.

"She probly don't even speak English," he said aloud, and realized that nobody else was present. He was all alone in his cabin in the woods, talking to himself, startled at his own voice. Even his dog was off wandering and hadn't come back for the night. He stared at the firelight flickering from the gaps in the stove and at the enclosing shifting curtain of utter dark.

8.

Even into his last years, when his arthritis and rheumatism sometimes made simple daily chores nearly impossible and two weeks of winter in the cabin would have killed him, Grainier still spent every summer and fall in his remote home.

By now it no longer astonished him to understand that the valley wouldn't slowly, eventually resume its condition from before the great fire. Though the signs of destruction were fading, it was a very different place now, with different plants and therefore with different animals. The gorgeous spruce had gone. Now came almost exclusively jack pine, which tended to grow up scraggly and mean. He'd been hearing the wolves less and less often, from farther and farther away. The coyotes grew numerous, the rabbits increasingly scarce. From long stretches of the Moyea River through the burn, the trout had gone.

Maybe one or two people wondered what drew him back to this hard-to-reach spot, but Grainier never cared to tell. The truth was he'd vowed to stay, and he'd been shocked into making this vow by something that happened about ten years after the region had burned.

This was in the two or three days after Kootenai Bob had been killed under a train, while his tribe still toured the tracks searching out the bits of him. On these three or four crisp autumn evenings, the Great Northern train blew a series of long ones, sounding off from the Meadow Creek crossing until it was well north, proceeding slowly through the area on orders from the management, who wanted to give the Kootenai tribe a chance to collect what they could of their brother without further disarrangement.

It was mid-November, but it hadn't yet snowed. The moon rose near midnight and hung above Queen Mountain as late as ten in the morning. The days were brief and bright, the nights clear and cold. And yet the nights were full of a raucous hysteria.

These nights, the whistle got the coyotes started, and then the wolves. His companion the red dog was out there, too—Grainier hadn't seen her for days. The chorus seemed the fullest the night the moon came full. Seemed the maddest. The most pitiable.

The wolves and coyotes howled without letup all night, sounding in the hundreds, more than Grainier had ever heard, and maybe other creatures too, owls, eagles—what, exactly, he couldn't guess—surely every single animal with a voice along the peaks and ridges looking down on the Moyea River, as if nothing could ease any of God's beasts. Grainier didn't dare to sleep, feeling it all to be some sort of vast pronouncement, maybe the alarms of the end of the world.

He fed the stove and stood in the cabin's doorway half-dressed and watched the sky. The night was cloudless and the moon was white and burning, erasing the stars and making gray silhouettes of the mountains. A pack of howlers seemed very near, and getting nearer, baying as they ran, perhaps. And suddenly they flooded into the clearing and around it, many forms and shadows, voices screaming, and several brushed past him, touching him where he stood in his doorway, and he could hear their pads thudding on the earth. Before his mind could say "these are wolves come into my yard," they were gone. All but one. And she was the wolf-girl.

Grainier believed he would faint. He gripped the doorjamb to stay on his feet. The creature didn't move, and seemed hurt. The general shape of her impressed him right away that this was a person—a female—a child. She lay on her side panting, a clearly human creature with the delicate structure of a little girl, but she was bent in the arms and legs, he believed, now that he was able to focus on this dim form in the moonlight. With the action of her lungs there came a whistling, a squeak, like a frightened pup's.

Grainier turned convulsively and went to the table looking for—he didn't know. A weapon? He'd never kept a shotgun. Perhaps a piece of kindling to beat at the thing's head. He fumbled at the clutter on the table and located the matches and lit a hurricane lamp and found such a weapon, and then went out again in his long johns, barefoot, lifting the lantern high and holding his club before him, stalked and made nervous by his own monstrous shadow, so huge it filled the whole clearing behind him. Frost had built on the dead grass, and it skirled beneath his feet. If not for this sound he'd have thought himself struck deaf, owing to the magnitude of the surrounding silence. All the night's noises had stopped. The whole valley seemed to reflect his shock. He heard only his footsteps and the wolf-girl's panting complaint.

Her whimpering ceased as he got closer, approaching cautiously so as not to terrify either this creature or himself. The wolf-girl waited, shot full of animal dread and perfectly still, moving nothing but her eyes, following his every move but not meeting his own gaze, and the breath smoking before her nostrils.

The child's eyes sparked greenly in the lamplight like those of any wolf. Her face was that of a wolf, but hairless.

"Kate?" he said. "Is it you?" But it was.

Nothing about her told him that. He simply knew it. This was his daughter.

She stayed stock-still as he drew even closer. He hoped that some sign of recognition might show itself and prove her to be Kate. But her eyes only watched in flat terror, like a wolf's. Still. Still and all. Kate she was, but Kate no longer. Kate-no-longer lay on her side, her left leg akimbo, splintered and bloody bone jutting below the knee; just a child spent from crawling on threes and having dragged the shattered leg behind her. He'd wondered sometimes about little Kate's hair, how it might have looked if she'd lived; but she'd snatched herself nearly bald. It grew out in a few patches.

He came within arm's reach. Kate-no-longer growled, barked, snapped as her father bent down toward her, and then her eyes glassed and she so faded from herself he believed she'd expired at his approach. But she lived, and watched him.

"Kate. Kate. What's happened to you?"

He set down the lamp and club and got his arms beneath her and lifted. Her breathing came rapid, faint, and shallow. She whimpered once in her ear and snapped her jaws but didn't otherwise struggle. He turned with her in his embrace and made for the cabin, now walking away from the lamplight and thus toward his own monstrous shadow as it engulfed his home and shrank magically at his approach. Inside, he laid her on his pallet on the floor. "I'll get the lamp," he told her.

When he came back into the cabin, she was still there. He set the lamp on the table where he could see what he was doing, and prepared to splint the broken leg with kindling, cutting the top of his long johns off himself around the waist, dragging it over his head, tearing it into strips. As soon as he grasped the child's ankle with one hand and put his other on the thigh to pull, she gave a terrible sigh, and then her breathing slowed. She'd fainted. He straightened the leg as best he could and, feeling that he could take his time now, he whittled a stick of kindling so that it cupped the shin. He pulled a bench beside the pallet and sat himself, resting her foot across his knee while he applied the splint and bound it around. "I'm not a doctor," he told her. "I'm just the one that's here." He opened the window across the room to give her air.

She lay there asleep with the life driven half out of her. He watched her a long time. She was as leathery as an old man. Her hands were curled under, the back of her wrists callused stumps, her feet misshapen, as hard and knotted as wooden burls. What was it about her face that seemed so wolflike, so animal, even in repose? He couldn't say. The face just seemed to have no life behind it when the eyes were closed. As if the creature would have no thoughts other than what it saw.

He moved the bench against the wall, sat back, and dozed. A train going through the valley didn't wake him, but only entered his dream. Later, near daylight, a much smaller sound brought him around. The wolf-girl had stirred. She was leaving.

She leaped out the window.

He stood at the window and watched her in the dawn effulgence, crawling and pausing to twist sideways on herself and snap at the windings on her leg as would any wolf or dog. She was making no great speed and keeping to the path that led to the river. He meant to track her and bring her back, but he never did.

9.

In the hot, rainless summer of 1935, Grainier came into a short season of sensual lust greater than any he'd experienced as a younger man.

In the middle of August it seemed as if a six-week drought would snap;

great thunderheads massed over the entire Panhandle and trapped the heat beneath them while the atmosphere dampened and ripened; but it wouldn't rain. Grainier felt made of lead—thick and worthless. And lonely. His little red dog had been gone for years, had grown old and sick and disappeared into the woods to die by herself, and he'd never replaced her. On a Sunday he walked to Meadow Creek and hopped the train into Bonners Ferry. The passengers in the lurching car had propped open the windows, and any lucky enough to sit beside one kept his face to the sodden breeze. The several who got off in Bonners dispersed wordlessly, like beaten prisoners. Grainier made his way toward the county fairgrounds, where a few folks set up shop on Sunday, and where he might find a dog.

Over on Second Street, the Methodist congregation was singing. The town of Bonners made no other sound. Grainier still went to services some rare times, when a trip to town coincided. People spoke nicely to him there, people recognized him from the days when he'd attended almost regularly with Gladys, but he generally regretted going. He very often wept in church. Living up the Moyea with plenty of small chores to distract him, he forgot he was a sad man. When the hymns began, he remembered.

At the fairgrounds he talked to a couple of Kootenais—one a middle-aged squaw, and the other a girl nearly grown. They were dressed to impress somebody, two half-breed witch-women in fringed blue buckskin dresses with headbands dangling feathers of crow, hawk, and eagle. They had a pack of very wolfish pups in a feed sack, and also a bobcat in a willow cage. They took the pups out one at a time to display them. A man was just walking away and saying to them, "That dog-of-wolf will never be Christianized."

"Why is that thing all blue?" Grainier said.

"What thing?"

"That cage you've got that old cat trapped up in."

One of them, the girl, showed a lot of white in her, and had freckles and sand-colored hair. When he looked at these two women, his vitals felt heavy with yearning and fear.

"That's just old paint to keep him from gnawing out. It sickens this old bobcat," the girl said. The cat had big paws with feathery tufts, as if it wore the same kind of boot as its women captors. The older woman had her leg so Grainier could see her calf. She scratched at it, leaving long white rakes on the flesh.

The sight so clouded his mind that he found himself a quarter mile from the fairgrounds before he knew it, without a pup, and having seen before his face, for some long minutes, nothing but those white marks on her dark skin. He knew something bad had happened inside him.

As if his lecherous half-thoughts had blasted away the ground at his feet and thrown him down into a pit of universal sexual mania, he now found that the Rex Theater on Main Street was out of its mind, too. The display out front consisted of a large bill, printed by the local newspaper, screaming of lust:

One Day Only Thursday August 22
The Most Daring Picture of the Year
"Sins of Love"
Nothing Like It Ever Before!

SEE Natural Birth
An Abortion
A Blood Transfusion
A Real Caesarian Operation
IF YOU FAINT EASILY—DON'T COME IN!
TRAINED NURSES AT EACH SHOW

On the Stage—Living Models Featuring
Miss Galveston
Winner of the Famous Pageant of Pulchritude
In Galveston, Texas

No One Under 16 Admitted

Matinee
Ladies Only

Night
Men Only

In Person
Professor Howard Young
Dynamic Lecturer on Sex.
Daring Facts Revealed

The Truth About Love.
Plain Facts About Secret Sins
No Beating About the Bush!

Grainier read the advertisement several times. His throat tightened and his innards began to flutter and sent down his limbs a palsy which, though slight, he felt sure was rocking the entire avenue like a rowboat. He wondered if he'd gone mad and maybe should start visiting an alienist.

Pulchritude!

He felt his way to the nearby railroad platform through a disorienting fog of desire. The Sins of Love would come August 22, Thursday. Beside the communicating doors of the passenger-car he rode out of town, there hung a calendar that told him today was Sunday, August 11.

At home, in the woods, the filthiest demons of his nature beset him. In dreams Miss Galveston came to him. He woke up fondling himself. He kept no calendar, but in his very loins he marked the moments until Thursday, August 22. By day he soaked almost hourly in the frigid river, but the nights took him over and over to Galveston.

The dark cloud over the Northwest, boiling like an upside-down ocean, blocked out the sun and moon and stars. It was too hot and muggy to sleep in the cabin. He made a pallet in the yard and spent the nights lying on it naked in an unrelieved blackness.

After many such nights, the cloud broke without rain, the sky cleared, the sun rose on the morning of August 22. He woke up all dewy in the yard, his marrow thick with cold—but when he remembered what day had come, his marrow went up like kerosene jelly, and he blushed so hard his eyes teared and the snot ran from his nose. He began walking immediately in the direction of the road, but turned himself around to wander his patch of land frantically. He couldn't find the gumption to appear in town on the day—to appear even on the road to town for anyone to behold, thickly melting with lust for the Queen of Galveston and desiring to breathe her atmosphere, to inhale the fumes of sex, sin, and pulchritude. It would kill him! Kill him to see it, kill him to be seen! There in the dark theater full of disembodied voices discussing plain facts about secret sins he would die, he would be dragged down to Hell and tortured in his parts eternally before the foul and stinking President of all Pulchritude. Naked, he stood swaying in his yard.

His desires must be completely out of nature; he was the kind of man who might couple with a beast, or—as he'd long ago heard it phrased—jigger himself a cow.

Around behind his cabin he fell on his face, clutching at the brown grass. He lost touch with the world and didn't return to it until the sun came over the house and the heat itched in his hair. He thought a walk would calm his blood, and he dressed himself and headed for the road and over to Placer Creek, several miles, never stopping. He climbed up to Deer Ridge and down the other side and up again into Canuck Basin, hiked for hours without a break, thinking only: Pulchritude! Pulchritude!—Pulchritude will be the damning of me, I'll end up snarfing at it like a dog at a carcass, rolling in it like a dog will, I'll end up all grimed and awful with pulchritude. Oh that Galveston would allow a parade of the stuff! That Galveston would take this harlot of pulchritude and make a queen of her!

At sunset, all progress stopped. He was standing on a cliff. He'd found a back way into a kind of arena enclosing a body of water called Spruce Lake and now looked down on it hundreds of feet below him, its flat surface as still and black as obsidian, engulfed in the shadow of surrounding cliffs, ringed with a double ring of evergreens and reflected evergreens. Beyond, he saw the Canadian Rockies still sunlit, snow peaked, a hundred miles away, as if the earth were in the midst of its creation, the mountains taking their substance out of the clouds. He'd never seen so grand a prospect. The forests that filled his life were so thickly populous and so tall that generally they blocked him from seeing how far away the world was, but right now it seemed clear there were mountains enough for everybody to get his own. The curse had left him, and the contagion of his lust had drifted off and settled into one of those distant valleys.

He made his way carefully down among the boulders of the cliff, reaching the lakeside in darkness, and slept there curled up under a blanket he made out of spruce boughs, on a bed of spruce, exhausted and comfortable. He missed the display of pulchritude at the Rex that night, and never knew whether he'd saved himself or deprived himself.

Grainier stayed at home for two weeks afterward and then went to town again, and did at last get himself a dog, a big male of the far-north sledding type, who was his friend for many years.

Grainier himself lived over eighty years, well into the 1960s. In his time he'd traveled west to within a few dozen miles of the Pacific, though he'd never seen the ocean itself, and as far east as the town of Libby, forty miles inside Montana. He'd had one lover—his wife Gladys—owned one acre of property, two horses, and a wagon. He'd never been drunk. He'd never purchased a firearm or spoken into a telephone. He'd ridden on trains regularly, many times in automobiles, and once on an aircraft. During the last decade of his life he watched television whenever he was in town. He had no idea who his parents might have been, and he left no heirs behind him.

Almost everyone in those parts knew Robert Grainier, but when he passed away in his sleep sometime in November of 1968, he lay dead in his cabin through the rest of the fall, and through the winter, and was never missed. A pair of hikers happened on his body in the spring. Next day the two returned with a doctor, who wrote out a certificate of death, and, taking turns with a shovel they found leaning against the cabin, the three of them dug a grave in the yard, and there lies Robert Grainier.

The day he bought the sled dog in Bonners Ferry, Grainier stayed overnight at the house of Dr. Sims, the veterinarian, whose wife took in lodgers. The doctor had come by some tickets to the Rex Theater's current show, a demonstration of the talents of Theodore the Wonder Horse, because he'd examined the star of it—that is, the horse, Theodore—in a professional capacity. Theodore's droppings were bloody, his cowboy master said. This was a bad sign. "Better take this ticket and go wonder at his wonders," the Doctor told Grainier, pressing one of his complimentary passes on the lodger, "because in half a year I wouldn't wonder if he was fed to dogs and rendered down to mucilage."

Grainier sat that night in the darkened Rex Theater amid a crowd of people pretty much like himself—his people, the hard people of the northwestern mountains, most of them quite a bit more impressed with

Theodore's master's glittering getup and magical lariat than with Theodore, who showed he could add and subtract by knocking on the stage with his hooves and stood on his hind legs and twirled around and did other things that any of them could have trained a horse to do.

The wonder-horse show that evening in 1935 included a wolf-boy. He wore a mask of fur, and a suit that looked like fur but was really something else. Shining in the electric light, silver and blue, the wolf-boy frolicked and gamboled around the stage in such a way the watchers couldn't be sure if he meant to be laughed at.

They were ready to laugh in order to prove they hadn't been fooled. They had seen and laughed at such as the Magnet Boy and the Chicken Boy, at the Professor of Silly and at jugglers who beat themselves over the head with Indian pins that weren't really made of wood. They had given their money to preachers who had lifted their hearts and baptized scores of them and later rolled around drunk in the Kootenai village and fornicated with squaws. Tonight, faced with the spectacle of this counterfeit monster, they were silent at first. Then a couple made remarks that sounded like questions, and a man in the dark honked like a goose, and people let themselves laugh at the wolf-boy.

But they hushed, all at once and quite abruptly, when he stood utterly still at center stage, his arms straight out from his shoulders, and went rigid and began to tremble with a massive inner dynamism. Nobody present had ever seen anyone stand so still and yet so strangely mobile. He laid his head back until his scalp contacted his spine, that far back, and opened his throat, and a sound rose in the auditorium like a wind coming from all four directions, low and terrifying, rumbling up from the ground beneath the floor, and it gathered into a roar that sucked at the hearing itself, and coalesced into a voice that penetrated into the sinuses and finally into the very minds of those hearing it, taking itself higher and higher, more and more awful and beautiful, the originating ideal of all such sounds ever made, of the foghorn and the ship's horn, the locomotive's lonesome whistle, of opera singing and the music of flutes and the continuous moan-music of bagpipes. And suddenly it all went black. And that time was gone forever.

Reading *The O. Henry Prize Stories 2003*
The Jurors on Their Favorites

Each juror read all twenty stories without knowing who wrote them or where they were published.

Jennifer Egan on "Train Dreams" by Denis Johnson

The nettlesome task of picking a favorite from among such a fine and disparate group of stories has had an unexpected payoff: it forced me to examine—and to some extent redefine—the qualities I value most in a piece of short fiction.

In one sense, my reading priorities have been consistent since childhood: I want to be riveted by what I read, and I want to be moved by it. As I've gotten older, the sort of fiction that can produce these effects in me has shifted toward works whose language and construction feel unique. Yet in judging these stories, I had to put aside my usual criteria. "Train Dreams" was not the one that moved and compelled me the most, nor did it wow me instantly with its rhythms and structure. Its protagonist is opaque to the point of cipherdom, and its leisurely, episodic unfolding seems perversely old-fashioned against the sly compression of some other stories. But weeks after reading them, it's the one that continues to float into my thoughts with the persistence of a dream, or some troubling relic of my own experience. Why?

First, there's the density of historical detail, the meticulous chronicling of logging and bridge building, flora and fauna of the American West, which make for an otherworldly atmospheric richness. But the story's real power lies in its mystery, its reluctance to reveal itself. What is this *about*? I kept asking myself as I read—A man's life? A supernatural transaction involving curses and wolves? The real answer is something much larger, I think, suggested only in the most glancing ways until the devastating last line: the cataclysmic changes wrought by the twentieth century, and the corollary disappearance of a certain kind of American life.

There is a tendency in short fiction—I feel it when writing myself—to conclude and resolve. "Train Dreams" ignores that expectation and many others as well, offering in their place what I can only call a kind of strangeness. A mystery. For me, that proved more powerful than anything else in the collection, and more lasting.

Jennifer Egan is the author of the novels *Look at Me* and *The Invisible Circus*, and a story collection, *Emerald City*. Her short stories have been published in *The New Yorker*, *Harper's*, *GQ*, and *Ploughshares*, among other publications, and her nonfiction appears frequently in *The New York Times Magazine*. She lives with her husband and children in Brooklyn.

David Guterson on "Train Dreams" by Denis Johnson

"The entire history of the short story," writes Daniel Halpern, "is passed down, generation after generation, like a relay runner's baton, and the art of the story continues."

It has been 170 years since Poe's "MS. Found in a Bottle," and the baton has gotten heavy indeed. The contemporary writer of ambitious short stories has emerged from under Gogol's "Overcoat" to find Calvino, Borges, Barthelme, Kawabata, Kafka, Oates, and George Saunders. It's a load to carry, with much to sort, and no prevailing certainties. Add to this the imperatives of the moment (not to mention the myths and tales preceding Poe by centuries), and a writer might well be brought to his knees by the weight of too much history.

Denis Johnson's "Train Dreams" is a sweeping tall tale, an homage to Bret Harte, a work of North American magical realism, a yarn of the supernatural variety, and finally the biography of a widower and hermit, Robert Grainier, who weeps in church, fears his dreams, and dies in 1968 without having used a telephone. Is it a short story? That's difficult to say. Perhaps there's no longer such a category.

Where everything is reduced to a "general death" by the fire that took his wife and only lover, Granier finds his woodstove "lying on its side with its legs curled up under it like a beetle's." He imagines that at the fire's inception "a magazine curled, darkened, and flamed, spiraled upward and flew away page by page, burning and circling." Such attentiveness to detail gives this story credence, but its greater power lies in its visitations, its haunted moments of sadness and yearning in which the world appears otherworldly and aggrieved even while infused with comedy.

I admire this story for its celebratory quality, its skillful blending of forms and traditions, its consistently exquisite use of the English language, and in the end for its emotional appeal. I carried it afterward into my dreams: on the night following my second reading, a lynx or bobcat visited me, having crossed over from Denis Johnson's "Train Dreams."

David Guterson is the author of the novels *Snow Falling on Cedars* and *East of the Mountains*, as well as a story collection *The Country Ahead of Us, The Country Behind*. He also wrote *Family Matters: Why Homeschooling Makes Sense*. He lives on Bainbridge Island in Puget Sound.

Diane Johnson on "The Thing in the Forest" by A. S. Byatt

Though it was hard, I've decided I liked the first story the best: "The Thing in the Forest." In some ways it is the most old-fashioned of the stories, with its circular ending and classical ingredients of ghost story. Or is it a ghost story? Was it maybe a real Loathly Worm they saw? The delicate handling of the supernatural along with the possible and the historical impressed me. The actual local tradition of the Loathly Worm gives us both a natural explanation and affirms the existence of the supernatural. The fate of little Alys is well handled—were those her tiny bones? Of course not, yet the writer so skillfully suggests that the awful creature consumed her. When Penny finds all the odd, repulsive things in the Thing's lair, all kinds of horrifying history is suggested, against the backdrop of the war and the frightening experience of dislocation and being in effect orphans.

I so admired the treatment of Primrose and Penny, and of the way English social-class differences dictated the subsequent lives of the two little girls and prevented them from really bonding at the end. Each is so well drawn, each so unlike the other, yet both are sympathetic. The line about the worm's having done them both "no good," is chilling in its matter-of-fact way of suggesting lives blighted by what they saw, to say nothing of what was done to them by the whole experience of being evacuated in the war, for which the Thing is in some way a metaphor. The writer has a quiet and powerful way of describing unearthly sights that convinces the reader utterly, and makes the natural world, with its "sinister hoods of arum lilies," vividly present.

Diane Johnson is the author of, most recently, *Le Mariage* and *Le Divorce*. She wrote the screenplay for Stanley Kubrick's *The Shining*, and the biography *Dashiell Hammett, A Life*. Her criticism appears often in the *New York Review of Books*. She divides her time between Paris and San Francisco.

Writing *The O. Henry Prize Stories 2003*
The Authors on Their Work

Chimamanda Ngozi Adichie, "The American Embassy"
Some years ago, I was at the American embassy in Lagos to apply for a student visa. I was furious at how Nigerian soldiers flogged people and how these people apologized profusely even though they had done nothing wrong; how rude the American embassy staff were and how the people humored them just to get in and get a chance at America; and later, how adults bawled when they were refused visas. Most of all, I was struck by the curious mix of humiliation and hope there.

I wanted to capture that in a story but I also wanted to write about somebody who was ambivalent about being there. The first draft of this story was written from the point of view of a girl reluctantly fleeing Nigeria with her political activist father. It didn't work, because it was too righteously angry and, although it merged the embassy experience with some political realities of Nigeria's military regime, it did not capture the subtle complexities of either. I like to think that this version does. It took some months to conceive, but I wrote it in a couple of days and was delighted when *Prism International* accepted it. The editors at *Prism* were nifty enough, also, to suggest shortening the title from "Talking to God at the American Embassy."

Chimamanda Ngozi Adichie was born in Nigeria in 1977 and grew up in the quiet university town of Nsukka. She moved to the United States to attend college and majored in communication and political science. Her short fiction has been published in the *Iowa Review*, *Prism International*, *Calyx*, *Wasafiri*, and *Other Voices*. In 2002, she was short-listed for the Caine Prize for African Writing. Her stories have also been selected for the Commonwealth Broadcasting and the BBC short story awards. Her first novel, *Purple Hibiscus*, will be published by Algonquin in the fall of 2003. She is working on a second novel, about the Nigerian civil war. She divides her time between the United States and Nigeria.

T. Coraghessan Boyle, "Swept Away"

"Swept Away" is the first of the new stories I wrote after completing my last novel, *Drop City*, and it had the quickest turnaround time (completion to print) of any story I've ever done. I finished it at the end of December, mailed it out, and it appeared in *The New Yorker* two weeks later, a truly happy turn of affairs—if only all stories were so quick to appreciate. At any rate, *Drop City* was my first attempt at a noncomic realistic novel, and I felt I needed a change of pace with the new stories, and so decided to revisit the mode of some of my earlier work—the absurdist stories of *Descent of Man*, for instance, or magical pieces like "The Miracle at Ballin-spittle" from *If the River Was Whiskey*. I feel very comfortable with this sort of story, especially as two of my enduring heroes are García Márquez and Calvino, whose best work has the whimsical charm of the folktale, a charm that is often unavailable to stories in the realist mode. And so, "Swept Away" began with a single amusing notion, that of the flying cat. I had read of the prodigious winds in the Shetland Islands and of how these winds were prone to lifting various objects and depositing them elsewhere, cats, of course, included in the description. I saw Junie Ooley stepping off that boat and getting coldcocked by a hefty tom, and once I'd established my narrator, all the rest just raveled out from there. Incidentally, I must confess that I've never been to the Shetlands (not yet, but there's still hope), though the coldest five hours of my life were spent in a fishing boat out of Oban one grim July afternoon, so I know something of the meteorological conditions off the Arctic coast of Scotland. But poor Robbie. And poor Junie. Life just shouldn't be like that, should it?

T. Coraghessan Boyle is the author of nine novels and six collections, including *Drop City*, *The Tortilla Curtain*, *The Road to Wellville*, *Water Music*, *After the Plague*, *Without a Hero*, and *Greasy Lake*. He has been the grateful recipient of a number of awards and honors, including the PEN/Faulkner Award in Fiction for *World's End* and the PEN/Malamud Award for his work in the short story. Since leaving the Iowa Writers' Workshop in 1978, he has taught fiction writing at the University of Southern California in Los Angeles.

A. S. Byatt, "The Thing in the Forest"

All I really want to say about the story is that it is an attempt to explore the possibilities of combining the worlds of story and history. It goes back to the time of my childhood—wartime Britain—though it carefully doesn't specify—and the local myths of the English North from which I come—the laily Worm—without saying so. It is to do with being gripped by the worm of the past which gets longer and stronger as one gets older.

A. S. Byatt is internationally acclaimed as a novelist, short-story writer, and critic. She is the author of a tetralogy consisting of *The Virgin in the Garden*, *Still Life*, *Babel Tower*, and, most recently, *The Whistling Woman*. Educated at York and Newnham College, Cambridge, she taught at the Central School of Art and Design, and was senior lecturer in English at University College, London, before becoming a full-time writer in 1983. She was appointed CBE in 1990 and DBE in 1999.

Evan S. Connell, "Election Eve"

"Election Eve" is the third story about Marguerite and Proctor Bemis. All three derive from an obvious, deepening, and threatening rift in this country between liberals and conservatives. Fiction writers, actors, poets, cartoonists, and other members of that fraternity almost invariably are liberal, which is to say inventive, which is to be expected because whatever they do emerges from a half-conscious or thoroughly conscious dissatisfaction with the status quo. One of a writer's problems, therefore, is to prevent his bias from influencing what he writes to the extent that the story degenerates into propaganda. But how does he know? Who can draw the line? It's a matter of taste, experience, sensibility, judgment, and nobody knows what else. And in the end who shall decide whether he failed or succeeded? But that, of course, is why writers and their accomplices obsessively chase what can never be caught. Next time, they believe, next time. So it is with Marguerite and Proctor. Next time, each believes, the other half will understand.

Evan S. Connell was born in Kansas City, attended Dartmouth, the University of Kansas, Stanford, and Columbia. He was a Navy pilot during World War II. Among the books he's written are *Mrs. Bridge, Son of the Morning Star, Diary of a Rapist, The Connoisseur,* and *Deus lo Volt!* He is working at present on a biography of Goya.

Adam Desnoyers, "Bleed Blue in Indonesia"

"Bleed Blue in Indonesia" is part of my novel-in-stories, which centers around the narrator, Cliff.

My stuff gets a little dark and I really wanted to write a nice love story. But then it took a turn. I became more interested in the Big Unrequited Moment—the idea that everybody has "something" that they wish they'd done in their past that would have made their lives drastically different. I'm not sure if the story ended up being about Will's "something" or about Cliff's.

This story was my first to be accepted for publication.

Adam Desnoyers is a graduate of the Syracuse University Creative Writing Program. His work has appeared in *Fence* and the *Idaho Review*. He teaches part-time in the English Department at the University of Kansas.

Anthony Doerr, "The Shell Collector"

This story started with an old Slazenger tennis ball can. It was green and yellow, rusted around the rims, and heavy, a talisman of my childhood; they don't make tennis ball cans that heavy anymore. I dug it out of a closet in my parents' house. When I pulled off the cap, a deeply familiar smell rose: the smell of dead snails. Inside the can were bits of coral and hundreds of tiny seashells: murexes, butterflies, olives. It wasn't until I poured them out on the floor that I remembered that they were mine, that I had collected them on Sanibel Island during a family trip.

I reclaimed a dozen or so and put them on my desk and would finger them idly while I worked. Memories kept surfacing: We used to drive back to Ohio from Florida, I remembered, with bounty for my brother's aquarium: crabs in gallon jugs of seawater, octopi in sloshing pails. I remembered shelling a sandbar and getting trapped by the tide; I remembered getting stung by jellyfish over and over again in the water off Hilton Head. I remembered, for the first time in years, an island off the coast of Kenya that was hardly more than a shoal, maybe fifty yards long, composed entirely of broken seashells; I spent a whole afternoon on my knees there, sifting through them.

I think the character of the shell collector started there, with the tactile pleasure of holding shells and the associations they fired in me. It took a lot of drafts before I learned how to explore the metaphor of making the shell collector's life like a shell itself, how he tries to retreat into it but cannot.

The story owes a debt to Kenneth Brower's "On the Reef, Darkly," and other profiles of the blind physical scientist Geerat Vermeij, who more than demonstrates that a sightless observer can contribute significantly to the study of mollusks.

Curiously, a year after I wrote the story, I learned that a biotech company in Silicon Valley designed an analgesic pain drug called Ziconotide from cone venom. With a few alterations, rather than block specific neural pathways in the brain, the drug merely inhibits them, not shutting down brain cells, but "muting their excitability." In trials, Ziconotide has successfully controlled the severe chronic pain caused by cancer and AIDS, and is expected to be on the market by the end of 2003.

Anthony Doerr's first collection of stories, *The Shell Collector*, was a *New York Times* and *Publishers Weekly* Notable Book of 2002, as well as a winner of the New York Public Library's Young Lions Award. He is currently a Hodder Fellow at Princeton University, where he is finishing his first novel. His story "The Hunter's Wife" was included in *The O. Henry Prize Stories 2002*.

Molly Giles, "Two Words"

I was daydreaming over my keyboard one summer morning when I looked out my window and saw my neighbor Tim, bald from chemo and totally naked except for a pink feather boa, waving a coffee cup and brandishing a garbage can lid at a large buck who had just leapt into his corn patch. I loved this image and although I was never able to fit it into "Two Words," it gave me a glimpse into Tim's sweet crazy courage and provided the impetus for the story.

Molly Giles is the author of two story collections, *Rough Translations* and *Creek Walk*, and a novel, *Iron Shoes*. She commutes between Woodacre, California, and Fayetteville, Arkansas, and directs the Programs in Creative Writing at the University of Arkansas.

Ann Harleman, "Meanwhile"

I began writing "Meanwhile" at the most alone, most desperate moment of my life (so far), when a balance between my own survival and that of others for whom I was responsible seemed as far away as heaven. By the end of the first draft I found that, like a child with an imaginary friend, I had made myself some company. The finished story retains the fractured, clamoring quality of the kind of experience it deals with. It was a hard story to write, and it may be a hard story to read. Certainly it was a hard story to typeset.

Ann Harleman is the author of *Happiness*, which won the 1993 Iowa Short Fiction Award, and *Bitter Lake*, a novel. Among her awards are Guggenheim and Rockefeller fellowships, two Rhode Island State Arts Council fellowships, the PEN Syndicated Fiction Award, and the Berlin Prize in Literature. She teaches writing and literature at the Rhode Island School of Design. "Meanwhile" is one of the stories in her just-completed second collection, *Will Build to Suit*.

Denis Johnson, "Train Dreams"

Denis Johnson is a novelist (*The Name of the World, Already Dead, Resuscitation of a Hanged Man, The Stars at Noon, Fiskadoro, Angels*), poet (*The*

Incognito Lounge), writer of short fiction (*Jesus' Son*), playwright (*Shoppers Carried by Escalators into the Flames of Hell*), and journalist. His stories and essays have appeared in *Esquire, Rolling Stone, The New Yorker, Paris Review,* and *The Atlantic Monthly.*

Tim Johnston, "Irish Girl"
I have no memory of where "Irish Girl" came from, but I do remember having no idea where it was going. I remember worrying that the youngish, blunt, undazzling voice I was hearing was not the stuff of great fiction, but I let it go on anyway. I began to hear a train in the distance, and the train grew louder, and larger, and still I didn't know what it was doing there. I didn't know it was Chekhov's gun-over-the-mantel-in-Act-I till the thing went off in Act III. When that happened, not a comma sooner, I realized why the voice of this story sounded the way it did: it was the voice of a boy *still* stunned, years later, by the events of his twelfth birthday. It was the voice of permanent shock.

   Which is only to remind myself, in front of everybody, of how little I need to know when I begin a story, but how well I need to listen.

Tim Johnston's first novel was *Never So Green* (2002). He was born in Iowa City, Iowa, and now lives in Los Angeles, where he is at work on his second novel.

Marjorie Kemper, "God's Goodness"
My friend Andrea has always maintained that her favorite book is the Book of Job. I'm the kind of person whose favorite book is Charles Portis's *Norwood*, so I'd always thought hers a pretty bleak choice. Since writing this story, I'm not so sure. The story went through a great many permutations. The one constant in all of them was Ling's voice and her steely determination to find God's goodness in the world. She just wouldn't give up on it. In the end, I couldn't either.

Marjorie Kemper's short fiction has most recently appeared in *New Orleans Review,* the *Greensboro Review, The Atlantic Monthly,* and the

Chattahoochee Review. Her first novel, *Until That Good Day,* was published in 2003. She lives in California.

William Kittredge, "Kissing"

During the winter of 1991, on my first trip to Europe, my companion, Annick Smith, and I put four thousand kilometers on a little rented red Renault. After Paris, we drove and drove; saw Venice and Florence, the Alhambra and the Prado. Heading back to Paris, we seized at a chance to visit archaeological sites along the Verzey River—the vicinity of Lascaux and a heartland of European prehistory. On a bright sweet morning we walked a path through an ordinary field to be escorted through the narrow passages of the cavern known as Font-de-Gaume. There, we saw the reindeer kissing. We were encouraged to acknowledge the degree to which we cared for one another. Our story was sort of like this one.

William Kittredge's most recent books are *The Nature of Generosity* (2000), *Southwestern Homelands* (2002), and *The Best Stories of William Kittredge* (2003). He ranched in southeastern Oregon until he was thirty-five, and taught for three decades in the Creative Writing Program at the University of Montana.

Robyn Joy Leff, "Burn Your Maps"

This story was one of the most unconscious things I've ever done. A mentor of mine called it "a gift," but at the same time I was writing, it felt more like a curse, like some kind of heavy black smoke that had to be expelled. It began, like most stories, almost benignly. I have always been fascinated (perhaps obsessed) by obsessions, and was interested in children who get into a "costume phase." I liked the sort of sad-funny notion that a child might already want to escape his indeterminate identity at the age of nine. In part, this was inspired by my own childhood and that of my twin brothers, who for months on end wore faded bathroom towels as capes and dubbed themselves, inexplicably, "Fatman" and "Batman" (but not *that* Batman). Yet, somehow, the story became not so much about Wes as about his parents' reactions to him—about the precariousness that tilts their own world and the tenuousness of their bonds to one another and the ways in which they nevertheless cling to one another in the face of all that.

Originally, almost eerily, the character Ismail was an Afghani, which I reluctantly changed just before publication (in the wake of September 11, 2001) in order to relieve the story of any outer politics, while hopefully leaving its inner politics intact. Once completed, the story never altered much. It only ever seemed to be able to end one way: with a cape and a clutch.

Robyn Joy Leff has published stories in such journals as *Quarterly West* and *ZYZZYVA*. She lives in Los Angeles, where she writes motion picture press kits and is at work on a novel.

Douglas Light, "Three Days. A Month. More."

The story came to me one early autumn afternoon in Harlem.

The day was hot, a remnant of summer. An elementary school. I was passing when the bell rang. Class was dismissed. The children exited the school, screaming and pushing. On the street, a woman selling flavored shaved ice competed with the Mister Softee ice cream van for the children's business. Both were positioned less than fifteen yards from the school's front doors. The woman was to the east. Mister Softee the west.

I sat on a bench a block from the school and watched the children file past on their way home. All under twelve, they acted much older. They cursed and spat. Complained that summer break was too short. The girls flirted. One bragged that she was wearing her mother's lace bra. A couple of the boys swaggered, like they'd accomplished something remarkable before even hitting puberty.

Though not an extraordinary moment, the scene left a strange impression on me. Pulling out some paper, I wrote the words "ice cream" and "underwear." Then "three days."

Then the story came. It came quickly.

I wrote the first draft while sitting there on the bench. Over the next two weeks, I made revisions. Lena, Maria, and Raho developed. The bed was stripped. The mother was gone for good. The bodega man spoke. The television, always on, became a member of the family.

Initially, I wasn't certain who the story was about. But with each revision, Lena stepped forward, claiming more and more of the piece until finally it was hers. It's her story.

Douglas Light lives in New York City. He has recently completed his first novel and is currently working on a story collection. "Three Days. A Month. More." is his first published story.

Bradford Morrow, "Lush"

I wanted to write about the fragility of redemption. To give each a voice that would balance, as if on a crystal fulcrum that threatened to shatter at any moment, rich rapture with chaos and even annihilation. I had no interest whatever in making a cautionary tale as such, which was why I discarded an early draft written in third person. My pity toward James Chatham and his wife, Margot, struck me, along with the inescapable anguish I felt for them, as paradoxically judgmental. The draft seemed merely well written and fictional.

James, I realized, needed to unveil his own pure love and terror of alcohol, without some narrator in the nearby shadows trying hard not to judge or save him. Too, his commitment to his doomed wife and their shared religion of liquor felt like his story to tell. And since Ivy Mattie, a casualty of coincidence not without her own frailties, experienced things James could not, her voice rose into life. A life and voice very different from but which also interweaved with his—flowers and spirits both being intoxicating—and so made a perfect analogue to their relationship.

The ending of this story still terrifies me, and while I'm not certain what James might do or say next, I am very aware that the illusory common sense behind his questioning comes from a place in all our psyches. This is true whether we're recovering from addiction or a broken heart, from any trivial mistake we may have made or cataclysmic error that might threaten to end all life. Even our smallest decisions are vast by implication.

Bradford Morrow is the author of the novels *Come Sunday*, *The Almanac Branch* (a finalist for the PEN/Faulkner Award), *Trinity Fields*, *Giovanni's Gift*, and *Ariel's Crossing*. In 1998, the American Academy of Arts and Letters presented him with the Academy Award in Literature. He is a professor of literature at Bard College and is founder and editor of the literary journal *Conjunctions*. He lives in New York.

Alice Munro, "Fathers"

I'm tempted to say that "Fathers" is an autobiographical story, until I think how much of it is pure invention. The "good" father, the "bad" father, their offspring, all the incidents. But it is about something quite personal—remembered feelings which interest me (those inspired by the behavior of the "good" father seem more complex and vivid, to me, than the natural horror of the "bad" father). Something here about the complexity of boundaries of power, between parents and children in that (lost) time?

Alice Munro was born in 1931 in Wingham, Ontario. Her most recent short-story collection is *Hateship, Friendship, Courtship, Loveship, Marriage*. She is a three-time winner of the Governor General's Literary Award, Canada's highest; the Lannan Literary Award; and the W. H. Smith Award. Her stories have appeared in *The New Yorker*, *The Atlantic Monthly*, *Paris Review*, and other publications, and her collections have been translated into thirteen languages. She divides her time between Clinton, Ontario, and Comox, British Columbia.

Tim O'Brien, "What Went Wrong"

Stories must speak for themselves. Whatever a writer may say about a work of fiction seems to me irrelevant and a little dangerous. Irrelevant, because everything of importance to a story is, or should be, contained within the story itself. Dangerous, because the effect of such commentary can be to fit the reader with prescriptive lenses, to impose prefabricated interpretations or conclusions, and thus to undermine the adventure of personal discovery. In the case of "What Went Wrong," I might be tempted to offer a paragraph or two about the destructive influence of Vietnam on the marriage of David Todd and Marla Dempsey. Yet unweaving a story's fabric—teasing out a single thematic strand and holding it to the microscope—seems to me reductive, simpleminded, and an injustice to the complex workings of the human heart. True, David's memories of the war do cause trouble, yet the corrosion in this relationship begins well prior to the war and has its sources within the characters themselves: David's suspicions and silences, Marla's misgivings about her ability to give or receive love. So what went wrong? I'm not sure. I don't want to be sure. Certainty dissolves mystery, and mystery fascinates me. Even the story's title bears an ambiguity I would hate to see explicated away. "What Went Wrong" can be taken as a simple declaration, but it can also be taken as a question, one that neither David nor Marla can ultimately answer, and one that a good many of us have trouble resolving in our own lives. Plainly, David and Marla care for each other. And despite their difficulties, despite their pain, they never stop caring. The great mysteries of the heart may forever be insoluble. What went wrong, perhaps, is that these two unhappy souls were born human.

Tim O'Brien was born in 1946 in Austin, Minnesota, and spent most of his youth in the small town of Worthington, Minnesota. He is the author of *Going After Cacciato* and *The Things They Carried*, winner of the National Book Award in fiction. Mr. O'Brien's other books are *If I Die in a Combat Zone*, *Northern Lights*, *The Nuclear Age*, *Tomcat in Love*, and, most recently, *July, July*. His short fiction has appeared in *The New Yorker*, *Esquire*, *Harper's*, *The Atlantic Monthly*, *Playboy*, and *Ploughshares*, and in *The Best American Short Stories* and *The O. Henry Prize Stories*. Mr. O'Brien is the recipient of literary awards from the American Academy of Arts and Letters, the Guggenheim Foundation, and the National Endowment for the Arts. Mr. O'Brien currently holds the Roy F. and Joann Cole Mitte Chair in Creative Writing at Southwest Texas State University.

Edith Pearlman, "The Story"

The story behind "The Story": I was told the central tale of heroic denial many years ago, in a sparer form. For those many years it seemed too tragic to repeat, too heavy to drop onto the unwitting reader. At last I hit on the idea of exploiting my own reluctance: telling the story and at the same time refusing to say a word.

Edith Pearlman's short stories have appeared in many prize anthologies: *The O. Henry Prize Stories*, *The Best American Short Stories*, *Pushcart Prize: Best of the Small Presses*, *New Stories from the South*, and others. Her own first collection, *Vaquita* (1996), won the Drue Heinz Literature Prize. Her second, *Love Among the Greats* (2002), won the Spokane Prize for Fiction. She lives in Massachusetts.

Joan Silber, "The High Road"

Before I wrote "The High Road," I wrote a story—loosely based on an incident someone had told me—in which a woman is humiliated by her dance coach. And then I wanted to give Duncan, the coach, his own story. I knew that he would end up a fool for love in some way and that this devotion without reward would do him good. Gaspara Stampa, an actual Venetian poet, is the teller of the next story. These are part of a ring of six stories, *Ideas of Heaven*.

Joan Silber is the author of a story collection, *In My Other Life*, and three novels, *Lucky Us*, *In the City*, and *Household Words*, winner of a PEN/Hemingway Award. Her stories have appeared in *The New Yorker*, *Ploughshares*, and *The Pushcart Prize XXV*. She's received awards from the Guggenheim Foundation, the National Endowment for the Arts, and the New York Foundation for the Arts. She teaches at Sarah Lawrence College.

William Trevor, "Sacred Statues"

William Trevor was born in 1928 at Mitchelstown, County Cork, and spent his childhood in provincial Ireland. He has written many novels, including *Fools of Fortune*, *Felicia's Journey*, and most recently *The Story of Lucy Gault*. He is a renowned short-story writer and has published thirteen collections, from *The Day We Got Drunk on Cake* to *The Hill Bachelors*. Mr. Trevor now lives in Devon, England.

Recommended Stories

Publications Submitted

The O. Henry Prize Stories 2004 will be based on stories originally written in English and published in Canada and the United States in 2003. Because of our compressed publishing schedule, it is essential that those stories reach the series editor by November 1, 2003. Magazines may submit fiction in proof or manuscript. Stories may not be nominated or submitted by agents or writers.

The address for submission is:

> Professor Laura Furman, O. Henry Prize Stories
> English Department
> University of Texas at Austin
> One University Station, B5000
> Austin, Texas 78712-5100

The information listed below is up-to-date as *The O. Henry Prize Stories 2003* went to press. Inclusion in the listings does not constitute endorsement or recommendation.

580 Split
Mills College
P.O. Box 9982
Oakland, CA 94613
five80split@yahoo.com
www.mills.edu/SHOWCASE/F99/
    580SPLIT/580.html
Annual

96 Inc
P.O. Box 15559
Boston, MA 02215
Julie Anderson, Vera Gold, Nancy
    Mehegan, Editors
Annual

African American Review
English Department
Indiana State University
Terre Haute, IN 47809
Joe Weixlmann, Editor
web.indstate.edu/artsci/AAR
Quarterly

Agni
236 Bay Street Road
Boston University Writing Program
Boston, MA 02215
Sven Birkerts, Editor
webdelsol.com/AGNI
Biannual

Alaska Quarterly Review
University of Alaska-Anchorage
3211 Providence Drive
Anchorage, AK 99508
Ronald Spatz, Editor
www.uaa.alaska.edu/aqr
Quarterly

Alligator Juniper
Prescott College
301 Grove Avenue
Prescott, AZ 86301
aj@prescott.edu
www.prescott.edu
Annual

American Literary Review
University of North Texas
P.O. Box 13827
Denton, TX 76203-1307
Lee Martin, Editor
americanliteraryreview@yahoo.com
www.engl.unt.edu/alr/main.html
Biannual

Another Chicago Magazine
3709 North Kenmore
Chicago, IL 60613
Barry Silesky, Editor and Publisher
editors@anotherchicagomag.com
anotherchicagomag.com
Biannual

Antietam Review
41 South Potomac Street
Hagerstown, MD 21740
Susanne Kass, Executive Editor

Antioch Review
P.O. Box 148
Yellow Springs, OH 45387
Robert S. Fogarty, Editor
www.antioch.edu/review/home.html
Quarterly

Appalachee Review
P.O. Box 10469
Tallahassee, FL 32302
Barbara Hamby, Editor
Biannual

Arkansas Review
Department of English and
    Philosophy
Box 1890
Arkansas State University
State University, AR 72467
William M. Clements, General Editor
delta@toltec.astate.edu
www.clt.astate.edu/arkreview
Triannual

Ascent
English Department
Concordia College

901 8th Street South
Moorhead, MN 56562
W. Scott Olsen, Editor
ascent@cord.edu
www.cord.edu/dept/english/ascent
Triannual

Atlanta Review
P.O. Box 8248
Atlanta, GA 31106
Daniel Veach, Editor and Publisher
www.atlantareview.com
Biannual

The Atlantic Monthly
77 North Washington Street
Boston, MA 02114
C. Michael Curtis, Senior Editor
www.theatlantic.com
Monthly

Baltimore Review
P.O. Box 410
Riderwood, MD 21139
Barbara Westwood Diehl, Editor
Biannual

Bellevue Literary Review
Department of Medicine, Room
    OBV-612
NYU School of Medicine
550 First Avenue
New York, NY 10016
Ronna Wineberg, JD, Fiction Editor
www.blreview.org
Biannual

Beloit Fiction Journal
Box 11
Beloit College

700 College Street
Beloit, WI 53511
www.beloit.edu/~libhome/Archives/
    BO/Pub/Fict.html
Biannual

Black Warrior Review
University of Alabama
P.O. Box 862936
Tuscaloosa, AL 35486-0027
www.sa.ua.edu/osm/bwr
Biannual

Bomb
594 Broadway, 9th Floor
New York, NY 10012
Betsy Sussler, Editor-in-chief
bomb@echonyc.com
www.bombsite.com/firstproof.html
Quarterly

Border Crossings
500-70 Arthur Street
Winnipeg, Manitoba R3B 1G7
    Canada
Meeka Walsh, Editor
bordercr@escape.ca
www.bordercrossingsmag.com
Quarterly

Boston Book Review
30 Brattle Street, 4th Floor
Cambridge, MA 02138
Kiril Stefan Alexandrov, Editor
BBR-Info@BostonBookReview.com
Monthly

Boston Review
E53-407, MIT
Cambridge, MA 02139

Joshua Cohen, Editor-in-chief
bostonreview@mit.edu
www.bostonreview.mit.edu
Six issues yearly

Boulevard Magazine
6614 Clayton Road, Box 325
Richmond Heights, MO 63117
Richard Burgin, Editor
www.richardburgin.com
Triannual

Briar Cliff Review
3303 Rebecca Street
P.O. Box 2100
Sioux City, IA 51104-2100
Tricia Currans-Sheehen, Editor
www.briar-cliff.edu/bcreview
Annual

Callaloo
English Department
322 Bryan Hall
University of Virginia
Charlottesville, VA 22903
Charles Henry Rowell, Editor
www.press.jhu.edu/press/journals/
    cal/cal.html
Quarterly

Calyx
P.O. Box B
Corvalis, OR 97339-0539
calyx@proaxis.com
www.proaxis.com/~calyx
Triannual

Canadian Fiction
P.O. Box 1061
Kingston, Ontario K7L 4Y5 Canada

Geoff Hancock, Rob Payne,
    Editors
Biannual

Carolina Quarterly
Greenlaw Hall CB#3520
University of North Carolina
Chapel Hill, NC 27599-3520
cquarter@unc.edu
www.unc.edu/depts/cqonline
Triannual

Chariton Review
Truman State University
Kirksville, MO 63501
Jim Barnes, Editor
Biannual

Chattahoochee Review
2101 Womack Road
Dunwoody, GA 30338-4497
Lawrence Hetrick, Editor
www.gpc.peachnet.edu/~twadley/cr/
    index.htm
Quarterly

Chelsea
P.O. Box 773
Cooper Station
New York, NY 10276-0773
Richard Foerster, Editor
Biannual

Chicago Review
5801 South Kenwood Avenue
Chicago, IL 60637-1794
Andrew Rathmann, Editor
www.humanities.uchicago.edu/
    review
Quarterly

Cimarron Review
205 Morrill Hall
Stillwater, OK 74078-0135
E. P. Walkiewicz, Editor
www.cimarronreview.okstate.edu
Quarterly

Colorado Review
Colorado State University
Department of English
Fort Collins, CO 80523
David Milofsky, Editor
creview@colostate.edu
www.coloradoreview.com
Biannual

Commentary
165 East 56th Street
New York, NY 10022
Neal Kozodoy, Editor
editorial@commentarymagazine.com
www.commentarymagazine.com
Monthly

Concho River Review
P.O. Box 1894
Angelo State University
San Angelo, TX 76909
James A. Moore,
    General Editor
www.angelo.edu/dept/english/
    river.htm
Biannual

Confrontation
English Department
C. W. Post Campus of Long Island
    University
Brookville, NY 11548-1300
Martin Tucker, Editor-in-chief

Conjunctions
21 East 10th Street
New York, NY 10003
Bradford Morrow, Editor
www.conjunctions.com
Biannual

Crab Orchard Review
Southern Illinois University at
    Carbondale
Carbondale, IL 62901-4503
Richard Peterson, Editor
www.siu.edu/~crborchd
Biannual

Crazyhorse
English Department
University of Arkansas-
    Little Rock
Little Rock, AR 72204
Ralph Burns, Lisa Lewis, Editors
www.uair.edu/~english/chorse.htm
Biannual

Cream City Review
University of Wisconsin-
    Milwaukee
P.O. Box 413
Milwaukee, WI 53201
www.uwm.edu/dept/english/
    creamcity.html
Biannual

Cut Bank
English Department
University of Montana
Missoula, MT 59812
cutbank@selway.umt.edu
www.umt.edu/cutbank
Biannual

Denver Quarterly
University of Denver
Denver, CO 80208
Bin Ramke, Editor
www.du.edu/english/
    DQuarterly.htm

DoubleTake
55 Davis Square
Somerville, MA 02144
Robert Coles, Editor
www.doubletakemagazine.org
Quarterly

Epoch
251 Goldwin Smith Hall
Cornell University
Ithaca, NY 14853-3201
Michael Koch, Editor
www.arts.cornell.edu/english/
    epoch.html
Triannual

Esquire
250 West 55th Street
New York, NY 10019
Adrienne Miller,
    Literary Editor
www.esquiremag.com
Monthly

Faultline
English and Comparative Literature
    Department
University of California-Irvine
Irvine, CA 92697-2650
faultline@uci.edu
www.humanities.uci.edu/faultline
Annual

Fence
14 Fifth Avenue, 1A
New York, NY 10011
Rebecca Wolff, Editor
rwolff@angel.net
www.fencemag.com
Biannual

Fiction
English Department
City College of New York
New York, NY 10031
Mark Jay Mirsky, Editor
www.ccny.cuny.edu/fiction/
    fiction.htm
Biannual

Fiddlehead
University of New Brunswick
P.O. Box 4400
Fredericton, New Brunswick
    E3B 5A3 Canada
Ross Leckie, Editor
Fid@nbnet.nb.ca
Quarterly

First Intensity
P.O. Box 665
Lawrence, KS 66044
Lee Chapman
leechapman@aol.com
www.members.aol.com/leechapman
Biannual

Five Points
English Department
Georgia State University
University Plaza
Athens, GA 30303-3083

David Bottoms and Pam Durban,
    Editors
www.webdelsol.com/Five_Points/
Triquarterly

Florida Review
English Department
University of Central Florida
Orlando, FL 32816
Russell Kesler, Editor
www.pegasus.cc.ucf.edu/~english/
    floridareview/home.htm
Biannual

Fourteen Hills
Creative Writing Department
San Francisco State University
1600 Holloway Avenue
San Francisco, CA 94132-1722
hills@sfsu.edu
www.userwww.sfsu.edu/~hills
Biannual

Georgia Review
University of Georgia
Athens, GA 30602-9009
T. R. Hummer, Editor
garev@uga.edu
www.uga.edu/garev
Quarterly

Gettysburg Review
Gettysburg College
Gettysburg, PA 17325
Peter Stitt, Editor
pstitt@gettysburg.edu
www.gettysburg.edu/academics/
    gettysburg_review
Quarterly

Glimmer Train Stories
710 SW Madison Street
Suite 504
Portland, OR 97205-2900
Linda Burmeister Davies, Susan
    Burmeister-Brown, Editors
www.glimmertrain.com
Quarterly

Grain
Box 1154
Regina, Saskatchewan S4P 3B4
    Canada
J. Jill Robinson, Editor
Quarterly

Grand Street
214 Sullivan Street
Suite 6C
New York, NY 10012
Jean Stein, Editor
info@grandstreet.com
www.grandstreet.com
Quarterly

Green Hills Literary Lantern
P.O. Box 375
Trenton, MO 64683
Jack Smith, Ken Reger, Senior Editors
www.ncmc.cc.mo.us
Biannual

Greensboro Review
English Department
134 McIver Building, University of
    North Carolina at Greensboro
P.O. Box 26170
Greensboro, NC 27402-6170
Jim Clark, Editor

www.uncg.edu/eng/mfa/review/
   Grhompage.htm
Biannual

Gulf Stream
English Department
FIU Biscayne Bay Campus
3000 NE 151 Street
North Miami, FL 33181-3000
Lynn Barrett, Editor
Biannual

Hampton Shorts
P.O. Box 1229
Water Mill, NY 11976
Barbara Stone, Editor-in-chief
hamptonshorts@hamptons.com

Happy
240 East 35th Street
Suite 11A
New York, NY 10016
Quarterly

Harper's Magazine
666 Broadway
New York, NY 10012
Lewis Lapham, Editor
www.harpers.org
Monthly

Harrington Gay Men's Fiction
Thomas Nelson Community College
99 Thomas Nelson Drive
Hampton, VA 23666
Thomas L. Long, Editor

Hawaii Pacific Review
Hawaii Pacific University

1060 Bishop Street
Honolulu, HI 96813
hpreview@hpu.edu
Annual

Hayden's Ferry Review
Box 871502
Arizona State University
Tempe, AZ 85287-1502
www.statepress.com/hfr
Biannual

Hemispheres
1301 Carolina Street
Greensboro, NC 27401
Selby Bateman, Senior Editor
selby@hemispheresmagazine.com
www.hemispheresmagazine.com
Monthly

High Plains Literary Review
180 Adams Street
Suite 250
Denver, CO 80206
Robert O. Greer, Jr., Editor-in-chief
Triannual

Hudson Review
684 Park Avenue
New York, NY 10021
Paula Deitz, Editor
Quarterly

Idaho Review
Boise State University
English Department
1910 University Drive
Boise, ID 83725
Mitch Wieland, Editor-in-chief

www.english.boisestate.edu/
  idahoreview/
Annual

Image
3307 Third Avenue West
Seattle, WA 98119
Gregory Wolfe, Publisher and Editor
image@imagejournal.org
www.imagejournal.org
Quarterly

Indiana Review
Ballantine Hall 465
1020 East Kirkwood Avenue
Bloomington, IN 47405-7103
Brian Leung, Editor
inreview@indiana.edu
www.indiana.edu/~inreview/ir.html
Biannual

Inkwell
Manhattanville College
Purchase, NY 10577
Biannual

Iowa Review
308 English/Philosophy Building
University of Iowa
Iowa City, IA 52242-1492
David Hamilton, Editor
www.uiowa.edu/~iareview
Triannual

Italian Americana
University of Rhode Island
Feinstein College of Continuing
  Education
80 Washington Street

Providence, RI 02903-1803
Carol Bonomo Albright, Editor
Biannual

Journal
Ohio State University
English Department
164 West 17th Avenue
Columbus, OH 43210
Michelle Herman,
  Fiction Editor
thejournal05@postbox.acs.ohio-
  state.edu
www.cohums.ohio-state.edu/
  english/journals/the_journal/
Biannual

Kalliope
Florida Community College at
  Jacksonville
3939 Roosevelt Boulevard
Jacksonville, FL 32205
Mary Sue Koeppel, Editor
www.fccj.org/kalliope/kalliope.htm
Triannual

Karamu
English Department
Eastern Illinois University
Charleston, IL 61920
Annual

Kenyon Review
Kenyon College
Gambier, OH 43022
David H. Lynn, Editor
kenyonreview@kenyon.edu
www.kenyonreview.com
Triannual

Kiosk
State University of New York at
    Buffalo
English Department
306 Clemens Hall
Buffalo, NY 14260
eng-kiosk@acsu.buffalo.edu
www.wings.buffalo.edu/kiosk
Annual

Laurel Review
Department of English
Northwest Missouri State University
Maryville, MO 64468
William Trowbridge, David Slater,
    Beth Richards, Editors
m500025@mail.nwmissouri.edu
Biannual

Literal Latté
Suite 240
61 East 8th Street
New York, NY 10003
Jenine Gordon Bockman, Publisher
    and Editor
Litlatte@aol.com
www.literal-latte.com
Bimonthly

Literary Review
Fairleigh Dickinson University
285 Madison Avenue
Madison, NJ 07940
Walter Cummins, Editor-in-chief
tlr@fdu.edu
www.webdelsol.com/tlr/
Quarterly

Long Story
18 Eaton Street
Lawrence, MA 01843

R. P. Burnham, Editor
TLS@aol.com
www.litline.org/ls/longstory/html
Annual

Louisiana Literature
SLU-10792
Southeastern Louisiana
    University
Hammond, LA 70402
Jack B. Bedell, Editor
Biannual

Malahat Review
University of Victoria
P.O. Box 1700
Victoria, British Columbia
    V8W 2Y2 Canada
Marlene Cookshaw, Editor
malahat@uvic.ca
www.web.uvic.ca/malahat
Quarterly

Manoa
English Department
University of Hawaii
Honolulu, HI 96822
Frank Stewart, Editor
www.hawaii.edu/mjournal

Massachusetts Review
South College
University of Massachusetts
Box 37140
Amherst, MA 01003-7140
Jules Chametzky, Mary Heath, Paul
    Jenkins, Editors
www.massreview.org
Quarterly

McSweeney's
424 7th Avenue
Brooklyn, NY 11215
David Eggers, Editor
mcsweeneys@earthlink.net
www.mcsweeneys.net
Quarterly

Michigan Quarterly Review
University of Michigan
3032 Rackham Building
915 East Washington Street
Ann Arbor, MI 48109-1070
Laurence Goldstein, Editor
www.umich.edu/~mqr
Quarterly

Midstream
633 Third Avenue, 21st Floor
New York, NY 10017-6706
Joel Carmichael, Editor
info@midstream.org
Nine issues yearly

Minnesota Review
English Department
University of Missouri-Columbia
110 Tate Hall
Columbia, MO 65211
Jeffrey Williams, Editor
williamsjeff@missouri.edu
www.theminnesotareview.org
Biannual

Mississippi Review
Center for Writers
University of Southern Mississippi
Box 5144
Hattiesburg, MS 39406-5144
Frederick Barthelme, Editor

rief@netdoor.com
www.orca.st.usm.edu/mrw
Biannual

Missouri Review
1507 Hillcrest Hall
University of Missouri
Columbia, MO 65211
Speer Morgan, Editor
www.missourireview.org
Triannual

Nassau Review
English Department
Nassau Community College
1 Education Drive
Garden City, NY 11530-6793
Paul A. Doyle, Editor
Annual

Natural Bridge
English Department
University of Missouri-St. Louis
8001 Natural Bridge Road
St. Louis, MO 63121
Steven Schreiner, Editor
natural@admiral.umsl.edu
www.umsl.edu/~natural
Biannual

Nebraska Review
Writer's Workshop
Fine Arts Building 212
University of Nebraska at Omaha
Omaha, NE 68182-0324
James Reed, Fiction and Managing
    Editor
www.unomaha.edu/~fineart/
    wworkshop/nebraska.review.htm
Biannual

Neotrope
P.O. Box 172
Lawrence, KS 66044
Adam Powell and Paul Silvia, Editors
apowell110@hotmail.com
www.brokenboulder.com/
  neotrope.htm
Annual

Nerve
520 Broadway, 6th Floor
New York, NY 10012
Susan Dominus, Editor-in-Chief
info@nerve.com
www.nerve.com/nerveprint
Six issues yearly

New Delta Review
English Department
Louisiana State University
Baton Rouge, LA 70803-5001
new-delta@lsu.edu
www.english.lsu.edu/journals/ndr
Biannual

New England Review
Middlebury College
Middlebury, VT 05753
Stephen Donadio, Editor
NEReview@middlebury.edu
www.middlebury.edu/~nereview
Quarterly

New Letters
University of Missouri-Kansas City
5100 Rockhill Road
Kansas City, MO 64110
James McKinley, Editor-in-chief
newletters@umkc.edu
www.iml.umkc.edu/newletters
Quarterly

New Orleans Review
P.O. Box 195
Loyola University
New Orleans, LA 70118
Ralph Adamo, Editor
noreview@beta.loyno.edu
www.loyno.edu/~noreview
Quarterly

(News from the) Republic of Letters
120 Cushing Avenue
Boston, MA 02125-2033
Saul Bellow, Keith Botsford, Editors
rangoni@bu.edu
www.bu.edu/trl
Biannual

The New Yorker
4 Times Square
New York, NY 10036
Deborah Treisman, Fiction Editor
www.newyorker.com
Weekly

New York Stories
La Guardia Community College/
  CUNY
31-10 Thomson Avenue
Long Island City, NY 11101
Daniel Caplice Lynch, Editor-in-
  chief
Triannual

Night Rally
P.O. Box 1707
Philadelphia, PA 19105
Amber Dorko Stopper, Editor-in-
  chief
NightRallyMag@aol.com
www.nightrally.org
Triquarterly

Nimrod
University of Tulsa
600 South College
Tulsa, OK 74104-3189
Francine Ringold, Editor-in-chief
www.utulsa.edu/NIMROD
Biannual

Noon
1369 Madison Avenue
PMB 298
New York, NY 10128
Diane Williams, Editor
noonannual@yahoo.com
Annual

North American Review
University of Northern Iowa
1222 West 27th Street
Cedar Falls, IA 50614-0156
Vince Gotera, Editor
nar@uni.edu
www.webdelsol.com/
    NorthAmReview/NAR
Five issues yearly

North Carolina Literary Review
English Department
East Carolina University
Greenville, NC 27858-4353
Margaret D. Bauer, Editor
BauerM@mail.ecu.edu
www.personal.ecu.edu/bauerm/
    nclr.htm
Annual

North Dakota Quarterly
University of North Dakota
Grand Forks, ND 58202-7209
Robert W. Lewis, Editor

ndq@sage.und.nodak.edu
Quarterly

Northwest Review
369 PLC
University of Oregon
Eugene, OR 97403
John Witte, Editor
jwitte@oregon.uoregon.edu
Triannual

Notre Dame Review
Creative Writing Program
English Department
University of Notre Dame
Notre Dame, IN 46556
John Matthias, William O'Rourke,
    Editors
English.ndreview.1@nd.edu
www.nd.edu/~ndr/review.htm
Biannual

Now & Then
Center for Appalachian Studies and
    Services
Box 70556
Johnson City, TN 37614-0556
Jane H. Woodside, Editor
cass@estu.edu
www.cass.etsu.edu/n&t
Triquarterly

Nylon
394 West Broadway, 2nd Floor
New York, NY 10012
Gloria M. Wong, Senior Editor
nylonmag@aol.com
www.nylonmag.com
Monthly

Oasis
P.O. Box 626
Largo, FL 34649-0626
Neal Storrs, Editor
www.oasislit@aol.com
Quarterly

Ohio Review
344 Scott Quad
Ohio University
Athens, OH 45701-2979
Wayne Dodd, Editor
www.ohio.edu/TheOhioReview
Biannual

One Story
P.O. Box 1326
New York, NY 10156
Hannah Tinti, Editor
www.one-story.com
About every three weeks

Ontario Review
9 Honey Brook Drive
Princeton, NJ 08540
Raymond J. Smith, Editor
www.ontarioreviewpress.com
Biannual

Open City Magazine
270 Lafayette Street, Suite 1412
New York, NY 10012-3327
Joanna Yas
editors@opencity.org
www.opencity.org
Annual

Orchid
3096 Williamsburg
Ann Arbor, MI 48108-2026

Maureen Aitken, Keith Hood,
    Cathy Mellett, Editors
editors@orchidlit.org
www.orchidlit.org
Semiannual

Other Voices
English Department (MC 162)
University of Illinois at Chicago
601 South Morgan Street
Chicago, IL 60607-7120
Lois Hauselman,
    Executive Editor
othervoices@listserv.uic.edu
Biannual

Owen Wister Review
University of Wyoming
Student Publications
Box 3625
Laramie, WY 82071
Annual

The Oxford American
303 President Clinton Avenue
Little Rock, AR 72201
Marc Smirnoff, Editor
www.oxfordamerican.com
Bimonthly

Oxford Magazine
English Department
356 Bachelor Hall
Miami University
Oxford, OH 45056
Oxmag@geocities.com
www.muohio.edu/creativewriting/
    oxmag.html
Annual

Oyster Boy Review
P.O. Box 77842
San Francisco, CA 94107-0842
Damon Sauve, Publisher
staff@oysterboyreview
www.oysterboyreview.com
Quarterly

Paris Review
541 East 72nd Street
New York, NY 10021
George Plimpton, Editor
www.parisreview.com
Quarterly

Partisan Review
236 Bay State Road
Boston, MA 02215
partisan@bu.edu
www.partisanreview.org
Quarterly

Phoebe
George Mason University
4400 University Drive
Fairfax, VA 22030-4444
phoebe@gmu.edu
www.gmu.edu/pubs/phoebe
Biannual

Playboy Magazine
680 North Lake Shore Drive
Chicago, IL 60611
Jonathan Black, Managing Editor
www.playboy.com
Monthly

Pleiades
English and Philosophy Departments
Central Missouri State University

Warrensburg, MO 64093
R. M. Kinder, Kevin Prufer, Editors
www.cmsu.edu/englphil/
    pleiades.html
Biannual

Ploughshares
Emerson College
120 Boylston Street
Boston, MA 02116-4624
Don Lee, Editor
www.pshares.org
Triannual

Post Road
853 Broadway, Suite 1516, Box 85
New York, NY 10003
David Ryan and Jaime Clarke
dwryan@bellatlantic.net or
    jaimeclarke@yahoo.com
http://webdelsol.com/Post_Road
Biannual

Potomac Review
P.O. Box 354
Port Tobacco, MD 20677
Eli Flam, Editor and Publisher
potomacreview@mc.cc.md.us
www.meral.com/potomac
Quarterly

Pottersfield Portfolio
P.O. Box 40, Station A
Sydney, Nova Scotia B1P 6G9
    Canada
Douglas Arthur Brown, Managing
    Editor
pportfolio@seascape.ns.ca
www.pportfolio.com
Triannual

Prairie Fire
423-100 Arthur Street
Winnipeg, Manitoba R3B 1H3
    Canada
Andris Taskins, Editor
prfire@escape.ca
www.prairiefire.mb.ca
Quarterly

Prairie Schooner
201 Andrews Hall
University of Nebraska
Lincoln, NE 68588-0334
Hilda Raz, Editor-in-chief
www.unl.edu/schooner/psmain.htm
Quarterly

Prism International
Creative Writing Program
University of British Columbia
Buch. E462-Main Mall
Vancouver, BC V6T 1Z1 Canada
Billeh Nickerson and Mark Mallet,
    Editors
prism.arts.ubc.ca
Quarterly

Provincetown Arts
650 Commercial Street
Provincetown, MA 02657
Christopher Busa, Editor
Annual

Puerto del Sol
P.O. Box 30001
New Mexico State University
Las Cruces, NM 88003-8001
Kevin McIlvoy, Editor-in-chief
Puerto@nmsu.edu
Biannual

Quarry Magazine
P.O. Box 74
Kingston, Ontario K7L 4V6 Canada
Andrew Griffin, Editor-in-chief
quarrymagazine@hotmail.com
Quarterly

Quarterly West
371 Olpin Union Hall
University of Utah
Salt Lake City, UT 84112
David Hawkins, Editor
dhawk@earthlink.net
www.webdelsol.com/
    Quarterly_West
Biannual

Raritan
Rutgers University
31 Mine Street
New Brunswick, NJ 08903
Richard Poirier, Editor-in-chief
Quarterly

Rattapallax
523 LaGuardia Place
New York, NY 10012
Martin Mitchell, Editor-in-chief
rattapallax@hotmail.com
www.rattapallax.com
Biannual

Red Rock Review
English Department, J2A
Community College Southern
    Nevada
3200 East Cheyenne Avenue
North Las Vegas, NV 89030
Richard Logsdon, Editor-in-chief
Biannual

River City
English Department
University of Memphis
Memphis, TN 38152-6176
Thomas Russell, Editor
rivercity@memphis.edu
www.people.memphis.edu/~rivercity
Biannual

River Styx
634 North Grand Boulevard,
    12th Floor
St. Louis, MO 63103-1002
Richard Newman, Editor
www.riverstyx.org
Triannual

Rosebud
P.O. Box 459
Cambridge, WI 53523
Roderick Clark, Editor
jrodclark@rsbd.net
www.rsbd.net
Quarterly

St. Anthony Messenger
1615 Republic Street
Cincinatti, OH 45210-1298
Pat McCloskey, O.F.M., Editor
StAnthony@AmericanCatholic.org
www.americancatholic.org
Monthly

Salamander
48 Ackers Avenue
Brookline, MA 02445-4160
Jennifer Barber, Editor
Biannual

SALMAGUNDI
Skidmore College
Saratoga Springs, NY 12866
Robert Boyers, Editor-in-chief
pboyers@skidmore.edu
Quarterly

Salt Hill
Syracuse University
English Department
Syracuse, NY 13244
Biannual

Santa Monica Review
Santa Monica College
1900 Pico Boulevard
Santa Monica, CA 90405
Biannual

Seattle Review
Padelford Hall
Box 354330
University of Washington
Seattle, WA 98195
Colleen J. McElroy, Editor
Biannual

Seven Days
P.O. Box 1164
255 South Champlain Street
Burlington, VT 05042-1164
Pamela Polston, Paula Routly,
    Coeditors
sevenday@together.net
www.sevendaysvt.com
Weekly

Sewanee Review
University of the South
735 University Avenue

Sewanee, TN 37383-1000
George Core, Editor
rjones@sewanee.edu
www.sewanee.edu/sreview.home.html
Quarterly

Shenandoah
Troubador Theater, 2nd Floor Box W
Washington and Lee University
Lexington, VA 24450-0303
R. T. Smith, Editor
Quarterly

Sonora Review
English Department
University of Arizona
Tucson, AZ 85721
sonora@u.arizona.edu
www.coh.arizona.edu/sonora
Biannual

South Carolina Review
English Department
Clemson University
Strode Tower, Box 340523
Clemson, SC 29634-0523
Wayne Chapman, Donna Jaisty
Winchell, Editors
cwayne@clemson.edu
Annual

South Dakota Review
Box 111
University Exchange
Vermillion, SD 57069
Brian Bedard, Editor
sdreview@usd.edu
www.sunbird.usd.edu/engl/SDR/
index.html
Quarterly

Southern Humanities Review
9088 Haley Center
Auburn University
Auburn, AL 36849
Dan R. Latimer, Virginia M.
Kouidis, Editors
www.auburn.edu/english/shr/
home.htm
Quarterly

Southern Review
43 Allen Hall
Louisiana State University
Baton Rouge, LA 70803-5005
James Olney, Dave Smith,
Editors
jolney@lsu.edu
Quarterly

Southwest Review
Southern Methodist University
307 Fondren Library West
Dallas, TX 75275
Willard Spiegelman, Editor-in-chief
www.southwestreview.org
Quarterly

StoryQuarterly
431 Sheridan Rd.
Kenilworth, IL 60043
M.M.M. Hayes, Editor
storyquarterly@hotmail.com
Annual

StringTown
93011 Ivy Station Road
Astoria, OR 97103
Polly Buckingham, Editor
Stringtown@aol.com
Annual

Sun
107 North Robertson Street
Chapel Hill, NC 27516
Sy Safransky, Editor
sy@thesunmagazine.org
www.thesunmagazine.org
Monthly

Sundog
English Department
Tallahassee, FL 32311
sundog@english.fsu.edu
english.fsu.edu/sundog
Biannual

Sycamore Review
English Department
1356 Heavilon Hall
Purdue University
West Lafayette, IN 47907
sycamore@expert.cc.purdue.edu
www.sla.purdue.edu/academic/engl/
    sycamore/
Biannual

Talking River Review
Division of Literature and
    Languages
Lewis-Clark State College
500 8th Avenue
Lewiston, ID 83501
Biannual

Tameme
199 First Street
Los Altos, CA 94022
C. M. Mayo, Editor
editor@tameme.org
www.tameme.org
Annual

Tampa Review
University of Tampa
401 West Kennedy Boulevard
Tampa, FL 33606-1490
Richard Matthews, Editor
Biannual

Texas Review
English Department
Sam Houston State University
Huntsville, TX 77341
Paul Ruffin, Editor
eng.pdr@shsu.edu
Biannual

Third Coast
English Department
Western Michigan University
Kalamazoo, MI 49008-5092
Shanda Hansma Blue, Editor
Shanda_Blue@hotmail.com
www.wmich.edu/thirdcoast
Biannual

The Threepenny Review
P.O. Box 9131
Berkeley, CA 94709
Wendy Lesser, Editor
wlesser@threepennyreview.com
www.threepennyreview.com
Quarterly

Tikkun
60 West 87th Street
New York, NY 10024
Thane Rosenbaum,
    Literary Editor
magazine@tikkun.org
www.tikkun.org
Bimonthly

Tin House
P.O. Box 10500
Portland, OR 97926-0500
Rob Spillman, Editor
www.tinhouse.com
Quarterly

Transition Magazine
W.E.B. DuBois Institute
Harvard University
69 Dunster Street
Cambridge, MA 02138
Henry Louis Gates, Jr., and Kwame
    Anthony Appiah, Editors
transition@fas.harvard.edu
www.transitionmagazine.com
Quarterly

Triquarterly
Northwestern University
2020 Ridge Avenue
Evanston, IL 60208
Susan Firestone Hahn, Editor
www.triquarterly.com
Triannual

1 West Range
P.O. Box 400223
Charlottesville, VA 22903-4223
Staige D. Blackford, Editor
vqreview@virginia.edu
www.virginia.edu/vqr
Quarterly

War, Literature & the Arts
English and Fine Arts Department
United States Air Force Academy
Colorado Springs, CO 80840-6242
Donald Anderson, Editor

donald.anderson@usafa.af.mil
www.usafa.af.mil/dfeng/wla
Biannual

Wascana Review
English Department
University of Regina
Regina, Saskatchewan S4S 0A2
    Canada
Michael Tussler, Editor
Michael.tussler@uregina.ca
www.uregina.ca/english/
    wrhome.htm
Biannual

Washington Review
P.O. Box 50132
Washington, DC 20091-0132
Clarissa K. Wittenberg, Editor
www.washingtonreview.org
Bimonthly

Washington Square
Creative Writing Program
New York University
19 University Place, 2nd Floor
New York, NY 10003-4556
Washington.square.journal@nyu.edu
www.nyu.edu/fas/program/cwp/wsr
Annual

Weber Studies
Weber State University
1214 University Circle
Ogden, UT 84408-1214
Sherwin W. Howard, Editor
weberstudies@weber.edu
www.weberstudies.weber.edu
Triquarterly

West Branch
Bucknell Hall
Bucknell University
Lewisburg, PA 17837
Joshua Harmon, Editor
www.westbranch@bucknell.edu
Biannual

West Coast Line
2027 East Academic Annex
Simon Fraser University
Burnaby, British Columbia V5A 1S6
    Canada
Roy Miki, Editor
wcl@sfu.ca
www.sfu.ca/west-coast-line
Triannual

Western Humanities Review
University of Utah
English Department
255 South Central Campus Drive,
    Room 3500
Salt Lake City, UT 84112-0494
Barry Weller, Editor
whr@mail.hum.utah.edu
www.hum.utah.edu/whr
Biannual

Whetstone
Barrington Area Arts Council
P.O. Box 1266
Barrington, IL 60011-1266
Sandra Berris, Marsha Portnoy, Jean
    Tolle, Editors
Annual

Wind
P.O. Box 24548
Lexington, KY 40524

Charlie Hughes, Leatha Kendrick,
    Editors
books@windpub.org
Biannual

Windsor Review
English Department
University of Windsor
Windsor, Ontario N9B 3P4 Canada
Katherine Quinsey, General Editor
uwrevu@uwindsor.ca
Biannual

Witness
Oakland Community College
Orchard Ridge Campus
27055 Orchard Lake Road
Farmington Hills, MI 48334
Peter Stine, Editor
Biannual

Worcester Review
6 Chatham Street
Worcester, MA 01609
Rodger Martin, Managing Editor
www.geocities.com/Paris/LeftBank/
    6433
Annual

Wordplay
P.O. Box 2248
South Portland, ME 04116-2248
Helen Peppe, Editor-in-chief
wordplay@maine.rr.edu
Quarterly

Writers' Forum
University of Colorado
P.O. Box 7150

Colorado Springs, CO 80933
C. Kenneth Pellow, Editor-in-chief
kpellow@mail.uccs.edu
Annual

Xavier Review
Xavier University
Box 110C
New Orleans, LA 70125
Thomas Bonner, Jr., and Richard
    Collins, Editors
www.rcollins@xula.edu
Biannual

Xconnect: Writers of the
    Information Age
P.O. Box 2317
Philadelphia, PA 19103
D. Edward Deifer, Editor-in-
    chief
xconnect@ccat.sas.upenn.edu
www.ccat.sas.upenn.edu/xconnect
Annual

Yale Review
Yale University
P.O. Box 208243
New Haven, CT 06250-8243

J. D. McClatchy, Editor
yalerev@yale.edu
Quarterly

Yalobusha Review
P.O. Box 186
University, MS 38677-0186
yalobush@sunset.backbone.
    olemiss.edu
www.olemiss.edu/depts/english/
    pubs/yalobusha_review.html
Annual

Zoetrope: All-Story
916 Kearny Street
San Francisco, CA 94133
Tamara Straus, Editor
www.zoetrope-stories.com
Quarterly

ZYZZYVA
41 Sutter Street
Suite 1400
San Francisco, CA 94104-4903
Howard Junker, Editor
editor@zyzzyva.org
www.zyzzyva.org
Triannual

Permissions